"BELOVED VIKING is a powerful love story that reaches back into the midst of time. I couldn't stop reading."

Billie Green, award winning author of A SPECIAL MAN—

"From the first page I was hurled back to America as it was before Columbus, a world filled with adventure and savage romance. It left me breathless."

Nancy Gramm, award winning author of THEN CAME LOVE—

SHELTER IN THE STORM

Eric lay awake a short distance from Shala, listening to the rain falling outside the dwellings, painfully aware of his leg throbbing with each beat of his heart. Had he caused it further injury by walking so far on it? Even so, he felt no regret. If he had not done so, Shala might well be dead.

He looked at her, wondering at the feelings she stirred deep inside him.

She lay there, covered with nothing but her cape, a slender arm projecting from beneath. He studied her slim hand, fingers in a curl, and he thought it was the most beautiful hand he had ever seen. His eyes moved to her face, exquisitely made, as though sculptured by one of the masters. Here and there wisps of black hair poked out from beneath the covering, blowing gently against her cheek.

"Shala," he whispered, his voice a husky caress.

Her heart jolted and a dizzying current raced through her. She held her breath, feeling almost mesmerized by his gaze. His arms tightened around her, his head dipped down, lips hovering only inches above hers.

"Sweet, sweet, Shala . . ."

FEEL THE FIRE IN CAROL FINCH'S ROMANCES!

BELOVED BETRAYAL (2346, $3.95)
Sabrina Spencer donned a gray wig and veiled hat before blackmailing rugged Ridge Tanner into guiding her to Fort Canby. But the costume soon became her prison—the beauty had fallen head over heels in love!

LOVE'S HIDDEN TREASURE (2980, $4.50)
Shandra d'Evereux felt her heart throb beneath the stolen map she'd hidden in her bodice when Nolan Elliot swept her out onto the veranda. It was hard to concentrate on her mission with that wily rogue around!

MONTANA MOONFIRE (3263, $4.95)
Just as debutante Victoria Flemming-Cassidy was about to marry an oh-so-suitable mate, the towering preacher, Dru Sullivan flung her over his shoulder and headed West! Suddenly, Tori realized she had been given the best present for a bride: a night of passion with a real man!

THUNDER'S TENDER TOUCH (2809, $4.50)
Refined Piper Malone needed bounty-hunter, Vince Logan to recover her swindled inheritance. She thought she could coolly dismiss him after he did the job, but she never counted on the hot flood of desire she felt whenever he was near!

Available wherever paperbacks are sold, or order direct from the Publisher. Send cover price plus 50¢ per copy for mailing and handling to Penguin USA, P.O. Box 999, c/o Dept. 17109, Bergenfield, NJ 07621. Residents of New York and Tennessee must include sales tax. DO NOT SEND CASH.

BETTY BROOKS

BELOVED VIKING

ZEBRA BOOKS
KENSINGTON PUBLISHING CORP.

ZEBRA BOOKS are published by

Kensington Publishing Corp.
475 Park Avenue South
New York, NY 10016

First Printing: February, 1994

Printed in the United States of America

Dedicated to my sister, Daisy,
who reminds me of the flower
that shares her name

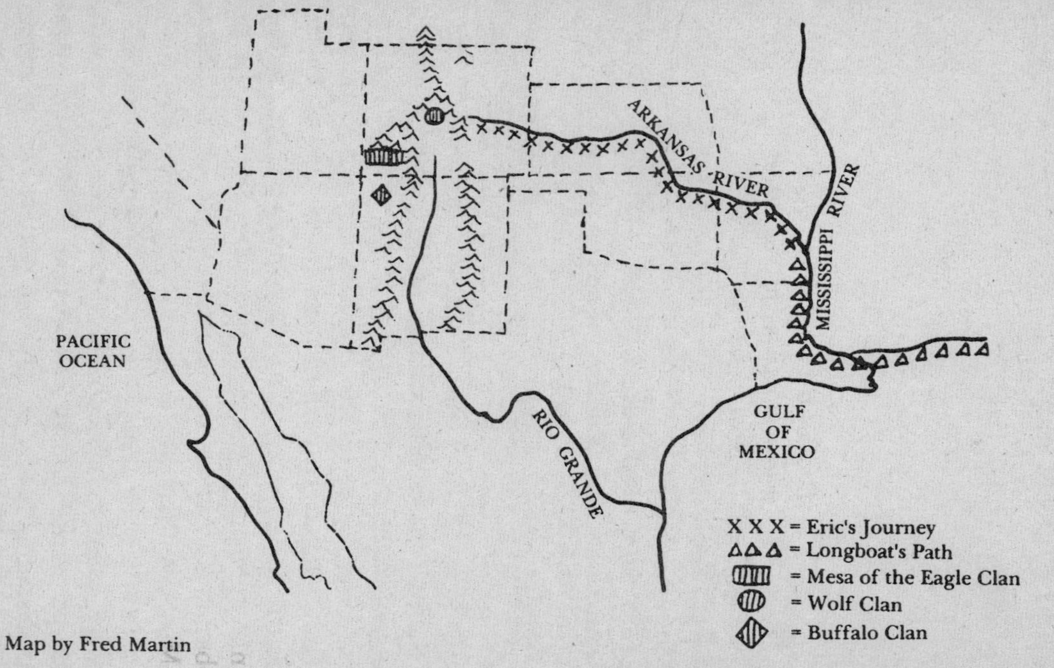

Map by Fred Martin

Foreword

Scholars theorize that Vikings sailed up the Mississippi River, then up the Arkansas River during the year one thousand. This supposed route would have brought the Norsemen very near the Mesa Verde cliff dwellings in Colorado.

Archaeologists have been digging among the ruins on Mesa Verde since the cliff dwellings were discovered in the late nineteenth century. From the artifacts and bones uncovered, scientists have learned much about the people who lived there.

Anasazi, the Navajo called them. The Ancient Ones. What they called themselves we will never know, for they left no written records. We recognize them by their deeds: they were cliff dwellers, builders in stone, the ancient people of the rock. Much of their life is still a mystery, piquing the curiosity and tantalizing the imagination. They were farmers who found the means to irrigate crops where no water existed. And they were craftsmen, skilled at making pottery in its most advanced form.

For approximately seven hundred years they occupied the mesa, growing corn and squash and building complex stone dwellings. Then, as suddenly as they came, they vanished, leaving nothing behind to show where they went or from whence they came.

The odds are great that at some point in time these two great peoples, the Vikings and the Anasazi, came together, forever placing a mark, no matter how imperceptible, upon the very soul of history.

One

1213 A.D.

A sharp January wind bit at Eric Nordstrom's ears as he shrugged on his pack. Snow had fallen the night before, leaving the trees and bushes frosted, the ground crunching beneath his feet. Leaden skies told him he could expect more of the same today.

Even so, he felt no fear. Winters in his Norwegian homeland had hardened him to conditions worse than any he could imagine in this new land. Still, should the situation worsen, the heavy fur coat he wore was designed to keep the chill at bay.

Finally laden, he surveyed the land he meant to explore this day. Already, as he had traveled the river, he had discovered mazelike canyons, hillocks and boulders.

He should have turned back before now, had meant to until he saw the mesa ahead and once again the lure of the unknown called out to him.

After all that had happened, one more day, one more night would mean little.

Using a twisted storm-rent limb as a staff, he began his upward climb. Branches pulled at his coat and tugged at his trousers as he wended his way through the trees.

His journey into this new land had been ill fated almost from the start. Dreams of riches and slaves to fill his longboat had brought him and his men here instead of to the Far East as they had intended.

He had made his first grave mistake by sailing from the gulf up the big muddy river that twisted and turned, its waters deep and rough. Still he had gone on, determined not to allow a mere river to conquer him, until, after a bitter storm, the river had won, seizing Eric's longboat in the grasp of a muddy shoal.

Shivering from the combined cold of the wind and the memory, Eric pulled his coat tighter around him. The higher he climbed, the colder the bite of the wind became.

He and his men had spent weeks trying to free the longboat, but in the end they had failed. Finally Eric had realized the boat was stuck until the spring thaws filled the river again.

Rather than waste an entire winter at the site, he had left six of his men with the longboat and started west with the other five, following one of the tributaries that branched off the wide muddy river.

Now he maneuvered his way around a boulder. This land was beautiful in a strange, splendid sort of way, but too soon he had discovered that it was also savage and brutal.

Thor had been the first man he lost, felled by an immense black bear. With the aid of the others, Eric had managed to down the beast, but not in time. Thor had died in his arms.

Ansel and Uric were next, killed by the *skraelings,* the savages who occupied this wild land. Then Odin and Fergus had sickened and died from some unknown illness. After Eric had torched their funeral pyres, only he was left of the original party.

It was imperative that he make it back to his men before the spring thaw, else he would be trapped in this world forever. He would start back, too, as soon as he explored the mesa ahead.

A few more days would put him in no danger.

The heavy snowbanks slowed his progress, and it was late afternoon when Eric reached the top of the mesa. He found several tracks made by deer and elk, which didn't surprise him, but he also found other signs that baffled him. They were oblong in shape but were totally absent of hoof or claw marks.

He was still puzzling over them when he came across the fields.

Although the fields were fallow now, the rows and rows of dried and broken stalks peeping through the blanket of snow told him farming people had once lived here.

He broke off one of the yellowed stalks, wondering what it was. Certainly nothing he had ever seen before in all his travels. How long had the fields been fallow? Why was there no sign of dwellings, of the farmers who would tend the fields?

Tossing aside the dried stalk, he continued on his way, his gaze wary now, searching carefully lest he be taken by surprise by man or beast.

When he found the dwellings, he was taken by surprise. They stood, stark and desolate, seeming as abandoned as the fields had been.

But were they really? In good condition, they were built of stone, with vertical walls and flat roofs, then joined together to make long rows. They were quite unlike the conical dwellings of the nomadic people he had encountered in other areas.

His gaze ran over the complex structures. The *skraelings* who built them were obviously craftsmen, skilled in architecture. And yet, they were farmers as well. Could such people really be savages? Had he come across a tribe of highly intelligent beings?

Intrigued by the thought, he wandered through the abandoned buildings, through rooms that had been designed to hold at least a hundred people, finding several pieces of broken pottery, further proof that craftsmen once inhabited this place.

Why had they left after building such complex dwellings? he wondered. Had they been driven out by their enemies, or had there been some other reason for leaving? Moisture would not be abundant on the plateau, so perhaps there had been a lack of water for their crops. He realized he would never know the answer. Whatever their reason, the people were gone, but the buildings they had left behind would provide overnight shelter for him, would keep the cold wind at bay as well as the wild animals that might want to make a meal of him.

Realizing he would need a fire, he tossed his pack and crossbow in the corner and went in search of wood. His arms were almost full when he found himself near a deep V-shaped canyon.

He strode along the rimrock while the wind—stronger near the edge—howled around him, whipping his golden hair across his face and blowing snow into his eyes.

It had begun to snow again, and the white flakes floated and twirled in the wind as he looked out over the canyon that had been gouged out eons ago by ancient waters. His sweeping gaze took in the panoramic view, reddish orange sandstone cliffs that would be impossible to climb, dropped to the cliff overhang, then below to the natural amphitheater carved out of the cliff face. He was on the point of turning away when a movement below the cliff overhang caught his eye.

Eric's gaze narrowed on the spot, focused on a tiny figure standing beside a tall spruce tree located halfway down the cliff. Was it a mountain goat? As he watched, the figure moved along a narrow ledge, making for the head of the canyon.

Excitement surged through Eric, sent a smile streaking across his face. That was no mountain goat. The creature walked upright. Could it be one of the *skraelings* who built the abandoned city?

Eric's gaze remained fastened on the creature, watching its every step as he wondered where the savage was headed.

A moment later he had his answer.

Why had he not seen it before? he wondered. Even now he could hardly believe his eyes. In the recess, hidden from view from above and below, was a massive building, similar to the one he had found on top of the mesa, comprised of rooms and towers bound together in a single mass of shaped and fitted sandstone that rose, curved and dipped, and was squared with a grace and delicacy that seemed to mask its sheer bulk.

The *skraelings* had left their home on the mesa, but they had not traveled far. Instead, they had built another city halfway down the cliff.

"Amazing," Eric muttered in awe-stricken tones. "They left the mesa above to build where no enemy could reach them."

The implications of what he was seeing struck him like a blow. He need not return to the longboat empty-handed. The cliff city was large, like the one on the mesa's top, and although undoubtedly primitive, the occupants must have a moderate degree of intelligence, plus an enormous amount of persistence. How else could they have devised the plans for the cliff dwellings, then completed the project?

He found the whole situation fascinating and looked forward to capturing one of the creatures. It should be an easy task for such as he. He was a skilled swordsman, more than competent with both arrow and spear. He anticipated no problem in taking at least one prisoner.

Becoming aware of the fading light, he turned back across the mesa. Morning would be soon enough to devise a plan. Right now his belly needed filling.

He was unaware of the mountain lion until he heard it scream.

In a small cave, located perhaps two hundred feet below the Viking, a small fire burned, warming the girl who knelt beside it feeding wood to the flames from the stack beside the hide-covered opening. She had seen her sixteenth summer, but instead of wearing her dark hair short as custom demanded when she reached a marriageable age, she defied convention and left it hanging loose.

So it was with Shala. She was different from the other women, had never enjoyed learning the things—basket and pottery making, tanning hides and weaving blankets—that girls must learn.

Ofttimes when she went berry picking with the other women, something in the trees whispered to her and she slipped away from the others to spend the day dreaming in the woods or climbing rocks with the boys.

But those days were long past now. She was alone. And the droop of Shala's shoulders spoke plainly of her sorrow for which she could find no relief. It was a huge, painful knot twisting inside her chest. The misery of her life haunted her, making her constantly aware of what she had lost.

There had been times during the long winter months when she had regretted the actions that brought her to this state, and if she could have reversed her decision, then she would surely have done so. But it was too late. The time for choosing was long since past. Shu, the shaman of the Eagle Clan, had chosen another for mate and, for Shala's rejection, had condemned her to live alone, apart from the rest.

Although Shu thought he was condemning Shala to certain death, he had underestimated her will to live, had underestimated, too, his son, the crippled one, Nampeyo.

Without Shu's knowledge, the young man had befriended Shala. He had taught her how to make and set snares to capture small game, but more importantly, he had also taught her the art of spear throwing.

Shala was aware of her indebtedness to Nampeyo. Because of his teachings she was more than proficient with a weapon and was now able to defend herself. She could also provide meat for her belly and hide for clothing, not simple tasks even for strong males.

She could never repay Nampeyo for the help he had given her, for even if there was a way, he no longer came to her, finding his father's wrath too great a barrier to cross. Shu had somehow discovered that Nampeyo was aiding Shala and threatened to destroy the young man's future if he continued to help her.

Shala could well understand Nampeyo's fear. He had been trained from childhood to take over as shaman when his father died. Should he be deprived of that position, he would lose his livelihood, for his crippled leg would not allow him to work in the fields with the rest of the men.

When he told her of his father's threat, he made her a promise. When the old shaman went to join his ancestors, Shala would be allowed to return to the cliff city. And all that had been taken from her—her home, her possessions, even her turkey-feather cloak—would be returned.

Shala's lips twisted with bitterness. Even though Nampeyo had made the promise to return everything, he could not do so. It was not in his power to return the years she would live apart from her People.

And it *would* be years. How could it be otherwise? Shu was still young by tribal standards and would undoubtedly have a long life since he was always careful to stay out of harm's way. Knowing his cruelty, she did not doubt that he would live forever, just to make certain she never returned home.

A terrible sadness shook Shala. She gripped the sacred stone she wore around her neck, hoping to draw comfort from it. The medallion—a deep turquoise, flecked with gold—was a gift from Nampeyo. A talisman, he said, to ward off evil.

She needed the stone's magic, needed it desperately. How else could she find the strength to live as she must, an outcast from her People, with no one to share her thoughts, no one to care whether she lived or died?

Expelling a heavy sigh, she crossed to the opening, pushed the hide covering aside and stepped outside. Wind Woman's icy breath struck her like a blow, and she pulled the rabbitskin cloak higher around her neck. Shala knew she should go back inside, but the urge to see the place of her birth was too great, too compelling.

She circled around a sheltering pine that blocked her view and gazed across the canyon at the cliff city.

Although the fading light hampered her vision, she knew the city by heart and was able to pinpoint the fire of Gryla, the woman who had given her birth. Just the sight of the fire and the knowledge that Gryla would be working nearby brought an ache to her heart and a sense of aloneness that was almost more than she could bear.

Her shoulders drooped as she turned away. Her leather foot coverings crunched across the frozen snow. With head bowed low, she headed back toward the small cave that had become home to her.

Shala's hand was on the hide flap when she heard the cougar scream. She stopped abruptly, stepping back and tilting her head, her gaze on the sandstone cliff as she tried to locate the source.

She had heard the sound often enough before to easily identify the animal. Immediately, the thought of another pelt to keep away winter's cold chill outweighed the danger involved.

The cougar screamed again, and Shala realized

it was on the mesa above her. Something must have disturbed the cat. She could only hope a bear was responsible, for then she could reap a double reward. Winter was unpredictable. The meat from a bear would be a welcome addition to her meager store.

Whipping aside the hide covering, she snatched up the spear left near the entrance and began the long climb to the mesa above.

The scream chilled Eric's blood. He dropped the armload of wood, snatched his sword from his belt and spun to face the mountain lion. At any other time he might have admired the graceful ferocity of the animal, but not at this particular moment. The big, tawny cat measured at least nine feet from its nose to the tip of its tail. It must weigh more than two hundred pounds, and he knew, having watched these lions in action before, that it could easily kill a two-hundred-pound mule deer with one fatal bite and have energy left over to drag the carcass uphill for miles to a rocky lair.

Now, however, there were no deer in sight. Only himself. And it looked to the Viking as if the animal fully intended him to be its next meal.

Eric, though, had no intention of being so accommodating.

He watched the tawny feline as it gathered its strength and crouched in readiness. Its ears were laid back, its tail swishing back and forth as though it might be playing with him, but he knew the beast well enough by now to be aware of its habits.

He had learned that the mountain lion had a well-defined territory where it hunted for game and from which it repelled invaders. Eric had invaded the big cat's territory.

Holding his sword in readiness, he waited for the cougar to attack, cursing himself for leaving his crossbow at the ruins. He would much have preferred shooting the animal from a distance rather than fighting at such close quarters as the sword required.

The cat opened its mouth and screamed out its rage, then crept closer to Eric. Its yellow eyes never wavered from the intruder who now stood only a few feet distant.

"Come on, big cat," Eric muttered, his muscles taut, his legs planted firmly apart in a fighting stance. "Either jump or, by Thor, leave this place!"

The mountain lion twitched its tail again and emitted another scream of rage. Eric, becoming impatient, swung his sword in a mighty circle. He hoped to convince the animal of his superior strength, but instead the mountain lion exploded in a short, swift charge.

Eric swung his blade toward the beast, leaping aside as he did so. His blade connected with the animal's flank. Blood spurted from the wound as the cat spun around. Its claws raked the Viking's shoulder, slicing through the heavy fur covering and ripping into the flesh beneath.

Pain streaked through Eric. He fought against

waves of dizziness, stumbling over a rock and flailing out while trying to regain his balance, then landed with a solid thud against the ground, striking it hard enough to jar the breath from his body and rip the sword from his hand.

Weaponless, he twisted around, his gaze searching for the sword. Sighting it, he spewed curses into the cold air. It had fallen beyond his reach. But the cat, with uncanny sense, stalked between him and his weapon.

A swift glance over his shoulder told Eric the cliff was a mere four feet away. His only hope seemed to be the gnarled juniper growing near the edge, its twisted trunk etched in sharp relief against the white snow, its branches stretched skyward as though in supplication to the ancient gods. If he could entice the cat into leaping, perhaps he could save himself by catching the lower limb while the cat plunged into the canyon.

Realizing he had no other choice, Eric pushed himself to all fours and backed slowly toward the edge, keeping his eyes on the animal. The cougar matched him step for step.

"Haaahh!" Eric shouted, waving his good arm at the cat, enticing it forward as he slid sideways, edging closer to the juniper.

The mountain lion's eyes followed him. Its head lowered, and its mouth opened again. Its flesh rippled with the pain from its wounded flank, and saliva dripped from its mouth. With another scream, it launched itself forward.

Realizing he was only seconds away from being mauled, Eric jumped up and out, his arms stretched to their fullest, reaching for the lower limb that would save his life. His fingers locked around rough bark, gripped hard. White hot pain flashed through Eric's wounded shoulder. How long could he hold on, he wondered, even as he breathed a silent prayer of gratitude to the gods for their help in defeating the lion.

Craa-ackk!

The sound chilled his blood.

Within that splintered fraction of a second, his searching gaze followed the limb down to its beginning where it joined with the trunk, and he saw the crack that quickly lengthened. The limb swayed beneath his weight, then dropped several inches, and with an almost overwhelming sense of fatality, Eric realized he had run out of time.

Was this to be his fate then? he wondered fleetingly as the line separating tree and branch lengthened. Was he meant to die alone in a strange land, with no kin to mourn his passing?

When Shala arrived on the scene, her eyes widened with disbelief as she saw the strange-looking man clinging precariously to a gnarled limb hanging over the cliff. He was of such magnitude that she wondered how the limb could possibly hold him.

But even before the thought was finished, she heard an ominous crack and the limb gave way beneath his weight, sending this hapless being plunging toward the ground that lay so far below.

Hurrying toward the cliff, Shala peered over the

edge, searching for the stranger who had surely fallen to his death. Her gaze found him, sprawled near the base of a juniper tree growing in a small patch of soil perhaps a hundred feet down the cliffside.

He lay still, completely motionless. His spirit had obviously departed his body, because no one, not even a giant such as he, could have survived such a fall.

Although he was a stranger, and of no import to her, Shala felt a mild twinge of regret at his passing. Such a pity, she thought, realizing he might have been saved had she arrived sooner.

Who was he, she wondered, this giant being, and where had he come from? The everpresent need to survive soon won out over her questioning mind, however, and realizing she would never know the answer, she dismissed the hapless individual and looked beyond him to the golden cougar that sprawled lifeless among the rocks.

Although the light was almost spent, Shala dare not wait for next light to skin the mountain lion; other eyes might see the mishap and claim the skin for their own.

Curiously, Shala went back the way she had come, picking her way down the cliff, using small depressions in the rocks for hand and footholds. Had the cougar fallen another fifty feet it would have landed just outside her cave. But since the animal had fallen short, she must skin it where it lay and roll the carcass into the canyon below. Otherwise, she would be bothered with wolves and other predators.

When she reached the level where the man creature lay, she knelt beside him, marveling at the long, wavy hair of a golden color that covered his head and lower jaw.

How strange he was.

Hesitantly, she reached out and smoothed her palm over his hair, feeling surprise to learn the texture was much like her own. Then she turned her attention to his clothing, a heavy garment of white fur taken from some animal unknown to her. Her gaze lowered, traveled down the length of him.

She marveled at his bigness. He easily stood a head taller than she. Where had such a creature come from? she wondered again.

Her gaze touched on his leg, bent at an awkward angle, and she felt a measure of regret. Even in death a man such as he—so magnificent a specimen—should have remained intact.

Taking her time to study him well, her roving gaze returned to his face. She focused momentarily upon his complexion, which was much lighter than her own coppery tan. The flesh was washed in a delicate shade of pink, very similar to the eastern horizon just before Father Sun woke and sent his fiery tongue creeping across the land.

Were the stranger's eyes different from her own?

Never having been one to leave her curiosity long unsatisfied, she lifted an eyelid and peered at the rounded orb beneath.

His eyes *were* different! Unlike her own night-dark ones, his were the color of new spring grass.

How could such a thing be possible? she wondered, having never heard stories of such a man existing. Not even from the travelers who came to the village to trade with the clan.

She bent closer, peering at the stranger's green eye, hoping to find some clue to his origin there.

Suddenly, without warning, his other eyelid popped open and that impossibly green iris rolled sideways and focused on her. Startled, Shala let a tiny yelp of surprise escape her before she jumped back and reclaimed the spear that was her only defense.

Two

Eric woke to numbing pain. He was instantly aware that he was no longer alone. He rolled his eyes toward the figure leaning over him, trying to focus his vision as the woman jerked away from him, snatching up the spear she'd left nearby. Spreading her legs in a fighting stance, she drew back her arm, pointing the deadly missile directly at him.

He fought against waves of dizziness, glaring ferociously at the *skraeling* woman who thought to intimidate him with her puny spear tipped with nothing more than a small stone arrowhead.

She jabbed the missile toward him. It penetrated the flesh of his upper right arm. Growling with rage, Eric reached for the spear. He yanked it from her hands and flung it aside.

Caught off balance, the woman sprawled heavily across him, sending the breath whooshing from his body as well as her own. He was acutely aware of every bruise, every painful claw mark the cougar had inflicted.

How he came to live through the fall was a mystery to Eric. He swallowed around his rising nausea, unwilling for the female to see his weakness lest she mistakenly take it for fear.

Breathing hard and fast, she scrambled once again for her weapon and snatched it up, her expression wavering between fear and challenge.

"Stop!" Eric grunted, realizing that he needed her help. When her expression remained unchanged, he resorted to sign language, pointing to himself first, then holding his hand, palm outward, in the universal sign of peace. "Friend," he growled, spreading his lips wide, hoping she would comprehend.

Silence stretched between them. Although she remained alert, she made no move toward him. He tried to ignore the pain in his body, focused instead on the woman in front of him. She was small—no more than five feet tall—and wore a garment made from the skins of rabbits. Her dark hair was long, flowing past her waist. He noted these things, then realized that his stare was returned. Her eyes pierced him as she accorded him the same type of intense inspection he was giving her.

His gaze lifted to her face again. He hoped her expression would have softened slightly, but it had not. He noticed also that the slim, strong fingers wrapped so tightly around her spear were tense with excitement. He knew without a doubt that she could, and would, with the slightest provocation launch the weapon with deadly aim.

Had he survived the fall from the mesa only to

be speared like a wild pig by a mere woman? No! He refused to let such a fate befall him.

Summoning every last remnant of his failing strength, Eric pushed himself to his elbows. He straightened his right leg. Immediately, excruciating pain stabbed through the injured limb, a pain so fierce his most valiant efforts could not stop the groan of agony which erupted from his lips.

He stared at the leg. Had he broken it?

A movement jerked his eyes back toward the woman. With immense relief, he found she was lowering the spear, apparently having decided he was in no condition to harm her. Propping the weapon against a nearby rock where it would be close to hand should her judgment be in error, she bent to administer aid to his damaged leg.

"Leave it be!" he said sharply.

Paying him not the slightest heed, she spoke in a guttural language, at the same time grasping his ankle with both hands and giving it a hard jerk.

"Thor's teeth!" The words spewed out of his mouth as spasms of tortured pain moved over him like waves. He clenched back further screams, fighting against the cloud of pain hovering around him. "Leave it be, woman!" he ordered harshly.

She ignored his outburst. She was obviously taking advantage of his weakness, he decided quickly, to torture him. When, without warning, she yanked on his leg again, the blackness that had been threatening finally descended, covering him with a smothering mantle and, thankfully, he knew no more.

Momentary panic flooded Shala's thoughts when she saw the stranger's eyes flutter closed and felt his body go limp. The panic soon subsided when she realized he was not dead but merely unconscious. Now she would be able to straighten the broken bones and bind them with wooden splints without his feeling the pain.

Worry creased her brow as she contemplated the problem of moving him. There was no way she could accomplish the task without some help, yet none was no available.

The problem seemed insurmountable.

She looked across the canyon toward the cliff city. If the occupants there knew of this man's presence they would be fearful. And perhaps with good cause. His very size made him formidable, yet, if they only stopped to think for a moment they would realize he was harmless with his broken limb, helpless against those who would harm him.

For his own safety, though, he must be moved. He must be taken to a safe haven before the shaman learned of his presence among the People.

Shala knew the clan shaman well, knew he had been actively searching for a scapegoat, someone at whom the finger of blame could be pointed. Harsh weather had wreaked havoc upon the People's food supply and had brought illness and death to many. The spirits must be very angry.

And now, with the appearance of this stranger, Shu would have someone to blame their anger upon. Who better to accuse, after all, than a stranger incapable of defending himself?

For several moments she studied the man's face. There was great strength etched upon his countenance. His fair skin was pulled taut against smooth cheek and brow bones. Although she had been aware of the harshness in his voice, she could not fault him for it. His pain must have been intense. Since he did not know her, he would, of course, think she was a danger to him.

But suppose she could change his opinion of her? Would he not then be an asset? A man such as he could provide well for her, could hold her enemies at bay.

As quickly as the thought came, it was followed by laughter. Her thoughts were racing far too fast. Before he would become her protecting warrior, she must first keep him alive.

Darkness settled over the land as Shala descended to the small cave where she lived. All doubts about what she was doing were excised as the clouds dissipated and the moon appeared to light her way with its golden glow. Even Wind Woman's breath had stilled by the time Shala entered the cave.

Gathering together the things she would need, she returned to the stranger. With string made from yucca fiber, she bound his leg to splints. After fastening the last knot, she settled back on her haunches, her eyes traveling over him in a possessive manner.

His shoulders were wide, his chest broad; the whole of his body spoke of strength and power.

He was the answer to her prayer, she realized with a growing sense of hope and expectation. Fierce though he was, he could do her no harm in his present state. That gave her time to know him, time to teach him, time to make him want to stay beyond his healing time. Surely that would not be so hard to do. After all, was he not a man? Would he not, therefore, have a man's desires? If she satisfied those desires, would he not be willing to stay by her side?

She felt excited by the prospect. She allowed her eyes to travel again over his body. His shoulders were strong; he might easily be capable of carrying a bear across them. He was broad-chested, the flesh gracefully narrowing at waist and hips. Despite the swollen damaged flesh of one leg, his lower limbs appeared strong and well muscled. He was no doubt a swift runner, but the large muscles bulging beneath the skin of his thighs suggested he must also be capable of a steadfast and unswerving stance. He would, most likely, stand firm against the most fearsome of enemies. She knew from her brief experience of him that he would not flinch at pain.

For several moments more she studied the stranger's physique. Her gaze paused for the merest slice of time upon the area of his maleness. He would, no doubt, be capable of making many babies, she decided, and she felt an involuntary twinge of delight at the thought. First things first, she admonished herself. Before he could become her mate, she must get him to safety. Before he could plant the seed of children within her, she must make certain he lived.

Her gaze traveled along the ledge, searching for shelter. She eyed a narrow opening in the cliff located beneath a protruding rock. It might be large enough to protect him from the chill weather until she was able to get him to her dwelling.

Placing her hands beneath his armpits, she tugged at him, putting her back into the effort. He remained unmoving, however. He was far too heavy for her puny strength.

Shala released him then, and sat back on her haunches, her brow creased into a frown as she took time to ponder the dilemma.

It was obvious, she realized with regret, that she would need help. But where was it to come from? Where could one shunned by her own clan ever hope to find help?

Thanks to Shu, everyone avoided her, fearing that by befriending her they would bring the shaman's wrath upon themselves. He had warned that on all those giving aid to one shunned, he would bring down his mightiest curses. Their spirits would then be doomed to wander forever in the eternal void, and there would be no peace for their restless souls.

She looked across the canyon at the city built into the cliff. There was one slight glimmer of hope to be found there. If she could find Nampeyo, could speak to him without his father's knowledge, he might be willing to help.

And, although Nampeyo was crippled, their combined strength might be enough to lower the man to her cave.

She would have to go to the cliff city, she quickly decided. She would have to appeal to Nampeyo. It was the only way.

The cold night air surrounded her, and she pulled her cloak higher around the neck to keep out the chill as she crossed the mesa, her feet crunching against the frozen snow. When she reached the eastern slope just above the cliff city, she carefully descended the narrow trail that curved down to handholds cut into the stone a short distance north of the cliff dwellings.

Shala paused to catch her breath beneath the jutting overhang of the cliff's brow near the edge of the city. Her nostrils flared, assailed by the smoky scent of cooking fires, of roasting meat and roosting fowl. It was all so familiar, so symbolic of what she had lost by refusing the shaman's advances.

Hugging the shadows near the cliff, hoping she would remain unseen, Shala circled the nearest courtyard formed by the roof of a kiva below. Upon various levels, round walls enclosed the upper part of many more kivas dug into the cave's floor. From the roofs of each one, ladders protruded like fingers pointing the way to the blessed Star People.

Shala paid little attention to the kivas, for they had nothing to do with women. They were used totally by the men of the tribe for ceremonial purposes. Instead, she looked wistfully around the city that was aglow with firelight, moving steadily toward one particular fire, hoping beyond hope to find the woman who had suckled her.

Gryla.

When she first came upon her, the older woman was bent over her cooking, unaware of Shala's presence. She seemed smaller than Shala remembered, more bent, somehow. Almost shrunken. Her hair, white as the deep winter snow, glistened in the firelight, and her face was a shriveled caricature of the one Shala had known. Had she aged so much in one short season, or had Shu, aided by the evil Spirits, cursed her with feebleness, angered into doing so because she had given birth to one who would deny the clan shaman?

Shala longed to go to her, to touch her gently, to implore forgiveness. But Gryla looked so frail, as though a simple sneeze could knock her from her feet. Then, as if sensing another presence, Gryla looked up, her gaze probing the darkness until Shala, unable to resist, stepped out of the shadows and revealed herself.

Their eyes met and held, and in that long, silent moment, Shala realized her mother's grief over their separation was as deep as her own.

She silently cursed herself for causing her mother more pain. She should have gone about her business, should have left the poor woman unaware of her presence. Gryla made an involuntary movement toward the girl she had birthed and Shala shook her head, holding up a cautionary hand, her eyes flickering around them, fearing her mother's actions would be seen and commented on.

Gryla, made aware of the circumstance, looked furtively around to see if anyone had noticed her temporary lapse.

Shala swallowed hard around a knot of pain, feeling unaccountably hurt that her mother could not acknowledge her presence. Yet she knew Gryla had no choice. A mere nod of the head could incite the shaman's wrath, even against one as important as Gryla, who held a coveted position in the clan as Keeper of Memories.

Shala's lips twisted bitterly. The position was one that would eventually have come to Shala when her mother was no longer among the living. Now, however, because of Shu, it would never be hers. Another thing the shaman had taken from her.

One man should not hold such power, she told herself. It was not right. Was theirs not a matriarchal society with the women owning everything except the crops in the fields? Yet the shaman was all powerful, his word law.

Why, she wondered as she had many times in the past, should the position of shaman always fall to a man?

But even as she asked herself the question, she knew the answer. Tradition's mandate. *Because it had always been so.* It was, after all, the shaman who spoke to Father Sun and Mother Earth, interceding for the clan in all matters. Without his intervention there would be no sunlight to make the crops grow, no good soil in which to plant the seeds. To not have a male shaman was to risk the fury of the spirits.

Realizing at last that she had no time for musing, Shala cast aside her thoughts of clan traditions and angered spirits, and after one last painful glance toward Gryla, she hurried on toward Nampeyo's quarters, keeping well to the shadows. She could hear children's laughter, women calling to one another as they cooked the evening meal and countless other sounds, mingling, so familiar, so dear to her heart that tears stung her eyes. She stopped for a few precious seconds to squeeze her eyelids tight against the assault.

She blinked the last of the tears away, then hurried on. A scuffling noise to her left brought her to a stumbling halt. A tingling at the base of her neck gave her warning that she was being observed.

"Shala!" a voice hissed, coming from the shadowy darkness of a doorway. "Come to the storehouse. Now, Shala!"

Recognizing the voice, Shala immediately changed direction and headed deeper into the cavern behind the cliff dwellings where the winter stores of food were held.

The darkness was absolute in the inner recesses of the cliff overhang. Not so much as the light from the cooking fires could penetrate there.

Shala heard the whisper of yucca fiber sandals just before she sensed movement in the blackness. Then Nama, her childhood friend, stepped forward and reached through the darkness to touch Shala's arm.

"Why have you come?" Nama asked gravely. "You know it is forbidden."

"Because I need help," Shala replied.

Nama's voice filled with concern. "We have been forbidden to help you, Shala, as you well know. But Shu has gone from the village until next light, so perhaps we can give aid without his knowledge. Are you in need of food?"

"No," Shala said. "The help is not for me. It is for another."

"Another?" Curiosity echoed the concern in Nama's voice. "One of our clan?"

Shala shook her head. "He is a stranger."

"A stranger?" The tension drained from Nama's tone. When she spoke again, there was amusement in her voice. "Is the stranger a man?"

"Yes. But that is of little consequence."

"What is there about this man which causes you to go where you are not welcome? Why do you risk so much for one you do not know?"

"If I do not help him, he will die. I am concerned with keeping him alive." She grasped the other girl's forearm to emphasize the urgency.

"I came to ask Nampeyo for help," Shala said.

"Nampeyo is not here," Nama replied. "He has gone with Shu to the temple of worship to speak with Father Sun."

Shala's spirits sank, and she expelled a worried sigh. The temple of worship had been built on the highest peak of the mountain, a tribute to Father Sun. Nampeyo would not return this night.

Of that she could be certain. "Next light will be too late," she said, wondering what she could do. "The stranger must be sheltered from the cold and the predators that hunt at night." Her mind recalled Nama's slender form. Was the girl strong enough to help her move the man?

Shala's voice was hesitant when she spoke again. "There is no other in the village to call friend except you, Nama."

"Friendship with you can be costly," the girl replied. "To be your friend is to risk the wrath of Shu. Most fear it."

"But you do not?"

Nama shrugged her shoulders. "Much has happened since you left the city. Shu has promised me to Standing Wolf when the crops are again in the fields. He would not dare harm me lest he make enemies of the desert people."

"Standing Wolf?" Shala vaguely remembered the gnarled, bent old man that went with the name. He and several of his warriors had come to the cliff dwellings last summer. "You would mate with him? He is an ugly old man who has had many wives! Why does he seek another?"

"Because the last one crossed over to the spirit world, taken during childbirth," Nama muttered. "As did those before her. The desert people do not respect their women, nor do they offer any protection for them. It would have served me better to have been away when Standing Wolf came looking for a mate."

The girl's unbending acceptance angered Shala, but she could offer no words of advice. The clan shaman was all powerful, and if Nama stood against him, she too would suffer Shala's fate.

She considered Nama's unhappy situation. Perhaps becoming an outcast would be preferable to living with desert people, especially if one was to be mated to such as Standing Wolf.

"You could come live with me," Shala suggested.

"That did cross my mind," Nama admitted. "But it would not be so easy. Shu allowed you to live because he wanted others to think your refusal mattered little to him. But I fear he would not leave me alone. He is strongly in favor of creating a bond between our clan and the desert people. He has now decided that sending me to Standing Wolf is the best way to form that bond.

Shala's mind worried over the problem. Unfortunately for Nama, it could not be easily solved. Others of her clan might be of the same mind as Shu, believing such a match would bind the desert people and The People of the Rocks together. In many ways, such a bond would benefit both clans. Standing together, they would be strong enough to keep even the most evil of enemies from attacking. What tribe, after all, would risk bringing the wrath of two united clans down upon their heads?

Shala, realizing the problem would take much thought, dismissed it for the moment, vowing to consider it at length when she had more time. At this time, the stranger's fate was more urgent. "Will you help me?" she asked, bringing Nama's full attention back to the plight at hand.

"I will do my best," Nama gravely promised. "But you must leave first; then I will follow. Where did you leave the stranger?"

"Hidden in the rocks above my dwelling," Shala replied. "We must lower him down the cliff to my cave. Can you bring some rope?"

"I think so," the other replied. "My mother's husband braided a long piece of hide rope during the last light. He was in our kiva before you came. If he remains there, he cannot question my use of the rope."

"Then bring it with you," Shala said.

"Daughter." The word was no more than a husky whisper, breaking gently into their conversation, but Shala knew from whence it came. She turned, and in the barely perceptible light to which her eyes had become accustomed, she saw her mother approaching.

"You should not have come," Shala said, eagerly embracing Gryla. "You will lose your position if Shu finds out."

"I had to speak with you. Are you well?" Gryla looked long into her daughter's eyes. "Are you in need?"

"No. You need not worry about me. Nampeyo taught me to survive." She hugged her mother tight, feeling the frail bones barely covered with flesh. "Have you been ill, Mother?"

"Mine is an illness of the soul," Gryla replied. "My last child has been taken from me."

"Not taken completely, Mother," Shala said. "My home is only across the canyon. You have but to look and you will see me there . . . perhaps not with your eyes, but your heart will know. One day . . . one day soon we will be together again."

"Yes," Gryla said gently, patting Shala's long hair. "Yes, daughter. The day will come when we will live together again." She was silent for a long moment, then, "Are you in need?"

"No."

"Then why have you come here? You know it is dangerous."

"To see Nampeyo." She would not tell her mother the reason, fearing it would only worry the older woman to know of the stranger's presence.

"You must not come again, daughter," Gryla warned. "Much as I desire to see you, you must stay away."

"I know." Shala agreed painfully, hugging her mother again and stepping aside. "It is good to know that you fare well."

"Keep safe, daughter," Gryla said. "One day you will return. Nampeyo has promised me this."

Shala nodded. "He will keep his word. Of that I am certain. Farewell, Mother."

Shala left her mother then and, working her way silently past the network of kivas, returned to the mesa. Soon she was joined by Nama, who carried a long coil of rope looped over one arm.

"Were you seen leaving?" Shala asked.

"My mother knows, and although she disapproved, she will tell no other."

"You told her about the stranger?" Shala asked.

"No. Only that you needed me. Do not worry. She will turn a blind eye toward me. She is not happy about Shu's decision." Nama shrugged. "She understands, though, that her voice would not be heard above the shaman's."

When they reached the cliff where the stranger had fallen, Shala peered over the edge, but the moonlight was too pale for her to see below.

"We must go carefully," she told the other girl, taking the lead to show Nama the way down.

Wind Woman's breath was strong, and snowflakes swirled around them as they descended the cliff to where the stranger lay. He remained where she had left him, alone and unconscious. For a moment she thought him dead.

Dropping to her knees beside him, Shala felt along the side of his neck until she detected a tiny throb of life.

"Loop the rope around the tree," Shala instructed the other girl, using the other end to make a harness for the stranger.

Shala worked swiftly, securing the rope around the stranger. Then, using the tree for leverage, the two girls lowered him slowly down the cliff. He remained unaware of their efforts to save his life, his body limp and unconscious as their muscles strained with the effort to keep him from falling. Finally the Viking rested beside the piñon growing outside Shala's little cave.

She glanced skyward, noting the fast moving clouds. "We must hurry," she told Nama. "Before the storm is upon us."

When they had him installed on Shala's sleeping pallet, Nama slumped wearily against the nearest wall while Shala hurried to the firepit.

The flames had long since died from lack of wood. Shala raked through the ashes until she exposed some live coals. Then, reaching for the kindling she kept stacked nearby, she put a few pieces on the glowing embers, blowing until they caught flame and then adding broken limbs until the fire was blazing, sending its warmth throughout the cave.

After checking her store of wood to make sure there was enough to last through the night, Shala went to join her friend who sat against the wall.

"Your help is much appreciated, Nama. I could not have moved him alone."

"Your gratitude is unnecessary," the girl replied. "Friends should help each other when the need is there, no matter the cost involved."

"The cost is too high for most," Shala said bitterly.

"Do not blame them," Nama urged, grasping Shala's forearm and giving it a sympathetic squeeze. "The People are doomed to live under Shu's rule until he passes over to the spirit world." Her gaze went to the stranger. "What are you going to do with him?"

"He is strong," Shala replied, following her gaze. "He will make a good protector."

"It is good you found him. You are in sore need of a protector."

Shala shrugged her shoulders. "I have not suffered without one, but the need to be forever alert deprives the body of a sound sleep."

Nama went to the stranger and knelt beside him. "Where does he come from?" She reached out and stroked the man's golden hair. "His hair is unusual, like nothing my eyes have seen before. Even in sleep, he looks so fierce." She fingered the white fur cloak. "What is this skin he is wearing?"

Shala shook her head. "I have never seen such a fur before." She knelt beside the Viking and fingered the white robe. It was very thick, similar to a bearskin, but a white bear was unheard of. "The cloak must be valuable," she said, turning back to Nama. "Would you like to have it?"

"Me?" Nama's dark eyes widened. "You would give me such a valuable garment?"

"It is the least I can do in return for your help."

"You are more than generous," Nama said, her fingers already fumbling at the unfamiliar fastenings. Round pieces of wood poked through a hole held the garment together. When Nama had them separated, she pulled the cloak apart and stopped short. The man wore a white short-sleeved garment made from some kind of soft fabric. Claw marks had ripped through one shoulder and blood was slowly oozing through.

"The golden lion must have done this," Shala muttered. "Help me remove the cloak."

The two girls stripped the heavy fur cloak away from the man's arms and rolled him sideways until they could remove the garment. While Nama examined the fur cloak for damage, Shala went deeper into the cave and gathered some of the web Grandmother Spider had left behind when she vacated the premises.

Kneeling beside the man, Shala used her obsidian-bladed knife to slice through the shoulder of his white garment; then she washed his wound. She applied the web and pressed it down firmly to stop the bleeding. After determining that he had no further injuries, other than numerous scrapes and bruises and the broken leg, she sat back and studied his upper torso.

As she had previously noted, his shoulders were wide. His upper arms strong and corded with thick muscles, as were his broad chest and back. Such a body was a dangerous weapon in itself and could most certainly provide the protection she so badly needed.

Congratulating herself on her luck in obtaining such a fine specimen, Shala reached for her one good blanket, fashioned from yucca cordage and strips of rabbit fur, and covered his body.

"Where will you sleep?" Nama asked, noting her friend's actions.

"Beside him," Shala replied. "We will share our body warmth."

A smile stretched Nama's lips and glinted in her dark eyes. "You are wise beyond your years, Shala. He is big and should generate much heat." She took her own short rabbitskin cloak and laid it beside the sleeping mat. "He will need my cloak if I am to have his."

"I am sure he would thank you for it," Shala replied politely. "But you must keep it. You dare not wear the other until you leave the cliff city, lest others wish to know where it came from."

"You are right as usual," Nama said, rubbing

her chin against the white fur cloak. "Perhaps it would be best to leave the cloak here . . . just for a while."

"Perhaps so," Shala agreed. "Will you stay the night with us?" The question was only asked out of politeness because she knew Nama dare not be away from the village when the shaman returned.

"Your invitation is much appreciated," Nama said, using the formality that custom demanded, even among such close friends. "Even so, it must be refused," she went on, "but with much gratitude in my heart for having received it." She pulled aside the hide covering and peered outside. "I must leave before the approaching storm prevents my going."

Shala nodded. "I will go with you and offer my protection . . . such as it is." She added more wood to the fire then picked up her spear. "Come. We must hurry before the cliff's edge becomes slippery with ice."

With Wind Woman's breath chilling their exposed flesh, the girls climbed the cliff and set off across the mesa. They encountered no wild animals on their journey and very soon reached the rim above the hidden city. Shala waited until she was sure Nama had reached the lower level; then she hurried back across the mesa, intent on reaching her own abode, and the golden-haired stranger, before the fast-moving clouds covered the moon and made descent too dangerous to attempt.

Three

Shala spent a restless night beside the stranger, afraid to sleep too deeply lest he waken and attack her. But her fears were unnecessary. The man lay unmoving throughout the long, cold night.

When first light chased away the darkness inside the cave, Shala threw back the blanket and left the sleeping pallet to replenish the fire. Soon a small blaze sent heat through her dwelling, driving the cold chill before it.

Turning her attention to the man on her sleeping mat, she was struck by his absolute stillness.

She sucked in a sharp breath, fear surging forth as she studied his pale features. Had she failed in her efforts to keep his spirit lingering near his body? Had it flown away without a sound, like a butterfly leaving its cocoon?

Her heart beat with rapid thuds as she bent over him, placed a fingertip against the base of his neck and searched for some sign of life. Dread settled around her, pressing against her shoulders like a heavy load.

Suddenly it came. Barely discernible at first, then more distinct. It was there, beneath her fingertip, the faint throb that meant his spirit was still within.

He was alive!

Shala's breath, expelled with great relief, mingled with popping and cracking as flames licked hungrily at the dry wood in the firepit.

A frown creased her forehead as Shala puzzled over the stranger's condition. He was alive. She was certain of that. Could she not feel his spirit breathing inside his body?

She reached over again, pressed her finger against the pulse to reassure herself. Yes, it was there, throbbing beneath her fingertip, faint yet distinct. His spirit was still there, and yet his limbs remained motionless.

A horrifying possibility presented itself. Had the fall taken the life from his limbs?

Oh, no! Such a possibility was too terrible to even contemplate. The thought of such a man being paralyzed, being dependent upon another for his very survival was completely abhorrent. She knew without being told that any man facing such a plight would rather be dead.

Forcing such thoughts from her mind, Shala leaned over him again, pulling aside the rabbit-skin blanket to examine his shoulder. Although the wound was angry looking, the flesh around it swollen and red, Grandmother Spider's web had clotted his blood. Given time, the wound should heal.

So why did he continue to sleep?

Shala turned her attention to his head. A quick examination brought to light a big lump, located behind his right ear. She parted the hair to better examine his scalp. Although the skin was broken around the lump, she found nothing more of consequence.

Realizing she could do nothing else for him, Shala donned her leather foot coverings, designed simply as a circle gathered about her ankles and tied with leather thongs. Although she regretted leaving the stranger alone, she knew there was no other choice. It had been an exceptionally hard winter and her food stores were almost gone. There was little left except a few roots and herbs and a small amount of dried meat.

Her mouth twisted bitterly. Had she known sooner that she would be banished from her clan, she could have put aside more food. But her confrontation with Shu did not come until two moons before the great cold settled upon them. A great part of the time since then had been spent learning how to set her snares and use the spear. Now she lived one day at a time, depending on her snares for meat to fill her belly.

Having not the luxury of time to dwell on what she could not change, Shala shrugged on her cloak, picked up her spear and, after one last look at the stranger, left the cave.

She paused for a moment outside, breathing deeply, allowing the chilled fresh air to surge through her lungs and squinting against the morning sun that dazzled her eyes. Then she began the slippery climb up the cliff.

The snow was deep, impeding Shala's progress as she made her way across the mesa to the first of her snares, which she had strategically placed beneath a bush, following Nampeyo's instructions.

Disappointment flooded through her when she found the snare empty. She fared no better at the second one, but the third trap held a grouse, caught tight with the leather thong.

After removing the bird, she set the trap again, then tied the legs of the grouse to a strip of leather and looped it over her shoulder in order to leave her hands free should she need to use her spear.

Her thoughts were on the man in the cave, not on her surroundings when a snap in the junipers, accompanied by a snuffling sound, jerked her head around.

Just in time.

Shala's heart leapt with fear as she saw a wild boar dart from the woods, headed straight for her, its razor-sharp tusks gleaming beneath the morning sun.

Eric groaned in pain as he swam toward consciousness. His eyelids flickered and opened. For a moment he could not comprehend his condition; then he remembered what had brought him to this state. He had fallen from the cliff.

Where was he now? he wondered, gazing up at the smoke-stained rock above him. The last he could recall, a *skraeling* woman had been torturing him, grabbing the leg he had injured in his fall and twisting it mercilessly, obviously delighted by his anguish. He tried, once more, to move the tormented limb, and pain flared immediately.

He sucked in a sharp breath, trying to control the pain as he peered down the length of his body, his gaze dwelling on the crude splints fastened to his injured leg. Someone had tried to set it, obviously one of the *skraelings,* so perhaps they meant to keep him alive. At least for the moment. He took a small measure of comfort from that fact.

His gaze roamed the interior of the small room, skimming over the firepit where a small blaze burned, taking in the clay pottery painted with black geometric designs on a grayish white background, traveling farther to the stack of hides situated against the farthest wall. He recognized the reddish yellow fur that had belonged to a fox, the mottled brown and gray of rabbits and several gray skins that could have been squirrels. All were from small animals. He wondered why, but spent little time contemplating the matter.

His attention turned, instead, to the hide bags that rested beside the stack of furs, and he wondered what they might contain. Again, his attention shifted, going this time to the clay pot, shaped like a large pitcher. Protruding from the top was the long, slender stem of a gourd.

Could it be a dipper? he wondered, his tongue moving slowly over his parched lips.

He swallowed hard, becoming conscious of an almost overpowering thirst.

Pushing himself to his elbows, he stared across

at the pitcher, almost certain now that it contained water. And he needed a drink, needed desperately to quench his burning thirst.

With a great struggle, he pulled his good leg beneath him and, his weight on his arms, attempted to rise. The effort sent pain stabbing into his injured leg, sent his senses reeling, forced the dark shadows to hover closer as he danced in and out of consciousness. At last the darkness descended mercilessly, completely overwhelming him, enveloping him in a cloud of oblivion.

Realizing the boar was intent on making a meal of her, Shala raced toward the nearest tree, hearing the pig crashing through the underbrush as it followed.

She could almost feel the boar's hot breath on her, could imagine sharp tusks ripping through her flesh, its snout rooting through her stomach. Fear caused her breath to come in short gasps, her legs pumping swiftly as she ran for her life.

Then, suddenly, the tree was before her. Dropping her spear, she leapt for the lowest branch, swinging her legs up and over.

When she was safely installed on the limb, with her legs locked securely around it, she lay still, listening to the pounding of her heart while she tried to catch her breath.

The boar, having been deprived of its prey, stopped beneath the tree and snuffled at the snow. Only then did Shala realize she had dropped the grouse when she had leapt for the branch. Despite the immediate danger posed by the boar, disappointment lay like a heavy stone in the pit of her stomach as she watched the animal devour her bird. That meager meal finished, the wild pig took one last baleful look at the girl perched out of its reach, then with one final snort, turned and trotted back into the woods.

Disgruntled and hungry, her fear having departed with the animal, Shala swung down to the ground, picked up her spear and pinpointed the spot where the boar had entered the woods. Although her grouse was gone, the boar would make a fine substitute. One quick kill could provide her with meat for many days to come.

Strengthened by newfound determination, Shala followed the boar's trail, the spear within her hand poised and ready.

Karl Nordenskiold leaned against the rail of the longboat and studied the dense woods along the shoreline. He had thought he had seen movement only moments before, but perhaps he had been mistaken, for his probing gaze brought nothing to light.

"Why do you stare at the shore?" a deep voice queried from behind him. He did not need to turn to view the speaker, the voice was all too familiar, belonging to none other than his brother, Arn. "Did you see something?"

"I thought I did," Karl replied. "I hoped it was Eric and the others returning, but now I find there is nothing."

"Your eyes are seeing what your mind wishes to find," Arn said. "He has been gone so long that I fear for his safety. Would it not be better for us to go in search of them?"

"Eric told us to wait here and keep the boat safe from invaders. We must do so else he'll return and have no boat to carry him away from this place." He heaved a heavy sigh. "Surely he will come soon. The weather is warming. The snow will melt, and the river will be full again. He must come before then." He was turning away from the rail when a movement, barely seen in his peripheral vision, caught his eye. He turned back, fixed his gaze on the woods again and saw the figure of a man, dressed in furs, step out of the woods.

For a moment he thought it was one of his party—perhaps Eric—returning. Then the afternoon sun caught the man's dark hair, and his faint hope plummeted.

Shala came upon the beast quite suddenly. Luckily, she was downwind and the pig's attention was directed toward a rabbit it had killed. Drawing back her throwing arm, she prepared to loose her spear, but in that fleeting moment of time before she could act, the boar whirled, centering in on her presence.

Though aimed at the center point between the beast's eyes, the spear missed its mark, striking the animal instead in the fleshy area behind its neck. The wound only served to enrage the wild boar. It shook its head, trying to dislodge the spear while Shala searched for a place to escape its wrath should the need arise, realizing, belatedly, that she had forgotten one of the most important things Nampeyo had taught her—to insure a place of safety before launching an attack that might be returned.

A lone tree stood with branches outspread. Although the trunk was slender, she thought it would hold her weight. She edged toward it.

Too late.

The beast seemed to sense her intention. It spun with incredible speed to face her. In the next instant, it charged.

Fear filled her, making her every muscle tense and escaping from her lips in the form of a scream. Acting on impulse alone, Shala jumped to the side, swiftly dodging the beast, giving it no time to pause.

Without thinking, she hurled her body onto the boar's back, straddling its midsection and latching her fingers around the wooden spear, trying to drive it deeper into the animal.

With a squeal of rage, the pig turned and twisted its mighty head, spittle flying, as it attempted to gore her with its razor-sharp tusks. Her muscles strained, her fingers tightened as she fought to maintain her grip. In that moment of time, death seemed no more than a breath away.

The beast's strength seemed enormous. In its rage, it whirled and spun and squealed, twisting and turning and jerking in its all-consuming effort to dislodge her from its back. Shala's heart pumped madly, and the world twirled in a blur of white as the muscles in her legs strained to keep their hold upon the frenzied animal's back.

She fought with every ounce of strength she possessed to push the wooden spear deeper into the savage beast. She was totally unprepared when the pig slipped on the ice and fell. The spear shaft snapped in her hand, and the breath in her lungs burst past her lips as her body slapped against the ground.

She lay stunned while the wild pig tried to scramble to its feet, slipping and sliding on the patch of ice that had been its undoing. Shala told herself to move while the chance was there, to get away before the boar turned on her again, but her body refused to respond and she remained frozen. She could only gasp for lost breath like a fish flung upon the river's bank, fighting desperately to survive.

She opened her mouth to scream, and even as she did, she knew it would be a futile effort. Who would hear her? And even if her screams were heard, who would come to her rescue?

Her lips fell closed, and the sound of her scream died even before it was born.

Would this moment, she wondered fleetingly, be her last?

Nama was sewing a new cape, meant as a parting gift for her mother, when the woman joined her.

"You are sad, my daughter," Ona said.

"Yes." Nama could respond with no other words. Her sadness was almost overwhelming. She knew she should put her fate from her mind, for there was nothing she could do to prevent it, but this day, this hour, the thought of what was ahead lay heavy on her.

"Your thoughts are of the desert people?"

"Yes," she said again, pushing her bone needle into the leather to bind the two pieces together. She could not bring herself to look at her mother.

"If I could prevent your going I would," Ona said softly, caressing her daughter's cheek with the back of her hand. "But who listens to me? I am nothing but an old woman, amounting to little in the eyes of the shaman."

"No one can prevent what is to come," Nama said, blinking away the moisture from her eyes. "I must learn to accept my fate." Her breath expelled and she added, "But it is very hard."

"It is equally hard for me," Ona replied. "If I could take your place, then I would gladly do so."

Such words were unnecessarily spoken. Nama needed no words of assurance to know of her mother's love and devotion. She had always felt protected by her mother's love, but even Ona could not stand against the shaman. No one could. Nama felt the hopelessness of despair settle heavily upon her. Her fate was sealed. There was no way out.

Shala's heart thumped rapidly as she flung her body sideways, rolling, tossing herself out of the beast's charging pathway. Scrambling quickly as it moved past her, she saw that the boar had stopped only a few feet from her and was now turned, preparing for its next charge. She looked about her, searching for something to use for a weapon. Behind her, a solid wall of rock rose sharply, preventing her retreat. To her left, a dense thicket of brush and brambles formed an impenetrable barrier, and the boar, poised now in that final instant before charging, was angled so that movement forward or to the right was impossible. Her eyes fell upon the large stone in that same particle of time in which she became aware of the boar's body hurtling toward her again, and even as she lunged forward, grasping the heavy stone with both hands, she felt the beast's hot breath upon her and her body numbed with fear and it seemed that this must certainly be the end, for she became intensely aware of her body falling backward as the boar struck her, and even though she knew her arms were lifting the heavy stone high above her head as the assault was made, she was not aware of any struggle to lift the burden. The stone might as easily have been an eagle's feather, so effortlessly did her arms raise it, and as she felt the boar's tusk pierce the flesh of her thigh, she realized that the stone, like a feather, was now falling back to earth. Gently, slowly, liltingly did her arms bring the stone downward, and she could think of nothing more than its descent as the blackness of newfound pain enfolded her. In the next instant, the stone, the boar, the world were gone, replaced by blissful blackness and gratefully, Shala knew no more.

She knew not how long she lay there, senseless, before the darkness left her. Her first and foremost thought was of the immense silence surrounding her, and her eyes grew wide with stunned surprise as she looked downward and saw the boar lying motionless at her feet. A portion of the boar's skull was marked with the stone's impression, and blood was everywhere. Oozing from the animal's head wound, splashed upon the stone and ground, and pulsing profusely from her thigh where the boar's tusk had torn her flesh.

Reaching out quickly, Shala grabbed a tuft of the dead grasses that jutted out from the stone embankment behind her and used the brittle grass like a sponge to soak up the excess blood as her hand applied pressure to the open wound.

Thankfully, she realized the boar's tusk had missed muscle, bone and sinew. The wound was not too deep and would do no lasting damage.

Shala leaned against the rock embankment and breathed deeply, intensely aware of how lucky she was to be alive. Gathering her strength, she shoved away from the rock. Wisdom dictated that she could not manage the dead boar with her wounded leg. Therefore she must leave most of it behind. She would take the heart and liver, though. And as much more of the meat as she could carry.

Bending over the boar, she sliced it open and dug her hands into the moist warm cavern, pulling out the heart and liver. Gratefully, she consumed the warm meat, heedless of the blood that dribbled down her chin, feeling renewed strength flowing into her body.

After she had filled her belly, she cut away a large slab of meat, wishing she could carry more, yet knowing it was impossible. Then, arching her back to soothe the ache of bending over, happy with the taste of blood and fresh liver on the back of her tongue, she hoisted the meat across her back and began the long journey home.

It seemed an eternity before she reached the safety of her cave.

The big man lay where she had left him. His condition seemed unchanged. As before, he was motionless. Already the moon and sun had circled the sky, but still he showed no sign of waking.

Anxiously, she knelt beside him, feeling his neck for a pulse as she had done before. A breath of relief escaped her throat. His heart still beat. He lived.

Taking a few moments to properly dress her leg wound, cleaning it and applying spider web to absorb the blood and then wrapping her leg with a soft, tanned strip of rabbit hide, she felt her senses calm. Her own heartbeat began to slow, and she slumped down beside the stranger, leaning against the cavern wall, exhaustion sweeping over her.

Shala dropped her head against her left shoulder, closed her eyes and allowed the peace of her small cave to wash over her.

Finally, hunger forced her to move again.

Pushing herself upright, she added wood chips

to the live coals, blowing on them until they caught and flames danced upward to the logs she had placed above them.

There was work to be done. The meat would have to be washed and then cut into chunks to boil. Her mouth watered at the thought of stew.

When the fire was blazing to her satisfaction and she felt content that there would soon be enough coals to cook a pot of stew, she picked up her obsidian knife and went to work on the meat.

Once again, Shala regretted the loss of the whole pig. Had she been able to bring it home, the animal would have supplied her with meat for several weeks.

Her glance flickered to the stranger, and she wondered how much he would eat. She suspected he would need twice as much as she herself consumed. Perhaps even more. That could pose a problem. She would have to see that he recovered as quickly as possible, so that he could provide his own food.

After putting the chunks of meat in a blackened pottery cooking vessel, she added water and dried vegetables, then put it over the coals. Later, when there was time, she would scrape the rest of the meat from the hide and stretch it for curing.

With a sigh of relief, she sat back on her haunches and wiped the sweat from her brow, unaware of the dark splotch she left on her forehead, blood left on her fingers from the boar's vital organs.

She realized she needed to wash, but knew as well that she must wait until the pieces of boar's hide were disposed of. Otherwise, she would have to do it again, and her water supply was running low.

After stirring the contents of the cooking pot, Shala turned her attention to the man again. She decided to check his head wound. It was past time that she cleaned it.

She knelt beside the stranger and parted the hair around his wound. The bleeding had stopped, but there was dirt embedded in the scalp around the injury. She must clean it at once and she would need hot water to do so.

Regretfully, she went to her water supply, saw the water container was nearly empty.

Sighing, for she had no wish to go outside again, Shala took up a large, pitch-covered basket and left the cavern to fill it with snow. When she returned, she filled a blackened pot with the white cold and, regretfully, moved aside the boiling stew to make space over the coals for the pot.

Dipping her hands into the frozen slush, she cleaned them as best she could, then, while the snow was melting, she sat back to catch her breath.

Her gaze went often to the unconscious man, and she wondered again where he came from.

When steam began to rise from the pot, she picked up a scrap of hide to protect her hands from the heat, removed the vessel from the fire and replaced it with the stew pot.

Although the water was tepid, she was tired, anxious for a hot meal and her bed.

Carrying the bowl of water to his bed of juniper branches covered with hide, Shala set it down, then gathered up a scrap of soft buckskin and the root of the yucca plant.

She had already softened the yucca root by pounding it. Now she placed it in one of the bowls. She let it soak while she scooped up a handful of the cool water and poured it over his wound. Then, taking the yucca root in hand, she rubbed it and squeezed it until she had enough suds. After she laid it aside, she gently rubbed the area around the wound, taking care to cause as little pain as possible while she removed the grit, using much the same technique she had used when cleansing her own wound.

Afterwards she made a poultice for the wound and put it over the gash. She next mixed a tea of healing herbs, pinched his nostrils together until he opened his mouth and poured it down his throat.

Settling back, she studied him again. Had she done everything she could? Did he have other wounds?

Realizing she must know, Shala fumbled with the fastenings of his garment. When she had the shirt removed, she stared down at his massive shoulders and chest. Strength such as this could be dangerous if it wasn't controlled from the beginning.

Swallowing back a surge of fear, reminding herself that he could do her no harm—indeed, he could only be grateful to her for saving his life—she scooped up a handful of water and poured it over his chest, following it with scoop after scoop, making sure she wet down every part of his upper torso.

Then, dipping the soft buckskin into the sudsy water, she gently rubbed his chest with the cleansing froth. His flesh was scraped and bruised, especially around the middle of his torso. Grit was embedded in the abraded skin around his flat male nipples and she leaned forward, paying careful attention to them, rubbing her fingers softly across them to remove the embedded particles.

She felt an odd catch in her throat, her breath became quick and there was a fluttery feeling in the pit of her stomach.

How curious.

She wondered if she were sickening.

Perhaps she should drink some of the healing brew. She must not become ill, she told herself, she could not afford to. Not now, when there was no other to care for this man.

Her fingers raked across his flat nipples, and she felt them harden. How odd. She leaned closer, studying the reddened flesh, finding them curiously interesting.

Why should it be so? Naked chests were not unfamiliar to her. During the warm season the men of her clan wore nothing but a loincloth; yet there was something different about the body of this man.

Perhaps it was because he was so unlike the

men of her acquaintance, or perhaps it was because of the faint coloring of his hair and flesh.

Not only was his hair a strange color, never before had she seen so much on one man. His head and pale skin was covered with it, all of it of that same golden color.

She flicked a nipple curiously, watched it harden again, and at the same time she had that strange sick feeling in her stomach. Why should that be? She flicked the nipple again, and as before, her stomach reacted.

How strange!

How curious!

Feeling almost shaky, she finished washing his upper torso and turned her attention to his neck and face, intent on completing the task.

The soft buckskin dripped water as she washed his neck, then his chin, working upward to his mouth and across his jaw line.

Suddenly, the hairs on the back of her neck stood on end. Shala lifted her gaze and sucked in a sharp breath. His eyes were open, those eyes colored like new spring grass, and they were staring—straight into hers.

Four

Eric woke when the woman first began to wash his body, as she would surely have known had she looked down upon his maleness. But she had not, and by the time she realized he was awake, he had himself under control.

While the *skraeling* woman washed him, he was able to study her without her knowledge.

Why was she so intent on having him clean, when she was so uncaring of her own person? he wondered. It made no sense to him. He studied her long dark hair. It needed a good brushing to take the tangles out, needed to be confined in some way or another, for she was constantly shoving the shorter strands back with her forearms as she worked.

Even her face was dirty, he thought with disgust. Streaked across her forehead was a dark stain that looked very much like dried blood.

His nostrils flared slightly as he realized the *skraeling* woman even bore the faint coppery smell that he associated with blood. What had she been doing? Bathing in the stuff?

Eric sensed her curiosity with his person, noticed how much time she spent washing his chest and nipples and tried to remain passive beneath her ministrations. But it was difficult. Almost impossible, he found, for despite his best efforts, he experienced a slight tautening of his nipples, felt it in his loins as well, but he tried to disassociate himself to keep his member from hardening, was able to keep his conscious state from the woman until she looked up and saw his opened eyes.

She jerked back in alarm, her eyes opening wide, her mouth dropping open and then snapping to as though a door had been slammed to stop a scream from erupting. Her face was a mixture of emotions; fear gave way to confusion, which was followed by a flush that spread up her cheeks.

His lips twitched slightly. Was she blushing? He was almost certain of it, and found it oddly amusing to see this *skraeling* woman unsettled.

The blush deepened then, and she lowered her eyes. Almost immediately her lashes jerked up again and she lifted her chin and met his gaze straight on. Her lips thinned slightly, and he realized she was annoyed at being caught unaware.

She spoke abruptly, her words harsh and guttural, and there was defiance in her tone as well as a subtle challenge. Her flashing dark eyes held steady on his green ones. It was more than obvious she had regained her composure.

Thor's teeth! he thought with a growing sense

of annoyance. If only he could make her understand him! But he could not. There was only one way they could communicate with each other, and that left a lot to be desired. Nevertheless, sign language was his only hope.

Licking dry lips, he pointed to himself. "Eric," he grunted. "Eric." He jabbed his chest with his forefinger. "Eric," he repeated. Then, pointing to her, he asked, "And you? What are you called?"

Her eyes widened slightly, then narrowed on his mouth and she uttered more of those guttural words that he had no way of understanding.

"Eric," he repeated, again indicating himself. Then he pointed silently at her, raising his brows in a universal mime of questioning. "What are you called?"

She frowned at his finger, then tapped her own chest. "Shala."

"Shala?" Eric questioned.

She nodded her head, her eyes never leaving his. Eric realized the word she spoke might not be her name. She might only have asked him if he were clean enough. Or if he was interested in bedding her. He would not be surprised if she had done so, because, by any standards, he was a man to be desired. Also, he remembered her reaction to his body when she washed him.

If that was in her mind, she could rid herself of the notion. He had no interest in her as a woman, even though he had been without one for a long time, his need was not so great that he would go to such lengths.

But he must be wary, must handle the woman

with care, for it seemed there was no other to tend his needs until he recovered from his injuries. He was, it appeared, wholly at her mercy.

His stomach rumbled, sounding loud in the silence that hung around them. His nostrils twitched again, and he realized there was a scent in the air other than blood. It was the savory aroma of stewed meat.

By Thunder, he was hungry!

Even as the thought occurred, another need overpowered his hunger, the need that had made itself known before. He was thirsty. His mouth was so dry, his throat so scratchy that he could hardly swallow.

He looked at the jug across the room, the one he was almost certain contained water. "Bring me some water," he said imperiously, curling his right hand as though he were holding a cup, then bringing it to his mouth and tilting his head back, going through the motions of swallowing. "Water," he repeated. "Bring me water."

Instead of hurrying to do his bidding, she continued to stare at him, her expression completely confused.

His eyes narrowed, became hard. Was the woman stupid? Could she not understand the simple needs of his body?

Pushing himself to his elbows while choking back a groan of pain, he managed to assume an upright position. When he was sitting with his back against the cavern wall, he beckoned her closer.

For a moment she resisted, then, with watchful

eyes, she inched toward him. Although she remained wary, she was apparently unsuspecting.

It was almost too easy.

He struck with the swiftness of a snake, reaching out with a long arm, fingers curling, tangling in her hair.

She yelped with surprise, then lashed out at him with both arms. His grip tightened, causing tears of pain as he forced her to her knees.

"Water!" he demanded, yanking her face closer until it was only inches from his own. His thirst was so great that he had no compunction about pulling the bitch's hair out by the roots if that was needed.

Her eyes welled with tears, some of them spilling over to flow down her cheeks, yet he felt no regret. He gave another hard yank with his right hand. "Water!" he snapped, again making the drinking motion with his other hand.

Eric felt a thrill of satisfaction when she lowered her tear-clouded eyes and nodded meekly. Good. He had made her understand him.

He released her.

Instantly, she sprang away from him, snatched up a thick stick from her woodpile and struck him hard across the shoulders.

Whack!

She struck again. *Whack!* Again. And yet again. *Whack!* One of the blows landed on the side of his head, and he shielded his face with an outspread palm.

Whack! She hit him again, hard enough to send curses spewing from his mouth!

As blow after blow rained onto him, he fought to regain his senses, fought to ignore the pain, to concentrate on depriving her of her weapon.

When her weapon descended again, he was ready. His fingers reached out, fastened around the thick stick and tightened. Twisting it out of her grip, he held it before her. "Touch me again and suffer, wench!" To emphasize his contempt at her puny strength, he broke the stick in half and flung it away from him.

Tossing her head, she eyed him with cold triumph, and he knew in that long moment of time that he had made a bad mistake. Why had he been so foolish? He had thrown the broken stick out of his reach. Her teeth gleamed in a wicked smile as she curled her fingers around another stick, even larger than the one he had broken, and struck him a hard blow on the head that sent his senses reeling.

Whack!

The blow struck the back of his head and he heard a curious humming.

Whack!

The blow slid off the side of his head and struck his shoulder.

Whack!

Pain sliced through his skull as she struck him above his left ear.

Eric slumped against the wall, his body sliding lower and lower as he waited for the next blow to fall. There was no longer any thought of resistance. How could he resist when the humming was growing louder with each passing moment, while a red and gray haze formed quickly around him. He could hear the sound of thunder. . . . No! Hoofbeats! Distant hoofbeats throbbing in time with his own heart, growing louder all the time, and he recognized them for what they were.

Odin and his Spirit Warriors. They were coming for him, and he was ready to receive them.

But wait, a silent voice screamed. *You cannot enter Valhalla lest you die with your sword in hand!*

Eric's eyes opened, searching for his blade, but it was not to be seen.

So be it. Valhalla was not for him. With a sigh of release, he gave himself over to the spirit world.

Shala's breath came in quick, short bursts, keeping time with her thudding heart as she raised her weapon to deliver another blow. She was on the verge of bringing it down when she became aware of the stranger's unconscious state.

Her anger drained away, and she was besieged by regret. *Your rage killed him!* a silent voice accused.

"No," she protested meekly, slumping to the floor and dropping her club. "He did not understand that he must not have water so soon after drinking the healing brew. He was savage, caused me pain, but I did not mean him harm . . . only meant to teach him a lesson . . . just to subdue him . . . to show him he must be obedient."

Spoken aloud, the words sounded harsh and hateful. What gave her the right to make him a slave to her wishes? She was no better than the people who occupied the southern lands. The desert people and those others—the ones who lived beyond them—the people who populated the rain forests in the southern hemisphere.

Shala had never seen the others—none of her clan had—but the traders knew them. It was the traders who brought word of their existence and their way of life. It was said they worshipped strange gods, that they captured birds with many colored feathers—all the colors of a rainbow—and kept them in cages, and that they bought and sold other humans at will.

Had she sunk to that level?

"No! Not me!" she cried out, springing to her feet and going to the stranger.

Shala winced when she saw the marks left by the stick and her stomach clenched tight, guilt ripping away at her guts. With a trembling hand, she searched his neck for the pulse of life.

"It beats!" she exulted, feeling a great weight leave her shoulders. "His spirit remains. He lives."

Slumping back, Shala stared at him. There was an inherent strength in his face and a set to his chin—evident even beneath the hair covering his face—that suggested a stubborn streak, a trait she had already witnessed.

She dwelt long on his features. Her gaze lingered on the firm, sensual lips, remembering his attempt to make them smile, the way they had curled at the edges.

Sighing, Shala ran her hand across a reddened spot on his upper arm. She was responsible for the mark. Her blows had knocked him senseless. "It was necessary." She spoke aloud, taking comfort from the sound of her voice. "He had to be taught a lesson. He must learn to obey."

Obey? Like a slave? a silent voice questioned.

"No!" Her mind rejected the idea.

Not like a slave. That was against her people's nature. But the man had such strength, and he held such anger within him. What else could she have done?

She must either make him obedient or send him from her abode. And in his condition that would surely be the death of him.

No! She had acted correctly. He must learn to obey her. When that was accomplished, then he would make an ideal companion, someone to keep her company for the rest of the long cold that was upon them.

She studied him a moment longer, saw again the strength and magnitude of the man and realized he would be angry when he woke.

Expelling a frustrated sigh, she reached for a strip of braided hide rope and bound his wrists. Although she regretted the action, she dared not leave him free. Not until he understood that, to regain his freedom, he must become docile.

Although she kept a wary eye on her prisoner, she need not have worried. He remained unconscious throughout the night and was still so when she woke the next morning. She feared that she might have done him irreparable damage with the blows to the head.

She prayed she had not.

* * *

It was late afternoon when Shala went to check her traps again. One held a rabbit, the others were empty. She expelled a heavy sigh that was visible in the cold air. It was past time she moved the traps, but a quick glance at the lowering sun decided her. She would wait until tomorrow. Tonight, they would eat rabbit.

Father Sun was lingering above the western horizon when she reached the cliff above her small cave. Had he not been in that position, she would have missed the gleam of metal, almost hidden by the snow. Just one quick, silvery flash and then it was gone, but it was enough to draw her attention.

Curious, she tossed the rabbit on the ground, laid her spear beside it and leaned over, her hands scraping away the snow until she uncovered the object.

It was long and slender, almost the length of her leg. She grasped one end, obviously a handle, and hefted it, testing its weight, then ran a fingertip across the blade.

Sharp. Very sharp. Obviously a weapon, shaped like a huge knife.

Shala extended her arms, and with both hands wrapped around the thick handle, she swung the weapon, slicing through the air with a soft, swishing sound.

Could the weapon have belonged to the stranger? Even as she questioned that fact, she knew it must have. The blade was unfamiliar, as was the golden-haired man. They must have found their way up the mesa together.

A smile crept across her face, and she swung the weapon again. Swish, swish, swish.

Her smile widened. Although it was heavy for her slight frame, she could manage it nicely with both hands. It would be a heavy deterrent to her enemies.

With a laugh of exultation, Shala picked up the rabbit and her spear, and hurried to the cliff. She could hardly wait to examine the weapon more thoroughly.

When she entered the cavern, her gaze flew to the sleeping mat. Good! He was awake. Relief, strong and heartfelt, flowed over her. Outwardly, she remained uncaring, knowing the beating would have accomplished little if he knew how troubled she had been.

Ignoring him, she laid her spear and the strange weapon beside the entrance, then went about preparing the rabbit for their meal, skinning it and paying special attention to the hide. This one, added to the others she had snared, would finish the cloak she was making.

Suddenly, as Shala dipped one hand into the rabbit's belly, intent on gutting it, the stranger spoke, his voice loud and harsh, his words strange, unknown to her ears.

Jerking around with surprise–she had almost forgotten his existence–she met his overbright gaze. "Silence!" she snapped, hoping he would not notice her trembling hands.

Her eyes swept over him, making certain he was

still securely fastened; then she turned her back to him and went on with her work. But even as she finished gutting the rabbit, even as she skewered it over the flames, she was aware of the golden-haired stranger silently watching her every movement.

What had he said to her?

Although the words sounded harsh and unnerving, perhaps he only spoke of his hunger or requested water again. Surely enough time had passed that a little water could do no harm.

Shala flicked a quick glance at him, found him watchful, ever alert. She was turning away again when his tongue flicked out, ran across his lips.

He *was* thirsty.

She pitied the hapless man, but she ignored the impulse to offer him water. He must first learn what was expected of him, that he must bow to her wishes.

She turned her back to him once more.

Soon the savory aroma of roasting rabbit filled the cave, causing her mouth to water. When the meat was cooked to a turn, Shala removed it from the fire and separated a leg from the carcass.

Settling herself down against the furthermost wall, she nibbled at the meat, knowing that, all the while, the stranger watched hungrily.

When she had eaten her fill, Shala looked up at him.

Now was the time, she decided at last.

She smiled at him.

The golden-haired man looked startled, obviously caught off guard, but he quickly recovered and glared fiercely at her, obviously thinking to intimidate her with his look.

Deliberately, she picked up a stout stick and struck him sharply across the shoulders, inwardly wincing as the weapon smacked against his flesh, but outwardly showing no sign of emotion.

Snarling with rage, he jerked away, raising his bound hands to protect his head. Shala struck him again, pulling her face into a fierceness that no one could misunderstand, and striking him again and again.

Whack, whack, whack!

Breathing heavily from exertion, she dropped the stick and smiled at him again.

Harsh words spewed from his mouth and he glared at her, his green eyes sparkling with rage. Calmly, she reached for the stick, holding it in a threatening manner.

He looked at the club, then at her and slowly, his rage gave way to a puzzled expression.

Shala smiled once more, dropping the hated stick, hoping she was getting her point across, feeling almost certain he was beginning to understand. She was sure of it when his lips twitched, then pulled into a grimace that could have been a smile.

Good!

He did understand.

Pulling the rest of the roasted meat off the stick, she held it toward him. His lips twitched again, curling slightly upward. She came forward slowly, cautiously, the meat temptingly offered.

Holding up his bound hands, he spoke to her in that strange language she could not fathom.

"All right," she said, realizing by his facial expression that he must be asking her to release him. After placing the meat into a clay bowl near the fire so it would keep warm, she worked at the knots that bound him. "It is good you finally understand," she said, offering him a shy smile. "About time you realized you need me more than I need you." The last knot refused to give way to her fumbling attempts to release it. She threw him a nervous glance, hoping he was unaware of how his breath, falling softly against her ear, was affecting her senses. "There," she said, as the knot came loose and the rope fell away. "Is that bet—"

She broke off as his hands reached out and wound through her hair, yanking her hard against him.

He had tricked her!

Shala screamed with rage, pummeling his chest and upper torso with her fists, but he seemed immune to her blows. Her scalp tingled with pain from his grip, but her fury was so great that she continued to pound away at him.

Finally, realizing how futile were her blows, realizing as well that her face was pressed firmly against one of his nipples, she opened her mouth and bit down hard. Had her teeth connected with her target, she would have taken the nipple off, but alerted by her opening mouth, he reacted swiftly, yanking her head aside, and she connected with the hard flesh of his chest.

With a roar of rage, he yanked her loose and flung her away from him.

Shala landed with a hard thump against the far wall.

Spitting out flesh and hair and blood, she snatched up the strange weapon and sprung to her feet, facing the golden-haired stranger.

Five

Thor's teeth! The *skraeling* woman had bitten him! Eric spared a brief look at his bleeding flesh, then his gaze fastened on her.

There she stood, small feet braced, ready for attack, his sword held in both her hands. Could he wrest his blade from her? he wondered. Although his strength was greater than hers, she held the advantage. He was not yet on his feet, and his broken leg would slow down his reaction time considerably.

His stomach rumbled, reminding him of his hunger. *Odin's chariot!* he silently cursed. Why had he not left well enough alone? Eric realized his mistake now. The woman, Shala—was that her name?—had been on the point of feeding him. He would have fared better had he left her to it, had he kept his anger to himself until his stomach was full.

Such a pretense would surely not have been easy—servility was foreign to his nature—for his was a warring people, used to having others give way before them. The thought of pretending otherwise was completely abhorrent to him. And yet, he realized, there was little else he could do, injured as he was, unable to help himself. He had been a fool to think differently.

Perhaps, though, he could regain the advantage. For the moment he could let the *skraeling* woman think she had won—but only for the moment.

He held out his hand, palm outward. "Be calm, woman," he said gruffly, forcing his lips to curl upward in his best imitation of a smile. "You think to intimidate me with your puny strength, but you cannot."

Her expression became less fierce, and convinced he was deceiving her, he forced his lips wider. "You are dirty, unkempt, a disgrace to your sex, certainly the last person I would choose to be with," he went on, "but it seems I have no choice in the matter. We are alone here, and my throat burns for water and my belly cries out for food." He screwed his face into what he hoped was a subservient expression and pointed to the water. "Bring me a drink, you stupid woman." The words were spoken softly, his voice trying for a pleading note that was hard to induce. "When my strength returns you will soon learn who is the master." Being able to say what he felt, even though he forced himself to speak in a servile manner, made him feel better.

Apparently he succeeded in his attempt to make her believe he was thoroughly cowed, because she transferred the sword to her right hand and relaxed her stance ever so slightly.

"Water, Shala," he said, hoping his use of her name would settle her down. He pointed to the water jug. "Bring me some water, Shala."

Something flickered in her dark eyes and he could almost have sworn it was pleasure at hearing her name on his tongue.

"Water, Shala," he said again. "Bring me water."

Her knuckles whitened as her grip tightened on the sword, and for a long moment, Eric thought he had somehow angered her. Their gazes were locked, hers wary, his—he hoped—soft and persuasive.

"Come, Shala," he coaxed, "bring me water."

Another long, heart-stopping moment passed, then she took a sideways step toward the water jug. Keeping wary eyes fixed on him, she filled the drinking gourd, then cautiously approached him.

"Come on, Shala," he said softly, soothingly. "Bring it over here, you *skraeling* bitch. We will play your little game for the moment . . . since there is little else to do. But mark my words well. My day will come. My leg will heal and when it does, it will be a day of reckoning."

She was standing before him now, but well out of his reach, apparently unaware of his hostility, thinking she had so easily put him under her thumb. Let her think that way, he told himself. In doing so, she would not be expecting his move when he made it. There would be time enough for her to learn his nature later.

And she *would* learn. He would make certain of that.

Shala gripped the long blade with her right hand while extending the other—the one clutching the gourd dipper—to the golden-haired stranger who called himself Eric.

He acted quickly, with the swiftness of a striking snake, his arm reaching out, fingers extended, then curling, to wrap around the handle.

Shala retreated, scuttling backward, watching from a safe distance while he drank greedily, unmindful of the water spilling down his hairy chin, and yet, even as he drank, his green eyes remained fixed on hers.

When the dipper was emptied, he held it toward her. "Food!" he said abruptly, again using a word that she was unfamiliar with.

Shala cocked her head and stared curiously at him, wondering what the word meant. Did he want more water? She thought not. The word was not the same as the one he had spoken before.

"Food!" he repeated, jerking his lips into a smile, before gesturing toward the rabbit carcass.

Shala's own lips curled slightly as she realized he wanted something to eat, and was showing his good will by the smile. *Good!* she silently applauded. At the rate she was going, she would have the large man eating out of her hand in no time.

Feeling confident enough to lay the blade aside, she handed the meat across to him. He would need it all, because his frame was so big. Her gaze dwelt on his splinted leg for a brief moment. How long would it take to heal? How much time must pass before she could send him out to hunt for her?

Her eyes flashed back to his, and their gazes locked again. His grass-colored eyes had darkened until they were the shade of moss, unreadable and hard. Suddenly, as though a wall had lifted, she saw a flicker of emotion in them, so fleeting, gone as quickly as it came, but in that moment of time she saw hatred swimming in their depths . . . a hatred so intense that she sucked in a sharp breath and took an involuntary step backward.

Shala trembled inwardly, realizing how easily he had fooled her. The stranger—Eric—was a dangerous foe. One to be reckoned with. One who would not easily give way to her will.

Even as her mind recognized those facts, her brain was activating her body, causing her to bend over, to reach for the spear and the long-bladed knife, her fingers wrapping around them, clutching, gripping before she retreated swiftly, moving to stand with her back against the furthermost wall.

Feeling more secure with the width of the cavern between them, she studied him intently.

One thing was in her favor. The stranger—Eric—needed her badly. He would never be able to manage on his own. Not with his broken leg. Food was hard enough to come by during the winter with two good legs beneath one's body. Without her, he would surely starve to death.

Watching her warily, obviously unaware of her intentions yet needing to fill his stomach, Eric bit into the meat, tearing off a large chunk, chewing with a greediness that was easy to understand. But, although he obviously relished the food, he avoided wolfing his meat. Instead, unlike the men of her clan, Eric chewed each mouthful thoroughly before swallowing it.

"Where do you come from, Golden One?" she asked softly.

Other than a momentary pause, he gave no sign that she had spoken. "You pull your lips into a smile thinking to deceive me, yet all the time you wish to harm me," she went on, feeling a sudden urge to approach him, to stroke his golden hair the way she would a pet. But Shala resisted the urge, knowing she must not approach him.

Not yet. If she allowed herself the pleasure of giving in to such feelings, he would undoubtedly strike with the swiftness of a snake.

"I will wait," she whispered. "And, in time, you will learn that you must accept me. There is no one else to stand between you and starvation. Your leg will not heal before the cold weather leaves us. By that time you will want to stay of your own accord." She smiled wider, watching him go back to the business of eating, paying her no mind now.

Shala sank down against the floor, her back to the wall, her right hand clutching the spear although she thought she would have little need of it now. Eric seemed intelligent enough. He must realize his position, must see that he needed her for his own survival. And if so, they should get along well.

He finished eating, and instead of flinging aside the bones as the men of her clan did, he laid them in a neat pile as far away from himself as he could reach and gestured toward the water jug again.

Shala resisted the impulse to snatch up the dipper and fill it again.

First there was a lesson to be learned.

Her eyes held his steadily for a long, heart-stopping moment, and she made no movement, holding herself perfectly still until his lips twitched, then lifted at the corners. Although the smile was only slight, it was enough.

"Good. You learn fast, Golden One."

Laying her weapons aside, she filled the dipper and carefully placed it within his reach, backing quickly out of harm's way again. While he quenched his thirst, she tidied up her dwelling, gathering up the clay pottery that had been scattered by their altercation—a bowl made by her mother, painted in a black and white geometric design, a slender jug with two handles and a blackened clay pot used for boiling water—and placing them in an orderly fashion beside the wall.

When everything was in order, Shala turned her attention to Eric again, realizing she had only been delaying what must be done.

Her heartbeat picked up speed as she scooped

up the leather bindings and held them toward him. "Hold out your hands," she said, pressing her wrists together to let him know what she wanted of him.

Instead of obeying, he shook his head and spoke unfamiliar words to her. Shala had been expecting that. He refused to allow her to bind him again, but she must. She could not afford to trust him yet, would be a fool to sleep without first making certain he could do her no harm.

Expelling a heavy sigh, she reached for the stick she had used earlier and turned to face him again.

When Eric saw her reach for the stick, his muscles knotted tensely. She was apparently going to use it on him again. By Thor, he refused to allow it. He would wring her slender neck, show his contempt for her puny strength. He tensed, making ready to strike, to wrench the stick from her hands.

She paused, stick in hand, and spoke in the guttural language she had used before, bringing her wrists together again, obviously telling him to submit or be beaten. He was ready for her, he would—

Suddenly he paused, realizing he was doing it again. Thor's teeth! When would he learn that resistance was useless? He must be patient, must wait until his leg healed. Nothing would be accomplished by a show of strength. He was almost helpless and, to his utmost dismay, knew she was totally aware of that fact.

But, by Odin, the war between them was not over. She would soon learn it had only begun.

Gritting his teeth to control his fury, he reached out, fists clenching, wrists together. But even as he bent to her will, he deliberately flexed his biceps to show his greater strength, to make her understand that he was allowing himself to be bound again—by his own will, not hers!

"Well, are you going to stand there all night, or will you be tying me up again?" he asked, his lips curling contemptuously.

A curious expression—was it fear or pleasure?—crossed her face. Whatever she felt, she wasted no time looping the leather strips around his wrists and pulling them tight, apparently feeling the urge to put distance between them as soon as possible.

Bound securely again, Eric settled back on the sleeping mat, closed his eyes and ignored the woman who continued to watch him. He knew she was watching, though he did not look at her. He could feel the heat of her gaze on him.

Forget the wench! he silently ordered. *She is no danger, would already have killed me if that was her intention.*

Uttering a heavy sigh, he shifted to a more comfortable position and allowed his mind to drift, to return to his homeland. With winter well under way, his father and brothers would be in the great room where a fire was always kept burning. They would probably be seated at the long table, either drinking mead and trading stories or polishing and sharpening their weapons as was their usual practice at this time of year. Eric envisioned the scene in his mind's eye, adding his mother and sister seated beside the fire and occupied with their needlework, ever mindful of the needs of the men of the house.

A smile curled Eric's lips. How Brynna hated doing needlework. In fact, his sister disliked doing any of the things females were meant to do. Instead, she would rather be out hunting with Garrick. Even helping to birth a sheep with Olaf, who was the farmer, gave Brynna more pleasure than her sewing.

Eric wondered if his family had worried about him when he had failed to return home before winter set in, then quickly dismissed the idea. They would probably think he was still trading in the Far East, perhaps holed up there until winter was over.

He should have sent word to them, but when he had decided to follow the path of Leif Eriksson to the New World, it had been a spur of the moment thing, and few, except those involved, knew of his decision.

Perhaps it was best they knew nothing of his destination. That way, his mother and sister would not worry overmuch. In his mind's eye, his mother lifted her eyes from her sewing and smiled at him. With that vision in his mind, he allowed sleep to claim him.

The cavern was dark with shadows when Eric awoke. He stared into the blackness, searching out

Shala's presence, his ears attuned to the slightest sound. Her even breathing told him she was sound asleep. Carefully, he lifted his wrists to his mouth, using his teeth to open the knots until his hands were finally loose.

Then, silently, he moved toward her, biting his lips to stifle the pain in his injured leg. His progress was torturously slow, but soon he was beside her. He reached out, his hands brushing her shoulder. Her breathing halted, then continued. His big body moved over hers as his hands circled her neck, squeezed ever so slightly. He knew the exact moment she came awake.

Even in the gloom he could see the fear in her eyes. She squirmed beneath him, trying to throw him off, to free her arms and legs, but his elbows effectively pinned her arms until she could do no more than beat at his sides with her clenched hands. His legs, locked around hers, combined with the weight of his body to make her efforts ineffective.

He squeezed her neck again, then eased his hold, unwilling to cause her permanent injury. "I could easily take your life," he said softly. "I could squeeze the breath from you without even trying, but you are spared, wench. I only hope you are capable of understanding why, because I would rather not repeat this action. I find such closeness completely abhorrent."

Even as he said the words, he realized something curious was happening to his lower body. His manhood was reacting in an unexpected way to the curves pressed so tightly against him.

Why should that be? He had no desire to bed a *skraeling* woman. He attempted to bring his body under control before the *skraeling* wench noticed, but the sudden awareness in her expression told him it was already too late.

She knew. And that knowledge caused a rising fury that tightened his grip momentarily before he brought it under control and rolled away from her. But he was not yet finished. He had set out to teach her a lesson, and he was not done. Snatching up her spear, he broke it in half and tossed it aside.

With a cry of outrage, Shala sprang to her feet and made a dash across the cave. He realized her intention when she bent toward the woodpile and wrapped her fingers around the largest stick and spun around to face him. Eric yanked it from her fingers and broke it in half, tossing the pieces beside the spear. Then, giving an outward appearance of calm, he turned his back on her and sank down on her bed of furs, covering his sword with his own body.

Silence filled the cave when he closed his eyes, indicating he was going to sleep. He held his breath, waiting for what was to come.

The silence stretched out. One minute, two, then suddenly he heard her utter a harsh word into the blackness. His heart thudded with painful jolts as he waited for her to react.

What was she doing? Was she unsheathing the knife at her waist, perhaps even moving toward him on silent feet?

A moment passed, then another and another

while he held his breath. Then, suddenly, he heard the whisper of footsteps, moving away from him, crossing to the sleeping pallet he had abandoned. His relief was great to find he had made his point . . . and survived. At least for the moment.

Eric expelled the breath he had been holding and slowly allowed his tense body to relax. He lay there, unwilling to allow himself the luxury of sleep. The *skraeling* woman—Shala—could be biding her time. She might very well have just decided to kill him while he slept.

He was still awake when the dawn broke, sending fingers of pale light through the cracks at the side of the hide covering the entrance.

The night had been long for Shala. She had not slept a wink after the man had attacked her, afraid if she did he would use her helplessness against her. She wondered again if she had made a mistake by bringing him here. And yet, he could have harmed her—could even have killed her—but he had let the opportunity pass.

Perhaps he had only been trying to show her she had no need to fear him. She hoped it was so, for she needed desperately to have someone to depend on, someone to hunt for her and to chase away the loneliness that forever threatened, to fight her battles should that be needed. He would be a good fighter, she knew, for there was much power in his body. If she could win him over, could make him want to stay with her, then he would be the answer to a prayer.

She was so tired of living alone. Tired of it, still uncertainty plagued her. Had she really done the right thing by taking in the stranger?

Dawn was breaking when she pulled her weary body out of her bed and, after determining that the stranger still slept, filled a pot with water and placed it over the still glowing coals. When the water came to a boil, Shala took a small amount out of the pot to wash herself, then added meat and dried vegetables to the rest.

After she had completed her morning ablutions, she carried the bones from their previous meal outside, buried them deep in the snow, then moved closer to the edge of the cliff.

Wind Woman's breath was strong today. Her icy fingers pulled at Shala's long hair, whipping it around her shoulders, tangling it into a knot. Shala braced her feet against the strong current that threatened to topple her into the depths of the canyon as she fixed her eyes on the city beneath the overhang. It lay serene, gleaming ocher and orange, the outlines sharp and clear beneath the morning sun.

In her mind's eye, she visualized her mother bending over the morning fire and preparing the cornmeal mush that was her usual breakfast. Could Gryla see her daughter watching from across the canyon?

If only they could be together, Shala thought, as she had so often in the past. But that was impossible. She could not return to the city, and

Gryla could not leave it. As Keeper of Memories, she was needed by her People. Even if that were not so, her mother could never survive the harsh life Shala was forced to lead, sometimes going for long periods of time without food.

No. She was too old, too frail. A knot formed in Shala's chest and her hands curled into fists. If only the shaman would die.

She forced her eyes away from the cliff city, turning her gaze upward to the mesa above where she caught a flicker of movement. She narrowed her eyelids, focusing on the spot, and her breath quickened, excitement pulsing through her veins.

A white wolf stood there, its front feet braced against the wind, its coat as white as the snow beneath it. Although they were separated by the width of the canyon, she knew, somehow, that its yellowish gaze was fixed on hers. They stared at each other for long moments, her thumping heart sounding like a herd of buffalo frightened by a crack of thunder.

Why had the wolf come to her?

Did he come as an omen? she wondered. Did he come with a message?

Sweeping all thought from her mind, she focused her attention on the white wolf standing so near—only a canyon's width separated them—and waited for Wolf to make her understand, to explain the reason for his presence.

Suddenly, in a blinding flash, Shala knew. As surely as though the wolf had actually spoken to her, she knew the reason for his appearance. Her spirit guide had come to take away her doubts.

Wolf approved of the stranger. And Wolf approved of her actions in saving Eric's life.

She would accept that.

It was true. Eric had been sent to her, sent by her spirit guide, the white wolf.

Now, all Shala had to do was make Eric realize his future was permanently bound to hers.

A task that might prove to be difficult.

Six

Disappointment flooded through Shala when she stared down at the snare she had previously placed near a hare's run. It was empty. Realizing she would have to find another place for the trap, she picked it up and tucked it beneath her left arm.

A glance at the darkening sky quickened her steps. She must not delay. There was still another snare to be checked, and she must reach shelter before the storm that was threatening released its fury upon her.

Her body was tense, her movements awkward as she stumbled forward, forcing her way through the deep snow, pushing herself to the limit, all the while praying that her spirit guide, the white wolf, had put an animal in her second snare.

Shala had almost reached the trap when she heard the unmistakable flapping of wings. "Thank you, Brother Wolf," she cried, her wind-burned face cracking into a smile.

Eagerly, she dashed forward, felt her foot slide

into a hole hidden by the deep snow, lost her balance and tumbled forward. With a soft sighing sound, Shala felt the cold white snow surround her, its icy touch against her face, her ears, her neck.

Pushing herself upright, she sucked in a sharp breath, the cold rush of air filling her lungs to capacity.

Her empty belly reminded her of her catch. Her eyes swept the area around her, found the place where the snow had been trampled by wings, but there was no sign of her trap.

Whomp, whomp, whomp. The sound was accompanied by a loud squawk. It sent her searching gaze toward a plum thicket only a few feet away. Another *whomp, whomp, squawk,* sounded and her gaze slid downward, found the grouse hiding beneath a thorny bush that was bare of leaves, staring out at her with large, frightened eyes.

Grasping the bird around the neck, Shala muttered a quick apology, ending with, "Bless your meat, Sister Grouse. Be thankful that your flesh will be used to prolong my life."

Shala knew the grouse understood her words, saw it in the bird's large brown eyes and felt it when the bird stopped fighting, folding its wings against its body as though in supplication to the Blessed Star People who waited in the Great Beyond to receive its spirit.

Unwilling to prolong the bird's torment, Shala dropped the hand holding the grouse to arm's length and gave a quick jerk that broke its neck and sent its spirit soaring skyward.

After tying the grouse's feet together with a leather thong, she looped it over her left shoulder, then tucked the snare away with the other one. A quick glance at the sky sent anxiety surging through her. Was she mistaken, or were the clouds darker?

She shook herself, sweeping away the snow gathering on her clothing. Were the flakes larger than before? She watched them fall around her, swirling thickly, feeling the cold breath of Wind Woman against her face.

Anxiety froze her steps.

Should she turn back? she wondered. They would not starve. After all, she did have the grouse to keep hunger at bay. But how long would the bird provide food?

She studied the bird she had been so happy to find. It was barely enough for two meals now that she had Eric to feed. And the snares would be of no use unless they were set.

Shala realized she had no choice. She could not turn back. Not yet. Not before she had set the snares.

Sheer determination sent her feet moving farther away from the cliff and her warm cave tucked beneath it.

As though intent on swaying her determination, Wind Woman raised her voice, moaning softly around her, sending chills down Shala's backbone. She shuddered, then quickened her steps. She must hurry, must set her traps while there was still time. And she must consider, very carefully, the place that would be best suited for her purpose.

Perhaps the stream? Even though it was frozen over, she remembered a spot where an elk had broken through. The animals went there to water. Yes, she decided. That would be the best place for her snares.

Having come to a decision, Shala hurried forward, trying to ignore Wind Woman's voice that had become curiously vibrant, at times soft and whispery, then becoming louder and howling around her like a coyote calling to its companions beneath the light of a full moon.

The snowflakes were definitely larger now. They fell faster, swirling around her, while Wind Woman alternately moaned and howled, uttering her eerie warning, blowing big flakes of snow into Shala's eyes until she was almost blinded by them.

She longed to turn back, but knew she could not. Not until her traps were set. Her legs moved automatically, first one, then the other, carrying her forward through the deep snow.

Nearly there, she silently consoled herself. *Almost there. Just a few more steps, a little more time and the traps will be set.*

Wind Woman's fingers became cruel, whipping Shala's cloak around her body, stabbing at her exposed flesh like obsidian-tipped darts. Shala tried to brace herself against Wind Woman's strong breath, stumbled, lost her footing and fell, face forward, into a deep snowdrift.

Pushing herself upright, she brushed the cold snow from her eyes with her right palm, then swept her hand across her face, clearing away the freezing slush.

Shivering with cold, she found her direction, and pushed forward again, breathing a sigh of relief when she saw the frozen stream ahead.

By the time the first snare was set, her fingers had gone numb, and Shala realized then she must let the other snares go or risk losing her life.

She turned to retrace her steps, and Wind Woman pulled angrily at her cloak, tugging at her hood, snatching it from her head and sending it tumbling around her shoulders. Shala's long, dark hair whipped wildly, stinging her face as Wind Woman's cruel fingers tried to tear it out by the roots.

The snow danced and swirled around Shala, flakes falling heavy and thick until she could see nothing beyond two feet. She felt as though she had entered a world where nothing existed save the white cold that was intent on freezing her where she stood.

Numbly, Shala stumbled forward, endlessly it seemed, afraid to allow herself to rest, fearing if she paused for one moment, she would never be able to move again.

Wind Woman continued to howl around her, her icy breath stabbing into the exposed flesh of the girl who sought so desperately to escape her wrath.

Shala clutched her hood tighter around her chin, covering as much of her lower jaw as possible while she crossed the seemingly endless mesa.

And although Shala's body moved mechanically,

her mind whirled furiously, questioningly. Why was it taking so long to cross the mesa? Was she even going in the right direction? Suppose she was heading north instead of south? How could she tell when her sense of direction seemed to have deserted her completely?

Only the Wise One above could possibly know the way.

And the snow—it was so heavy . . . so icy, so slick. How could she possibly descend the cliff even if she could reach it.

In her mind's eye she saw the little cave . . . warm, snug, protected from the freezing cold that threatened to squeeze the life from her body.

White Wolf, Spirit Guide! she silently cried. *Help me!*

Suddenly, Shala's right foot slipped on an icy patch, then went into a hole, sending her tumbling forward, sprawling facedown, her body sinking into the white cold.

Wolf has deserted me! With the thought came a sinking, desolate despair. She was exhausted, unable to go farther. And if her spirit guide had left her, then she was surely lost.

Why did she continue to struggle, to push herself upright? It was no use. The battle was over.

Expelling a heavy sigh, she allowed herself to go limp. She lay there in the freezing cold, waiting for death to claim her . . . waiting . . . waiting.

Her pounding heart slowed its beat, and she closed her eyes. Soon it would be over. Soon she would sleep and never wake again.

Suddenly, a calm settled over the land, a calm so profound that Shala opened her eyes and gazed up at the forbidding sky. The endless fall of giant flakes continued to spin out of the murky clouds, but she was aware of nothing but the silence.

Where was Wind Woman's voice? Where was her fury? Did she grow silent now that Shala had admitted her defeat and was ready to embrace death?

Ready to embrace death? Shala's heart began to pound within her breast. Was she really ready to depart from the land of the living?

She pushed herself to her knees and searched the area around her for some sign. There was nothing but snow as far as she could see.

"Where are you, White Wolf?" she muttered. "Why have you deserted me?"

Perhaps the wolf's continued absence was the sign she had been waiting for. Perhaps his continued absence meant it was time for her to leave this world, to dwell with her ancestors in the place of the spirits.

If that were so, then all she had to do was lie down again . . . just remain still and allow the white cold to cover her body and—

No! her mind protested. If she gave in to death then Shu would have won!

Struggling to her feet, motivated by a new and driving will, Shala forced her legs to move forward again, to seek shelter from the cold that sapped all the strength from both mind and body.

* * *

Eric's eyelids flickered, then flew open. He stared up at the cream-colored limestone ceiling above. Why was it so cold? he wondered. Had Shala allowed the fire to go out?

Frowning heavily, he raised himself to his elbows and searched the shadows for the *skraeling* woman. It was bad enough that he must sleep on a bed so hard it made him painfully conscious of every scrape, every claw mark, every bruise on his body. And his leg—damn!—his broken leg felt as though it were being stabbed repeatedly with a white-hot poker.

"Shala?" His voice grated harshly in the otherwise silent cave.

There was no one to answer him. He was alone!

A curious flapping noise startled him, and he turned toward the entrance, saw the leather covering that hung there flapping wildly in the wind, shoving cold drafts into the cave with each inward movement.

Where is the wench? he silently questioned.

The howling wind outside told him of the storm's fury, so why had the woman left her cave?

Clutching the rabbitskin blanket tighter around his shoulders, Eric crawled toward the cave opening, knowing he could not long endure the freezing cold. He used several large rocks, placed conveniently to the right of the entrance, to secure the bottom of the hide.

Then, dragging his injured leg behind him, he crawled to the firepit and dug through the ashes until he found several live coals. After adding wood shavings, he blew on the coals until they caught, added larger pieces of wood to the resulting flame.

After settling himself on the sleeping pallet again, Eric huddled beneath the blanket, waiting for the flames to warm the cave, still wondering where the woman had gone.

The flames licked at the wood, hissing and spitting, cracking and popping, warming Eric's flesh. As heat filled the cavern, his eyes became heavy again. He sighed heavily, willing his tense body to relax. Then he slept.

Shala was unable to see the ruins until she was only a few feet away. At first, when she saw the wall of white looming before her, she thought she had come to the end of the world—until she reached out and touched it. Then, realizing what she had found, she moved along the wall until she found an entrance and stumbled inside, moving to the distant wall, as far from the driving storm as possible. Her body was plagued with countless aches and pains and refused to move her any farther.

Although Wind Woman howled around the dwellings, blowing heavy snow into the interior of the room, Shala found protection of a sort and curled herself into the tiniest ball possible, wrapping as much of herself in her rabbitskin cloak as was possible, wishing she had wood with which to build a fire, wondering if she would even wake from sleep.

She knew not how long she lay there, sleeping fitfully, numb with cold, before she felt a curious warmth seeping into her chilled body.

Curiosity gave her enough strength to open her sleep-dulled eyes, and she met the white wolf's yellow gaze.

Shala felt no elation, no curiosity, no fear. Why should she? Wolf, her spirit guide, had come. He would keep her warm, and he would keep her safe from predators that roamed the night.

Peace washed over her, and she fell into a deep sleep of exhaustion.

When she woke again, it was first light and she was alone, but beside her, imprinted in the earthen floor, was the shape of Wolf.

Shala stepped out into the crisp morning air, shading her eyes against the glare. Wind Woman's voice was hushed . . . and all around her the world was white.

She set off across the mesa, intent on reaching her small cave and the comfort she would find there.

The deep snow hampered her progress, causing her to stumble and fall time and again, yet Shala knew she must go on. Her joints ached, her legs were stiff and sore and the high drifts made slow walking.

To make matters worse, every time she fell, the freezing snow found its way beneath her garments and chilled her flesh.

Her heart pumped rapidly as she went along, and she was detouring around a heavy drift of snow when something brown caught her attention.

It was half-covered by a deep snow drift, and she almost went around it.

Then it moved.

In that instant of time she recognized it for what it was. A deer. Shala could hardly believe her eyes. As though sensing her presence, the deer lifted its head and looked at her with stunned brown eyes that were already glazing over.

How had it come there? she wondered.

Suddenly, she saw the wolf tracks in the snow and comprehension dawned. Wolf had known of her hunger and had apparently chased the deer into the snow drift. It had been left there to be found by her. This had to be Wolf's way of providing for her when she was unable to help herself.

"Forgive me," she said, kneeling beside the animal. "Your meat will give me strength while your soul finds relief in the blessed spirit world." With a quick slash of her knife, Shala sliced the deer's throat, ending its suffering.

"Thank you, Wolf," she cried, holding the bloody knife above her head to show Wolf she knew the part he had played in the kill. "I am grateful for your help."

Turning her attention to the dead deer, she went about getting it ready for the long walk across the mesa.

It was barely dawn and light fog clung tenaciously to the longboat when Karl Nordenskiold left his quarters and joined his brother on the deck. "Still quiet?" he asked, his gaze probing the area along the riverbank where he had seen the *skraeling* before. Gnarled oaks rose at intervals there, and a bayou twisted away from it.

"Still quiet," Arn replied. "But they are still there. You can smell the smoke from their fires."

Karl sniffed the air and realized Arn was right. There was the distinctive smell of wood smoke in the air.

"What do they want?" Arn muttered. "Why do they continue to wait there, keeping just out of sight, never coming into the open where we can get a good look at them?"

"Perhaps they only mean to observe."

"Observe? Or devise some plan of attack?" His frustration spewed into the moist air. "The waiting is driving me crazy."

"Perhaps that is their intention," Karl growled, sliding his gaze toward his brother. "Relax, Arn. Otherwise you will be in no condition to help when the attack comes."

"So you think there will be an attack?"

"We must be prepared for the worst."

"I wonder how many of them are out there," Arn muttered. "There are only six of us."

Karl smiled grimly. "But we are Vikings, brother. They are only *skraelings*. No matter the number, if they attack, they will soon regret having done so."

"I would feel better if the others were here," Arn said uneasily. "I wonder why they have not returned?"

Karl had been wondering the same thing.

* * *

Eric woke abruptly, feeling uneasy.

What had awakened him? he wondered. Had Shala returned?

He searched the small cave. It was still empty . . . silent. No change there. Perhaps that was what woke him. The total absence of sound.

Was the storm over, then?

He was aware of the warmth, knew he could not have slept long this time because the fire had not yet burned out.

Smoke tickled his nostrils, and a sudden hunger saturated him.

He crawled to the firepit, added more wood—the supply was becoming dangerously low—then dragged himself across to the narrow entrance, pushed the flap aside and squinted against the glare of the morning sun.

Although there was a snowdrift a few feet from the opening, a flat, overlapping rock protected the entrance from the blowing snow. It also blocked the valley from his view.

Feeling thoroughly chilled, he scooted backward and allowed the flap to fall into place again. His anxiety was a pounding knot, and the need to know the woman's fate was a palpable thing. If she had been caught out in the storm, she must surely have perished.

The thought of her death caused a curious ache deep inside his body.

Shala was only a *skraeling,* merely a savage, but she had done her best to care for him. It was only natural that he should feel loss at her death. Or was it?

Although his mind told him that she was dead, Eric found he could not accept the idea so easily. His ears strained as he listened for some sound . . . any sound.

Had he not been listening so intently, he might not have heard the soft thud from somewhere outside.

Was the sound accompanied by a human cry or had that only been his imagination? His thudding heart beat loudly in his chest as he waited for something, some other sound to tell him what had occurred.

Suddenly, the flap was pushed aside and the *skraeling* woman tumbled inside, sprawling forward onto the cavern floor.

Seven

Shala was surrounded by a delicious warmth. She floated on the edge of oblivion while her mind wandered along a twisted path with no beginning or end. She was aware of a voice above her, speaking words that had no meaning, and yet, she felt no concern.

"Shala!" The voice grated harshly on her ears, but she gave no sign that she had heard the speaker.

Callused hands moved over her face, ran through her hair, circled her head, feeling, probing. "Shala! What happened?"

She felt her forehead pulling into a frown. What did the speaker want with her? Why did he not leave her alone so she could sleep?

"Shala!" he said again, slapping her face lightly, obviously trying to make her wake up.

But she would not. Even though she drifted on the edge of consciousness, she was aware that her ordeal was finally over. She had reached the safety of her small cave, and whatever had happened to her, she was no longer alone.

No longer alone. The words filled her mind, made her wonder about her companion. Why had she been unable to understand his words?

She opened her eyes to a mere slit, and a stranger's face floated out of the misty haze. Who was he? Her eyes went beyond his face, touched on the halo of gold surrounding his head and remained fixed there. Had Father Sun come down from the sky to save her?

The idea sent the edges of her lips curling upward.

Her gaze moved to his eyes . . . his sparkling, grass green eyes, and her heart gave a sudden jerk of remembrance. The man who studied her so intently was the stranger!

Yes! The knowledge sent a surge of adrenaline through her, opened her eyes wider.

"Eric." Her voice sounded hoarse, and her throat hurt. It felt as she imagined it would if she had swallowed several obsidian-tipped darts.

Eric spoke again, his voice harsh and stern. And his hands, tugging at her body, were cruel and hard. She had only imagined his concern.

"N-no," she stuttered. "L-leave me alone!" She pushed at the hands, trying to make him stop tormenting her, but her words and her attempts to make him desist were useless. They only made him tighten his grip, made him tug harder on her limbs while he dragged her across the rocky floor toward the firepit.

Her frantic gaze fastened on the flames for a long moment. They leapt and danced as though driven by the same fury she sensed in the man forcing her toward them.

"N-no!" she said again, turning her gaze toward Eric, trying to determine his intention from his rock-hard expression. "W-what are you d-doing?"

Was he going to burn her?

Shala's throat was constricted by fear, but smothered by a gathering darkness, she was unable to resist his strength. She had no strength left, had used every last ounce she possessed to reach the security of her small cave.

Security? With a man like Eric just waiting for an opportunity like this? Fearfully, she watched a red haze forming around his head, moving closer to her in ever-widening circles, growing thicker with each circling movement, becoming heavy as encroaching fog, turning darker and darker, closing in around her, pushing, pulsing, swirling, over and over again until she moaned for relief and closed her eyes against it.

Shala was swamped with a sense of fatality as the darkness smothered her.

Pulling the girl's limp body to the sleeping pallet, Eric unfastened her cloak and stripped it away. Then, covering her with the feather blanket and pulling her into his arms, he shared his body warmth with her.

It was obvious she was half-frozen, having apparently been through a trying experience. How had she survived the storm?

He studied her pinched, wind-burned face. She

had no doubt suffered a great deal. The thought of her ordeal caused a feeling of protectiveness to surge within him. Yet, why should he feel anything for the *skraeling* woman? he wondered. She had done her level best to torment him ever since they had met.

His gaze traveled down her straight nose, stopping momentarily on her full lips. What would they feel like beneath his? They looked soft and pliant, moist as a dew-laden flower.

His heart thundered loudly in his ears as he ran his thumb across her lower lips, felt her breath warm against his touch. Her cheeks were curiously flushed, but perhaps it was only an illusion . . . or shadows cast by the firelight flickering in the firepit.

Shala, she called herself. Her midnight dark hair was spread out around her like a cloud of black velvet. He touched it, feeling the strands beneath his fingers, silky and smooth, the texture equaling the most delicate fabric he had found when he traded with the people in the Far East.

How could he have thought her ugly? he wondered. Even now, in her wind-burned condition, she was the most beautiful creature he had ever laid eyes upon. How could a creature of such delicate beauty hold so much strength in her small frame? Such courage?

Suddenly, a frown marred her forehead and she uttered a moan. "Eric!" she cried, her voice hoarse, strained.

She was obviously in the grip of some strong emotion, perhaps was even reliving her ordeal in a nightmare. Her voice, crying out to him so piteously, stirred something to life deep inside his cold heart.

Without stopping to ask himself why, he tightened his arms around her, pulling her still closer against him.

"Be not afraid," he murmured harshly, lowering his head to rest it against her silky hair. "You are with me now. I will keep you safe." The moment he uttered the words, he realized how incongruous they were.

How could he keep her safe when he could barely help himself?

Nama stood on the edge of the cliff, protected from the swirling snow by the protruding lip of the cap rock above her. Her anxious gaze searched the opposite cliff wall for some sign of movement, something that would tell her Shala was all right.

Although she strained her eyes, she perceived no movement.

"Which means nothing," she muttered uneasily. She sent her gaze lower, sweeping across the snow-covered trees and bushes growing from the canyon floor, probing farther, searching for some sign of the desert people. There was nothing, only stillness as far as the eye could see.

Breathing a sigh of relief, Nama lifted her eyes, and looked again at the canyon wall across from her. "Shala can take care of herself. She will be tucked inside her cave . . . maybe working on a carrying basket for roots and berries." Nama had seen Shala's old basket, knew it was worn and could easily break beneath a load.

Nama tried to picture Shala beside her fire, weaving dried grasses into a large basket, but somehow the vision would not come.

Why? she wondered.

Even as she asked herself the question, the answer appeared in her mind's eye. The face of a man. A golden-haired man, the stranger that Shala had saved. He was an unknown factor, with a body that spoke of such power Shala would never be able to stand against his strength if he chose to use it against her.

Shala should never have taken the stranger to her cave.

You helped her! a silent voice accused. *If anything happens to Shala, it will be your fault!*

"What else could I have done?" Nama said aloud. "She came to me for help!"

You could have refused! the silent voice replied.

"Who are you talking to, Nama?"

The voice, coming from behind her, caused Nama to whirl around. She looked at the child who had spoken, a little girl who had yet to see her fourth summer. But even at so young an age, the child was remarkably astute.

Nama thought quickly, wondering how she could reply to Sage Flower. To say she had been talking to herself would surely lead to endless questions. "I was . . . was speaking to . . . Wind Woman," Nama replied.

"Wind Woman?" Sage Flower leaned forward,

carefully peeping around Nama, mindful of having been told countless times to exercise great caution when near the edge of the cliff. She had even been witness, on one occasion, to the tragic results of carelessness and hoped never to see such a sight again.

Turning her attention to the snow-covered trees growing on the valley floor, Sage Flower studied them for a long moment, then lifted fearful eyes to meet Nama's gaze.

"The trees are not moving," she said. "Wind Woman must be sleeping. How can she hear you speak to her when she sleeps?" Without waiting for an answer, she continued. "I hope she stays silent. I was afraid of her last night. Her breath was so strong and she screamed so loud I thought she was angry with me." Her gaze became fearful. "Was she angry with me, Nama?" She gave a delicate shudder. "Do you think she was?"

"No," Nama replied, kneeling beside Sage Flower and smoothing her hair away from her face. "Wind Woman is our friend. When her voice is so loud, it is her way of warning us to stay out of the snow, to keep tucked in bed away from the deep cold. She would never deliberately harm little girls."

"Sometimes she hurts little girls," Sage Flower reminded. "Before the big cold came she pushed Little Owl from the ledge and sent her body down into the valley below." Sudden tears filled her eyes, and her lips quivered. "I miss Little Owl. She was my friend. Now she has gone to the spirit world. She will never play with me again. I wish—"

"That was an accident," Nama interrupted quickly. "Wind Woman spoke very loudly before Little Owl went onto the ledge, but your friend did not take heed. We must always listen to Wind Woman and never, never ignore her warning." It was imperative that she make the child understand, lest another such tragedy occur.

"I will listen to her," Sage Flower said. "But does she have to use such a loud voice when she warns us of danger?"

"Yes, she must," Nama said, rising to her feet.

"Why?"

"Because that is her way."

"Why?"

"Because you would not listen if she spoke softly." Nama smiled at the child and swatted her on the backside. "Now stop asking so many questions."

"Why?"

"Because I have no time to answer."

"Why?"

"Because I have other things to do."

"What things?"

"Sage Flower . . ." Nama took a deep breath, trying to find a way to discourage the child without hurting her feelings. "You must—"

"Sage Flower!"

Recognizing the child's mother, Gia, Nama sighed with relief. "Your mother is calling you!" Nama said.

She need not have spoken because the child had already heard. "Mother's calling me!" she cried, making a dash across the courtyard to where Gia waited. Halfway there, she turned back toward Nama. "See you later!" she called. Then, with a wave of her small hand, she joined her mother.

Nama watched Gia sweep the child up into her embrace, saw Sage Flower wrap her arms around her mother's neck and give her a squeeze. There was such love between mother and daughter, just as there was between Nama and her own mother, Ona. Was it always so? Would Nama's daughter feel that way about her mother? How could she if she were fathered by the man Shu had promised her to?

She heaved a dispirited sigh. Better to put thoughts of her future out of her mind for the moment. Time enough to worry about it later. Right now, there was Shala to worry about.

If only there were someone Nama could talk to, someone to share her fears about the stranger.

She was on the point of returning to her own dwelling when she looked up and saw Nampeyo warming his crippled legs beside the fire and whittling on a chunk of wood as he so often did.

Nampeyo was a strange, silent man who had once been a childhood friend. What had happened to that friendship? Nama wondered. The child had disappeared and the man was a complete mystery to her. Patiently, he endured the jokes and gibes and sometimes the open ridicule of the People. Having been crippled when he was no more than Sage Flower's age, he remained alone and aloof, apart from the others, seeming content to whittle on his wood, to carve beautiful figures of animals and birds.

Since the day Shu had proclaimed his son the next shaman of the Eagle Clan, Nampeyo's life had been easier. Although he remained alone, set apart from his peers, the open ridicule had at least stopped, for none dared set the future shaman against them.

As though becoming aware of her gaze, Nampeyo looked up at her, and without knowing why, Nama found herself changing direction and crossing the courtyard to join him.

The fog lay thick upon the wide river, blanketing everything farther than a foot from Gunther Volsung as he crossed the deck of the longboat in search of Karl Nordenskiold.

The sound of footsteps against planks jerked his head around. Whoever approached was still hidden by the thick fog. Although he changed directions, Gunther sent his voice ahead of him. "Karl?" he questioned sharply. "Is that you, Karl?"

"No," grunted Harold Grimolfsson. His large body became recognizable, even though fog was still wrapped around him, like clutching fingers determined to keep him prisoner. The illusion made Gunther uneasy. "It is only me," Harold went on. "Karl has only just left for his quarters and, hopefully, will get some sleep."

"Why does he insist on standing guard with the rest of us?" Gunther asked. "He was left in charge. Had Eric left me in charge, you would not find me standing guard at night. I would not shirk my duty, but neither would I deprive myself of sleep."

"That is the reason Karl was selected to be in charge," Harold said, clapping the other man on the shoulder. "Your penchant for making things easier on yourself is well known, my friend."

Gunther smiled, not in the least upset by the other man's words. Why should he be? There was no shame in selecting lighter duty for oneself. Everyone knew that, when it came to fighting, Gunther Volsung was one of the best, unequaled by few with sword and crossbow. A good man if one should need one's back watched.

"I am worried, Harold," Gunther said shortly. "So are the rest of the crew. The snow has melted away long ago and the days are becoming warmer all the time. Soon the rains will come, and we will be free of this mudbank. And still, Eric and the others have not come."

"What are you saying?"

Harold shifted uneasily. "We wonder where the *skraelings* went who watched us for so long."

"What does one thing have with the other?"

"Maybe the *skraelings* heard them returning. They might have attacked them. We could be waiting here for dead men that will never return."

"They will come back," Harold said gruffly. "Put such thoughts out of your mind, and speak no more of them."

"But if they do not? How long are we to wait?"

"Eric left word for us to leave when the longboat is free," Harold said reluctantly.

"That will be soon," Gunther said slowly, trying

again to penetrate the deep fog with his gaze. "I think they will not be back before then. It is my fear they will never return."

Harold remained silent. After all, what could he say when he was of the same mind?

Eight

Nampeyo had been watching Nama for some time and knew the exact moment she decided to approach him. Her coming caused mixed feelings to stir within him. Uppermost was the almost overwhelming happiness he always felt when she was near, but it was tempered by the painful anguish of knowing the girl he loved so deeply would never return his feelings—indeed, would never even know of them.

"I offer you greetings, Nampeyo," she said formally. "My mother and father also wish you well."

"Greetings to them and to you," Nampeyo replied, placing his wood carving aside and courteously nodding his head.

"Would you grant me a moment to speak with you?"

"Friends are always welcome at my fire," he said, aware that, while his voice remained calm, his heart beat in double time, threatening to batter through the bones of his rib cage. Nama was obviously unaware of his intense emotions. He was grateful for that, grateful she could not see that his heart, so strong in many ways, was so fragile in the face of love. No one but the Wise One above had occasion to know his pain, except perhaps, his spirit guide, and Nampeyo intended that it remain so. Such knowledge, were it shared, would surely drive a wedge between himself and the woman he loved.

"You seem troubled, Nama," he said.

"Do I wear my feelings for all to see?" she asked.

"Not all," he replied kindly. "But I know you better than most. We have been friends for a very long time."

"You and Shala and me," she said. "And it is Shala who occupies my thoughts." She looked about to determine if they were being observed, then apparently deciding it was safe to speak, did so. "It is not right that Shala was banished from the clan, Nampeyo. Not for such a reason."

Alarmed, he put a hand on her shoulder and gave a light squeeze. "Sshhh!" he cautioned in a low voice. "You must be careful what you say. My father has many eyes here, Nama. He would not take kindly to your words of complaint."

"I know," she said fiercely. "But I worry about her . . . living alone as she does. So much could happen."

"You are a good friend to her, and that is good for her, but could prove foolhardy for you. Already it has dealt you misery."

"What do you mean?"

Instead of answering her question, he asked

one of his own. "Were you not chosen for Standing Wolf's bride?"

"Chosen?" she asked, her voice rising with surprise, then quickly dropping again. "I thought Standing Wolf made a request for me!"

He shook his head. "No. I was there when his messenger spoke to my father. Standing Wolf asked only for a maiden from our clan. The choosing was left to the shaman."

Anger surged through Nama. Nampeyo was probably right. It would be just like Shu to have chosen her for the desert chief simply because he knew of Nama's longstanding friendship with Shala.

"You say you are worried about our mutual friend?" Nampeyo said, carefully omitting Shala's name in case they were overheard. "Is it because of the weather? Or is there another reason?"

"Another reason," Nama replied, setting aside her own problems for the moment. There would be time enough to worry about them later. Right now, Shala's situation seemed far more urgent.

Nama told Nampeyo what had occurred while he was away, then added, "The man is strange, like no other I have ever seen. A big man, larger even than Grandfather Black Bear, and the garment that covers him is made from some strange pelt."

Nampeyo's penetrating gaze darkened. Had Shala's mind wandered out of her head during the long winter months? It must be so. "There is no such being," he said.

"There is," Nama contradicted softly. "My own eyes have seen this man."

"You saw him?"

"Yes. I helped Shala take him to her cave. Believe me, Nampeyo, for I speak the truth. The stranger wears a golden halo, not only on his head, but it covers most of his face as well. And his eyes are different from ours. They are colored like the new grass that pushes from beneath the earth when the long cold has gone."

"How can this be possible?" he asked, frowning at her. "How could such a being exist without someone knowing?"

"Perhaps he comes from a great distance."

"Even so, the traders should have known about him. They travel everywhere, from the big salt water in the west to the one in the east, and they know all the people who populate our world. They would not have kept silent about such a being. Our Keeper of Memories would have been told." His gaze turned toward the opposite cliff, where, according to Nama, the stranger was. "How could such a being exist without anyone knowing?" he muttered again.

She shook her head. "I don't know. I only know he *does* exist. My own eyes have seen him. Over the strange garment he wore a white cloak, made from the fur of some unknown animal." Her eyes glinted with remembered pleasure. "The cloak is mine now. Shala has given it to me."

"You have it with you?"

"No," she said regretfully. "How could I bring

it here? Shu might see it and question its existence."

"He *would* do that," Nampeyo said grimly. "Shala should not have taken the stranger in. He could be dangerous. He might do her serious harm."

"I realize that now," Nama replied. "It is the reason I worry."

"You have every right to be worried. But nothing can be done at the moment. We must wait until the snow melts enough to make climbing safe. Until then we can only pray that her spirit guide will keep Shala safe."

"You will keep silent about the stranger?"

"Surely you need not ask. I would not break a confidence, even though it may be wrong. Such a man could be dangerous to all of us." He looked thoughtful. "But his presence will remain a secret, known only to the three of us. And there is one consolation, Nama. If the weather will not permit us to go to him, neither can he come here."

Picking up his wood carving again, he added, "When it is safe to travel I will see this stranger for myself. Until then, we can only hope Shala remains unharmed."

When Nama remained unmoving, he looked at her again. "There is another thing you wished to speak with me about?" Although he desperately wanted her company, he knew he must not allow her to know his feelings, and if she remained with him much longer, she would surely see the love he felt reflected in his eyes.

"Yes," she replied hesitantly. "I am disturbed that Shu chose me for the desert people. It is not my wish to leave my home in the cliffs."

Her words stabbed at Nampeyo. He wished with all his heart he could tell her she would not have to leave. But he could not. His father had made the decision. And, for the good of the People, the pact must be kept.

His silence apparently unnerved Nama, for she hurried to add, "It would be hard to leave my mother, Nampeyo. She would miss me greatly. She has already lost many children and will soon need someone to help her through her old age."

"Your mother would never be left to fend for herself," he reminded gently, wanting to take her in his arms and comfort her, knowing at the same time that she would not welcome his embrace. "You know the clan will look after her needs until she makes her journey to the land where the spirits dwell."

Nama's long dark lashes fluttered like bird wings, then dropped to hide her gaze from his. "I am deeply ashamed for having used my mother's name for such a purpose." She swallowed hard, then lifted her eyes to meet his again.

Nampeyo flinched inwardly when he saw the barely hidden fear reflected in her gaze. "My heart is heavy with fear," she admitted. "The Buffalo Clan who occupy the desert are a fierce people, always making war on their neighbors, and their chief, Standing Wolf, has already lost many wives to the other world. If I go with them, I think my feet will soon follow the other unfortunate wives to the spirit world."

Nampeyo fought against a fear so great that it brought a rising nausea. How could he put her fears at rest when he was of the same mind? Nama was such a delicate creature, far too fragile for such as Standing Wolf or any other man in the Buffalo Clan. Unlike Shala, who had insisted on being taught the things boys were learning—like how to make spear points and snares, and how best to track game—Nama had been interested in things totally female. She was fast becoming the finest seamstress in the clan, could make a mouth-watering stew and cook a rabbit until the meat fairly melted in the mouth. In fact, she would make some fortunate man a fine mate.

But why did it have to be Standing Wolf who benefited from all her training? How could a woman with her fine sensibilities stand up to the rigors of desert life, much less a man like Standing Wolf, who would break her before one moon had passed?

Oh, Wise One above! How could Nampeyo be a party to such a thing? And, yet, he thought sadly. How could he not? It did no good to rail against what was to be. He could not help her that way. Her only hope for survival was to accept her fate.

But it was so unfair! So unfair!

Nampeyo thought his heart would surely break and, to keep from crying out his pain, he searched for someone to blame. And soon the target was found. Shala! All that had taken place was Shala's fault!

If only Shala had not rejected Shu, then, perhaps Nama, the girl Nampeyo had always loved, would not have been chosen to be the wife of Standing Wolf!

To be Shala's friend was to be most certainly condemned!

"Can you not help me?" Nama whispered. "You are his son, the next shaman of our clan. Your word would carry much weight with your father."

Oh, Nama, his heart cried within his breast. *Do you not know that I have tried, time and time again, to intercede on your behalf? But it did no good! Shu was adamant. He has already given your name to the Buffalo Clan. To send another in your place now would only serve to anger the desert chief!*

"You must talk to your father for me," she went on, unaware of his thoughts. "Please, Nampeyo, have him select another."

"Which one would you choose?" he asked gently. "Which maiden would you have him send in your place? White Flower? Gentle Fawn? Night Moon? Laughing Duck? Kwana? Think about it for a moment." He tried to find the words his father had used on him to make the choice seem the most realistic one. "White Flower loves Lothi. And it has always been known that Laughing Duck and Flying Eagle would mate. And Gentle Fawn? She has not yet chosen her mate, but her health is so delicate that, before the desert people could reach their home, she would wither away like the mist that gathers before dawn only to disappear beneath Father Sun's fiery gaze. If that should happen, they would return for another maiden, which means you would be condemning two people. There is only Night Moon and Kwana. Night Moon is our healer. The clan cannot manage without her. And Kwana is but a child, having seen only eleven summers."

Nampeyo watched her hang her head in shame. "It seems there is no other," she said sadly. "I am the logical one. But fear does not listen to logic. It cannot be controlled by the knowledge of duty. What would happen if my spirit should depart my body before the desert people come? Who would be chosen then?"

Nampeyo felt a jab of fear as sharp as a knife. The fear twisted inside him, turning slowly around and around in his belly. "Don't even consider such a thing," he said, making his voice as stern as possible. "To take your own life would doom your spirit to wander forever in eternity. You would never be able to reach our ancestors who have gone before us." *Oh, Wise One above,* he silently prayed. *Chase such thoughts from her mind.*

"What would happen?" she persisted. "Would another be chosen then?"

"Yes. Either White Flower or Laughing Duck would have to go," he said. "Is it your wish to make them suffer?"

She shook her head. "No," she whispered. "But neither do I want it for myself."

"You will find the strength you need to get through whatever faces you," he said gently, his eyes hungrily devouring her features. Even as he said the words, he silently cursed himself. He did not want her to go! Not to any other man, much less one who was known for such harshness. But he could not stop what was to be. His father had taught him well the things a shaman must concern himself with. In all things—the welfare of the clan must come first.

"Thank you for listening to me," Nama said.

"There is no need for thanks among friends," Nampeyo replied. "It is my regret that I could not ease your mind."

"My mind will find no ease," she admitted. "Never again, in this world, will it feel happiness."

"Nama . . ." he began slowly, achingly. "Nama . . . I wish—"

"Enough," she replied, waving a slim hand in the air. "There is no more to be said on the subject. Just put your mind at rest. I will abide by my shaman's decision." With a heavy sigh, and without a second look back, she departed then to the solitude of her pain.

Put it out of my mind? How could I ever do that? Nampeyo's heart cried. *Just the thought of you in another man's arms is enough to turn my blood cold.* He watched her cross the courtyard to her own dwelling, saw her stop and speak to her mother and knew, from past experience, that she would be struggling to keep her mother from knowing how deep was her fear.

But he knew. Yes, Nampeyo did know. And, although he shared Nama's fear, there was nothing he could do to help her. Nothing at all.

* * *

Shala woke slowly, aware of a heavy weight pressed against her. Feeling slightly disoriented, she cracked her eyelids, saw a definitely male chest before her and jerked her eyes open wider, tilting her head back at the same time to meet impossibly green eyes.

The stranger! Eric!

She was cuddled tight against his body. Even now his arm lay across her back.

She drew a long deep breath, felt a flush of color creeping up her neck and staining her cheeks. Moistening her lips, she tried to pull away, but his grip tightened, preventing her escape.

"Please," she whispered huskily.

"Please?" He repeated the word questioningly, obviously not knowing the meaning of it. "Shala?" His warm breath, fanning across her cheeks, disturbed her senses, as did the hand that swept her long hair away from her face.

"Let me go!" she said, wriggling away from his embrace and pushing herself to a sitting position. She felt completely flustered now, unable to meet his gaze. Instead, she looked toward the entrance flap. Through a small crack at the side she could see the glare of Father Sun's hot gaze. It foretold fair weather.

"Shala," Eric said again. Her name was followed by other words that she could not understand, and his hand crept toward her neckline as he spoke.

What does he mean? she silently questioned,

trying to scuttle backward out of his reach while her heart fluttered like a trapped butterfly, captured beneath her breastbone.

He prevented her action by snagging her arm with his left hand while his right grasped her amulet tightly, lifting it toward her face. He spoke again in his language, words that had no meaning for her, but obviously were important to him.

"What about my amulet?" she asked him. "Do you want to know its meaning?"

He frowned down at her, spoke again in his language, his voice becoming harshly aggressive.

Tightening her lips, she jerked away from him, scuttled backward out of his reach and snatched up a stout stick from the woodpile.

His transformation was instant. "Shala," he said, his voice gentle, soft. Even so, his features expressed his frustration at not being able to make her understand.

Slowly, Shala laid aside the stick. Apparently he meant her no harm, had only been expressing an interest in her talisman. She herself felt frustration at their inability to communicate with each other. She must teach him her language. But how?

While she was studying over the matter, her stomach gave a loud rumble, reminding her that she was immensely hungry. The man must be as well.

There would be time enough to worry about communicating with each other. Right now there was work to be done. The deer that she had carried home over her shoulders and thrown over the cliff was outside—if the scavengers had not already made off with it.

Ignoring Eric, she pushed herself upright, then headed for the entrance flap, intent on preparing them a meal as quickly as possible.

The air remained crisp and cold, but inside the small cave it was cozy and warm. It had been several days since Shala's return, and she had completely recovered from her ordeal. The deer kept them supplied with food, and her absence must have softened Eric because the animosity he had held for her had disappeared. It was almost as though it had never existed.

Eric.

Such an unusual name, sounding strange upon her tongue when she spoke it, as she so often did these days. She had discovered he was very stubborn, capable of completely ignoring her until she caught his attention by using his name. Then he would listen carefully to what she said, his gaze flickering between her lips and her hands, which she used often to get her point across, and amazing as it seemed, they were actually beginning to communicate with each other.

She had taught him simple words. Like water, food, wood, fire and basket. And she had taught him other words, like she would a baby. Touching his hair, so crisp and silky, she would say the word before moving on to eyes, cheeks, lips, hands and fingers. And he would respond by repeating the word, then using the equivalent in his own language which he expected her to learn.

Shala had completely lost her fear of him, responding to his gentleness, and yet, for some reason, she remained wary, ever conscious of his eyes following her as she worked, preparing their meals and tending to daily chores.

Father Sun had slept seven nights before Eric devised a better way of learning. He had been watching her form a new bowl from the clay she had stored in the back of the cave, when suddenly he spoke her name and motioned her closer to him, a curious expression on his face that she likened to eagerness, to the excitement of discovery.

"Eric?" She asked curiously in her own language, searching his expression, "What do you wish?"

"Shala," he said again, motioning with his hand for her to come closer and speaking one of the Anasazi words that he had so recently learned. "Come, Shala."

Her curiosity piqued, she set her work aside and went to him.

"No," he said, still using her language. "Come." He pointed to the soft clay she had been working with.

Did he mean for her to bring the clay? Why should he want it? A grin twitched her lips when a possibility occurred. Maybe he wanted to learn how to make a clay pot, a curious pastime for a man. But then, she would be the first to admit that he was no ordinary man.

Scooping up the damp clay, she knelt beside him and handed it over. Before she could show him how to curve the clay, he tossed it to the earthen floor and flattened it with the heel of his hand.

"No!" she said sharply, slapping his hand. "Why did you do that?"

"Shala, look!" he commanded, meeting her eyes and holding them intently.

Puzzled, she looked down at the flattened clay, watched him use a sharp stick and make deep lines in the damp material. At first the lines made no sense, but she continued to watch, and soon, she began to see the shape of a big bird. Another line here and there and she knew it for what it was—an eagle!

Eric grunted a harsh word in that strange tongue of his, then waited until she met his eyes. Saying the word again, he pointed to the drawing. Was he telling her the name of the eagle in his language? That must be it.

"Eagle," she said, in the Anasazi language. "Eagle," she repeated, pointing at the drawing.

He smiled at her, repeated the word, then spoke in his language again, just the one word, over and over until she repeated it.

"Good," he said in her language.

Turning the clay over, he used the stick to draw again. The curious hump on the animal's back told her it was a buffalo. Again, he said the word, waited until she had repeated it, then said the word she gave him for the animal. The process was repeated over and over again. First he made a drawing, then they said the word for it in both languages until each had learned the new word.

Time passed swiftly, the daylight hours seeming to fly as they learned to communicate with each other. She learned many things about him, although she was puzzled about many others. He said he came from across the big salt water. She had heard of the place; traders sometimes came to the village and brought large funny-shaped shells to trade. They claimed they had come from the big salt water.

Their food was fast being depleted but that fact caused Shala little worry. Already the snow was melting from the face of the cliff, and soon she would be able to venture out to check her traps.

At the moment though, there was still food left, and time enough later to worry about the future. Right now she wanted nothing to intrude on their learning time together. She was intrigued by Eric, the man who called himself a Viking. When she asked him for an explanation for the word, he seemed at a loss for one. But the time would come when she could understand. Until that time she was content to spend her time with him, to wonder at the curious way he made her feel, at the stirring deep within her body that made her feel a curious sort of hunger that refused to be assuaged by mere food.

Even as the thought occurred, she looked across the cavern at Eric who was busy sharpening her knife. He seemed to sense her interest because, even as she watched, he looked up and met her gaze. His flashing green eyes darkened slightly, and something stirred in their depths. In response, something stirred in Shala's lower body, something that she could only liken to longing.

How curious, she thought. What did it mean? What was this feeling, this sort of aching emptiness that cried out for sustenance, yet refused to be satisfied by food.

Shala needed to know, wanted desperately to know, but how could she find the answer?

Nine

In the desert country two days from the mesa, the hot wind blew across a land that had seen no moisture for several seasons. Those who lived there, the Buffalo Clan, had hoped to find relief when winter's cold touch was upon them, but their hopes had been in vain. Not even a faint dusting of snow had fallen to relieve the terrible drought.

Standing Wolf, chief of the Buffalo Clan, stood on a rocky outcrop on a hillock behind his camp. From his vantage point he could see a great distance—as far as a man could walk in three days—but there was nothing there he wanted to see. Not even one of the great beasts—the buffalo—that his people needed so badly if they were to survive.

How had this happened?

Standing Wolf had been so careful when he chose this place for his camp only two summers ago. At that time there were many great herds of buffalo grazing within a day's walk of the village.

But times have changed, he silently told himself. *And we must change with them if we are to survive.*

He thought bitterly about his childhood friend, Eagle Claw. Once Eagle Claw had belonged to the Buffalo Clan but when he married a woman from another clan, he became joined with hers. Now he was one of Standing Wolf's worst enemies. Having become shaman for the People of the Rocks, Eagle Claw convinced his new clan to band together with the Coyote Clan who occupied the land to the east. Together, they made a formidable enemy. Caring nothing of the Buffalo Clan's prior claim on the desert land, they came in hordes, hunting the buffalo herds and pushing the great beasts farther to the north.

Although Standing Wolf's hunters had followed, the trek between the waterholes was long. The distance without water was hard on the old and weak buffalo. They collapsed. The cows grew gaunt and died, the herds were diminished, the skeletons of the dead marking their dusty path northward.

The desert chief knew there was nothing left here for them, nothing to do except find new hunting grounds. He also knew where the best hunting grounds were, and although they belonged to another clan, he had no reservations about taking what he considered his. Why should he? And why should the Buffalo Clan not do to others what had already been done to them?

Yes. He knew where they would go from here, had already laid careful plans to achieve his goal.

His eyes lifted, and he studied the high mountains in the north. From his position he could see the white line that denoted snow. Never, as far as he knew, had winter's cold touch failed to bring snow to the mountains, and where there was snow, there was plenty of water. And where there was water, the grass grew greener and the game grew fatter.

"Soon it will be time," he muttered. "Soon we will go to the mountain. And we will take what is rightfully ours. The Buffalo Clan will take more than the Eagle Clan will wish to give, but why should we not take what is rightfully ours? We are the Chosen People. This land was put here for our use. Soon the Eagle Clan will know that. Soon everyone will know it!"

Eric's leg was healing quickly. Although he used a stick for walking, he was able to get around well enough, but still not able to climb the cliff to the top of the mesa. For that reason he felt confined.

He looked across the small cave at Shala. Her head was bent over her sewing—she was making a blanket out of feathers. How could she appear so calm when he felt so restless, so restricted?

She lifted her head suddenly, breaking the silence to speak in her own language, a language that he found harsh and guttural but, at least, was coming to understand better with each passing day.

Although some of her words were still unfamiliar, he knew enough of her language now to understand that she was likening him to a cat that continually paced.

"Why do you not relax?" she asked.

He sighed with frustration and spoke in her tongue. "There is much that needs doing." He knew those words well. Had she not said them often enough when he tried to get her to speak of the blue stone hanging around her neck. She seemed to value it highly, but he still had no idea where it came from.

Perhaps he was just following a will-o'-the-wisp. Maybe, like the shells she showed him, the stone had come from a trader. But he must find out for sure. If such stones were found nearby, then he intended to fill his longboat with them. To delay his trip home and bring what was left of his crew back to this place to mine—or somehow get—the stones. He was almost certain they would bring a good price in Norway.

"What must be done?" she asked. "What is so important that it keeps you on your feet?"

He spread his arms impatiently. "The wood is almost gone and we need more meat."

She held his gaze. "I will hunt when it is safe to climb to the mesa. Until then you must be patient."

He seated himself near her and stretched his injured leg out in front of him. He wanted to know about the stone, but suddenly the need to know more about her was stronger. "Why do you live here alone?" he asked.

"Sometimes it is better to live apart from others."

Had there been something odd in her voice?

"Is that the way of your people?" He knew it was not. Had he not seen the abandoned dwellings on the mesa, the city built into the cliff? It was obvious theirs was a close-knit community.

It was a long moment before she answered, and when she spoke, it was in a subdued voice. "No," she muttered. "It is not the way of my people, but it is my way."

"You do not get lonely?" he pursued.

"No!" she denied emphatically. "There is peace to be found here, humble though my home is. I *like* living alone! I answer to no one, have only myself to think about. It is a good way to live."

He raised a golden eyebrow. "That is the reason you live here, separated by a canyon from the others?" Why was he so intent on making her answer? he wondered. Why did he feel such curiosity about her? "Is that the reason, Shala? Just because you answer to no one? Because you want to be left alone?"

Her eyes were evasive, seeming determined to avoid his. "My reasons are my own," she replied, bending her head over her work again, bent on ignoring him.

But Eric refused to be ignored. Again, he wondered why he was so intent on learning the truth of the matter. The answer escaped him. He only knew that she was hiding something and he longed to discover what it was.

Taking the unfinished blanket from her hands, he tilted her chin and forced her to look at him. "Have you no friends, Shala? No parents who worry about you? Why do you live on this side of the canyon while your people are on the other?"

"I will speak no more of this!" she said, tugging ineffectually at the hands cupping her face. "Do not make me sorry that I saved your life." When her efforts to make him free her only tightened his grip, she struck at him, landing a solid blow on his chest. "Release me, Eric," she demanded.

Her tone of voice as much as her demand caused him to do the opposite. His hands slid to her shoulders and he pulled her tightly against him. Ignoring her useless struggles, her puny fists beating against his chest, he dipped his head down and captured her lips beneath his own.

Shala sucked in a sharp breath, alarmed at the feelings his action caused. Her heart jolted at the first contact of her breasts with his chest, and her pulse raced, pounding in much the same way it had when she had fought the boar. Then his lips closed over hers, and startling though it was, she felt the most curious sensation in the pit of her stomach, a sensation that she could only liken to longing—to a tormenting ache, a hunger that could not be satisfied with food. What was this feeling? Why did it become stronger, more exciting as his lips moved against hers? What was he doing to her? Why did her nipples tighten and why did her loins feel strange?

Eric had only meant to show his superiority when he had exerted his strength over her. When his lips connected with hers, he was unprepared for the surge of desire that swept over him.

Not being one to curb his impulses, he shoved her to the floor and covered her body with his own.

"Ho-yeh! You here, Shala?" The shout came from just outside.

Breathing heavily, Eric pulled away from her. "Who is that?" he asked, frowning at the covered entrance before looking back at her.

She rolled away from him, brushing her hair away from her flushed cheeks. "It sounded like Nampeyo," she said, keeping her eyes averted from his.

"Who is Nampeyo?" His voice grated harshly.

Without answering, Shala scrambled to her feet and hurried to the entrance. With a trembling hand, she pushed aside the entrance flap. "Nampeyo!" she said unsteadily. "How good of you to come. What are you doing here?"

"Standing in the cold waiting for my friend to invite me into her home," he replied, his gaze sliding past her shoulder to stop on the man beyond.

"Please enter," she said formally, standing aside that he might do so. "How did you get down the cliff? You should not have risked the climb. It was foolhardy to . . ." Her voice trailed away as she realized that Nampeyo was not listening to her, instead, he was taking Eric's measure. "You have heard about Eric?" Although she asked the question, she already knew the answer. Nama must have told him, because he seemed unsurprised to see the Viking.

"Yes, I have heard." Nampeyo's words confirmed her belief. "Nama told me. Her description of the stranger was hard to believe, but I see she did not exaggerate."

Shala's glance flickered between Nampeyo and Eric, who was now standing upright, without the aid of the walking stick he usually used. She remembered how formidable he had looked to her own eyes when she had first beheld him. Obviously Nampeyo was reacting in the same manner, although he kept it well hidden.

"Does he speak our language?" Nampeyo asked her.

"You might ask me that question," Eric growled in the Anasazi tongue.

"There is no need to ask now," Nampeyo replied. "It is obvious that you do." His eyes swept over the other man. "Where are you from, stranger. And why are you here?"

"His home is across the big salt water," Shala hurried to reply, a feeling of apprehension surging through her. She must not set Nampeyo against Eric lest the shaman's son speak ill of him to the father. "He was traveling through our land when he was attacked and fell from the cliff."

"I can speak for myself, Shala," Eric said, striding to stand beside her. She wished he had stayed where he was. Close up, he was even more intimidating. "My name is Eric, and this land is unknown to me. It is only by chance that I came here. Shala has kindly offered me a place to stay."

"How long do you plan on staying?"

Nampeyo had only just come, but he had already asked the question that had been plaguing Shala for some time.

"Only until my leg heals enough for travel."

Although Shala had suspected as much, it was painful to hear the words spoken aloud.

"It would be well if others knew nothing of your presence," Nampeyo said. "My father is shaman, and he has no good feelings for Shala. If he thinks harming you would do her ill, then he would not hesitate for one moment."

Eric looked curiously at Shala, then back to Nampeyo. "Why would he wish her ill?"

"That is another story," Nampeyo replied.

"Will you sit at my fire?" Shala asked politely.

"Thank you," Nampeyo replied, sinking down on the floor and stretching his lame legs toward the warmth. "The cold has already seeped into my bones."

"Although you are welcome, you should not have come," Shala said. "The cliffs are dangerous . . . as you should know."

They talked together for a while, with Eric sitting apart from them, silently watching. Shala made a pot of herb tea and offered a cup to each man, then poured one for herself. All too soon Nampeyo said he must be leaving.

Shala uttered all the polite words, thanking him for his visit, then finishing with, "Be careful on your return journey."

"You need not remind me," Nampeyo said. "Do you have everything you need?"

"Yes. My spirit guide sent me a deer during the deep snow. We have not yet finished it."

"Your spirit guide has done well by you, Shala. Did you thank the deer for its meat?"

"Of course," Shala replied. "Did you not teach me yourself? I would never forget to thank an animal for allowing me to take its flesh."

"You are a good hunter, Shala." With a heavy sigh, he uncurled his lame legs and pushed himself to his feet. "I must go now. Stay well," he said. After nodding to Eric, Nampeyo left them alone.

Eric was silent for a long moment, then, "He is a good friend?" When she nodded her head, he said, "How is it he never came before?"

"He could not. His legs are weak. Did you not see?"

"I saw. How did he come to injure them?"

"He fell from the cliff before he had seen two summers. Both legs were broken, and they never healed right. The deep cold makes them ache in the bones." She looked curiously at him. "Why are you so curious about him?"

"My curiosity is natural. Since he fell when he was so young, I am surprised he was allowed to live. Who looks after him?"

Allowed to live? What did he mean? "The clan looks after him," she replied. "Nampeyo is the shaman's son, but even were he not, the clan would still look after him."

"A man who offers nothing to the tribe's welfare? That makes no sense."

"Would your people have killed him, then?" she asked sharply, feeling horrified at the idea.

"Not killed him. But he would have been allowed the dignity of death."

"There is no dignity in death," she replied. "Not where a child is concerned. You tell me your people are more advanced than mine, that we, here on the mesa, are primitive. May we always remain so if the result would make us less caring toward each other."

"We are not barbarians, Shala. We look to the future always. The search for a better way of life is eternal."

"And that way includes condemning innocent people?" Scorn ripped through her words.

"In Norway we know enough to put the crippled out of their misery," he said grimly.

What kind of man had she brought into her home? He was a monster, uncaring of less fortunate beings. How could she have been so mistaken about him? "You would have killed a child in such circumstances?"

"Not a child. No. But a babe. Yes. Babies have no soul, Shala. Were you unaware of that?" He went on to explain the ritual of birth. "When a babe is first born, it is carefully inspected by the father, who must decide whether the child be allowed to live." When she drew in a horrified breath, he went on to explain. "The winters are cold and long in Norway. Only the strong can survive there. Would it be kinder to give a child life, then have the harshness of its existence take that life away again?"

"What gives you the right to make such a decision about someone else's life?"

"I have made no such decision," he grated. "But if the circumstances were such that it was required of me, then I would not hesitate to do so."

"You could kill your own child?"

"We do not kill the babes," he said heavily. "If circumstances demand the child's death . . . if a babe is born weak or deformed, then it is rejected by the father, taken from the home and exposed to the elements. It dies, of course, but the child would not have survived anyway and it would be wasteful to give it food and attention when others are more in need."

Shala fought to control the nausea rising in her. "It is a cruel practice. Every living creature has a right to survive. The Wise One above has decreed it so."

"Your wise one above must be stupid, then," he retorted.

Shala shrank back in horror. "Do not say such things lest *He* release his wrath upon your head."

Eric laughed. "Do you really believe he could do that?" Reaching out, he snagged her wrist and pulled her close to him. "I am not fearful of your wise one above. He does not know me. The gods of Norway watch over me. I answer to no others."

Blasphemy! He should tremble before his words, and yet, he was calm, unstricken. Apparently the Wise One was biding his time. Who could say when He would strike the Viking down?

She drew a deep breath and prepared for a battle since she would not stay so close to him, but he surprised her by allowing her to wriggle free.

She saw immediately that his attention was directed elsewhere.

"Where did this stone come from, Shala?" He asked the question he had often put to her before, his eyes focused on her amulet.

"I have told you many times that Nampeyo gave it to me," she replied.

"Nampeyo?" he asked, his eyes flying to the entrance flap. "The man who was just here?"

"Yes," she said. "I told you his name was Nampeyo."

"Where did he get the stone?"

She shrugged her shoulders as she had done many times. "Who knows?"

"Nampeyo must know," he insisted.

"I suppose he does," she replied. "But he would not tell me. The stone is sacred. The place where it was found remains a secret to the People." Her lips twisted bitterly. "Have you decided the crippled man might just be good for something?"

"We were speaking of this stone, Shala. And where it might be found." He studied her thoughtfully. "I would like to speak to him about it. Is it likely he will come for another visit?"

"No," she said, feeling great satisfaction that she could reply in that manner. "It would be unwise for him to do so. Although he is Shu's son, he does not escape the shaman's wrath."

Evidently her words reminded him of what Nampeyo had said because he pinned her with his gaze. "Why does the shaman dislike you?"

"That is a long story," she replied, turning

away from him. "And there is no time to speak of it. I must check my snares before dark."

"Is that wise?" he asked. "The cliff will be slick with ice."

"If Nampeyo can climb down here, then I can climb to the mesa," she replied, stooping to pick up her rabbitskin cloak. She was determined to go out, to put some distance between the two of them. She had learned something terrible about him and needed time to think, to sort out her thoughts, her feelings.

The fresh air would do her good, would help to clear her mind and chase away the curious feelings that he had unleashed when his mouth had covered hers so possessively.

What did it all mean? she wondered. How could she feel such animosity for a man, yet still be filled with such longing for his touch?

Shala found no answer to her questions, knew she would not while he was near. She hurried out of the cave, leaving him and his disturbing presence behind.

Ten

Eric watched with mixed feelings as Shala left the cave. On the one hand, he wanted her to stay, but on the other, he felt the need to be alone, to be given time to sort out his feelings. For despite his constant denial, he did have feelings for her, feelings that were becoming harder and harder to suppress with each passing day.

And to allow her to know them, would be to show her his weakness. No! He must, at all cost, keep his feelings to himself.

Those very same feelings had been out of control when that idiot, Nampeyo, had come. But perhaps it was a good thing the lame one came. Another moment and Eric would have taken the girl, which could very well have proven disastrous.

Why should it be such a disaster? logic cried out. *What harm could really come from giving in to desires of the flesh?*

Perhaps he should take her. Would it be so bad to listen to the needs of his body? He could certainly be excused for those needs. He had been without a woman for a long time. He thought about that for a moment and realized it had been almost a year since he had taken a woman to his bed.

His lips twisted wryly. It was no wonder that his loins swelled, that his seed demanded to be spilled.

His only concern was that such a union might bring forth a child.

Suppose a child was conceived? he silently questioned. It need not overly concern him. Shala would see that it was cared for. He imagined a child with blond hair and deeply tanned skin. It would surely be a sight to behold.

Eric knew then that he would bed Shala, knew as well that it would be a delightful experience. The satisfaction gained from that knowledge was tempered by a measure of regret that he would not be around long enough to know if his seed had taken root, but it was only a fleeting thought, really of no consequence at all.

The watcher had been waiting since midmorning in the plum thicket near the cliff, hoping to see the girl who had been in his thoughts for some time. He had thought about her constantly while the snow was heavy upon the ground, wondering if her need had finally become so great that she would welcome his attentions, and yet, unwilling to climb down to her cave lest someone see him do so.

It was one thing to run into her accidentally. Quite another to deliberately seek her out.

His lips twisted into a smile.

No. He would not seek.

Rather, he would wait. Eventually, she would have to leave the cave where she lived to search for food. When she did, he would be waiting for her.

His eyes glinted darkly as his mind's eye conjured up a vision of her the way she had been last summer. He had seen her swimming, unaware that she was being observed. The water was so clear that, instead of covering her nakedness, it had only enhanced her darkly tanned skin, making it glisten beneath the pale moonlight spilling down on the glittering pool and the girl who swam there.

Just the memory tightened his loins.

Shala had not yet been banished from the clan, and it was only that knowledge that had kept him from leaving his place of concealment to capture her, throw her to the ground and mate with her.

Rape within the clan was forbidden and would not be tolerated, therefore the punishment for such a crime was severe. Castration. The word alone was enough to horrify any man, to make him keep his distance unless otherwise invited.

He had been invited many times. . . . There were always girls available, more than willing to service his needs, but somehow they did not appeal to him any longer. What he needed was a good fight. He wanted a girl who would cry out, who would fight tooth and nail to save her virginity.

He shifted his position. He could think of several things he would rather be doing than crouching here among the brush, waiting for a girl who might not appear. He pictured himself atop one of the maidens of the village, but his male member was unresponsive, passive. There was no excitement in such a union.

No! He needed more! Someone different. A girl who would fight and scratch and claw beneath him. He needed to see terror-stricken eyes below his, needed to see those very same eyes go dim with despair when he entered her and she realized fighting was useless.

He squeezed his male member, imagining the sound of ripping flesh as he tore through a virgin body with his maleness, conjuring up the smell of blood that resulted from the wound.

One part of his brain looked on in horror at his need while another concentrated on coaxing his manhood, on making it hard, ready at a moment's notice.

He could never take one of the village maidens, dared not do so. But Shala's own eagerness to resist Shu had made her an acceptable prey. She would be alone, easy to conquer—but not *too* easy. And there was no one to object.

Even more important, no one would condemn him if he was found out.

Yes, it would be perfect. It would be—

Suddenly, before his eyes, a head appeared at the edge of the mesa. It was followed by the upper portion of a girl. Shala. Without a thought of being observed, she leapt lightly to her feet and strode away from the canyon, unaware that he was only a short distance behind her.

Shala followed the trail that skirted the canyon with light steps. Spring wouldn't be long in coming now. She was certain of it. Right now Sky Man was wearing his bluest coat and Father Sun was sending down his fiery gaze upon the land, warming it, melting the snow. Soon, new grass would burst forth from the earth, and she would carry her digging stick, made from a tough juniper branch, with her and search out roots and greens and newly sprouted yarrows to use for seasoning.

Unaware of being followed, Shala held her newly fashioned spear loosely in her right hand. Usually she was not so careless with her weapon, but her mind was still occupied by memories of Eric and the way her body had felt, pressed so tightly beneath his. Just the thought of his maleness swelling against her lower body sent heat surging up her neck to stain her cheeks.

Eric.

He was so different from the other men of her acquaintance.

Eric . . .

So intelligent, so obviously male, and although at most times he tried to keep it hidden, she sensed the need for her lingering just beneath the surface.

It was strange because she also sensed the barely hidden contempt he held for her. And that hurt. It cut her to the quick that he would want her and at the same time feel scorn for her.

Yet was it not the same for her? She had felt horror when he had spoken of child sacrifice. Did he not recognize it for what it was? A cruel practice devised by men who sought to improve on the Supreme Being's plan for his children. How could Eric condone such a practice? The thought that he could do so angered and dismayed her; yet her innermost feelings for the man had not changed. She still desired him, would take him for a mate if he were so inclined.

Remembering how his male member had swelled against her, she felt he might be moved in that direction.

What would have happened if Nampeyo had not come calling? Would they have coupled? Shala considered it for a moment, then came to the conclusion that they would have done so.

Would that have changed his feelings about her? Would the scorn that was barely hidden beneath the surface have given way to admiration?

She thought not. Mating took no intelligence. The act took no special skills, no tools. One was born with the ability to mate. Why should the mere act alter Eric's opinion of her?

What did she have to impress him with? Her skills as a hunter? She bit her lower lip and grimaced. With their food almost gone, her hunting skills would impress no one.

What about her cooking skills? she wondered.

Eric had a voracious appetite, and she had learned early in life to prepare good meals. Even as the thought occurred, she quickly dismissed it. How could she prepare even the simplest dishes when there were very few foodstuffs to choose from?

She thought about the corn stored in the cliff city and spared a moment to wish she had some, then blithely dismissed it from her mind. It did no good to wish for what could not be.

There was nothing she could do at present, except check her snares and hope there would be meat there. But when spring came, she promised herself, she would show that green-eyed man what she could do. When the earth was green again, she would prepare mouth-watering meals for him and bask in his pleasure and astonishment.

Almost lost in her fantasy, she was jerked back to the present by a snapping sound coming from somewhere behind her.

Immediately, she felt alarm. Spinning on her heels, she brought her spear up—and found herself faced with one of her own clansman.

"Stalking Coyote! Why are you skulking about like your namesake trailing a rabbit. Are you following me?" she questioned sharply.

He spread his arms wide and strode toward her. "Following you?" he prevaricated. "Why should I follow you?"

Despite the fact that he carried his spear low, Shala felt unease, a sense of danger. "If you were not following me, why did you not call out to announce your presence?"

He grinned down at her, a burning light in his eyes. "That is not important. What is important is that I *am* here. And so are you." His dark gaze looked beyond her, then to each side before returning to meet her eyes again. Then he motioned toward the bushes. "Come," he said. "I wish to show you something."

"What?" she asked suspiciously, backing away from him.

Too late!

With a quick movement he bounded forward, snatched the spear from her hand and tossed it aside. Then, snagging her wrist between fingers as hard as flint, he yanked her against him.

Before she could react, thick arms wrapped around her middle, crushing her to the ground beneath his weight.

Struggling desperately against his greater strength, she twisted and turned, flailing out with her fists, kicking out with her legs, but he seemed impervious to her blows. His knee shoved between her legs as he attempted to part them. Realizing she had only one chance, she allowed herself to relax for one short moment.

It was obvious by the grin that spread across his face that he thought she had given up. Just that one moment was all she needed. When he relaxed his hold, she brought her knee up between his thighs with as much strength as she could, connecting with the softness there.

With a howl of pain, he rolled aside. Shala leapt to her feet and fled through the trees. Her fear was so great that she had no thought of the spear she left behind.

Hope, like a sliver of flint, rose sharp within her breast as she ran, blood surging frantically through her veins and her heart pumping madly. Her lungs heaved as she fled through the forest, swerving to avoid clutching branches that tore at her cloak and diving around a tall fir. Her lungs burned, but still she fled, her mind whirling with panic!

She had to get away! She must! If she was caught, he would rip through her body as though it was of no consequence at all, and when he was finished with her, he would see the life drain away before he left her. She was certain of it.

But she also knew there was one thing in her favor. Her body was whipcord thin, not an ounce of fat padded her firmly muscled flesh, and although she did not have a man's strength, she had a special balance and speed that gave her an advantage, however slight it was.

Over the pounding of her heart, she could hear brush cracking behind her and knew the man had recovered enough to give pursuit.

Spirit Wolf! she silently cried. *Help me!*

The late afternoon sun shone brightly down on the cliff dwellings as Nama left her quarters and crossed the courtyard, making her way toward the spring at the head of the canyon. All around her was the sound of the People. Children laughing, playing, and women talking together while they worked at various tasks. She passed Nampeyo's living quarters and paused, wondering for a moment if she should speak to him again, perhaps plead her case again, but immediately dismissed the idea. She would have to find another way out of the trap she was in. Nampeyo would think only of the People, not of the girl he had played with as a child, the girl whose heart was now weighted down by sorrow.

Eleven

Gryla peered around the door to her living quarters, watching Nama start up the trail toward the spring, wondering if the girl had been in touch with Shala, tempted to follow her and find out.

A heavy hollowness lay inside her breast as she thought of Shala. How could she stand the thought of her only child being abandoned, left alone to fend for herself? It was cruel, and yet, the shaman's word was all powerful. It was, and would always be, the way of their clan.

Stepping back into her dwelling, Gryla let her eyes wander around the shadowy interior. Her gaze came to rest on the pallet where Shala had slept . . . where each of Gryla's five children had slept while their spirits remained among the living. She experienced a curious emptiness of the soul. Two of her children, one a female, the other male, had died mysteriously in the night, their bodies already blue when discovered. One of her daughters had been bitten when a wolf tried to stop the child from taking its cub, and the wound had gone bad; evil had sneaked in to cause pus and corruption, and the girl child had died in fever. Another daughter had lasted five seasons before a black bear caught her picking berries. The bear's hide had covered Gryla and her mate until he had died. It still covered her; yet it was little solace for a dead daughter.

Last of all was Shala. She had been the strong one, the one who slowly turned into a slim young woman. Gryla had been so certain that she would marry well, that she would have strong sons to hunt for them.

But now Shala, too, was gone.

And Gryla might just as well be dead.

Unfortunately, she was not!

Neither was Shala. No! She was out there, somewhere, alone. Perhaps in trouble. And Gryla could not do one thing to help her.

It had been hours since Shala left the cavern, and Eric was worried about her. He remembered the last time she had left, how she had almost died. What would he do if something happened to her now?

Just the thought caused an ache in the pit of his stomach. Thor's teeth! Why had she gone?

He limped to the entrance, shoved the hide flap aside and peered across the canyon at the cliff city, wondering if perhaps she was there, but it was too far away to see her even had she been there.

Stepping outside, he sent his gaze up the cliff

above him. Could he climb it in his condition? If Shala did not return soon, then he would damn well try.

Shala crouched beneath a covering of leaves, listening for the quiet tread of leather-covered feet that would herald the approach of her attacker. High above her she could see streaks of reddish clouds flaming in the dying light of Father Sun. There was no sound around her, not even a stirring of Wind Woman's breath to mask the footsteps that slowly approached her hiding place.

He was going on by! *Oh, Spirit Wolf!* she silently breathed. *Thank you for your protection!*

She unfolded her legs and rose to her feet, brushing the leaves from her body.

Suddenly, she felt her shoulder gripped by iron fingers and whirled to face her tormentor.

Eric was unprepared for the fury with which Shala attacked him. "Thor's teeth!" he shouted, wrapping his arms around her body to still her flailing fists. "What is the matter with you?"

Instantly, her struggles ceased and she looked up at him. "Eric?" Her eyes were tearful. "Is it really you? How did you get here?"

"Yes, it is really me," he growled, "and I climbed up the cliff the same way you did. I had the mistaken idea that something had happened to you." He gripped her shoulders with cruel fingers and gave her a hard shake. "Why did you not return?"

"Something did happen to me," she said angrily, brushing the tousled hair away from her face and glaring fiercely at him. "Turn me loose! Your fingers are hurting me!"

His gaze was wary, his expression inscrutable. "What happened? What prevented your return?"

"I was attacked."

His fingers relaxed slightly while he sent his narrowed gaze around them, searching the bushes, the trees, looking for the danger that might still be lurking there. "Attacked by what?"

"Not by a thing. It was a man. One of my own clansmen."

"One of your own attacked you? Why? And where is he now?"

"I ran away from him." Her voice held only a slight wobble, a fact of which she was proud. "I am glad you are here."

"You should not have come. It is not safe for a woman alone."

"We need food," she reminded him angrily. "And whether it is safe or not, I am forced to hunt or go hungry." She paused, the anger draining away as a frown creased her brow. Her gaze went to his injured leg. "You should not be here. Your leg is not yet healed."

"The journey has not harmed it. The bone will soon be healed." He gripped her forearm. "Night will soon be upon us. We must return to the cave."

"I have not yet checked the traps," she cried, pulling her arm free.

"Forget it," he commanded gruffly. "My leg demands rest, and I will not return without you."

"You must," she said. "There is no other choice. We need meat and—"

"There is an easier way to get it," he said. "There is food in my pack. Enough to last until this leg is mended. If the pack is still there."

"A pack? Where did you leave it?"

"The abandoned city."

She frowned up at him. "That is where I slept before. When Wolf saved my life. But I saw nothing of a pack."

"Someone may have found it then. How far are we from the ruins?"

"They are close by."

"Good," he said, bending to rub his leg. "I could not travel far on this leg. Already it aches with cold."

"You rest here," she suggested. "I will go on alone."

"No. It would serve us better to stay together."

Since she had no desire to leave him behind, Shala made no objection. They took a northward path with her in the lead while Eric limped along behind her, all the time wondering if he had enough strength left to make it back to the cave.

Stalking Coyote, hearing the sound of voices—one of them definitely a female's—circled carefully toward the sound, safely hidden by the trees.

He was almost certain one of the voices belonged to Shala, but the other—the deeper, male voice—was unfamiliar to him.

His fingers tightened around his spear and he held it ready for attack as his path took him closer to the southern edge of the cliff—close to the abandoned dwellings on the mesa.

Why would Shala go there? he wondered. Did she think to hide in the buildings? She couldn't. He knew them like the back of his hand. Of course, there were hiding places there—the abandoned kivas for instance. It would take time to search them, but Stalking Coyote was determined not to leave without having mated with Shala and he would stay as long as required to accomplish that end.

Realizing they were traveling at a snail's pace, he hurried toward the abandoned city, hiding himself just inside where he would remain unseen.

The footsteps were growing louder now. He crouched behind the nearest wall, intent on remaining hidden until he knew the identity of the man with Shala. Already, he had a good idea who it was, because the person with her had a decided limp.

He smiled grimly. Shu would want to know if someone was helping Shala survive. Even if it proved to be his own son, Nampeyo. It was common knowledge that he had no love for his crippled son, that he had only taught him the duties of shaman because it was expected of him, because for generations the position had been handed down from father to son.

Shu might even reward the person who saw fit to inform on Nampeyo. He could certainly use any information that was detrimental to Nampeyo's character to his advantage.

Stalking Coyote had let his thoughts keep him busy too long. He realized that as Shala stepped into the building. She was unaware of another presence. She turned to speak to someone who remained outside Stalking Coyote's line of vision. The words she spoke gave the warrior pause—they sounded like gibberish—but he realized she was speaking in a language unknown to him.

A harsh voice sounded from the trees behind her. It was a deep voice, obviously male, and yet, Stalking Coyote could not pin the voice on the face of Nampeyo, nor any other man he knew.

Why? he wondered. He knew every one of the People. Was the man not Clan? How could that be? The whole thing became curiouser and curiouser.

Yes! Shu must be told of this!

He might have crept away unseen had chance not brought his foot upon a limb that snapped beneath his weight.

Immediately, Shala jerked her head around, her eyes widening as they met his, and in that moment, Stalking Coyote knew he was not going to slink off like a beaten coyote. Just the thought of doing it was so hateful to him that he drew himself up to his full height and stepped into view, challenging her and whomever followed, knowing full well that he could deal easily with the man who was crippled.

"Stalking Coyote!" Shala gasped, her voice showing her fear.

"So you thought to escape me so easily," Stalking Coyote said, striding toward her. "Who is with you? Nampeyo? Just wait until Shu hears—"

He broke off as the man came into view. Although he was leaning on a heavy stick, he was still formidable. In fact, he was the biggest man Stalking Coyote had ever seen. For a moment he wondered if he had made a mistake by not escaping when he could. Then he chided himself for a fool. The man was weaponless, obviously crippled. And Stalking Coyote was no coward.

With a grin of anticipation, he hurled his spear at the golden-haired man.

Eric was caught by surprise at seeing the *skraeling's* hostile act. He barely had time to skip aside from the deadly missile hurled his way. He felt the whisper of air as it sailed by his left shoulder, inches away.

The Viking braced himself, spreading his legs wide, as the *skraeling,* angered at having wasted his spear, drew his knife and launched himself at Eric.

Stumbling, trying to keep his balance with only one good leg, Eric lashed out with his fist, catching the other man on the side of his face before he was in striking distance with the knife. The *skraeling* sailed across the floor of the courtyard, landing with a hard thud near a hole in the ground from which protruded a wooden ladder.

Shaking his head as though trying to clear it, the man launched himself forward for another attack. Eric saw Shala join the fray, springing into her clansman's path, grabbing a fistful of hair and yanking back as hard as she could.

The man shook her off as though she were nothing but a feather, then rushed toward Eric again.

"Stay out of it!" Eric ordered sternly, bracing himself to meet the next attack.

But instead of obeying, Shala picked herself off the ground and sprang after Eric's attacker.

"I said stay out of it!" Eric roared, swinging his arm to meet the rush of the other man.

His attention had been diverted just long enough for the other man to get close enough to strike. Realizing how close he was to death, Eric jumped back, landed near the edge of the hole on his bad leg and lost his balance. His opponent, taking advantage of the moment, whirled and faced him again.

Realizing death was on the point of the gleaming obsidian blade, Eric ushered all of his strength to the fore and struck out with his doubled fist. He felt the drive of the knife into his flesh just before his fist connected with the other man's head. Then he was falling . . . falling . . . falling into the depths of the kiva. Something hard struck his head and he knew no more.

* * *

Shala's heart beat with dread as, after one glance at Stalking Coyote to determine that he lay unmoving, she leapt into the ruined kiva and landed beside Eric's limp body.

Oh, Wise One above! she silently cried, *don't let him be dead!* Tears flooded her eyes and spilled down her cheeks as she bent to examine him.

Relief flooded through her as she felt his breath against her cheek. He lived. She bent to examine his leg, found the splints remained intact and hoped there had been no further damage to the bone.

"Eric," she said huskily, lifting his head against her breast and patting his cheek gently. "Are you all right?"

He lifted his lashes and met her eyes. "Where is he?" he asked.

"Up there," she replied. "You knocked his head against a rock. I think he is dead."

"Go and make certain."

Shala knew she must, even though she hated the thought of approaching Stalking Coyote again. They must know for sure the man was dead. With a heavy sigh, she climbed the ladder to its topmost step and looked to where she had last seen her clansman.

He was gone.

Her heart sank with dread. She dared not tell Eric about Stalking Coyote's disappearance. The fight had left him in no condition to travel fast, yet travel they must. And it would have to be done at a slower pace.

"Wolf!" she cried aloud. "Help me! Delay

Stalking Coyote so that we will have time to reach the safety of my cave." Shala hoped her spirit guide would heed her cry, for she knew her clansman would waste no time informing Shu of Eric's presence. And Shu would surely set out to kill him.

She delayed returning for several minutes, wondering what to tell Eric. If she told him Stalking Coyote had fled, he would surely make her leave without him, would stay and face the danger alone. Since she was determined to remain with him, there would be an argument which would result in even more delay.

Would it really be so bad if she told an untruth just this one time?

Coming to a swift decision, she joined Eric again, and with a smile pasted on her face, she faced him with a lie. "My clansman's spirit has departed from his body," she said. "I covered him with rocks so no one will know what happened."

"That is good," he said huskily. "Because I fear I cannot make it back to the cave."

"But we must!" she cried urgently.

"Why?" He looked at her. "The pack is here. We have shelter. There is no reason we cannot stay the night."

Shala knew then she must tell him about the lie, yet she could not bring herself to do so. If he could not make it home, then he could not. They would just have to take the chance that Stalking Coyote would be too shamed to admit he had been bested by a crippled man.

She went after the pack.

Twelve

". . . and he was big as Grandfather Black Bear! His hair was the color of Father Sun at midday, and his strength was so great that it could demolish twice the numbers on both my hands with one blow." Stalking Coyote stood in the center of the courtyard, gesturing wildly with his hands, knowing with a certainty that every eye was upon him and secretly gloating over that fact.

He considered the possibility that Shu might even reward the messenger who carried news of the strange intruder.

What would be a just reward for such important news? he silently wondered.

"Such a thing is not possible!" the shaman said, dashing to the ground Stalking Coyote's dreams of being showered with gifts. The man had never even considered that he might not be believed.

"I saw him!" Stalking Coyote cried.

Shu's flat black eyes resembled the storm clouds that were gathering high above them. They were dark and dangerous. "If there were such a man, then I would know of him."

Realizing the extent of his mistake, Stalking Coyote hurried to remedy it. "Yes! You would know, Wise One . . . if the man was already here in our world." His eyes shifted, swept over the crowd, stopped on Gryla, Keeper of Memories, and he squirmed inwardly, like a packrat in a snake's hole.

What right did she have to look at him in that manner? Although her face was expressionless, her eyes bored into him, and he felt almost certain the woman could see right through him. But Gryla was the least of his worries. Right now the shaman waited for an explanation.

"What do you mean?" Shu asked.

"The stranger is not from this earth, Wise One. My own eyes saw him come into this world through a sipapu at the abandoned city. He has only just left the third world that we fled from so long ago. Now he is loose in ours."

"The third world?" Shu's gaze probed Stalking Coyote, and the hapless individual expected at any moment to be denounced as a liar—and a coward—but, astonishingly, Shu looked thoughtful. Tapping a long finger against his chin, he said, "Is such a thing possible? Could an evil spirit escape from that world into ours?"

Breathing a sigh of relief, Stalking Coyote was quick to take advantage. "It is possible, Wise One. And the evil spirit thinks to fool us by taking on the appearance of Father Sun."

The crowd surrounding Stalking Coyote surged

back a few feet as though suspecting he carried some kind of plague that he had caught from the evil one on his person.

"An evil spirit . . . loose in our world?" muttered Flying Eagle who was standing closest to Stalking Coyote. "How did he escape from the third world? Did First Man not dream a spell on the sipapu—the entrance to our world—to guard against such a happening?" He turned to Gryla for confirmation.

"Yes," she affirmed, her face showing no emotion whatsoever. "First Man *did* dream a spell on the entrance. There is no way an evil one could come through." She fixed accusing eyes on Stalking Coyote as though he were personally responsible for the spirit being let loose among them.

"Wait!" he cried, holding out a hand as though to hold back his accusers. "Listen to me!" Stalking Coyote's thoughts grappled for an explanation that would serve his purpose. "It was a long time ago. First Man dreamed the spell many years ago. The power of the dream must have been diminished by time, maybe even blown away by Wind Woman's breath."

"Blown away?" cried someone—a woman—nearby. "If that is so, there may be more of them!"

"Evil spirits," people muttered around him. "How many more have come."

"You saw only one?" Ona asked anxiously.

Stalking Coyote smiled reassuringly at her, then shifted his gaze to the rest of the crowd, feeling like a man who was granting permission for them to be happy again. "There is only one."

"Only one?" Shu asked. "How can you be sure? If the spell has gone–if it has been blown away by Wind Woman or weakened by time–then why has no other evil spirit entered our world?"

Feeling as though he were losing ground again, Stalking Coyote tried to focus the shaman's attention elsewhere. "Maybe one has!" he cried, turning flashing eyes on Gryla. "Maybe the Keeper of Memories has forgotten!" He pointed an accusing finger at the old woman.

Gryla's back stiffened at the insult. "Forgotten?" she asked quietly. "The Keeper of Memories does not forget!"

"No," Ona said quickly, stepping forward to stand beside Gryla. "You know the Keeper of Memories is chosen with care, Stalking Coyote. She is chosen by the Wise One above who gives her the power to retain all memory. If you insult our Keeper of Memories, then you insult our Supreme Being, the Wise One above who made First Man in his own image."

Stalking Coyote heard several people mutter agreement and dropped his eyes, feeling shame that he had allowed himself to go so far. *Shala's fault!* an inner voice cried. *This whole thing is Shala's fault. She should not have resisted, should not have brought in the stranger!* He should not have accused Gryla. His anger with Shala was responsible for his actions. He must be careful lest the Wise One above decided to punish him for his insults.

Stalking Coyote was no coward; yet he did have one deep, all-consuming fear—that when his spirit departed from the land of the living, it would not be allowed to go to the Great Beyond.

"I am sorry, Wise Mother," he said most humbly. "I do not doubt your memories. My tongue spoke without thought."

With a hard look at him, Gryla turned away from him and strode away, leaving him wondering if she had accepted his apology. He turned his attention to Shu again, and this time he spoke more quietly. "The man is there!" he said. "If you doubt my words, then come with me. You will see him with your own eyes."

The shaman cast a quick look at the dark clouds in the sky. "We cannot go now," he said. "A storm is brewing. Soon it will unleash its fury on us. Meanwhile I will cleanse myself and consult with the spirits about this matter. If there is actually such a man"—he eyed the marks on Stalking Coyote's face, then went on—"it is best to be prepared for the meeting."

"We cannot wait!" Stalking Coyote argued. "We must go now, while the stranger—the evil spirit is weak."

"Weak! You said he was strong! You said he had the strength of ten men!"

"He does. But I bested him. I threw him into a kiva, and he lay motionless."

"Motionless?" The shaman arched his brow. "Did you kill him?"

"I do not know," Stalking Coyote admitted. "I did not wait to find out."

"Not find out? But would it not have been better to have done so?"

"Perhaps," Stalking Coyote admitted. "But Shala was there, too, and—"

"Shala?" Shu's eyes hardened. "You did not mention her before? Was the evil one with her?"

"Yes," Stalking Coyote admitted.

"Perhaps there is no evil one." Wupatki laughed. "Perhaps Stalking Coyote mistook Shala for an evil spirit who escaped from the third world."

"Maybe that is what happened," Flying Eagle said scornfully. "He was unable to best her even when they were children! Is that it, Stalking Coyote? Was it Shala who attacked you? Did she give you that big bump on your head?"

A low rumbling of uneasy laughter sounded, but stopped abruptly as Shu snarled. "Since when do my People speak the name of an outcast!"

Instantly, silence fell around him. He glared at Stalking Coyote. "I have already said I will consult with the spirits. If it is their wish, then we will go look at the evil stranger. But for now we will speak no more of this."

Without another word, he stalked away from the crowd, headed, undoubtedly, for his kiva where he would cleanse his body with purifying steam, readying himself to speak with the spirit world.

Cra-a-a-ck!

The loud crack of thunder startled Stalking Coyote, making him jerk. It was followed by a jagged streak of lightning that split the sky and streaked downward as though reaching for him.

He stared up with frightened eyes. Had he angered the Wise One above with his tales of evil spirits? Should he hurry after Shu and take back everything he had said?

Stalking Coyote waited for some sign, but none was forthcoming. Relieved, he headed for his dwelling.

Cra-a-ack!

The loud crack of thunder sent Shala hurtling into Eric's arms, where she burrowed her head against his chest. He held her tight against him, tucking her head beneath his chin as they waited for more.

And waited, but nothing more came. Instead, there was silence around them.

When the silence continued, Shala pulled back slightly, tilting her head to meet his eyes. "I have shamed myself before you," she muttered. "I have no excuse for my cowardice. It has always been so. When thunder booms overhead I want to hide myself away until my ears can no longer hear its terrible voice."

"You have no need to fear thunder," he said gently. "It is nothing. Only a great booming noise, caused by Thor throwing his hammer."

"Thor?" Shala had heard him use the word before. Had it not been something to do with teeth?

"Yes," he said. "Have you never heard of Thor?" He smiled suddenly and answered his own question. "No. I guess you have not. He is one of our ancient gods, Shala. We have many of them in Norway." His lips twitched, and his eyes actually twinkled. He did not explain that Christianity had made its way to Norway several centuries ago. There would be time enough later to teach her, time enough to teach her other things as well, he decided, enjoying the feel of her in his arms.

Craa-ack! The sound was followed by a jagged streak of lightning that reached for the ground.

Uttering a yelp of fright, Shala burrowed her head against his chest again.

"Close your eyes and forget where you are," he said, patting her on the back. "Try to get some sleep."

"No!" she said, pulling away from him and twisting around to fix her eyes on the partially collapsed roof of the kiva. "Not here. We must find a safer place. One that will not be so vulnerable to attack." Even as she spoke, she felt a raindrop against her flesh.

"You are right," he agreed, following her gaze. "The buildings above would make a safer place." He gripped the ladder to hold it steady. "You go first."

By the time they were settled in a dry place that could offer both shelter and safety, the rain was coming down so hard that Shala knew they were safe for a time. Her clansmen would never leave the cliff city in such weather, nor would there be scavengers. Taking comfort from that knowledge, she curled up on the floor, covered herself with her cape and was soon fast asleep.

Eric lay awake a short distance from Shala, listening to the rain falling outside the dwellings, painfully aware of his leg, throbbing with each beat of his heart. Had he caused it further injury by walking so far on it? Even had he done so, he felt no regret for having come. If he had not, Shala might well be dead.

He looked across at her, wondering at the feelings she stirred deep inside of him.

She lay there, covered with nothing but her cape, a slender arm projecting from beneath. He studied her slim hand. It lay limp, fingers in a curl, and he thought it was the most beautiful hand he had ever seen. His eyes moved to her face, exquisitely made, as though sculptured by one of the masters. Here and there wisps of black hair poked out from beneath the hide covering, blowing gently against her face.

Blowing? His gaze flashed to the entrance, and he realized the wind was stronger, the storm was increasing in its fury.

Cra-a-ack!

The thunder boomed around them. It jerked Shala's eyes open and sent her scurrying fearfully toward him. He opened his arms to receive her.

"Easy," he murmured soothingly, smoothing a hand down her silky dark hair.

Crack!

Feeling her flinch, he tightened his arms around

her. He knew her heart was thudding as rapidly as a frightened bird's.

"You need not worry," he said, raising his voice over the furious cracks of thunder that continued to peal around them. It was as though all the furies in heaven had suddenly been released. "Need not worry," he repeated. "It is only Odin leading his spirit warriors into battle."

"O-Odin?" she stuttered, the word sounding as though it was spoken through clenched teeth. Her arms snaked around his waist, gripping him tightly. "W-who is O-Odin?"

"Odin, the one-eyed god. Father of Thor," he said. "Remember? I told you about Thor. He is responsible for the thunder. It occurs when he throws his magic hammer." Realizing she needed to be distracted from the fury of the storm, he proceeded to tell her about Asgard, the realm of the ancient gods and those who dwelt there.

Shala listened intently, her eyes moving often to his lips. By the time he stopped speaking, the fury of the storm had spent itself. Now there was only the gentle sound of falling rain.

"The noise has stopped now," she said in a hushed voice.

"Yes," he agreed, still caught up in his tales of the ancient legends. "Odin has finished his wild ride across the sky. Now he takes his seat in Valhalla with his two wolves beside him. He will throw them the food set before him, for he eats nothing. Instead, he drinks mead while two ravens perch on his throne whispering to him all that is happening in the world."

She shivered, feeling as though unseen eyes were boring through her. Could his god, Odin, the one-eyed, see them here? In this land that was an ocean's width from the place where he ruled with such fury? Eric had said he was in a place called Valla. "Where is Valla?" she asked.

"Valhalla," he corrected. "No man knows its location. Only the gods know. Valhalla is a place where the most valiant knights—warriors to you—who fell in battle are gathered together."

"It is a spirit place then," she said. "And as such cannot be described."

"Every Viking can describe Valhalla," he said. "It is a huge hall of dazzling gold; it is sumptuously decorated, and there is no limit to the size of assembly that can be held there. It is so big that it contains five hundred and forty doors which are so wide that each one can admit eight hundred warriors walking abreast."

Shala could not comprehend the numbers he was using, but that fact did not bother her. She allowed his voice to wash over her, so soothing, so soft that it canceled out the frightening vision of the mighty Odin and his spirit warriors.

The tension had drained away as though it had never been, and Shala allowed her head to fall back against Eric's shoulder.

He stopped speaking, and she looked inquiringly at him, saw he was watching her intently, but something in his moss green eyes held her still.

"Shala," he whispered, his voice a husky caress.

Her heart jolted and a dizzying current raced

through her. She held her breath, almost mesmerized by his gaze. His arms tightened around her, his head dipped down, his lips hovering only inches above hers.

"Sweet, sweet, Shala," he muttered.

Her pulse accelerated as his mouth lowered, then closed over hers with tantalizing gentleness as though testing her response. Or waiting for something. Should she be doing something herself to help him? Even as she asked herself the question, the pressure of his lips increased and his mouth coaxed hers to open.

The intrusion of his tongue piercing her lips was swift, accomplished with sexual expertise. Wildfire coursed through her veins, accompanied by a fluttery feeling in her stomach as though a thousand butterflies had taken wing.

When his tongue probed the moist cavern within, raking over the roof of her mouth, an icy chill spread through her, working its way along her spine as though Wind Woman were playing a tune and using her backbone for a musical instrument.

Feeling his lower body swell against her, Shala felt a vague sense of satisfaction, and yet, she remained in hunger, completely unsatisfied, left wanting in some obscure way. Was this what the maidens spoke of in whispers after they had coupled with a man?

She wriggled beneath him, aware of Eric's body, hard against her own. His rough hands slid beneath her cape and caressed the hillocks of her small breasts, and she gasped, wondering at the pleasure the small act caused. His hands were eager, caressing, and her nipples grew taut beneath his fingers even while his tongue continued to work its magic in her mouth.

Shala was no longer passive beneath his touch, could not remain so with his manhood so hard, throbbing with such passion as it pressed against her lower belly.

Her body arched against him while her arms slid around his neck, her fingers tangling in his golden curls.

This was so right. She belonged to Eric, just as he belonged to her. No matter what tomorrow brought, they would face it together. For the rest of their lives. From this moment on, she would see to his needs as he would see to hers.

And right now she needed his loving, needed to feel him inside her body.

She pulled her mouth away from his. "Eric," she murmured, "please, Eric. Take me now."

Instead of heeding her plea, he used his lips to blaze a trail of fire down her neck to the curve of her breast and to cover her left nipple. The warm moistness of his mouth, teasing first one nipple and then the other, caused delicious shudders that stoked the fire already burning in her lower extremities.

Shala moaned low in her throat, wriggling beneath him, trying to get closer, his rough hands on her thighs, her skirt sliding up them, then his eager fingers searching out the moistness between her legs.

Shala was startled by the touch; when his fingers moved gently, shock coursed through her, causing her to spasm slightly, then push hard against his hand. A sudden sense of urgency drove her, and when his hand continued to stroke her, she moved in rhythm, her heart thumping rapidly in time with the movement.

"Eric," she moaned, softly supplicating. "No more, Eric." She was nearly begging in her need, but he seemed uncaring of that fact.

Suddenly, he moved away. She thought he had misunderstood her words, was going to leave her this way, unfulfilled. Her cry of protest was barely uttered before he was back, sliding over her with bared flesh, covering her with his maleness. She slid her legs apart, wanting the completion of their union. There was a moment of pain, then her woman's membrane separated and he plunged into her.

He rode her until she was mindless with pleasure, leaving only an aching need to be satisfied. His shaft drove deeper and swifter until she thought she could stand no more. Then, in a burst of ecstasy that left them both exhausted, they reached completion together. Her body arched with the need to prolong such pleasure, and then he rolled to his side, carrying her with him, still locked tight in his embrace.

Although Shala wanted to savor the feeling they had shared, the warmth emanating from his body, and the exhausted state of her own, combined to work against her. She succumbed to sleep.

* * *

The sun was streaming through the doorway when Eric woke the next morning. His lips twitched as he remembered their lovemaking of the night before. He had been surprised at her response and was tempted to mount her again, but the sight of his pack in the corner reminded him of his hunger. There would be time enough later for lovemaking. After they reached the safety of her cave.

He reached out, intending to wake Shala, and stopped abruptly, his gaze fixed on a bruise on her lower jaw. How did she come by it? Had the mark been put there by the man who attacked her? That thought brought about another question.

Why had she been attacked by one of her own clansmen?

Suddenly, her eyes opened and she smiled lazily up at him.

"I was about to wake you," he said gruffly. "It is time we left this place."

Sudden awareness of their whereabouts set her in motion. "We should have left before now," she said, springing to her feet, driven by urgency.

Shouldering his pack, Eric followed her across the mesa. Shala seemed uneasy about something and continually turned her head to look behind them. Eric attributed her nervousness to having been attacked the day before. Again, he wondered why her clansman had set upon her, but when questioned, she evaded an answer.

Shala stood near the cliff, staring across the canyon at the cliff city for a long moment. Eric followed her gaze, realizing there was something different about the place. It took a moment before he realized there was little movement there, and where usually, there was sound—the high-pitched laughter of children, people calling to one another—now there was only silence.

Was something happening there? Something that took the laughter from the children, that made the occupants fearful of using their voices? Even the fowl were curiously silent.

He turned to question Shala, but she was already moving, grasping a protruding rock and lowering herself over the cliff.

When they were inside the cave, he tossed his pack onto the earthen floor and sank down against the nearest wall.

"Are you in pain?" she asked, dropping to her haunches beside him.

"A little," he said gruffly. Actually, his leg felt as though it were being jabbed with a hot poker.

"I have something that will help." She went to the back of the cave and searched through the bags stored there. Withdrawing one of the smallest sacks, she brought it to him. "This contains extract made from willow bark. It will help ease the pain."

He opened the bag and looked inside. "You have so little of it. Perhaps we should save it."

"No. You need it. I can make more later. It is a simple task, requiring only that the bark be peeled and boiled and the residue scraped up and stored for later use."

He popped some in his mouth while she delved

through his pack and found dried onions and meat. Then she put the onions on to boil, shaved the meat thin with her knife and added it to the boiling pot.

Soon the small cave was awash with the smell of a stew cooking.

"Shala, come sit by me." He patted a spot beside him, waited until she had seated herself, then said, "Now tell me why one of your clansmen was chasing you. Are such things allowed among your people?"

She swallowed hard. Would he think less of her at finding out that she was an outcast? She had tried to avoid his questions, but apparently the time had come for him to know.

She sighed heavily. "No. It is not allowed. But I am no longer considered one of the Eagle Clan."

"Not one of the clan," he asked, arching a golden eyebrow. "Why?"

"Because our shaman, Shu, has cast me out."

His expression softened. "Why? Tell me his reason."

"He wanted to mate with me," she whispered, her lashes fluttering down, then quickly lifting again. She must be honest with him, and must not evade his eyes. "And it was not my wish to do so."

"And for this you became an outcast?"

"Yes," she replied, pushing her dark hair away from her face and lowering her eyes. "The clan must comply with the shaman's wishes. He is all powerful. Since I would not do his bidding, I can no longer live among my People. Indeed, they think of me as having departed from the land of the living." She lifted her eyes and met his, and he flinched at the pain he saw in them. "Even my own mother dare not recognize my existence. To her I am dead."

He felt a deep stab of pity. "Apparently not all of them think that way. Nampeyo ventured here to see you, and then, of course, there is this other one . . ."

"Stalking Coyote!" The name spewed from her mouth. "He wants to mate with me."

Sudden rage surged through Eric, but outwardly he remained calm. "And that is not your wish?"

"I would sooner mate with the animal from which he took his name!" she spat out.

Pleasure replaced the anger. "My question is answered. Perhaps I should speak to your shaman."

"No! You must not let him see you!" she gasped. "To do so would only mean trouble."

Little did they know that trouble was already brewing. At the moment, it was headed toward the abandoned dwellings, in the form of Shu, Stalking Coyote, and four other warriors, all prepared to do battle with the evil spirit who had escaped from the third world into their own.

Thirteen

Nampeyo sat beside his morning fire, his nimble fingers carving the lines of a delicate head from the piece of white wood in his hands. Sage Flower squatted on her haunches nearby, her eager eyes following each slice of the knife as she tried, which she often did, to guess what he was carving before it became apparent.

"Is it a sage hen, Nampeyo?" she asked, leaning closer to the carving. "It looks a little like a sage hen."

"No," he replied. "It is not a sage hen."

Although he presented an outward calm, the manner was hard to maintain. Inwardly, he was filled with trepidation. Earlier, he had watched his father and several of his clansmen—armed to the teeth with bows and spears—leave the cliff city, and it worried him.

Why had Shu chosen to go with them? Under ordinary circumstances, he would have stayed behind. Had he gone because he hoped to incite his clansmen, to make certain Shala was fatally wounded in the fight that was sure to come? Was it not enough that he had banished her from the clan? Sentenced her to live alone, apart from others of her kind?

But then, that was no longer true. She was not alone now. A vision of the golden-haired stranger appeared in his mind's eye. He was strong, would make a mighty opponent, even though he was injured. There was sure to be trouble. Shu must never learn that his son had seen the stranger. Whatever happened, he must never know. Not only for Nampeyo's sake, but for that of his clan.

Nampeyo's reasons for keeping silent were many. He was certain there would come a time when his people would need not only a shaman, but a good leader. When that time came, Nampeyo would be there, ready and willing to satisfy that need. He had learned much from his father, had learned well. He intended that his People would benefit from his knowledge.

"Nampeyo! Are you listening to me?" Sage Flower's voice cut into his thoughts. "Are you making a turkey?"

"No. Not a turkey."

"Is it a snake?" Sage Flower asked, following the outrageous suggestion with a giggle that told Nampeyo she didn't believe it was.

"No," he said again, turning his attention to her. Screwing his face into a frown, he growled low in his throat. "And it is not Grandfather Black Bear either. Now go away, little girl, and do not bother me."

"I knew it was not Grandfather Black Bear,"

she said, giggling harder and wrapping her arms around her upper body. "You look funny, Nampeyo."

Nampeyo felt a curious stab of hurt. He knew the little girl had not meant to wound him with her words, but his twisted legs had always made him different from the others of the clan and this difference he would never be able to overcome. "You should not make fun of people, Sage Flower," he reprimanded quietly. "It is not a nice thing to do."

The little girl looked stricken. Tears welled in her eyes. "I was not making fun of you," she said, her lips quivering suddenly. "I was just . . . you looked so funny with your face all . . . frowny and y-your laughing ey-eyes." The tears overflowed and slid down her cheeks, and she bounded to her feet, backing away from him and sticking her thumb in her mouth.

Remorse stabbed at him, jabbing with the pain of an obsidian knife blade. "Sage Flower," he said gruffly, "I am sorry. I thought—" He broke off as she ran away, across the courtyard to her mother's arms.

Gia scooped the crying child up and dipped her head low to hear what her crying daughter was saying. Nampeyo waited for her to come to him with angry words for causing Sage Flower to cry, but instead Gia spoke at length to the child, who finally lifted her head and looked across the courtyard toward him.

"What is the matter with Sage Flower?" The voice was at his elbow.

Nampeyo turned toward the speaker, already knowing who it was. He would not fail to recognize Nama even if he were blind. He knew her by her walk, by her voice, even by the smell of her body.

"I hurt her feelings," he said, meeting Nama's concerned eyes.

"I am sure it was unintentional."

"Yes. It was. But the result is the same one way or another." He waved toward the courtyard wall. "Seat yourself, and let us speak of why you have sought me out."

Her eyes widened slightly. "Should there be a reason?"

"There usually is."

A red flush stole up her neck to stain her cheeks and she dropped her eyelashes to avoid his gaze. "Have you forgotten how we used to play together . . . when we were children?"

"No," he said quietly. "I have not forgotten. But I thought perhaps you had."

Her gaze flew up to his. "No. I have not. But things are different now. I am older. No longer a child. And you are . . . well, you are who you are. Shu's son. The one he has chosen to be the clan shaman."

Also I am the one with the twisted legs, he thought. They didn't matter when we were children. But that very fact sets me apart from the others, keeps me from ever being considered for a mate.

"It is not your legs, Nampeyo," she quietly assured him, guessing the path his thoughts had taken. "You are special to me, and you will always be. But since we are older now, things are different. It is not seemly for us to be special friends anymore. The rest of the clan might resent it—after you become shaman. Anyway, such a place should be reserved for your mate."

"When I have a mate, then she can take your place and become my special friend," he said noncommittally, knowing he would never take a mate. He wanted no other except Nama. "Now let us put aside this talk and speak of what concerns you."

"It is that story Stalking Coyote told. You heard him! He saw the golden-haired stranger with Shala. And yet he lied. We both know he did not see the golden one enter this world."

"Yes," Nampeyo agreed. "We do know that."

"Then why did you not speak out? Why did you not tell your father Stalking Coyote was lying?"

"You know why." His gaze was penetrating. "If a part of the whole were told, the rest would surely be brought to light."

"How you came to know of the stranger's presence."

He nodded his dark head. "Yes. Shu is smart. He would know someone had told me about him, and he would not rest until he found that person."

"Then you were protecting me."

"In part. And myself as well."

"Stalking Coyote had the marks of battle on his face, and the warriors went well armed, carrying spears, knives and bows and arrows. They were not on a peaceful mission. I fear Shala will be harmed."

"As I do. Shu bears her a grudge." A deep sadness entered his eyes. "I am afraid the trouble brewing between Shu and Shala has come to a head. With Stalking Coyote's lie to give him the excuse he needed, nothing can stop him from exacting his revenge."

The fire crackled and popped, sending flickers of yellow light to play on the soot-thick ceiling. The air was filled with the scent of boiled stew, giving Eric a warm and cozy feeling.

Not so Shala. She seemed restless. Although he wanted her beside him, she had claimed work as an excuse to stay apart from him. Firelight played in her shimmering hair as her agile fingers worked supple leather, trimming cured hide with her obsidian knife, trying to make it fit snugly against a matching piece for a new cape she was fashioning—a cape that she said was for him.

He liked to watch her work, but wanted her nearer. Their lovemaking the night before had left him wanting more; yet she remained apart from him, seeming uneasy about something, continually cocking her head as though listening to—or for—some distant sound.

He listened as well, wondering what was troubling her. Suddenly, he heard something outside, as though a shower of stones had struck nearby. The sound brought her to her feet, sent her streaking toward the entrance where she snatched up her spear and pushed aside the hide flap.

Alerted, he followed her, but, out of necessity, at a much slower pace.

"See!" Stalking Coyote said, pointing his finger into the kiva. "There is where the stranger entered our world from the third one."

"I see a sipapu," Shu replied. "But there is no one there. Nothing to show an evil spirit's entrance into our world."

"If you were an evil spirit would you have stayed and waited for us to come destroy you?" Stalking Coyote asked. "He must have gone with Shala to her dwelling."

"Then we will go there," Shu said, glad for the excuse. "Although she is an outcast, no longer spoken of by her clan, if she harbors an evil spirit then she must be destroyed for doing so."

Feeling well satisfied with Shu's plan, Stalking Coyote followed the others across the mesa.

The shower of stones had stopped falling by the time Shala was outside. She stood, feet braced apart, ready to use her spear if it became necessary. She was aware of Eric, stepping beside her, the heavy blade in his hands.

She stood as still as lightning-struck dead wood when she saw the big white wolf, motionless, settled on its haunches, its tail curled around its front legs. It stared at her with glowing yellow eyes that burned into her soul.

She sensed movement at her elbow and turned to see Eric on the point of striding forward, his sword raised in combat.

"No!" she cried, snatching at his arm. "He will not harm us."

"The wolf is dangerous!" he said grimly.

"He is my spirit guide," she said. "He has come for a reason. Leave him alone."

Reluctantly, he lowered his sword, his eyes never leaving the wolf.

Suddenly, without warning, the fur rose on the big wolf's neck, sending a chill down Eric's spine. The animal's lips drew back to expose flashing canines, and the muscles bunched under its sleek hide, the sunlight gleaming in its rippling coat.

"Get behind me!" Eric growled, yanking her toward him. "Only a fool would think he meant no harm. The wolf is on the point of attack, ready to tear us limb from limb."

"No. Not us." She looked up the cliff, saw movement near the edge. "Them," she said, pointing toward the mesa.

Keeping a wary eye on the wolf, he sent a quick look winging upward, then pinpointed the figure of a man leaning over the edge. "Your kinsmen?" he asked.

"Yes."

"Why are they here?"

"Probably because you are."

"Nampeyo told them about me?"

"No. Not Nampeyo," she admitted. "Stalking Coyote."

"Stalking Coyote! You said he was dead!"

"I told you an untruth," she admitted.

He threw her a dark look. "We will speak more of that later," he said grimly. "Are your clansmen here to start trouble?"

"There could be no other reason for their presence. I believe they mean to kill us." Her lips thinned, and her eyes glinted. "But they will have a hard time of it. I chose this place with care."

Before he could respond to that there was a shout from above. "Shala! Are you there, Shala?"

"I am here!" she called, raising her voice to be heard.

"Shu wishes to speak with you."

"Then let him!" she cried.

"You must first come up here!"

"I am no fool!" she called. "If the shaman wants to converse with me, then he must come down!"

There was a moment of silence, and she supposed they were considering her words. Finally, a head peeped over the cliff. She recognized Flying Eagle. "You will allow us to come without harm?"

"Shu!" she answered, cupping her mouth to make certain they understood. "I will allow Shu to come. But he must come alone."

Flying Eagle withdrew his head, but a short moment later, peeped over the cliff again. "Will you allow me, Flying Eagle, to approach?"

She need not think about that request. Flying Eagle was a man to be trusted. "Come ahead!"

He slid over the cliff, foot searching for purchase, found it, then lowered himself to the next indentation. Shala stood poised, waiting for others to follow, ready to act if the need should arise, but the man descended alone.

Finally, he stood in front of her, his eyes flickering from her to Eric, then the wolf before returning to meet her eyes again. "Stalking Coyote has spoken to the shaman about your companion, Shala. Shu wishes to meet him."

"Is that all he wants?" she asked, her gaze probing his. "Just to meet Eric? Or has he something else in mind?"

"I cannot say." His gaze left hers, found the wolf and stayed there. "Your spirit guide is here to help you. While he is here, you need fear no harm."

"And Eric? Will Wolf protect him too?" When the man did not answer, Shala continued. "Why are you here?"

"Because Shu commanded it," he replied honestly. "He has spoken to the spirits, and we follow their wishes."

"Do you?" she asked haughtily, "or do you act on Shu's wishes alone?"

"I did not come here to argue, Shala. I came to deliver a message, to make you see you must go to Shu . . ." —his eyes flickered to Eric, then back to hers again— ". . . you and the stranger."

"Then go! You have delivered your message."

"You must go to him, Shala!"

"No! I will not!"

"He is our shaman."

"Not mine," she replied calmly. "I am an outcast."

"Then you refuse?"

"Yes."

"He will order you killed."

"He may. But tell him my spirit guide has come to offer his protection in the form of a man." She pointed to the wolf. "Behold his body." She pointed to Eric. "Behold him now."

His eyes widened. "The golden-haired stranger is your spirit guide?"

"Yes," she claimed, hoping the Wise One above would understand her reason for telling the falsehood. "Stalking Coyote attacked me, and my spirit guide took this form in order to protect me. He will be with me from now on. Go and convey my words to your shaman."

She watched him leave with trepidation. Would Shu accept what she claimed? She was almost sure he would not. Almost certain such a thing would have to be proven. And there was no way Eric could make such a claim hold up.

No way at all.

Fourteen

Shu crouched beside the cliff, waiting impatiently for Flying Eagle's return. The very air around him was charged, electrified by his anger and hatred. How did Shala dare give refuge to a stranger?

It seemed an eternity before a head appeared at the edge of the mesa and Flying Eagle reached out, wrapping his hands around the trunk of the gnarled juniper, gripping it tightly before he scrambled over the edge. He lay there for a long moment trying to catch his breath.

The shaman loomed over the man, trying to control his expression, staying the hand that wanted to grip the man's hair and pull him upright. Such a show would surely set the others against him when he needed their combined strength to face whatever lay below.

Finally, Flying Eagle's breathing slowed and he raised himself to face the shaman. The look in Shu's dark eyes sent a cold shiver down his spine.

Flying Eagle's mouth moved, but no words

came out. Clearing his throat, he tried again. "Sha—" He broke off quickly, horrified that he had almost used the name of the outcast. "She r-refuses to come to you." His voice was guarded, as though there were more to tell, yet he was hesitant to impart the news.

Again, Shu controlled the urge to release his fury on the man. "Refuses to come?" he echoed.

"She—she said you must come to her!"

Shu clenched his fists with rage. He glared at Flying Eagle as though the man were personally responsible for Shala's failure to appear. The girl was an outcast! If she had any sense, she would be trying to pacify the shaman, hoping to gain entry into the clan again. Yet she remained as rebellious as the day he had cast her from the tribe. "She dares to defy her shaman?" he growled, taking a threatening step toward the cliff.

"She . . ."

The warrior's voice trailed off as though he had thought better of the words he was about to impart, but Shu turned on him again, pinning him with his gaze. "There is more?"

"She said—" Flying Eagle broke off, swallowed hard, then continued. "Yes, mighty shaman. There is more. The outcast claims she is protected by her spirit guide. That he is there with her now!"

Shock mingled with fear in the expressions of the men around Shu. A dull rage filled his black eyes, rearranged the flat planes of his face, but when he spoke, his voice was even. "And does she think her spirit guide is more powerful than mine? Will he hurl spears at us while we descend the cliff?"

"He m-might," the warrior stuttered. "But I saw no spear except for the one carried by the outcast. The stranger wields a mighty blade the length and breadth of a man's leg. It looks as though it could slice any of us in half."

"What nonsense is this?" Shu's obsidian eyes glittered with rage. "The outcast has bewitched you. There is no such weapon."

"I saw it with my own eyes," Flying Eagle claimed. "The man is as tall as Stick Legs would be with an extra pair of legs. And he is wider than Laughing Duck."

"Taller than Stick Legs?" muttered one of the warriors. "He is the tallest among us."

"Wider than Laughing Duck?" questioned another. "She is so wide that a man cannot wrap his arms around her."

"He must be a spirit in human form," said another.

"Perhaps he is only a trader," suggested a warrior in an uneasy voice. "Some of them are tall. And wide too. Especially the traders who come from the land located beside the big salt water."

"Fools!" Shu spewed the word into the morning air. "The being below is not a man! You heard Stalking Coyote! He saw the spirit enter our world through a sipapu. He saw it take the form of a man to fool us. If we do not act swiftly then others will follow and take over our world. It must be killed. And the woman too, for harboring him."

"We only have Stalking Coyote's word that the being is an evil spirit," Flying Eagle muttered, marveling at his bravery in pointing out that fact to the shaman even though his stomach protested his foolhardiness. What would he do if Shu's rage became directed at himself? "The outcast claims the being is her spirit guide, Wolf. If that is so, then he is a good spirit, not one who is evil as Stalking Coyote claims." He pinned the man in question with his gaze.

"He *is* an evil spirit!" Stalking Coyote cried, backing away from his clansmen as though suspecting they would turn on him at any moment. "I saw him enter our world from the sipapu with my own eyes! Yes, he is big. But that is surely what an evil spirit would be. Why should a spirit who is able to change its shape take the form of something small, easily vanquished. We are warriors with courage. But it is harder to overcome a large warrior than a small one."

A heavy silence fell around them as each man retreated into his own thoughts. If Shu ordered an attack, they would have to abide by his decision, but he did not. Instead, he held the words back, feeling uneasy about the situation.

Shu knew something the others did not. The spirits did not talk to him. At least, if they did speak, he was unable to hear them. He had no spirit power at all. Sometimes he wondered if he ever had. But no other living being was aware that he was a false shaman. Not even his crippled son Nampeyo knew. And it was Shu's intention that no one ever acquire that knowledge. It was a secret that he would carry to the spirit world with him.

The man waiting below could very well be a trader, and if he—or any of his clansmen—harmed a trader, then no others would come to the Eagle Clan. They would be shunned forever by other traders, and there would be no more brilliantly colored feathers found in the far south for the Eagle Clan. Nor would there be any more of the seashells that Shu had acquired last summer. He hoped eventually to have enough for a necklace to hang around his neck, knowing it would attract quite a lot of attention during ceremonial dances.

And, even more important, the traders brought news of other tribes, of their ways, of their movements. Without the traders how would Shu have known about the desert people's migration north? Why else would he have offered a wife to Standing Wolf, if not to protect their land from invasion?

No. The Trader's Law must be honored at all cost. No trader must be harmed else the clan who broke that law be shunned forevermore. But, even as Shu made that decision, he knew that he must act in some manner. His clansmen were watching him, and he must not lose face. His powers would surely be diminished. His position threatened.

How to get out of this situation that Flying Eagle had created?

"I must consult with the spirits," he said at last.

Stalking Coyote met his eyes with a long look. "If the spirits are long in answering . . . as they were before . . . the evil one will most likely be able to hide himself—and the outcast as well."

"Who can say how long it will take?" Shu said angrily. "Spirits cannot be hurried. But I will consult with them in this very spot. That way the spirit—if it is one—cannot take the woman away from here." He glared hard at each of them. "No sound will be made while I speak with the spirit world."

Grimly, he stepped nearer the edge, dug into his hide bag of spirit dust and pulled a few of the sacred stones out of it and threw them to the four sacred directions. The ones cast to the north struck the ground behind him, while the stones cast to the other three directions drifted down into the canyon. With the directions satisfied, he lifted his arms skyward, closed his eyes and began the spirit chant. "Hey, hey! Haw, yah! Hey, hey, haw, yaw!"

While he chanted, his mind worried over the problem. He must come up with some kind of solution to handle this. He felt almost certain the stranger did not come from the spirit world, yet he came from somewhere. And he knew Flying Eagle would not have lied about what he'd seen. So the stranger's proportions must be huge indeed. Therefore, he must be handled with care.

Shala was in an impregnable position. She would be able to spear each man as he climbed down the cliff were she of that mind. She did not really need the stranger beside her to hold her position. And although Shu cared little for his clansmen, he did worry about his own hide. He also worried about keeping his revered position in the clan safe.

"Hey, hey, haw, yaw!"

Continuing the chant, he opened his eyes to a mere slit and stared out over the canyon, looking for an answer to his dilemma. His gaze fastened on the ledge beneath the cliff overhang, locked on the figure standing near the edge of the cliff city, and his lips thinned slightly as a plan began to take form in his mind.

A hundred feet below the chanting shaman, Eric leaned against a huge rock, his wary gaze fixed on the cliff. His mind was otherwise occupied.

Why had Shala lied to him about Stalking Coyote? She had said the man was dead. Surely the lie had not been spoken to protect the man. He had attacked them, would have killed them—at least Eric—had he been able to do so. Instead, because she had lied, the man had escaped, and had brought the whole clan down upon them.

How many were there? he wondered. A hundred? Even more? Perhaps Shala was right and the two of them *could* hold off an attack. But for how long? Certainly not forever. Eventually, they would have to leave the cave and check the traps, would have to hunt food on the mesa. If they were under siege by the warriors of her clan, the position that had seemed so safe in the beginning might very well become their prison.

Clunk! Something struck him sharply on the forehead.

Not moisture, so it was not rain. Instead, it had been hard. Had it been thrown from the cliff?

Puzzled, and more than a little alarmed, he tilted his head back farther, searching the edge of the cliff. A movement, barely perceptible, gone in the blink of an eye, caught his attention.

Had someone been there in that small measure of time? Had he—or she—thrown something over the cliff?

Eric raked a hand through his hair and came away with a few grains of sand and a larger object. Something hard, perhaps the size of a pebble. Holding it before his eyes, he stared in amazement. It was a multicolored blue stone, similar to the one Shala wore around her neck.

"What is it?" Shala asked.

He held out his palm, watched the color leave her face when she recognized the blue stone.

"What is wrong?" Eric asked, grasping her forearm. "Why does the sight of the stone cause you such fear?"

"It is one of the sacred stones," she replied in a strained voice. Her throat worked as though she swallowed around an obstruction. "Shu cast some over the cliff. He is seeking help from the spirit world."

Eric did not believe in their spirit world, but he did want to know more about the stones. Apparently they were in plentiful supply if the shaman threw them so carelessly over the cliff. If they lived through the fight that was sure to come, he would make it his business to find out more about the stones.

* * *

Nampeyo stood beside the spruce tree, staring out over the canyon to where Shala and Eric stood, sheltered in part by a large, flat, leaning rock. His gaze touched on the white wolf, barely visible from this distance. Amazing though it was, it seemed Shala's spirit guide was with her, visible to all who cared to see.

Would the shaman order an attack, even while knowing Wolf stood ready to defend the woman he had made an outcast? Or was his father even aware the white wolf was Shala's spirit guide? Nampeyo suspected the shaman was; for there was little going on at the cliff city that he did not soon learn about, and it had been three years since Shala had gone on a vision quest—a journey usually undertaken only by boys approaching manhood. But Shala, being the willful termagant that she had always been, had gone. She had returned after three days, gaunt, weary from lack of sleep, but victorious, and she had told all who would listen of the white wolf who had come to her. Told how her mind had blended with Wolf's, and how the ground had felt beneath her paws, how new and sharp everything smelled with her newly acquired nose.

Yes, Nampeyo decided. The shaman must certainly know about the white wolf's association with Shala. The event had been too unusual for him not to have known.

Nampeyo's lips twisted slightly. Although he felt Shala was at the root of all Nama's problems,

Nampeyo still had no wish to see her harmed. Had they not been childhood friends? And had Shala not defended him many times against those children who found pleasure in taunting him. He owed her for that, and would help her if it were possible. But it was not. He was helpless to do anything for her. In the eyes of the clan, he was next to nothing. Even though he had been chosen for the next shaman, the position might never be his. Who could say how long his father would live? That was the reason Nampeyo must remain silent. Shu's word was law. None dared stand against him. Not even his own son.

With his slitted eyes still fixed on his crippled son, Shu finished his prayer chant; then, having found the solution to his problem, he turned around to face his clansmen. "All is decided." He spoke in a heavy monotone, as though he were in a trance. "The spirits have spoken to me. They wish to test the one I have chosen to be your next shaman. They demand that Nampeyo go. That he speak with Shala and the stranger. He must demand the stranger—be he spirit or man—leave our land."

"Nampeyo?" questioned Flying Eagle.

"The crippled one?" muttered another man.

"You mean to send Nampeyo?" Flying Eagle asked harshly. "What can he accomplish that I could not? And have you not considered that such an act might anger the spirit?"

"Silence!" Shu snapped, fixing Flying Eagle

with a baleful glare. "Nampeyo has been chosen to go."

"But he is young, untried—"

"Do you question the wisdom of the spirits?" Shu roared, his dark eyes flashing. "And do you think I would send my own son into danger if the spirits had not told me to do so?"

"No. Of course not," said the man, lowering his eyes to avoid the shaman's piercing stare. "As you say, he is your son." His gaze locked on the tiny figure standing near the edge of the canyon. Even though Nampeyo was shaded by the cliff overhang, Flying Eagle could make out the crooked staff clutched in the crippled one's hand.

How can Nampeyo stand against spirit power when he cannot stand very long without the support of a staff? Flying Eagle silently questioned. *The young man has not the strength to harm a living soul.*

Suddenly, he thought he knew. "Now I see the wisdom of such a move," he told Shu. "Nampeyo can offer little resistance to the man—or spirit—who waits below, therefore there would be no need for such a being to harm him." He looked back at Nampeyo. "It is a brilliant plan."

Stalking Coyote had been listening silently to the interchange. He alone knew the plan for what it was—a calculated attempt by Shu to save his own skin even at the cost of his only son's—and it was then that his feeling for his shaman changed. Where before he had feared Shu's power, he now felt only a growing contempt. The man had no spirit power. He was a false shaman. And he was a coward. Although Stalking Coyote wanted to denounce Shu for what he was, he knew such a move would be dangerous. Too many of his clansmen were under the shaman's power, would obey his every command.

Even though he was no longer in awe of the shaman, he had to admire Shu's quick thinking. See how he had tricked them into thinking the move to save his own skin was, in fact, a wise decision made by the spirits.

No! He could not denounce Shu. Not right now. But he would watch carefully. The shaman would make a mistake. And Stalking Coyote would be there to see it and use the moment to his own advantage.

"How long do you think they will stay up there?" Eric asked, flexing tired shoulder muscles.

"I do not know," Shala replied. Although she found the waiting interminable, she dare not relax her guard.

Would they be attacked? she wondered. And could she actually kill one of her own clansmen if the need should arise?

Her gaze went across the canyon, and she saw Nampeyo there near the cliff city, his face turned toward her as though he were either watching her or those above her. Her eyes slid up the face of the cliff, wondering if the shaman had sent for others of the clan, wondering if he was preparing to launch an attack.

Suddenly, while her gaze was fixed on the mesa above the cliff city, a movement caught her attention. Her heart jolted to a stop, then picked up speed. There was someone there! Just above the cliff city, and he was descending.

"What do you see?" Eric asked from beside her.

"Shu has sent for more warriors," she said wearily.

"Do not worry about it," he said calmly, wrapping an arm about her waist and pulling her against him. "They cannot reach us here. We can pick them off as they descend."

"It is not my wish to kill my own People!" she exclaimed.

"We will do whatever is necessary to stay alive," he said.

"Why did this have to happen?" she asked bitterly. "Even if we win the battle, we can never remain here."

"To remain here was never my intention," he said grimly. "Put the future from your mind. We will sort things out later. After this is over."

Will it ever be over? she wondered.

The western sky blazed with color as Father Sun hovered just above the horizon, intent on hurrying to his rest. Shala stood in the circle of Eric's arms, taking comfort from his nearness, knowing that the weapons they had placed nearby might soon have to be used.

A small shower of stones from above alerted them to movement on the cliff. Eric's arms fell away and, simultaneously, they reached for their weapons and held them in readiness.

Shala saw a pair of legs drop over the edge of the cliff, followed by the rest of a man's body.

"Nampeyo," she muttered, her gaze fixed on the twisted leg. "Shu sent for his son."

"So I see," Eric said, his mouth twisting with contempt. "I wonder what the shaman hopes to accomplish by sending a cripple to us?"

"Who knows?" She continued to watch Nampeyo's halting descent.

Soon, he stood beside them and explained what had been taking place above them, ending with Stalking Coyote's lie about Eric.

"Telling falsehoods seems to be common in your clan," Eric said contemptuously.

Nampeyo let the words pass without comment. "I cannot accuse him of telling a falsehood," he went on. "I dare not tell the others I saw the stranger before Stalking Coyote did." His gaze held Shala's. "You know what would happen if I did, Shala. Shu cares nothing for me. He would use my actions against me. He would surely choose another to train for shaman."

Shala knew how important it was for him to become shaman. Knew as well that the clan would greatly benefit from his leadership. Unlike Shu, Nampeyo would be fair, impartial. "No. You cannot take the chance," she agreed, her thoughts spinning wildly as she sought a solution. "So . . . they think my Viking is an evil spirit who escaped from the third world, do they?"

Eric had been silent while they spoke together, and she wondered how much of the conversation he had understood. Since she was more proficient in his language than he was in hers, she explained to him, using the words he had taught her. She finished her explanation with, "It is good they believe you a spirit, Eric. But we must convince them you are not evil. They *must* believe you are my spirit guide in human form."

"Why must they be told what is not true?" he asked harshly. "Have you not yet learned that one lie always leads to another?"

A flush rose up her neck and stained her cheeks. She knew he was referring to the falsehood she had told him about Stalking Coyote being dead, but there was no time for explanations now.

"If they knew you for the man you are, they would not hesitate to attack."

"Shala is right," Nampeyo interjected. "Since the tale is told, then it must stand. Otherwise—even if they leave right now—they will wait for you to leave here, to hunt or gather food, and they will attack when you are least expecting it." He looked uneasily at the big white wolf nearby. "And it is not such a big lie. Shala's spirit guide is here, ready to protect her."

"Yes, he is," she hurriedly agreed, hoping to mollify Eric. "Although I do not know how long he will stay."

"It does not matter," Nampeyo said. "What matters is that he is here now. Here, for the others to see. I will tell them it is as you claimed. That Wolf saw you needed help and came to protect you. That his body remains here—without his spirit. That it has gone into the man." He looked up at Sky Man who wore his brightest clothing. "The spirits will surely forgive me for telling the falsehood since one of them has come to help you." He was on the point of turning away from them when he paused and met Shala's gaze. "Be wary, Shala. My father's hatred for you is strong. He will not be content to leave you with a companion. He banished you from the clan, satisfied that you would be forever alone. Be wary of his wrath."

"You have no need to remind me," she said. "But thank you for doing so."

With mixed feelings, Shala watched Nampeyo leave them. Then she turned her attention to Eric. His chin was thrust forward, and as she watched, a muscle twitched along his jaw. His long, sturdy Viking legs braced him as he faced her. He covered the distance between them and gripped her shoulders hard. His strong fingers bit deeply into her flesh and his grass green eyes were cold as a winter's storm.

"It is past time you explained yourself," he said grimly.

Shala knew what Eric meant. He was angry at her, furious that she had lied about Stalking Coyote. Could she make him understand why she had done so? She opened her mouth to speak, then closed it again. She was too weary to face an argument, tired to the point of exhaustion.

With a heavy sigh, Shala met his flashing green eyes. "Not now, Eric," she muttered. "We will speak of Stalking Coyote later. I am too weary to think straight right now."

His fingers dug deeper into her flesh, causing her to wince with pain. Then his grip relaxed slightly and suddenly she was free. His face was unreadable when he turned and stalked away. He put several feet between them before settling himself down against a large rock with his weapon beside him.

Although Shala knew she should go to him, should try to make him understand, she let the moment pass. She spun on her heels and stepped into the cave. She could sleep now, content that, between them, Wolf and Eric would keep their enemies at bay. But she knew she had only put off the inevitable. The day of reckoning could not be postponed forever.

Fifteen

Shala stirred, feeling a delicious warmth against her back. Her lips curled into a smile when she realized it was Eric's body giving off the heat. As the remnants of sleep drifted way from her like fog dissipating beneath Father Sun's early morning rays, she opened sleep-fogged eyes. She found Eric already awake, his eyes fastened on her, wary, alert and watchful.

"Did you sleep well?" she asked, hoping to delay the inevitable. She should have known he would not allow her to do so. The time of reckoning had come.

When he spoke, his voice had a harsh note to it. "Why did you lie about Stalking Coyote? Why did you say he was dead? Was it to protect him?"

"No!" she quickly denied. "You were hurt, Eric. You needed time to regain your strength before traveling home. He was gone, and with the storm brewing, I saw no need to worry you about him." Tears filled her eyes, and she swallowed around a lump in her throat. "I know it was wrong, but do you not see? He was gone and could do us no harm. Not before morning, and I knew we would be gone before he could bring others to help him."

"So you told the falsehood for me?"

"Yes," she said, lowering her eyes, unable to meet his gaze although her words were truthful. "My lips uttered the lie, but my heart was not happy with it. I was going to tell you the truth of the matter. Please believe me. I would not have let the lie remain between us."

Did his features soften ever so slightly?

"That was your only reason?" he asked gruffly. "You wanted to give me time to regain my strength?"

"What else?" she asked, meeting his eyes again. "Believe me, Eric. I thought only of you."

He smoothed her hair back from her face. "I do not like liars, Shala. You must never again tell me what is not true. Promise me."

She would have promised him anything to take the scowl from his face. "I promise," she whispered. "Do not be angry with me, Eric."

Threading her fingers through his golden hair, she lifted her face and kissed him softly on the lips, needing his kiss to take away the taste of his displeasure. He complied, kissing her thoroughly.

The next few days were the happiest Shala had ever known. Although she was still uneasy about Shu's intentions, he left them alone to hunt as they wished, almost as though he refused to recognize their existence. And yet Shala knew they had not been forgotten, realized the shaman waited only for a time when he could prove their claims about Eric being her spirit guide in human form were false.

Surprisingly, Wolf had not left them. He kept guard outside the cave, resting on his haunches, tail curled around his front legs, moving only his head to follow the movements of anything that caught his attention.

Eric's injured leg continued to heal, becoming stronger with each passing day. Soon he began to accompany Shala on hunting trips.

So did Wolf. The animal was amazing, seeming more like a mountain goat the way he climbed the rough trail leading up to the mesa. Shala continuously marveled at Wolf's agility. But then, she reminded herself, why should he not be able to accomplish such feats? Was he not her spirit guide?

Eric proved to be a good hunter, leaving her little to do.

He showed great contempt for the smaller animals that she found in her traps. One day, shortly after he had killed a mule deer when her traps had yielded nothing more than a grouse, he suggested leaving the bird behind. He was startled by her horrified expression.

"Leave the meat to rot?" she cried. "Never! The grouse gave its life to feed us. We would never be forgiven if we allowed its flesh to go to waste." She reminded him of the need to replenish their store of dried meat.

He looked thoughtful for a moment, then

agreed, adding, "We will need a good supply of dried meat for our journey."

Although something clicked in her mind, she was occupied with removing the grouse from her trap and resetting it, and did not think to question his words. But later, when they were home again, she thought about what he had said. "You spoke earlier of a journey, Eric. Are we going somewhere?"

"Of course," he said. "The snow is melting now. Spring will soon be here, and that means the rivers will swell and run strong."

"Why is that important?" she questioned, her eyes on the dampened clay she was patting into shape. "What is going to happen when the rivers are full?"

Instead of answering, he frowned at the hunk of clay, studying its oblong shape. "What is that thing supposed to be?"

"What thing?" Her eyes flashed up to his.

"That thing," he said, pointing to the hunk of wet clay in her hands. "What are you making?"

"It is a drinking mug," she replied, her lips quirking with amusement while she poked two holes in the center and began to dig clay from one of them. "Can you not see from the shape?" She knew he could not, and yet she could not resist teasing him.

His frown deepened. "A mug? You mean a cup? You expect to drink from it?"

She nodded her head, felt her hair fall across her cheek. "Yes," she replied, digging her fingers into the soft clay, shaping one of the holes that would one day—hopefully soon—contain a very potent wine.

"I see it now," he said gravely. "Since there are two holes, you must be making two cups."

"Yes."

Although his voice was serious, his eyes twinkled with merriment. "I hate to tell you this, Shala, but you will not be able to separate them. The clay is too thin where they are joined together."

"I will not separate them."

"You intend to leave them conjoined?"

She nodded again and smiled her secret smile. "That is my intention."

"Are they only for decoration?"

"No. They are used for ceremonial purposes." She was deliberately keeping her explanations short, not yet ready to explain the purpose of the double mugs which were used in marriage ceremonies.

"Are you not going to explain further?"

"Not yet."

"Then put your work aside and come here."

The deep huskiness in his voice was enough to tell her what was on his mind, and with an eagerness that was almost shameful, she hurried to do his bidding. She covered the clay with a wet cloth so it would stay damp, washed her hands, then went to him.

Dropping to her knees, she slid her arms around his neck, twined her fingers through his bright hair and pressed her body hard against his.

Lifting her chin to receive his kiss, she met his eyes.

"Does everyone feel this way when they mate?" she asked softly, burrowing closer against him.

"What way?" he muttered, his lips brushing hers in a light caress that left her wanting more.

"Like now," she whispered, her lips opening slightly, allowing her tongue to trace a moist path across his neck. "Like this. I feel all tingly and hot. Like a fire is burning inside my belly. Is that always the way of it? Does everyone feel the way I do when your lips cover mine?"

"Not always." His voice was a husky growl. "Sometimes there is nothing but heat. A heat so intense that—"

"Sometimes?" she questioned, drawing away from him and licking lips that had suddenly gone dry. "You have mated many times?" Shala wondered why the thought irritated her.

"Many times." He laughed huskily, his fingers tightening on her shoulders, pulling her back into his embrace. "Now stop that."

"What?" she asked, pushing at his chest, trying to escape from his hold.

"That!" he said sternly. "You keep pulling away from me. I want you here. In my arms where you belong." His hands slid down her dress to her thighs and he pulled her skirt up. "Help me get this out of the way."

For some reason she no longer wanted to mate with him. She slapped at his hand, trying to make him loose her. When he continued to resist, she kicked his shin.

"Thor's teeth!" His hold loosened, dropped away, and he stared at her with amazement. "What has come over you, woman?"

"Nothing!" she said, scrambling away from him. "There will be time enough later for things of that nature. Right now I have work to do." Her gaze fell on the corpses of two ground squirrels that she had left over the coals to dry. "The squirrel meat will be burned to a crisp if they are left over the heat."

"Are you angry with me?"

"Why should I be angry?" she asked, striving for indifference. Perhaps she was, though, she silently admitted. No woman liked hearing her man speak about making love with other women.

Shala put the dried squirrel—left whole to dry—in a clay bowl and found one of the hand-sized stones she used to pound meat. Then, seating herself beside a flat rock, she began to pound the dried squirrel into paste.

Throwing a quick glance at Eric, she found him watching her with a most peculiar expression. He seemed almost puzzled about something. Was she so different from the women he had known? What were they like anyway?

"Why do you look at me that way?" she questioned.

"What way?"

"Like . . . well, like you think me different, unlike other women."

"You are, Shala."

"Tell me about your homeland, about the women there. What are they like?"

"I have already told you," he muttered, obviously irritable at having her avoid his touch. "Probably too much."

"Do you have a wife?" she asked.

"No." His answer was abrupt. "No wife."

"A special woman then, someone waiting in your homeland for your return?"

Eric's lips thinned. Shala was the most aggravating woman he had ever met. And the most surprising. None of the other women he had bedded wished him to speak of their rivals. He thought about Maudya, who had been his mistress for years. He supposed she was special. "Yes, there is one," he admitted.

She bowed her head quickly and drove the pounding stone harder against the squirrel meat. "Is she good to look upon?"

He narrowed his eyes on her, saw her dark hair, glistening like polished wood, tumbling carelessly down her back. Her face was flushed a delicate pink. Was it the heat, or was she jealous? Could it be possible? If she was, then why did she continue to question him? He had thought women were much the same the world over. But perhaps he was wrong. After all, she was from a primitive tribe, unlike any woman he had ever known. And, although she was a virgin when he had taken her, she had been eager for his possession. Perhaps she would have been the same with any man. He rejected that thought, unwilling to accept it.

"I would rather not talk about Maudya," he grated.

"Why not? If she is someone special to you,

then you should be happy to tell of her virtues." Her lips thinned. "If the woman has any."

Maudya? Virtues? The woman was without virtue, but she did know how to pleasure a man. That thought brought a smile to his lips.

"Does she?" Shala asked, her dark eyes flashing.

"What?"

"Have any virtues?"

"Maudya? She has no need of them," he said wryly.

"Can she make better stew than me?"

He laughed harshly. "Make stew? Maudya cannot cook."

"Cannot cook? How does she live?"

"Others cook for her."

Shala expressed no surprise. "Then she is a hunter."

Again he laughed. "No. Maudya is a lady of leisure."

"Does she sew?"

"No. Not that either. Her clothing is made for her."

"She is a woman of such importance?" Her voice was scornful. "What then, is her role in society?"

"She has no role, does nothing, and devotes all her time to learning how best to please a man."

"What an odd place you live in," she said. Her lips were compressed tightly as she turned her attention back to her work.

Thwarted in his attempts to coax her into his arms, Eric took up his knife and the sharpening stone and proceeded to put a fine edge on his blade.

Although Shala felt his gaze on her often, she ignored it, feeling unsettled and somehow hurt by the knowledge that Eric, the man she had thought to be her own, had a woman waiting for him in his homeland.

She continued to worry the matter over in her mind as she finished pounding the squirrels into paste, mixed dried berries with the meat paste, then laid it aside.

What sort of woman spent all her time finding ways to please a man? she silently wondered while stoking the fire with more wood and heating fat until it was melted. And what would such a woman do if she suddenly found herself alone?

Her face glistened with sweat from the heat and Shala shook aside the sweat-dampened ends of her hair where they clung to her forehead. If the woman, Maudya had no need to do anything except please a man, then she must be very good at that.

Anger drove her as Shala shoved handfuls of meat and berries into cleaned intestines taken from a recently killed mule deer. After each handful, she poured hot fat into the ropy sack, ramming home the whole lumpy mass with a stick until the gut bulged from being overstuffed.

It was Eric who broke the long silence. "The food will taste good on the long trail that awaits us."

His words jerked her back to the present. "Long trail?" she asked, having completely forgotten he had mentioned a journey before. She lifted her head and met his eyes with a questioning gaze. "What long trail?"

"The trail that leads to my longboat."

She frowned at him, still not comprehending, and yet, feeling a constriction in her chest, a curious foreboding. "You speak of the boat that brought you across the big salt water? It is your plan to fetch the boat?" Before he could reply, she went on. "What use do we have for such a boat here, Eric?"

His lips twitched with amusement. "There is no use here for my boat. Nevertheless, it will be used. The boat will carry us to my home in Norway."

His words stabbed through her, and Shala felt as if her breath was cut off. Norway? His homeland? Her stomach churned with anxiety, and her heart pounded with dread as she sat back on her haunches, wiped her hands on her skirt and gazed up at him. "You mean to return there?" Her voice was a husky whisper.

Something flickered in his green eyes, causing them to darken to the color of moss. "I have always meant to return, Shala. Surely you knew that?"

She wrapped her arms around her upper torso, hoping to stop the chill that slowly spread through her. "No. You never said anything about going home, Eric. I thought you meant to stay here."

He smiled wryly. "Why should I do that? This is a primitive land, populated by primitive people. Look at you . . . down on your hands and knees, stuffing dried corpses and bear fat into guts with a rock." He went to her, pulled her to her feet, holding her steady when she would have stumbled. "In my land, Shala, you would have servants to wait on you, to prepare the meals and clean your dwelling. You would wear garments made from the finest cloth available. You would—"

"Be welcomed by your people?" she asked quietly, a dull pain spreading through her chest. "Would I be the same there as the woman, Maudya, who is special to you? Would I be looked upon with favor by the angry gods who rule your land? No. I think not. Such a place would not make me feel welcome. Neither the gods nor the people would want me there." She spoke the words that would send him away from her, wishing to recall them even as they were uttered. "If you go, Eric, then you must go alone."

"You are being foolish, Shala!" he snapped, his fingers digging into her shoulders as he gave her a hard shake. "You will go with me!"

"No!"

"Yes. Too much has passed between us for me to leave you behind. You are my woman now. Why do you even question my right to take you? There is nothing here for you. Only a hard life among savages. With me you will have riches, everything you could ever want. You *must* come with me."

To compete with the other women of your tribe for your favors? she silently cried. *How could I compete with them? You called me a savage.* "I will not go!" she cried violently. "You cannot make me!"

He circled her shoulders with his right arm and

roughly jerked her against him. "I cannot leave you here," he said harshly. "You belong to me, Shala. Have you not realized that? You are mine. No other shall have you." Lifting her chin, he kissed her hard upon the lips, bruising them with his need.

His action sent a wild burst of longing through her, but it was accompanied by a feeling of desperation. He would not stay and she would not go—no matter what he said—so they would soon separate. Forever. How could she stand losing him? It did not bear thinking about.

Wrapping her arms around his neck, her legs about his waist, she put everything she had into the kiss. She must make each moment they had left together count for a lifetime of memories.

His mouth moved eagerly beneath her own and they sank together on the floor, each consumed by their need for each other. The flame that sparked to life soon turned into a raging inferno that could only be put out by that final, explosive burst that would send them both spiraling toward the stars.

Sixteen

Fate took a hand in Shala's future. Shu, descending the cliff with careless haste, missed his footing and fell to his death. The only witness to the mishap was Stalking Coyote. If an argument had preceded the fall, there were none to attest to that fact. The warrior would not, and the deceased shaman could not.

Word spread quickly throughout the community, and it was unlikely there was even one person who mourned him. He had been a harsh, unjust man. Not only to those who did not quickly obey his wishes, but to his only son as well.

As was their custom, Shu was taken to his final resting place—a hole dug in the refuse dump—and placed there in the usual position, upright with knees drawn up to the chest. No disrespect was meant by the place of burial. It was just common sense. The ground above was still frozen, too hard to make digging a grave feasible. After Shu's limbs had been arranged to their satisfaction, dirt was thrown into the hole to cover the dead shaman. With their duties completed, the burial detail left the refuse dump and began preparations for a celebration.

The People gathered willow and pine boughs and piled them in the middle of the central courtyard, making bonfires that crackled high, sending wreaths of sparks to glow orange-red against the cliff overhang. The People danced, lifting their voices in song to accompany the departing spirit of Shu, then welcoming the new shaman to his duties. Soon they would feast, the huge fires flaring so the spirits might see them rejoicing in their new shaman.

Nampeyo had finally come into his own. He sent word that Shala and Eric were invited to join them in celebration, obviously laying the groundwork for her return to the clan. Eric had said no more about leaving, and Shala held her own silence on the subject, hoping he had changed his mind. Now she stood outside her cave, listening to the music of both drums and flutes that drifted across the canyon to them.

"The People are happy again," she said aloud, watching the flames of the distant bonfire leap higher beneath the cliff overhang.

"Who are you speaking to?" Eric asked from beside her. "Wolf?"

"No. Wolf is no longer with us."

"He is gone?"

"Yes." She turned to meet his eyes. "Can you not see he is no longer needed?" She waved her hand toward the cliff city. "Look at my People. See how happy they are. Listen to their laughter."

He cocked his head to the side and grinned at her. "It is obvious they do not mourn their shaman's death."

"No. Most have suffered in some way because of him, whether the misery inflicted be on themselves or on someone they love. As was my mother's case."

"What about his son? Are they happy about Nampeyo taking over?"

"Nampeyo has no enemies. He is a gentle man and will not abuse his position as clan shaman." Her gaze dropped to the canyon floor several hundred feet below, where a small patch of green told her that winter was fast losing its grip. Soon the earth would be warm again. Even now the warm air off the canyon floor rose with the night, sending pleasant dry breezes upward, accompanied by the gentle scent of sage, juniper and pine.

A high-pitched shriek, coming from the cliff city, jerked Shala's eyes upward. Her heart gave a jolt of fear, then quickly settled down as she realized it was only laughter.

"Do you hear them, Eric?" she asked. "Do you hear the sound of their laughter? It is long since my People have laughed so much."

The large, crackling fire had been laid in the center courtyard. The dancing flames reflected yellow bronze tones off the high arch of the overhanging sandstone. Shadow patterns leapt and jumped in accordance with the rising and falling of speech animated by happy laughter.

Over it all the night sky stretched endlessly. The stars sparkled in brilliant radiance as each point of light glimmered and danced in the velvet night.

It was a happy sight, and yet, Shala felt a sadness welling deep within her. The warmth of the night made her very aware that time was growing short. She was certain Eric had not changed his mind about leaving, but she could not go with him. Even though she loved him desperately, she could not!

"Nampeyo will be wondering where we are," he said, taking her arm and turning her toward the path that led up the cliff. "Now be careful. One misstep and we may be joining that shaman of yours—wherever he is."

The reunion between mother and daughter was a happy one. "At last you are with me again," Gryla said, embracing her eagerly. "I thought this day would never come."

Shala introduced Eric to her mother and saw that Gryla was impressed by the height and breadth of him. Not being one to mince words, Gryla spoke what was in her mind. "You will make strong babies for my daughter. Babies that will be able to survive in this harsh land of ours." A sad expression crossed her face. "Shala will not know the heartbreak of losing her children."

What would Gryla think if she knew of Eric's people's custom of doing away with infants that were not perfect? Shala wondered. She would never tell her mother of that. For some reason, she wanted her mother to think highly of the man she loved.

The celebration had been under way for some time when Shala saw her friend, Nama, standing at the corner of her dwelling. Her demeanor was puzzling, sad, as though she had lost a loved one. Why did she look that way? Had something happened that Shala was unaware of?

She crossed the courtyard, seeking out her friend. "You do not look well, Nama," she said. "Are you ill?"

"Yes," the other girl replied. "But not with a sickness of the body. Instead, I suffer from a sickness of the mind, caused by dread of what the future holds for me."

"You worry about the desert clan? But surely you no longer have to worry about them. Shu is dead, and the promise he made to Standing Wolf died with him."

"The promise did not die," the other girl said, wiping a tear from her eye. "The promise lives on. Nampeyo has deemed it so."

"He would not!" Shala protested. "Nampeyo has always thought highly of you. He would not see you suffer at the hands of the desert people."

"It is Nampeyo who told me I must honor the promise," she said bitterly.

"That is hard to believe," Shala said.

Becoming aware of other eyes upon them, and realizing that Nama was almost on the point of tears, Shala hooked her fingers around the other girl's arm and led her deeper into the shadows.

"Now tell me what has happened," she said grimly.

"I told you. Nampeyo has said I must honor the promise his father made to the desert clan."

"Why does he speak of it now? Why not wait awhile? Is there something else that remains untold?"

"A messenger came today from the desert people," Nama said in a trembling voice. "He told the council Standing Wolf and his people will come for me in four days." Her face was pinched with anxiety. "I cannot go with them, Shala!" she cried desperately, her shoulders hunching in misery. "I would rather put an end to my life."

"No!" Shala exclaimed, taking the other girl's hand. "You cannot even consider such a thing. You know what would happen. Your spirit would be doomed to wander eternally in the place of the shadows."

"Better that than to go with the desert people," Nama cried, squeezing her eyelids shut to stop the tears from spilling over. Her efforts were in vain. She swiped at the escaping moisture with the back of her hand and turned away from Shala. "I thought you would understand," she muttered. "You were cast out by the clan, shunned by our people and cursed by Shu for refusing to be his mate. You already know how miserable it is to live apart from the clan."

"There were many times when I wished to be given a chance to reconsider my decision," Shala admitted. "Times when I would gladly have embraced his loathsome presence . . . just to be back among my people. But that was because I was entirely alone. You will have other people around you, Nama. And they cannot help but love you."

Although her words were meant for encouragement, they served only to strengthen Nama's resolve. "See!" the girl cried. "You would have done anything to be among our people. But I will not be among them, will not find comfort anywhere. It would be better to be alone than among such savages." Her voice became bitter. "It is easy for you to dismiss my trouble, for you have found love with the golden-haired Viking. Your future is secure with only happiness in store. Not so mine. There will be no chance for love in my life. With the desert people I will be doomed to a life of misery. All chance for happiness would be gone."

Love with the golden-haired Viking. Your future is secure. The words mocked Shala, and she ducked her head quickly, blinking her eyes to dry the tears that suddenly threatened. "There will be no future for me with Eric," she said unsteadily.

"You say those words hoping to make me feel less miserable," Nama said sternly. "But they do not. If they were true, then I would feel sadness for you, but it would not help me face the future with any more courage."

"My words are true. There is no future for the Viking and me. He will soon return to his homeland."

Nama's features softened. "I know how distressed you must feel, but at least you will no longer be alone. Now that Shu is dead you can return to the clan. Nampeyo has said so. He has even lifted the curse from your spirit."

"Nampeyo will be a good shaman." Shala tried to shrug away her own problems, tried instead to think only of the trouble that plagued her friend. "You must appeal to him for help. He would not refuse you."

A flood of fresh tears streaked Nama's face. "He has refused. I told you so."

"Had he consulted with the elders?"

"Yes. They are of the same mind. They dare not risk the wrath of the desert clan by withdrawing Shu's offer. Nampeyo said I must resign myself to going with them. But I will not! They cannot make me! I will see myself dead first!"

"No!" Shala protested, alarm streaking through her. "Do not say such things. Do not even think such thoughts."

"Perhaps it is the best way after all. My People cannot be held responsible for my death. With Shu and me both dead . . ." Her voice trailed away.

"Do not act with undue haste," Shala said sternly. "The desert clan will not come for another few days, and perhaps by then another way will be found."

"There is no other way. If I am here, I will be forced to leave with them." She covered her face with her hands and began to sob bitterly.

It was obvious that Nama had thought everything out very carefully. Still, she must be dissuaded from taking her own life. There were other possibilities that had obviously not yet occurred to her.

In her mind's eye, Shala saw herself on the mesa, her face turned to the north as it had been earlier in the day. From her position, the desert below was not visible, but the ridges of distant mountains rose against the skyline, one after the other. Although Shala had never been off the mesa, she had heard tales of the game that abounded there, heard the animals stood still, just waiting for a hunter's lance to pierce their vital parts, their earthly bodies more than willing to feed the People with their flesh, and all they wished in return was for their spirits to be sung to the nether world among the stars.

Such a place would be suited for two girls, one experienced at hunting and the other having much to learn. They could live there for years . . . would most likely have to, because they would no longer be welcomed into their clan.

Was that what Shala wanted?

No! Not when Nampeyo had just lifted the curse placed on her. Not when she would finally be able to return among the Eagle Clan. But it seemed the choice was not hers. Eric had made it plain that, when he left the mesa, he would not leave her behind.

A painful lump filled her throat, threatened to choke her. She squeezed the words past. "If you left the mesa, the clan might think you dead. When the desert people came, you would be gone from here, out of their reach."

"How would I survive?" Nama asked, obviously

willing to be persuaded, for her eyes had taken on a glitter. "I do not have your ability with a spear, Shala. I would starve to death—if the animals did not eat me first."

"No," Shala replied grimly. "You will not starve."

"I will not?"

"No. I will be with you. Together we will find another place to live."

"You speak nonsense, Shala. Why should you go away from our people, leave everyone you love? Now? When Nampeyo has given you permission to return to the Eagle Clan?"

"Because of Eric. He means to take me away with him."

"Take you away? Where?"

"To his homeland."

"But he cannot! He lives far away from here. Clear across the big salt water."

"Yes. That is why I cannot go."

Nama's face softened. "Maybe it would not be so bad as you think, Shala."

"You would not say that if you knew about the angry gods that rule his people. He has told me much about them. They ride horses and—"

"Horses?"

"Yes. He drew me a picture of one. It had fire coming from its mouth, and it rode across the sky among bolts of lightning thrown by another of his gods. Such gods would never accept me as one of their mortal beings. They would turn the people against me, would turn Eric against me; and he would send me to live apart from him."

Her eyes took on a misty glaze. "I saw this in my dreams," she went on. "His is a land of great cold, where ice covers everything. It is a place that is inhabited by strange beasts and warring people, where women are treated like animals. He believes we are the savages, but it is not so. His are the savage people. I will not be taken there and left alone. Never!"

"Why do you think he would leave you alone?" Nama inquired. "Would Eric not keep you beside him? He loves you. Has he not told you so?"

"No. He has never said such a thing. He likes to mate with me. But he likes to mate with others as well."

"You imagine such things. And, even if they are true, he would always keep you from harm. He is a good man."

"A good man that I cannot trust," Shala replied.

"But you love him!"

"Yes." She nodded her head. "I do love him. So much that the fire of love burns constantly deep inside my belly. I never dreamed I could love a man in such a way. But there is something about him that makes me fearful, something he keeps hidden from me."

"You are afraid of him?"

Yes, she was afraid. And that made her all the more determined to escape . . . to leave while she had the chance. "There is another reason I must leave," she said grimly. "I am with child, and I would not see it destroyed."

"Destroyed!" Nama's expression showed her confusion. "Who would destroy your baby?"

"Eric."

"No! He would not do such a thing."

"He told me so himself."

"That he would destroy your babe?"

"In his world a man decides whether a babe will live or die. I fear he will not keep the child." She shuddered. "I could not see anything happen to a child of my flesh." She shook her head. "No. I must leave here. Go where he will not find me. After he leaves for his boat, then I will return to claim what is mine." Her eyes met Nama's in a long look. "Perhaps then, there will no longer be the threat of Standing Wolf to worry you. He will have come and gone by the time we return. Whatever happens will already have taken place."

"How soon can we leave?" Nama asked eagerly.

"Tomorrow night. That way we will have the light of the full moon to guide us and we will have time to collect food and clothing for our trip. Can you hide some away?" When Nama nodded, Shala continued. "Wait until everyone is asleep, and go to the abandoned dwellings. I will meet you there."

Nama's excitement showed in her face. "It will be done," she said. "We will be well away from this place before anyone learns of our intentions."

Seventeen

The decision to leave Eric appeared—in the cold light of day—to be a foolish, thoughtless plan. What had possessed her? she wondered. How could she even consider leaving the man she had come to love so dearly? It would be like tearing the heart from her body!

As though sensing her troubled thoughts, Eric woke suddenly, opening eyes that bored into hers. A frown darkened his brow, making her wonder if he guessed her innermost feelings. Shala lowered her thick black lashes and pulled her trembling lips into a smile to reassure him.

Apparently she succeeded, because his face relaxed slightly and he returned her smile, then yawned widely, displaying strong, white teeth. As quickly as his eyes had opened, they drifted shut again, allowing her time to study his features that were still relaxed from sleep.

I must have been wrong about his intentions, she told herself. *Even if it is the custom of his people to rid themselves of weak infants Eric would never deliberately harm his own child.*

No! She had only been letting her imagination run wild. She would be foolish to leave him.

Nama. The name drifted into her consciousness just before the girl's face appeared. Shala had almost forgotten about the girl's dilemma. She sighed heavily. She would consult Eric. He would help them. Together, they would find an answer to Nama's problem.

Feeling somewhat better about the situation and fully intending to approach Eric about the situation as soon as he woke, Shala tossed aside the blanket and slipped off the sleeping mat to begin preparations for the morning meal.

Soon the aroma of mush and corn cakes filled the air, teasing Eric's nostrils, making him open his eyes to a mere slit. "Why are you up so early?" he groaned.

"It is not early," she replied calmly.

"It feels early," he grumbled. "Come back to bed." He held out a beckoning hand.

Although she was tempted to go to him, to know again the ecstasy she experienced in his arms, she resisted. "If I join you on the sleeping mat, your meal will grow cold. Are you prepared to eat cold mush?"

He grimaced wryly. "You present me with a problem, woman. My body wants you in my arms, but my stomach argues that it wants hot food, not cold mush."

"Which will win?" she asked softly, finding herself moving toward him.

He pushed aside the rabbit skin blanket and sat up. "My stomach," he growled. "It needs hot food to settle that stuff I drank last night. What was it anyway? Every time I emptied my cup someone filled it again."

"It was a drink made from berries. The men of my clan drink it when they celebrate, but from what I have seen, a little goes a long way."

"The stuff is certainly potent. It has more kick than mead."

"You should not have drank so much." The slightest irritation crept into her voice. "I was afraid you would fall from the cliff coming home."

"Me?" He gave an abrupt laugh. "It takes more than overripe berry juice to make me clumsy." He squatted down beside her and scratched the curly golden hair on his chest and yawned widely. "Dish me up some mush, woman, and sweeten it with plenty of honey." He curled his fingers around her neck and planted a hard kiss on her lips; then, as easily as he had captured her, he set her free.

Although Shala remained silent throughout the meal, Eric appeared not to notice anything out of the ordinary. After finishing his meal, he left on his morning hunt.

With trepidation, Shala watched him go. Although she had meant to speak of the babe she carried snuggled deep in her belly, she could not bring herself to do so out of fear for the child's welfare. How could she love Eric so much and still think he could harm their child?

Her mind told her she was being foolish; yet she remembered Eric's expression when he had first met Nampeyo. The look on his face had been indescribable. She had been made uneasy by that incomprehensible look, by his eyes that had darkened with something very much like pity. Or had it been disgust that she had seen in them? If it had been the latter, then would he feel that same disgust for their child if it arrived into this world less than perfect?

Shala sighed deeply. She was unwilling to believe that Eric could hurt their child, but there was no way she could know for sure. She should have brought her worries out of hiding, should have faced him with them, but she had not, fearing his reaction.

Although Shala fully intended to face Eric with her news when he returned from hunting, she knew it was best to be prepared for the worst and spent the morning hours packing the things she would need if she were forced to flee from him. She filled parfleches made from deerhide with dried strips of venison until they were almost bursting, then stuffed another with pemmican—dried meat, berries and bearfat—and laid them aside. Then she added a small leather pouch of medicinal herbs, gathered up her rabbitskin cloak and a blanket and tossed them on the other supplies, and finally filled a clean pig gut with water and placed it beside the growing pile of supplies. When she had her supplies together, she carried them to the abandoned city on the mesa and secreted them there.

Having done all she could to secure a quick departure if it should prove necessary, she returned home and spent the early afternoon hours sharpening her spear point and knife blade to keener edges, knowing if she went through with her plan, she would be traveling in unknown territory and must be ready for whatever came her way, whether it be hunger or an enemy, human or otherwise.

The rest of the day passed with the pace of a turtle making its way across a desert, Shala waiting impatiently for the Viking to return.

Father Sun hung at the top of the world, smiling down upon his children, warming the earth with his golden gaze that was so like Eric's hair; then the bright yellow ball of his face began a lazy, slow descent that would eventually lead to his rest for the night.

And still Shala waited for Eric to come.

The afternoon was long, endless; the air calm and still. It remained that way until late in the day, but when the bright yellow ball of Father Sun's face hovered over the horizon, painting Sky Man's cloak with slashes of orange and red and purple, Wind Woman began to blow softly.

Shala stood near the edge of the canyon, her rabbitskin dress flattened against her slight frame by the cold, brisk air. Her dark, tousled hair danced across her cheeks, obscuring her vision. She shoved it back impatiently, tucking the long strands behind her ears, looking anxiously up the face of the cliff while she searched for sign of her Viking.

Nothing.

Where was Eric? she wondered. When he had left that morning she had had no idea he would be gone so long.

Sighing heavily, she went back inside and began preparing the evening meal. He would be hungry when he did come home.

Worry continued to plague her as she prepared rabbit stew and corn cakes, all the while listening for any sound that might announce Eric's arrival.

Nothing.

Time passed and still Shala waited.

She knelt beside the fire in the center of her small cave and dug into the ashes for one of the balls of corn cakes left there to bake. When her horn spoon struck against one, she raked it from the ashes and, after brushing it clean, broke it open. It was firm all the way through, done to a turn and ready to eat. As was the rabbit stew simmering in the blackened pot over the coals. Even now the aroma teased at her nostrils, making her aware of her hunger.

She threw a quick look at the entrance, then, with deepening frown, turned back to the firepit. Where was Eric? Why had he not yet returned?

Knowing she dare not wait longer lest the corn ash cakes burn to a crisp, she raked the rest of them from the ashes, brushed them clean, then dropped them in a large clay bowl. After covering them with a clay lid, she lifted the simmering stew from the coals and set it nearby to keep warm. Now, assured that their meal would not burn, she left the cave.

Father Sun had already gone to his rest, and Wind Woman's breath was colder without his face to warm it. But still there was no sign of Eric.

Unable to keep still, she entered the cave again. Fearing the soup would congeal, Shala picked up her horn spoon and stirred it, her thoughts returning to another place, another time. She knew he had waited as she was now doing. And she had been in trouble.

Was it the same with him? Had he encountered something he could not handle?

Dread replaced anxiety. She must find him—as soon as possible.

Urgency drove her as she snatched up her spear and started out of the cave. It was then she heard the falling rock and knew someone was descending the cliff.

Hope sent her scurrying outside, swept her gaze toward the man who was descending, a pig slung across his shoulders.

Eric! He was back!

Her relief was so great that tears filled her eyes. She quickly wiped them away before he could reach her.

When he was finally beside her, Eric flung the carcass of the gutted hog on the ground; then he grinned down at Shala. "What do you think about that one?" he asked. "Have you ever seen such a big hog?"

Shala shook her head, her eager eyes roaming over his face, his body, assuring her that he was unharmed. Finding him so, she finally looked at his kill. "He is very big," she agreed, her voice husky with emotion. She kept her eyes on the pig, resisting the urge to throw herself into his arms and bawl like a babe in arms. She could not allow herself that luxury. If she did so, he would surely want an explanation.

No! She dare not allow him to see how much she was hurting, because he would surely demand a reason and she had no answer to give him. Not until she was certain of how he would react to the news of their unborn child, not even then if she was still uncertain about the babe's future.

Shala swallowed around the lump stuck in her throat, praying that she would not be forced to leave, that she would not be forced to meet Nama and carry out their plans, that Eric would want their child, no matter how imperfect it might be.

But what if he did not? What if she had to leave him? Would he care that she was gone?

Perhaps.

Would he miss her?

Maybe.

But even if he did, he would soon get over it. When he reached his homeland there would be many women wanting his attention. Many who would not be afraid of his gods, who would gladly embrace all of his customs just to be held in his arms.

Tears stung Shala's eyes, and she choked back a sob. Those women—the unknown women who waited in Eric's future—would soon make him forget that Shala ever existed.

Despite her efforts at control, the tears that she fought to keep back flooded Shala's eyes, and she turned quickly away, entering the cavern and blinking rapidly to rid her eyes of their moisture.

She heard his booted feet thumping on the hard ground as he followed her inside, felt his hand gripping her shoulder just before he turned her around. With his other hand he tilted her chin and forced her to meet his darkening eyes. "Come here," he said gruffly, pulling her into his arms. "Tell me what troubles you."

Had he seen the tears? *Oh, no!* He would surely ask the reason for them.

"Are you feeling neglected, Shala?" he asked gently, kissing her moist eyelids. "It was thoughtless of me not to ask you to go hunting with me, but you seemed so distracted this morning that I thought you might need some time alone. Was I wrong?"

She shook her head. "No," she whispered, feeling his breath warm against her face. "I had . . . had things to do." She swallowed hard, her arms circling his neck, her fingers threading through his bright hair. "I am being silly, I know. It is just that—that I missed you so terribly."

"So terribly?" He slanted a smile down at her just before claiming her mouth in a hard kiss that set her heart pounding and left her wanting more. "You can show me how much I was missed after I finish cleaning this pig. Too bad there will not be time enough to cure the hide, but we can give it to Nampeyo. It will make a nice parting gift."

Releasing her, he dropped to his haunches and set to work slicing meat from the hog's shank while Shala put the pot of stew over the coals to heat.

She watched him uneasily. The time was not right for questions, but she must ask them anyway. "Eric," she began hesitantly.

"Ummm?" He never looked up from his work.

"Eric, you spoke before about your people's customs."

He threw a swift glance at her, then returned to his work. "We have many customs, Shala. Which one interests you?"

"The one about a newborn babe," she replied slowly. "You said . . . if a father rejected his child it was allowed to die."

"It was a custom older than time," he said, hacking through a joint, chopping through gristle and wrenching the leg loose and laying it aside. Blood covered his forearms, but he seemed unaware of its existence as he turned his attention to another leg.

Shala's heart pounded with fear. There had been no emotion in his voice when he'd spoken of killing babies. No emotion whatsoever. How could he so easily dismiss another human life?

"Hand me the sword," he said grimly. "My blade has gone dull."

She passed it to him, then set the covered bowl containing corn cakes near the coals. Her heart was a dull ache beneath her breast. She had her answer now. There was no need to question him further. He would see their child dead if it reached the world less than perfect. And she would not allow that.

Heaving a despairing sigh, she removed the food from the heat. Eric was disposing of the remains of the carcass by the time the stew was heated.

"Thor's teeth!" he exclaimed, settling down against the wall and stretching his long legs out while rubbing taut neck muscles. "This has been one long day." He eyed the pallet of sleeping furs nearby. "That bed will feel good after my belly is filled."

Shala felt a sinking despair. Was he going to sleep without loving her one last time?

Trying to keep her disappointment concealed, she filled their bowls with savory stew, and watched him set to with an eagerness hard to ignore. Although Shala had not eaten since early morn, she found herself with no appetite and merely pushed her food around the bowl, spooning a bite into her mouth every now and then, mostly when he chanced to look her way.

When he finished his meal, Eric washed his food down with a dipper of water, stripped away his clothing, then sprawled out on the sleeping mat as naked as the day he was born. Although it had become his custom to sleep in that manner, the sight of his well-muscled body tightened her lower belly.

When his voice came, it startled her. "Will you be long in retiring?"

"I can do so now if you like." Did she sound too eager? If she did, he seemed not to notice.

"No," he replied gruffly. "I imagine you want to finish that basket you were weaving last eve.

You should finish shortly, and I am so tired that you will not disturb me. Stay up as long as you like. I could sleep through a grizzly attack." The last words were barely uttered before he rolled over with his back to her, pulled the sleeping robe over his lower body and became still. His even breathing told her he was already asleep.

Tears closed Shala's throat, constricting tears that welled into her eyes, threatening to overflow while she stared at him in dismay. How could he dismiss her so easily? Could he not see how badly she wanted him? Did he even care about her needs?

Turning away from the sleeping man, Shala retrieved the unfinished basket from the corner where she had left it and began to weave. Although her mind was busy, troubled by Eric's lack of interest, her fingers were nimble as they worked the yucca strands in and out.

Her gaze went often to Eric, but his motionless body and his even breathing told her that he was still fast asleep.

She resented that fact.

Why had he gone to sleep? How could he have done so? Tonight of all nights, he should have held her in his arms, should have whispered sweet words into her ears. Instead, he lay there, sleeping like a log.

She threw him an anguished look, and the fingers that had been working the yucca strands stilled. She laid the basket aside.

She was only wasting time on it. Neither she nor Eric would have the use of it. Since others would, then they could very well finish weaving it.

With a sigh of frustration, she moved to the entrance, pushed the deerhide flap aside and stepped out into the night air. Darkness had settled over the land. Shala looked up at the blessed star people, glittering so brightly in the night sky. Even Moon Woman was at her fullest and her gaze outlined the cliff city across the canyon.

It was quiet there. The children had been put to sleep, and the last voice had died down; the last flute had long since been silenced.

It was time for her to go, and yet she could not make herself do so.

Why did she delay? she wondered. Eric was sleeping soundly and she could easily slip away without his knowing. Nama would be at the meeting place, waiting to start their journey, but even so, something intangible held Shala back.

Fresh tears surged forth, stinging her eyes as she went back into the cave.

She looked at the sleeping man and wondered again how she could bear to leave him. She loved him so much. But even as she questioned her ability to go, she remembered her reason for doing so—the secret she held close against her heart—and knew she had no choice. She could not remain with him.

She must leave. The life that was only beginning must have its chance to survive. But how it hurt to leave her golden-haired Viking!

She picked up her knife, strapped it around

her waist, took spear in hand, then cast one last look at Eric.

He lay unmoving. It was so unfair, she thought. So unfair. He had fallen asleep and stolen what could have been her one last night of ecstasy.

How could he dismiss her so easily?

As though sensing her troubled thoughts, he muttered her name, tossed restlessly, then became still again.

Eric! her heart cried. *Remember me always! Never forget what we were to one another!*

Again, he stirred. "Shala," he mumbled. "What are . . . ?"

Her heart surged with gladness. He was thinking of her. Even in his sleep, his thoughts remained with her. Although she knew she should leave before he woke, she could not make herself do so. Instead, she put aside her weapons and hurried to the sleeping pallet.

He lay motionless again, his restless state having already passed. His back was facing her, his body relaxed in a lazy curve. He was totally unaware of her gaze, unaware as well of her inner turmoil.

I cannot leave you! she silently cried, dropping to her knees beside him. *I cannot go, Eric. Not without knowing your loving one more time.*

Never mind that Nama was waiting in the abandoned city. Never mind that if Eric woke, Shala might have lost her chance to leave. No! Never mind all that! The only thing that mattered was satisfying this urgency that was suddenly so overwhelming.

Stripping away her clothing, Shala tossed it

carelessly aside, then pulled the rabbitskin covering off Eric, her eyes feasting on his naked body as she crawled onto the sleeping mat beside him. Her nostrils twitched as she breathed in his purely male scent, and she rubbed her cheek against his shoulder and whispered his name.

"Eric." Would he hear the pain in her voice? "I love you, Eric. There will never be another man for me. Only you."

She kissed his shoulders and neck, delighting in the salty taste of his flesh while she rubbed the inside of his thigh with her right palm. "Love me," she whispered in his ear. "Just one more time let me feel your body on mine."

Eric sighed heavily and made small noises in his throat as if trying to speak. Wrapping her fingers around his manhood, she gently squeezed it, feeling it grow in her grasp as she continued whispering in his ear.

His eyes fluttered open, and he turned his head until his sleep-drugged eyes were able to meet hers. He mumbled something that was too low for her to understand, then closed his eyes again.

A new feeling surged forth, coming from somewhere deep inside her, dulling the pain that had been with Shala since she had decided to leave her Viking. It was called irritation. How could he ignore her when his manhood was pulsing with so much eagerness?

Unwilling to allow him to sleep again without giving her body satisfaction, she released his member and shoved him on his back.

"What are you doin'?" he mumbled, his eyelids flicking up, then drifting down again.

Determined to wake him fully, she knelt above him and nipped at his throat with her teeth. Although his breath quickened, he gave no other sign that he was aware of her touch.

Opening her mouth, she spread moist kisses from his neck to his chest, pausing momentarily when she reached his flat male nipples circling each of them in turn with her tongue. She knew he was fully awake now and totally aware of her ministrations. She could feel his heart pounding inside his chest, knew that if she ceased her efforts he would not be able to let her go.

But she had no intention of stopping. Not now. She had initiated the contact between them, and she would continue in this vein. She would show him how much he had taught her.

And she did. Her mouth and tongue continued to blaze a trail across his chest. All the while she could feel his member growing beneath her lower body, throbbing impatiently. Yet still, she left him unsatisfied, continuing the slow, sensual path she traced across his flesh, always moving in a circular downward motion, trailing lower and lower until finally, she reached his concave belly. Shala stopped there for a long moment, dipping her tongue into the hollow of his navel, then streaking a trail of fire even lower until she felt his quivering flesh beneath her chin.

His breath came in quick gasps, harsh and raspy, until suddenly, as though unable to bear the sweet torture she was so effectively delivering with her hot tongue, Eric grasped her upper arms and pulled her upright. "Thor's teeth!" he grunted. "No more!"

Pulling her over him, he impaled her with his throbbing member, driving it deep into her body, pushing onward until it was completely enfolded with her soft woman's flesh, and all the while, he caressed her back with his callused palms.

A small series of explosions began deep inside Shala, building to a crescendo until she found herself biting her lip to keep from screaming. Eric continued to move beneath her, thrusting upward, harder and harder, and each thrust seemed to loosen something deep inside her until finally she could hold back no longer. A scream erupted from her, a loud wailing sound that shook her whole body. It sounded nothing like Shala. Instead, it was shrill and piercing, inarticulate and completely shameless.

Suddenly, she collapsed, feeling replete in the afterglow of Eric's lovemaking. She lay beside him, responding to his kisses, pressing her body against his, wanting to keep the night of loving locked deep in her memory in the years ahead, years that would of necessity, exclude Eric.

When the Viking was fast asleep, she pulled herself from his arms and went about the business of dressing as warmly as possible. She had gathered up her weapons and headed for the door when she remembered a promise given.

The Viking's robe. Long ago she had promised it to Nama. Now the promise must be fulfilled.

Taking the white robe from the stack of furs, she paused for one last look at Eric.

He looked so young, so vulnerable in his sleep. But Shala had occasion to know the magnitude of his strength. Even though she had covered him with the rabbitskin blanket, the memory of his well-muscled torso was firmly entrenched in her mind. She could still taste his kiss upon her lips.

Feeling as though her heart must surely break, she turned away from him and left the cave. Tears streamed down her face while she crossed the mesa to the abandoned dwellings.

She found Nama waiting at the assigned place. "Where have you been?" Nama cried. "I thought something had happened to keep you from coming."

If only it had, Shala thought silently, but gave no hint of those feelings to her friend. "Are you ready?" she asked, not bothering to explain her delay in coming.

"Yes," the other girl said, looking curiously at Shala. If she guessed the reason for the delay, she kept it to herself.

They traveled throughout the night, grateful for the light cast down by Moon Woman. By the time dawn broke, they were descending the mesa.

When they reached the edge of the large plain below, they stopped for a short rest and a bite to eat.

"Do you think they know we are gone yet?" Nama asked, her gaze moving toward the mesa again, before returning to her friend.

Shala would not look behind her, could not

without pain. Leaving Eric had been harder than she had ever imagined. "They will not suspect anything for a while. We could be anywhere—fetching water from the spring, digging roots or visiting each other. It will be some time—perhaps noon—before anyone starts looking for us. By then we will be so far away they will not catch us." Instead of making her feel better, the words seemed to seal her fate.

"Unless Nampeyo suspects what we have done as soon as they know we are missing," Nama said gravely. "He knows me better than most, knows as well how fearful of Standing Wolf I am. He may guess what has happened and send runners after us."

"That is a possibility," Shala replied. "That is why we must take steps to cover our tracks. If we can delay them long enough, the animals and Wind Woman's breath may help us deceive them."

"Show me what to do," Nama said quickly. "Surely the two of us can outwit them."

Even as Shala wiped away their trail, she wondered at her actions. Could she really go through with this? Could she really leave the Viking behind?

Eighteen

Thunk, thunk, thunk. Although the noise was curious, rousing Eric from a state of sleeplessness, he spent no time wondering what caused the sound. He already knew. It was the hide covering the entrance, flapping back and forth. The noise and the annoying rays of sunlight piercing his eyelids were the reasons he stirred. He struggled from the cobwebs of sleep.

"Shala," he muttered, "are you awake?"

Although he waited for her to answer, there was nothing but silence.

His mouth felt incredibly dry, as though he were traveling across a great desert as he had done last year when his travels took him to Egypt. He sighed and licked parched lips. He need not get up, he decided. Shala would bring him water. "Shala," he said again, eyes still closed. "Time to get up, Shala."

Again, there was only silence.

Could she still be asleep? Eric cracked his eyelids to a narrow slit and reached out for her, intending to shake her awake. She could bring him a dipper of water and secure the entrance flap while she was up.

His hands swept over nothingness.

Opening his eyes to their full width, he swept them around the shadowy interior of the small cave.

No Shala.

With the memory of last night fresh in his mind, he expelled a disappointed sigh. He had hoped she would lie with him for a while, but it seemed he was doomed to disappointment.

Eric was not really surprised to find her gone, and certainly not the least bit worried.

Unlike him, Shala usually woke abruptly in the morning. It was her habit to spring from the sleeping mat the instant she woke, hurry outside, and breathe deeply of the morning air.

At first he had found this habit irritating because he liked to stay abed for a while. This was especially true since the two of them had become so intimate. But his annoyance at Shala's waking habits had soon vanished. After all, they were part of her.

Although thirsty, Eric continued to laze on the sleeping mat, hoping she would soon return and join him on the bed of furs. The memory of their last joining surfaced in his mind. His lips curled into a satisfied smile. She had been so eager last night for his loving. Never had he seen such a passionate woman. And her tongue . . . Thor's teeth! It had driven him almost to the edge of sanity. The mere memory caused his lower body to pulse, to throb with anticipation.

He stared eagerly at the entrance, watching the deerhide flap swing in time to the throbbing of his ardent heart. *Thunk, thunk, thunk! Thud, thud, thud.* Why did she not return? he wondered impatiently.

What was taking her so long?

The two girls traveled throughout the day, across dry, sparse land dotted with sagebrush and sandy hillocks and little else. They rested whenever they could, hiding from Father Sun's fiery gaze beneath the shade of a scraggly juniper that somehow managed to survive in the dry wasteland surrounding them.

When the round, bright ball blazing above them reached its zenith, Shala called a halt. "We will stop a moment and rest," she said, sliding the water gut from her shoulders and handing it across to Nama.

Shading her eyes from the glare, Shala stared at the distant mountains which seemed so far away. They were indistinct, hazy, seeming as wispy as the clouds pushed along by Wind Woman's breath.

How long would it take to reach them? Shala wondered, slumping down on the ground beside a sagebush. She gave it a mere passing glance before returning her attention to the mountains. The bush was no higher than her knees and could offer no comfort whatsoever. The mountains would. If they could reach them.

"Do you think they know we are gone yet?" Nama asked, handing the water gut back to Shala and wiping her mouth with her arm.

"Perhaps," Shala replied shortly. "But it does not matter. I doubt they will leave the mesa to look for us." She handed the other girl a piece of dried venison and helped herself to some. They remained silent. Each was lost in her own thoughts, reflecting on the future that awaited her, until it was time to resume their journey again.

By the time the western sky was blazing with the orange and red color that preceded the end of day, they found themselves in a small valley divided down the middle by a narrow river edged with willow trees that would shelter them while they slept.

Nama, staggering with weariness from the journey, stumbled to the nearest tree, tossed her pack to the ground and sat with her back against the trunk. "Will we be safe here?" she asked fearfully, her eyes probing the shadows gathering beneath the willows as though suspecting some danger of lurking there. "What about scavengers? Will they not attack us?"

Shala sighed and slumped down beside her friend, laying her spear aside but keeping it within easy reach. "We will rest awhile, then look for a safer place." She rubbed her throbbing temples with her fingers.

Although she presented a fearless front to the

world, it was only that. A front. A face put on to deceive others, to make them think her strength was greater than it was.

"Nothing frightens you, does it?" Nama asked suddenly. "Is it because of your spirit guide, Shala? It must be comforting to know Wolf will come whenever he is needed."

Come when he is needed? The words caused Shala's lips to curl in a humorless smile. Nama knew nothing of the times Shala had pleaded—in vain—for the help of her spirit guide. She knew nothing of the ways of the spirit world.

"Do you think the spirits would honor me with a guide?" Nama asked, breaking the long silence.

"You could seek one," Shala replied, throwing her friend a curious look. "There is no guarantee that one would appear, but it would do no harm to seek one."

"A spirit guide would be good to have," the other girl replied. "Especially now, when we are away from other help." She looked hopefully at Shala. "You survived the quest for a spirit guide. Surely I could do so as well."

"Perhaps," Shala said thoughtfully. "But the quest must not be taken lightly. It is a hard, dangerous path to follow. I was near starving to death by the time Wolf finally revealed himself to me."

"When you were lost as a child," Nama said, taking up the story she already knew. "Does that mean I must starve before I can find one?" She looked longingly at her pack. "I am so very hungry, Shala. Perhaps Wolf would be obliging enough to protect both of us for a while."

"We cannot rely on help from anyone—or anything—but ourselves," Shala said shortly. "Not even my spirit guide, Nama. The spirits do not always concern themselves with our needs. I think . . ." She stopped, wondering how best to explain her thoughts. "Maybe they have other duties to perform and our lives go unnoticed by them for a while. Perhaps that is the reason Wolf does not always come when he is needed."

Since she had left the mesa, Shala had looked for Wolf, had hoped he would join them in their trek to the mountain, but she had seen no sign of him. Although that did not mean he was not with her, she was still worried. What if Wolf did not approve of her actions? The spirits surely meant humans to use the sense the creator gave them to stay out of trouble. When Wolf had come to protect her at the cliff, the trouble was through no fault of her own. This time it was different. This time she had left the safety of her cave voluntarily.

It was for that reason that she could not—dare not—rely on Wolf's help.

Her gaze flew around the clearing, but she saw nothing that would provide shelter from animals. Farther downstream there was a pile of logs, cut by Brother Beaver in the recent past. Could she use the fallen trees for shelter?

She ran her eyes across the length and breadth of the pile, mentally measuring them while she did so.

Coming to a quick decision, Shala turned to

the silent girl beside her. "Help me make a shelter from the fallen trees."

A short time later the two girls had constructed a crude shelter from the logs. They placed them atop each other at right angles, lashing them with strips of hide. Although there was a wide space between each pole, there was no possibility that a wolf—or any other scavenger—could take them by surprise.

Feeling some measure of security, Shala curled beside her friend on one of the two hides they had brought; then, after pulling the other hide over themselves, she allowed herself the luxury of sleep.

She dreamed of Eric that night. She could see him clearly, even though it was dark. And she knew, somehow, that they were sleeping together somewhere on a vast rolling desert. Even though she felt joy at his presence, something disturbed her. What? Was there another presence near them? A vague, shadowy figure that crept closer under cover of darkness?

She tried to open her eyes, but found her lids locked tightly together. Her fear was so great that she moaned softly. A twig snapped somewhere nearby, as though the shadowy figure in her dream had inadvertently stepped on it.

Thud, thud, thud! Shala's heart pumped with dread as she willed herself to wake up. She must rouse herself from this dream that was slowly becoming a nightmare. She must!

But she really had no need to awaken herself. Someone else did that for her.

She was vaguely aware of the shadowy form leaning over her, but totally unaware of the fingers twining through her long, dark hair. Until she felt the sharp tug that stung her scalp and jerked her eyes open wide.

In the dim light of the full moon she could see him clearly. A tall man. "Eric!" she cried, her heart jerking with gladness. As soon as she said the name she knew she was wrong. He was not her Viking lover. Instead, he was a stranger. And not a very friendly one, she judged. Her gaze went past him to the warriors standing beyond, all armed to the teeth with both bow and spear.

The stranger leaned closer. His grip tightened on her hair, and his lips pulled back into a ferocious snarl that sent chills through her.

Standing Wolf could see the mesa ahead of him, and already he felt a sense of possession. Soon the flat mountain top would belong to the desert tribe. Their hunters would have no need to search for days for game that remained absent. Hunger would be a thing of the past, for there would be a plentiful supply of food, both meat and growing things, on the mesa. He thought about the people who presently inhabited it; imagined his blade slicing through their flesh. They would be caught by surprise.

Should he kill them all, or should he allow some to survive? The traders that came so often to visit the desert clan had many stories to tell. Standing Wolf's favorite tale concerned the people who lived far away in the south. The traders spoke of clothing made from a colorful array of materials, of slaves who tended to their every need, of buildings designed for beauty and comfort. Why should the people in the south live better than the desert tribe?

A king. That was the name the traders used for the ruler of that faraway place. Well, they were no better than Standing Wolf. He, too, desired to be a king. He tested it on his tongue. "King of the mesa." It bore a good sound. Yes, he decided. He would be king of the mesa.

His lips pulled into a grim smile, and his dark eyes glittered. The people of the Eagle Clan had been so easily fooled. They had accepted his words at face value, thinking he needed a bride.

A bride! Why should he want one of their maidens for a bride? Did they have more beautiful maidens than the desert tribe? He thought not, but since he had not actually seen the one chosen for him, he could not know for certain. Perhaps he would seek her out when he had overpowered the clan. And if she was beautiful to look upon, then he might keep her for a while to serve his needs. Or, he just might turn her over to his warriors. They would deserve a reward for their efforts.

Yes, perhaps that is what he would do. He would tell them she was a reward for their fierce fighting. They would like that and would feel indebted to him for giving them the woman who was promised to him.

His smile widened, and his dark eyes glittered

brightly. Victory—and the mesa—would soon be his.

They would reach the mesa before the day was at its end.

The afternoon sun beat down on Shala's head as she was alternately pushed and pulled along behind her captors. They seemed to be headed for the distant range of mountains that had been Shala's destination. They traveled fast, as though feeling the need to put as much distance as possible between the mesa and them before daylight.

Did they think they would be pursued by the Eagle Clan? Shala wondered bitterly. Would they slow down if they knew the girls were on their own?

Shala thought not, so she decided to keep quiet. The worry that warriors might be following close behind kept their captors on guard, afraid to stop long lest they be attacked. That was a good thing. As long as they continued to travel, the girls would not be subjected to their lust.

As long as they traveled . . .

Suddenly, Shala stumbled over an unseen rock and sprawled forward into the dirt. The man behind her bent, curled his fingers around her upper arm and yanked her to her feet. She swayed as the strain of the long walk began to tell on her muscles.

"Go!" he grunted, pushing her forward again.

"Are you all right?" Nama asked from her position behind Shala.

"Yes," Shala muttered, hurrying forward to ease the pressure applied to her arm.

Using her free arm, she wiped the perspiration from her forehead, then shoved back the damp tendrils of hair that curled wetly around her face.

She was so hot, so thirsty. She knew from the prickling of her skin that Father Sun's rays were burning her flesh. Her hide dress seemed almost to have doubled in thickness, and she found it smothering.

Spirit Guide, she silently cried. *Have you completely deserted me?*

She scanned the countryside, hoping for a glimpse of Wolf, but, other than themselves, there was no sign of anyone.

The walking was becoming more difficult now as they encountered rough, broken canyon country, dotted here and there with mescal, prickly pear and an occasional bush. The mountains were closer now, and Shala knew their situation was becoming more desperate. She had no idea how far it was to their captor's village, but she feared time was running out for them. If they were going to escape, they would have to do so soon, but for the life of her, she was unable to devise a plan that would see them free.

It was near dusk when they entered the foothills of the mountains. There was a distinct trail now, winding upward, and they would be forced to go single file as the way narrowed to an alarming degree.

Perhaps now was the time. While the men were

occupied with the narrow trail. Yes. She would wait for the first opportunity and—

In the instant that she made her decision, she became aware that her captors had shrugged off their packs and were preparing to make camp. Shala could have screamed with disappointment. With their minds no longer occupied with reaching their village, the men might turn their thoughts toward the captive women and what they had to offer.

Her eyes met those of the nearest man, a wide-shouldered individual who looked as though his role in life was to make those around him suffer. The look in his eyes was almost a promise, a threat of what was to come.

She looked across at Nama, saw the girl was quivering with fear. "Do not let them see that you are afraid," she whispered.

"What are they going to do?" Nama asked, her frightened gaze fastening on her friend and holding there, as though she were afraid to look at their captors.

"We will soon know," Shala said in a low voice. "Whatever happens, try to remain calm. Some men like to hear a woman scream and cry. To do so will only make them hurt you more."

"I cannot bear it," Nama said. "They might as well kill me now."

"You can and you will bear this!" Shala said sharply. "We will get through this night—somehow! We *will* survive."

Noticing the leader—the fiery-haired man they called Red Fox—watching her, Shala shrugged off her pack and let it fall to the ground. "Drop your pack," she told the girl beside her. "Offer to cook the rabbits they killed."

"Cook for them?" Nama's voice was outraged. "Why should we cook for them? Let them eat the meat raw like the savages they are!"

"Hush!" Shala said, keeping her voice low. "Do not anger them. Can you not see we must keep busy lest we become prey to their lust?"

Nama's eyes were wide with fear, and she moaned low in her throat. Her gaze darted here and there, seeking help that was not forthcoming. Her gaze touched on the leader, then moved rapidly to Shala again. "See their leader—the one they call Red Fox—his hair is unlike any other I have seen. Do you think he could be Eric's kinsman? Perhaps we could bargain with him, tell him where Eric is and—"

"I do not think so," Shala said, meeting the eyes of the man in question. He held her gaze, obviously aware that he was the object of their discussion. "Eric said his ancestors were here before him. Perhaps the man was born from their seed, but he is no Norseman."

Suddenly, fingers of iron curled around her upper arm, jerking her around. It was a skinny warrior with a hooked nose. Although his frame was narrow, she knew from his grip that he was strong. She met his eyes, hoping to dim the lust she saw there. "Let me make you some food," she offered. "You must be hungry."

His thin lips curled into a knowing smile. "Hungry for more than food," he replied.

"You have traveled a long way today," she said, hoping to stall him. "Let me fill your belly first."

Hearing a shriek from Nama, Shala jerked her arm away from her captor and darted toward the girl and the man who had pulled her to the ground. "Release her!" she cried, yanking at his arm, trying her best to pull him off.

A short word from Red Fox caused Nama's captor to let her go, and the girl scuttled toward Shala.

"Cook the food," the redheaded man said. "I have hunger in my belly." His glance slid from Nama to Shala, where it held for a long moment. "There will be time for other things later."

Shala knew the words for what they were. She was being told that he would not again interfere with the men's plans for them.

But perhaps he could be made to change his mind. "We need wood for a fire," she said, pointing to a fallen log nearby to make certain he understood.

He sent one of his men to fetch it. Shala knew they must prepare the best meal possible because it was their only hope for a reprieve at the moment. She delved into a hide bag and removed the small store of spices she had brought along. Nama rigged up a tripod to hold the buffalo stomach she had brought for cooking—it was much easier for packing and much lighter in weight than a clay pot—added water to the "pot" and then dried vegetables.

Shala realized they were using up their precious store of food, but what did it really matter? If they did not escape there would be no need for food anyway.

Soon the air around them was permeated with the smell of a stew cooking. They served two at a time from their own bowls and were rewarded with grunts of satisfaction and many calls for more.

"Good," commented Red Fox after he had emptied the last bowl. He threw a quick glance toward Shala. "You have learned the art of cooking well . . . as a woman should."

She returned his smile. Her plan had worked. At least, the first part had. Now for the second part. "I am glad you approve. And I will continue to make good meals for you. But I insist on being left alone. Only then will I serve you and your people."

The nearest man, the one with the hooked nose, laughed loudly and smacked his lips. "You can start by serving me, girl!" He lumbered to his feet and pulled her roughly toward him.

"Stop!" she cried, trying to jerk away from him, trying to catch the eyes of Red Fox. He was their leader. He must be made to help her. "I have knowledge of someone—one of your kin. Stop this attack and I will tell you!"

"I have no kin," Red Fox said.

Taking his words for encouragement, Shala's captor hooked his fingers in the neckline of her dress and ripped it open, exposing her breasts to his view.

"Release me!" she demanded, twisting out of his grip and lashing out at him.

He laughed, leaned closer, his fetid breath almost gagging her as he twisted her left nipple with cruel fingers. Her fist connected with his nose, and he roared with pain. She tried to hide the fear threatening to overcome the outrage she felt at being used in such a manner. Angered to the point of fury, her attacker shoved her violently, throwing her to the ground. Raw pain ate into her arms and legs as gravel and dirt dug into her sunburned flesh. Blood pounded in her ears, and her heart thudded against her rib cage like a trapped bird trying to free itself.

"Eric!" she screamed, pushing the word through her dry throat, crying out with every fiber of her being even while she knew the man she called for would never be able to save her. "Eric! Help me!"

Nineteen

Eric, help me!

The words seemed to reverberate all around him, halting Eric in midstride, jerking his head up and sending his gaze skittering through the junipers growing in such abundance on the mesa as he searched for some sign of the girl who had called out to him.

But he saw nothing there. At least nothing out of the ordinary. Nothing except the other searchers. The trackers who had been sent to help him look for Shala and the other girl, Nama, who had disappeared at the same time.

"Shala!" he called, cupping his mouth to make his voice carry farther. "Shala! Where are you?"

Noticing the curious looks he was getting from Flying Eagle, Eric beckoned him over. "Did any of you hear anything?"

"Hear what?" asked Flying Eagle.

"I could have sworn Shala called out to me."

"I heard nothing."

Eric stifled his disappointment, wondering if

his anxiety was responsible for making him hear things that were not there. He had been so certain Shala had called out to him, but apparently he had imagined her voice. Come to think of it, his ears had not heard the words. He had heard them in his head. "Never mind," he said quietly. "I must have imagined her voice."

Flying Eagle nodded his head as though he understood and went back to searching the brush for footprints.

Eric called himself all kinds of a fool while he, along with several of Shala's clansmen, searched the mesa for some sign of the missing girls. *Why did you not go to the cliff city as soon as you woke and found her gone?* a silent voice questioned.

He could not answer, because he had no excuse. To have waited so long—until darkness covered the land—was inexcusable.

If only he had not been so eager to obtain more of the turquoise stones! Granted, he could find a good market for them in Norway, but at what cost? Shala's life?

The mere thought was agonizing, making him despise the stones he had worked so hard the day before to obtain.

He remembered how it had all come about.

He had been lazing in bed, waiting for Shala's return when Nampeyo came to visit. Upon finding Shala gone, Nampeyo stayed to visit with Eric. They had talked about various things, but the conversation had eventually turned to a topic that was of considerable interest to Eric . . . the amulet Shala wore around her neck.

Upon learning about Eric's interest in the stones, the shaman had offered him one, saying it would protect him in times of need. The size of the stone had taken the Viking's breath away, but when questioned, Nampeyo refused to divulge the place where he had found it, saying only that it was a holy place and must be kept secret.

The shaman had barely left when Eric had begun his search for the stones. It was his nature to be stubborn, and when he wanted something, he was not easily discouraged.

He had spent the rest of the day looking for the stones, and so was unaware that Shala remained absent until he returned that night. Still, not unduly alarmed, thinking she had gone to the cliff city, he went there. That was when he discovered that her friend, Nama, was also missing.

"Why did I wait so long to start a search," he muttered, feeling the weight of guilt heavy upon his shoulders. "She could be in trouble, maybe even dead by now."

And all because of me, his heart cried. *All because I was so obsessed with a blue stone. A mere object that could have no possible use except to be made into trinkets.*

Suddenly, Eric became aware of a hush falling upon the group around him. He looked up, saw Jumping Hare, the tracker, who had gone ahead of them, running toward them. His heart jolted with fear.

What had happened?

Why was the man in such a hurry? Intent on learning the reason, Eric hurried forward at a ground-eating pace.

Nama's heart pounded furiously as she took in the scene before her. Shala lay on the ground, staring up at the warrior who had thrown her there. He looked around at his companions as though making certain they were watching him, then, with a harsh laugh, reached for her.

Shala rolled quickly aside, striking out with her foot. She caught him on the upper thigh with a hard kick. His expression darkened with rage, and he curled his fingers around her ankle. He jerked her toward him while his left hand fumbled with his loincloth. His intentions were all too clear.

Released from its confinement, his manhood stood away from his body.

Nama's blood froze in her veins, and she tried to stop the anguished sounds that rose in her throat as she stared at the hideous, fearful, pulsating thing. *Do not let them see your fear!* The words Shala had spoken surfaced in Nama's memory.

Biting down on her quivering lip, she welcomed the ensuing pain. She was determined not to give in to her panic. But the scene in front of her was so horrible, so intense, that she could not stop the small, mewling sounds—like those of a lion cub caught in the paws of a wolf—from erupting.

This brutality—this horrible forced mating that was about to take place—was what she had fled the cliff city to escape. And now she was faced with it anyway. She took a backward step, closing her eyes to shut out the horror. But in her mind's eye she could still see Shala, being attacked by the monster.

A sudden thought intruded. It halted her cowardly flight.

The child! Oh, Wise One above! The brutal rape will cause the death of the child!

Suddenly, courage that Nama had never known she possessed swelled to the surface, covering her fear of the unknown. Her dark eyes blazing with hate, she launched herself at Shala's tormentor.

"Leave her alone!" she cried, lashing out at him with her fists and feet. "She carries a babe in her belly! Only a coward would attack a woman who is with child. Leave her alone!"

Casually, as though she were but a fly, he knocked her aside, sending her sprawling to the ground while he renewed his attack on Shala.

The western sky blazed with orange and gold as Father Sun slipped out of sight beneath the horizon. Nampeyo sat in his usual place beside the fire, his nimble fingers working the wood, carving the delicate head of a thrush. Beside him squatted Sage Flower, watching the carving turn into something beautiful before her very eyes. Even as she continued to plague him with her endless questions, his mind was trying to deal with the fact that Nama and Shala had disappeared.

They would surely be found, Nampeyo consoled himself, just as he had consoled Eric. Meanwhile, he must use all his mental capabilities to find another way to placate the desert clan so that Nama need not be sacrificed.

Would Standing Wolf be willing to forget the marriage if the Eagle Clan agreed to share the hunting grounds on the Mesa? Surely they would be willing to do so if the reason they had given Shu—the desire to unite the two clans in order to extend both people's hunting grounds—was a true one.

Would the elders agree to such a thing? Nampeyo knew they were cautious, would be watching him closely for a while, weighing each decision he made. And that was only right. He was young. As yet untried.

Dare he even try to find a way out for Nama? Would it not undermine his own position?

Even as the thought occurred, he quickly dismissed it. He would do everything in his power to stop such a marriage from taking place. The thought of Nama at the mercy of Standing Wolf made him shudder.

Nampeyo had seen the way she cringed with fear when he told her of the council's decision. He had wanted to tell her of the decree himself and assure her in the same breath that he would not allow such a thing to happen. But he was not given a chance. Nama had been summoned before the elders and told that the marriage would take place as promised.

Since then, Nampeyo had not laid eyes on her.

"Nampeyo, why does Father Sun have to sleep if he is so powerful?" Sage Flower's voice intruded on his thoughts.

He looked at the little girl. "Father Sun must sleep so the creatures who depend on the night for cover can hunt for their meals," he replied.

"Like Sister Owl and Brother Fox?" she asked.

"Yes. And Brother Coon and Brother Ring-tailed Cat," he replied, turning the carving over in his hand to chip away at the underside of a wing. "Without the night to cover them they would be eaten by larger animals. Then the food chain would be broken."

"Why?"

"If Sister Owl did not eat the crickets there would be too many crickets. They would eat all the corn in the fields, and we would have none to make our bread." The little girl already knew what it meant to be without bread in the winter when game was scarce. Although she was only three, she still remembered the hunger that plagued her belly during the long cold. "You can see how important it is for Sister Owl to be able to hunt. It is also true of the other animals. They have a purpose in the spiral of life. If they cannot serve that purpose, then all human creatures will suffer."

"If we could–" She broke off suddenly, staring

beyond Nampeyo's shoulder with a wide-eyed look.

Nampeyo turned to see the golden-haired Viking approaching with a scowl on his face. "Run along, Sage Flower," he said gently. "We will speak more of the spiral of life later."

Silently, still staring at Eric, she scuttled away, hurrying toward the rooms she shared with her family.

"You did not find them?" Nampeyo asked, knowing the answer before it came.

"No. But we found something else," Eric said grimly. "I think you are on the point of being attacked."

"Attacked? By whom?"

"Flying Eagle called them the Desert Clan. He sent me to warn you."

"They must have come for Nama," Nampeyo said grimly. "But they are here early. We did not expect them yet." He sighed and pushed himself to his feet. "I must think of a way to tell them about Nama. They are expecting a wedding celebration."

"I think not," Eric said shortly. "From the looks of them, they have come for another purpose."

"What other purpose could they have?"

"Perhaps they want the mesa."

"They expect to have access to our hunting grounds after the marriage takes place."

"I think they are after more than access," Eric said. "They are carrying their weapons with them."

"They will not bring them to the village. It

would be an act of war to do so. They will leave their weapons elsewhere."

"I think not," Eric said again. "They were hiding their weapons within their clothing as we observed them. It looks as though they intend to attack when they gain access to your city."

"This cannot be!" Nampeyo exclaimed. "You are sure about this?"

"Yes."

"It is good we were forewarned. Now we can be ready for them." He eyed Eric. "You will fight with us?"

"I am not interested in your fight," Eric said grimly. "I need to find Shala before she comes to harm. But I need a good tracker to go with me, and Jumping Hare refuses to accompany me until you bless his journey."

"I cannot send him away while the village is in danger. We will need every man here to defend our home and families."

"If I fight with you, will you lend me the tracker?" Eric asked.

"Yes. Jumping Hare can go if he survives the fight and if the spirit world approves that decision."

"Thor's teeth!" Eric exclaimed. "Shala is in terrible danger and still you must consult with the spirits! I should have known you would take that stand. What else could I expect from a people ruled completely by superstition!"

Nampeyo would have laughed if the situation had not been so grave. How could Eric make rude comments about superstition when his own people were ruled over by so many different gods—all of them vengeful?

He watched the Viking stalk away from the cliff city, wondering if he would wait to see if the spirit world looked on the journey with favor.

Cold sweat beaded Shala's forehead as she stared up into the night, where Moon Woman hung among the Blessed Star People. If the red-haired warrior had not stopped the brutal attack on her by his fellow clansman, her spirit would surely have gone to live among the Star People even if her body had remained on this earth.

The nightmarish assault was still before her, and her body shook uncontrollably at the memory. She could feel her attacker's fists pummeling her flesh, could smell the scent of him in her nostrils.

She squeezed her eyes shut, an icy chill sweeping over her. His manhood had been probing between her legs when the leader—Red Fox—had called a halt to the brutality.

Her ears rang with the pounding of her blood. Her heart began to thud with dreaded remembrance. She squeezed her hands into fists, strained her muscles against her bonds.

She had to escape. Must get away. But how?

She was bound so tightly that her hands had grown numb from lack of circulation. She fought against tears that threatened to choke her.

Eric! she silently cried, as she had done so many times before. *Eric! Help me!*

Even as she beseeched her love, she knew it was in vain. There was no one to help her! Even her spirit guide, Wolf, had deserted her.

Twenty

Eric was deeply troubled when he left the cliff city and climbed the ladder leading to the mesa above. Troubled and indecisive. He was no tracker, had missed the sign found by Jumping Hare, so how could he possibly follow a trail that had long since gone cold?

He needed Jumping Hare! Eric was certain of that, just as he was sure that Shala was in danger. But what kind of danger? he wondered. Was she threatened by man? Was she held at bay by predators? Perhaps it was only her surroundings that presented the danger. Whatever it was, she needed help. He was positive of that!

Something nagged at the corners of his mind, begging to be recognized but he was unable to grasp it. What was it? he wondered. If he could figure it out would he know where Shala was? Would he know why she had left?

His fingers curled tightly as he reached the top of the ladder, clenching into fists. She would not have left voluntarily. Not after joining with him in such a manner. He knew he was not mistaken in thinking that had been an act of love.

That left him with only one conclusion.

Shala had not left voluntarily. She had been forcibly taken from him.

But by whom?

Stalking Coyote? No. The man was in the village, and if he had stolen Shala he would be with her.

Eric had turned his steps toward the small cave he shared with Shala when he heard a shout coming from the north. "Shala," he muttered, spinning on his heels and hurrying toward the sound.

Hope swelled within his chest. Hope that his fears were all for nothing. The hope died quickly when another yell sounded, quickly followed by a shriek of pain.

He crashed madly through the brush as he hurried toward the cries, realizing it was the sounds of battle that he was hearing. There was no longer any doubt in Eric's mind about which road to travel. Shala's people were threatened by Standing Wolf and his warriors. She would not want him to abandon them in their time of need. And, even as he drew his sword and joined the battle, he wondered if the desert clan was responsible for her disappearance.

Shala pushed her tongue against the front tooth Hooked Nose had loosened with his fist and felt it move. If the blow had not been a glancing one, she was sure the tooth would have fallen out. She had not been so lucky with her left eye. It was swollen shut now. Still, she reminded herself, it could have been worse. He might have closed both her eyes before he stopped beating her. Or he might have kicked her in the stomach instead of her ribs.

She was lucky to be alive, lucky to feel her babe moving inside her belly.

Shala looked up at Sister Moon with her one good eye. The round, yellow ball hung still in the night sky above them. Shala imagined there was sorrow in that yellow face, sorrow that her sisters could be treated in such a manner by her brothers.

The Blessed Star People—the souls that had already departed this world—twinkled down at Shala, seeming to offer encouragement, assuring her that things would soon be better.

Or was it only Shala's imagination that made her think in such a manner? Imagination and a way of life?

She turned her head slightly, wincing from the soreness in her neck where Hooked Nose's fingers had dug into her flesh. On the other side of the fire the warriors lay sleeping. The sight of Hooked Nose enraged her.

How dare he abuse her in such a manner! She was not a woman who would be subservient to a man's needs, not a woman who had no recourse except to tolerate whatever man decreed.

No!

Shala hunted for herself, supplied herself with both meat and hides. She had learned to protect herself from man and beast. She was equal to any man.

What then, was she doing lying here, tied up like a pig waiting for slaughter?

Grimly, she lifted her hands to her mouth and, with her teeth, tugged at the leather thongs binding them. Very soon she learned that she could not bite through the restraints. They were too strong, too thick.

Undeterred, she wriggled around, moving as silently as a tree lizard, pushing herself to a sitting position, and sending her sweeping gaze around her as she searched for something—some way—to free herself.

Her gaze passed over Nama, sleeping soundly despite the danger that surrounded them. It stopped on the spear beside the firepit ringed with stones. Shala's one good eye widened. The enemy had been careless, leaving the weapon unguarded.

She knew from its size—shorter than the average one—that the weapon belonged to her. She knew, as well, that the spearhead was sharp. Had she not taken the time to put a keen edge on it? She could put that edge to good use now. If she could just reach it, she could slice through her bindings with it.

Her heart thudded rapidly as, using her bound hands for lifting power, she inched her way toward the fire. Her progress was painfully slow. Her aim was to get there without making a sound.

Cra-a-ack!

The sound came out of nowhere, startling her

with its sharpness, freezing her body as though it had been turned to solid ice. Her heart picked up speed, seeming to jerk rapidly about within the confines of her rib cage like a trapped creature intent on escape.

Her gaze sought the enemy again; she waited breathlessly for them to awaken. They remained unmoving, silent and motionless, obviously unaware of anything out of the ordinary.

Releasing the breath that she had been holding captive, Shala continued her silent journey toward the firepit and the spear that lay just beyond.

Time ceased to exist for her. She had no idea how long it took before she reached the weapon, but she finally had it in her grasp.

Then, wedging it between two rocks, she worked the leather bindings across the edge of the tip, uncaring of the flesh she scraped in her attempt to free herself. Her progress was agonizingly slow, but the bindings finally yielded to the sharpness and separated.

Elation flowed through her.

She had done it! She was free!

It took only moments to cut away the bindings on her ankles and less time to reach Nama. After putting a cautionary hand over the other girl's mouth so she could not scream, Shala shook her awake.

"Ummmmph!" Nama grunted, her eyes widening in terror. The fear faded away to confusion when she recognized her friend. Only then did Shala remove her hand from Nama's mouth.

"Quiet!" Shala commanded fiercely.

Nama nodded. She turned her head quickly toward the sleeping warriors. It took only moments to cut away Nama's bindings. When she was free, Shala turned her attention to the men who had thought to hold them captive.

Her eyes glittered with vengeance, and her mouth thinned grimly as her fingers tightened around the rounded spear shaft. She would make the enemy pay dearly for their misdeeds. She would see them all dead.

Her feet crunched on gravel as she started toward them again. She froze, waiting for the shout that would tell her they had awakened.

Silence.

"No!" The word uttered with such passion by Nama was yet spoken so quietly that Shala's ears barely caught it. She met the eyes of her childhood friend; realized that Nama was right. She dared not seek retribution for their treatment. One slip on her part, one voice uttering a warning to the others, would surely prevent their escape.

She stood motionless, poised on the balls of her feet, still hesitating, torn between an overwhelming urge to slice the throat of Hooked Nose, the man who had so brutally attacked her, and an overpowering need to put as much distance between their captors and themselves as possible.

A turning-over feeling in her stomach made her aware of her unborn child at the same time Nama clasped firm fingers on her elbow and urged her toward the dense forest of pine. Shala allowed herself to be persuaded, realizing she had little choice in the matter. She could throw away her own life for revenge, but not that of her unborn child. Nor could she deliberately subject Nama to further danger.

Lowering her spear, Shala followed Nama to the sheltering pines. They left the camp on stealthy feet, leaving their packs behind them, knowing that any undue noise would wake the men.

Bull Elk, the man Shala thought of as Hooked Nose, had wakened abruptly at the first sign of noise when Shala was still trying to reach the spear beside the fire. At first he had kept silent because he wanted to watch her attempts to free herself, intended to taunt her the moment she realized she was unable to do so. To his surprise, she had cut herself free. He would have stopped her at that point, but decided, since she hurried straight to her friend, that he would allow the both of them a moment or two of freedom before sounding the alarm. Then, with all as witness, Bull Elk would accuse Red Fox of being careless. When the elders of the tribe were told of the incident, they would surely realize that Bull Elk was a better choice for leader than the warrior with red hair.

He was ready to call out when both girls were free, but something stopped him. Another idea that he liked even better. Red Fox would be discredited, even if the girls were still in camp, but he was still the leader and his command must be obeyed for the duration of the journey. That meant Bull Elk would be forced to leave the girls alone.

A grin slowly spread across Bull Elk's face as another idea began to take form. Suppose he allowed the girls to go free, to escape the camp . . . and then, when they least expected it, caught them off guard and took them captive again. Only this time there would be no Red Fox to interfere with his plans. He could use them for his own purposes with no interference from anyone. Use them . . . for the rest of their lives.

He wondered how long they would be able to survive what he had in mind for them.

A low moaning alerted Shala to Wind Woman's restless state. The sound was followed by icy fingers trailing along her flesh and a definite darkening of the shadowy world around them.

Shala stumbled over a fallen log, then threw a quick look at the sky. Storm clouds were gathering there. Already they covered the faces of the Blessed Star People. All too soon they would cover the face of Sister Moon as well, would stop her from sending the pale light that allowed the two fleeing girls to find their way.

"We must hurry," Shala said sharply. "Soon the path will be too dark to travel."

Shala forced herself to the edge of endurance as she jumped over sage and other obstacles, fully aware of the risks of running too fast through unknown territory. Pain stabbed through her sore ribs with each step she took. Her starved lungs fought for air. The back of her throat burned hot and dry and her tongue stuck to the roof of her mouth when she tried to swallow. The tremble of fatigue lay just beyond the threshold of her exertion. That point was finally reached when they came across a stream.

Wading out into thigh-deep water, Shala sank into its icy depths, aware of Nama stopping beside her. "Are you all right, Shala?" she asked.

"Yes," Shala muttered.

"The water is cold. You should not cover yourself with it."

"It feels good against my bruises, and my body heat will soon dry my clothing," Shala replied. She peered at the distant shore, studied the dense shadows there. The thicker ones must be bushes and trees, she decided, barely able to make them out.

"It is getting darker," Nama said fearfully. "A storm is brewing and we must find shelter from it."

"No," Shala contradicted. "Rain will cover our tracks." She peered at the farthest bank. "We must take precautions even if it rains, Nama. The ground looks soft over there. I think it would be better to wade upstream until we find rocky ground. That way, if the people from the north pursue us, they will have trouble finding our tracks."

"Do you think they will come after us?"

The memory of Hooked Nose's face formed Shala's answer. "Yes. They will come."

"What will we do against so many?"

"Whatever we must."

Silently, they resumed their journey, wading upstream for a long while until they found a suitable place to leave the water. Then they continued on, traveling without words, saving their breath for climbing since the trail they were on circled higher and higher into the mountains.

The rain that had threatened held off, and the clouds slowly thinned, then completely disappeared. By the time the sun peeped over the horizon, topping the pine trees with a glorious burst of color, Shala felt unable to take another step.

She must find a place to hide from their enemies. A place where she could keep watch on their back trail while they rested.

"Do you think they know we are gone yet?" Nama inquired fearfully.

"They know," Shala replied. "Their leader would have had them up before daybreak. They are surely searching for us now, but they will not find our trail an easy one to follow."

A grin spread across her face as she imagined her captors' consternation when they woke to find the girls gone. The grin faded when she realized they would be swarming after the two girls like angry bees after a bear that has found their beehive.

"We cannot continue to travel at this pace," Shala said. "We must find a place to hide from them."

"But . . . you said the water would hide our trail from them," Nama protested. "And was that not why we left the stream across the rocks? So the water would dry and they would not be able to find our tracks?"

"It will only work for a while," Shala replied. "If they search both ways—and they surely will—they will come to the conclusion that we used the rocks to deceive them."

"Why would they think that?" Nama asked.

"The absence of tracks will give us away."

"Then they will find us," Nama said.

"Do not be so easily discouraged," Shala urged. "We will outwit them."

"How?"

"That is something I do not know. But believe me, Nama, we *will* find a way."

"They have our food and water, and we have none."

"We cannot allow that to stop us," Shala snapped, wishing Nama would show a little more courage. She tilted her head back and looked up the mountain toward the snowline. "There will be water up there," she said in a softer voice. "And there will also be caves where we can hide ourselves from our enemies."

Although the air was chill, there was evidence of spring all around them. Already they could see green shoots bursting through the ground where the snow had melted, and Shala knew there would be edible roots somewhere beneath.

They continued their circling path up the mountain, stopping every little while to check the trail behind them. Even though it remained empty, Shala was still worried. She had a deep premonition that their escape had been too easy, that they would soon find themselves captives again.

Twenty-one

All the clans had one thing in common. They avoided fighting while darkness covered the land, believing the soul of any warrior killed during that time would be unable to find its way to the spirit world. That was one reason Standing Wolf chose that particular time for attack. He was confident that he would not be among those killed, and he counted on the element of surprise, as well as fear of being killed at night, to overcome the cliff dwellers.

He counted on too much!

The element of surprise was gone. . . . The quarry had been alerted. And, with the golden-haired stranger fighting beside them, his mighty blade felling anything or anyone that came near to him, the Eagle Clan's fear of the unknown had departed.

Standing Wolf had no way of knowing the cliff dwellers believed Eric to be a spirit in human form. And, to their way of thinking, a spirit who fought beside them would surely call upon other spirits to lead them through the darkness to the Great Beyond should it become necessary.

No. Standing Wolf only knew that he would have called back his warriors if it were at all possible. But it was not. The desert clan were no longer concerned with conquering the mesa and its people. They fought now because they had no other choice. After all, if a warrior finds himself on the blade end of a knife he must do what he can to save his own skin.

When the battle was finally over, and none of the would-be conquerors were left standing, Eric searched among the dead and dying until he found one body that still contained a breath of life. He knelt beside the warrior, meeting the eyes of the dying man.

"The women," Eric growled. "What have you done with them?"

Although pain wracked the desert warrior's features, his eyes were glazed, uncomprehending, and Eric realized the man had little time left on this earth. Had he not understood the question, Eric wondered, or was the dying man too far gone to answer?

A movement in his peripheral vision brought his gaze around, and he saw Flying Eagle approaching. Eric beckoned him over. "I think he cannot understand my way of speaking," he said. "Ask him about Shala. Find out where they are being held before he dies."

Flying Eagle pulled his knife from his belt and knelt beside the man, holding his blade in a threatening manner against the other warrior's throat. "Where are the women?" he growled.

"What women?" the desert warrior muttered.

"The women you took captive!" Flying Eagle said harshly, pushing the tip of the blade into the man's throat until beads of blood dotted his skin. "Tell me where they are!"

"We took no women," the wounded man replied, his voice growing weaker all the time. "No women."

"He said they took no women," Flying Eagle told Eric, easing his grip on the man beneath him.

Eric had no need of the explanation. Although the wounded man had seemed not to understand him, Eric had enough knowledge of the Anasazi language to translate the reply. "If he is truthful, then there must be another explanation for their disappearance."

"He would not speak untruths just before joining the spirits," Flying Eagle said, looking at the man who lay unmoving, his eyes closed as though the lids were too heavy to keep open.

Eric looked at the arrow protruding from the warrior's left side. Although there was an enormous amount of blood leaking from the wound, the man might have a chance at recovery. "It may not be a mortal wound. He may not be leaving this world as soon as you think."

A smile quirked Flying Eagle's lips. But it was not a smile of amusement. "There is no doubt about his departure," he said grimly. With a quick, almost casual movement, he dug his blade into the wounded man's throat and sliced the flesh deeply from ear to ear. Then, as though nothing unusual had occurred, he regained his feet and stared toward the eastern horizon where dawn streaked the sky with delicate shades of pink and gold. "Father Sun comes to chase away the lingering shadows. That will make it easier to find the tracks of their passing."

Although Eric heard the other man's words, he remained silent, troubled by the easy way Flying Eagle had disposed of his enemy. He obviously felt no compunction in killing a wounded man, but then why should he? This was a harsh, cruel land, and given the same chance, the man would just as easily have killed the warrior from the Eagle Clan.

Eric's thoughts were troubled as he strode to the edge of the mesa and searched the land below. It was desert, dry and arid, and so alkaline that it was mostly white. Vegetation was sparse there, with only a few sagebrushes and a stubble of desert scrub.

Shala could not be there, he assured himself. Not in that barren land below. She was somewhere on this mesa, unable to reach him for some reason.

Fear shuddered through him as he wondered what that reason could be. Had the desert warrior told the truth? Could Shala have been captured by the desert clan and taken from the mesa before the attack came? That must be so, otherwise, she would have returned home long ago.

A raw and primitive grief overwhelmed him.

Would he ever see her again? The thought that she might be lost to him forever shattered him.

He was drawn from his wretchedness when he heard the sound of approaching footsteps. Spinning on his heel, he saw several warriors approaching. He recognized one of them as Jumping Hare, the tracker.

"Ho-yah!" Flying Eagle greeted them. "Did not our brother, Eric, fight a good battle? Many of the desert people fell beneath his blade." A quick smile split his face. "In the years to come he will father many brave warriors that will strengthen our clan until no enemy will dare attack us again." With those simple words he let his fellow warriors know he believed the Viking was no spirit, that he was a man, not unlike them, who would fight for his people, or, in this case, his adopted people.

His gaze locked on the weapon hanging at Eric's side. "No man who owns a blade such as his need fear any other man."

"The sword is yours if you help me find Shala," Eric said grimly.

Flying Eagle looked startled for a moment, his gaze swinging up to meet the Viking's. "There is no need to bargain away your weapon," he said quietly. "We owe you a great debt for fighting beside us. We stand ready to repay that debt."

A small measure of relief washed over Eric. With the help of the Eagle Clan, he just might be able to follow Shala's trail. "You have my gratitude."

"Do not concern yourself," Flying Eagle said.

"Jumping Hare can follow a trail that no other eyes can see." He motioned toward the tracker who was busy collecting the weapons scattered among the dead. He was a short, skinny, individual who looked as though a stiff wind would blow him over.

As though sensing their eyes upon him, the tracker stood upright and glanced their way, holding Eric's gaze for a long moment. Then, handing the confiscated weapons to the nearest man, he loped away through the scattered junipers.

"Before the fighting began, Jumping Hare found several tracks near the eastern slope of the mesa. He is certain they belong to Nama," Flying Eagle explained. "He has gone there now to search for other signs."

"Good," Eric grunted. "If he is as good a tracker as you say, he will find something there, something to tell us what happened . . . and who captured them."

Flying Eagle's dark eyes flickered, and the Vikings saw something there that made him uneasy. "There will be no tracks except for those of the two girls," the warrior said. "There cannot be."

"How can you know that?"

"Jumping Hare knows. He said the girls travel alone, and they carry supplies with them."

Pain stabbed into Eric, squeezing his gut, coiling it into an agonizing knot while he tried to deal with the knowledge that Shala had not been forced to leave him, but had gone of her own accord.

Why? his heart cried out. *Why would she do such a thing?*

He had no answer that would satisfy his pain. He only knew that she had gone! Shala had run away and left him behind!

Shala and Nama continued following the trail that wound up the side of the mountain. The area they were traveling through now was thickly wooded. Blue spruce and aspen stretched out on both sides of the path, while above them, seeming just out of their reach, billowing white clouds were piled like snowdrifts across Sky Man's bluest cloak.

Slightly below her, Shala could hear the sound of rushing water, and she knew the stream would soon become a raging river as more snow melted farther up.

She grabbed the narrow trunk of a spruce to steady herself and paused to catch her breath, realizing suddenly that it was coming in quick, short bursts, probably caused by the higher elevation.

"Can we stop for a while?" Nama gasped, slumping down on the ground, her back against the trunk of a slender pine. "I think I cannot go another step." Her words were quick, jerky, as though she, too, was having trouble breathing.

"For a few moments," Shala agreed. "But Father Sun is growing tired. He will soon be sleeping, and we must find a place where we will be safe for the night before then." Shala was uneasy.

They could not rest—must not rest—until they found a safe haven.

Were the warriors who had captured them following them now? Or had they given up and continued on their way?

Remembering the promise of retribution in Hooked Nose's eyes, Shala had little doubt that he, at least, was on their trail.

Oh, Spirit Guide, she called silently. *Come to me! Show me a safe haven!*

She looked hopefully for some sign that Wolf had come, but he remained conspicuously absent. Perhaps she just could not see him, she thought.

Her searching gaze swept over the large boulder that nestled against the mountain, and she realized that, from that vantage point, she should be able to see the valley below.

Hurrying to the huge rock, Shala wound her fingers around a protrusion, found a foothold and started the climb upward. Upon reaching the top, she discovered she had an excellent view of the area below, all the way to a clearing on another level below them.

It was a peaceful setting, the ground literally covered with blue columbines, purple mountain laurels and an assortment of pink and red and yellow blossoms that she did not recognize.

Shala stood there for a long moment, admiring the display of color. She was on the point of turning away when a movement somewhere near the edge of the clearing caught her eyes.

She narrowed her gaze, pinpointing the object.

A man.

Her heart gave a jolt of fear. Who was he? Certainly no friend; most likely an enemy. With fast-beating heart, she scrambled down the boulder and hurried to Nama. "We must go now," she said, hoping to keep the fear from her voice.

Apparently she succeeded, for Nama protested loudly. "No, Shala! We have only just stopped. Surely we can take more time to rest. My back hurts and my legs are weary and I am so tired that—"

"Do you wish to become a prisoner again?" The question spewed into the air around them, the words bitter, the tone full of torment.

Nama glanced uneasily behind her and scrambled to her feet. "Someone is coming!" she blurted.

Shala nodded abruptly. "A man follows us."

"Only one?" Hope filled Nama's large, ebony eyes, and she looked at Shala's spear. "Could you use your weapon to kill him?"

"I can do no less than try," Shala replied, her gaze skittering around them, taking in the narrow trail, the lack of a place to hide from the man who pursued them. "But this is not a good place to confront whoever is following us, Nama. It is too open. If my aim is not true, then there will be no way for us to escape his wrath."

She turned and hurried up the trail again, urging the other girl to hurry. Nama did so, moving swiftly at first, then slower until she began to lag behind. Shala became impatient. She knew Nama was tired, because her own back and legs ached with weariness and the spear she carried seemed to bear the weight of a muledeer, but they could not slow down yet. They dared not.

Her heart pumped with exertion, her breathing became labored, coming in short bursts again, but she forced herself to go on, even though the going was harder now, the climb steeper.

Before long they encountered patches of snow that soon became thicker and deeper with each step they took. Soon the snow was thicker than the patches of ground until finally they were crunching through frozen snow that covered the pathway completely.

They made their way gingerly across the slippery surface, climbing higher all the time until they had almost reached the summit. The sound of water below them had become a muted roar when Shala rounded a curve and stopped short, staring in consternation at the path ahead. It had narrowed until it was a mere ledge, no wider than the length of a man's foot.

Shala realized they could not traverse the path any farther, and yet, neither could they go back. She searched for a way out of their predicament.

The mountain rose sheer on their left, while on their right the path fell away to join the creek below them. Its waters were swollen from its banks, and the reason for its condition was apparent. Straight ahead of them torrents of water cascaded down the side of the mountain, plunging over a ledge and into a pool that overflowed its banks and filled the creek below beyond its normal capacity.

Are we trapped here? she silently asked herself.

"What are we going to do?" Nama asked, gripping Shala's arm fearfully, and hugging the cliff behind her.

"I must think of the answer," Shala replied, all the while knowing she could do nothing.

The Wolf Clan was behind them, and the raging torrent and the mountain blocked their path ahead.

There was nothing to do except go back.

Jumping Hare led the others down the mesa to the edge of the plains. There, Flying Eagle called a halt.

"We can go no farther, Eric," he said regretfully. "Even though we defeated the desert clan, we cannot leave the city undefended. We have too many enemies who would take such an opportunity to attack our homes."

"Then I must go on alone," Eric said wearily.

"Not alone," Flying Eagle said. "Jumping Hare will go with you. Nampeyo instructed him to follow the trail. To find Nama and take her home."

"And Shala?" Eric questioned. "Has he no instructions about her?"

"None. Shala may go or stay as she desires. She has earned that right. But Nama must be brought back. She is bound to the Eagle Clan. She must return to her People."

Eric's expression was grim as he watched the men leave. Now there was only he and Jumping Hare were left to follow the trail the two girls had left behind.

The Viking tried to empty his mind of thoughts of Shala, tried to concentrate his efforts instead on following a trail that was barely visible to him, but it was hard to do. Despite his efforts, her face kept appearing in his mind's eye. He remembered the way her lips would quirk whenever she was amused, remembered the way her dark lashes would sweep down across her cheekbones when she tried to hide her expressive eyes from him.

He could not lose her! He must not!

Even now, Eric refused to admit to the depth of feeling he had for the wild, untamed girl of the Eagle Clan. He only knew that she could not escape him. He would follow her to the ends of the earth if necessary. And he would bring her back, would keep her in chains if he must, would do anything that was required to keep her by his side.

Lost in his misery, Eric had followed along behind Jumping Hare, stopping when the tracker needed to examine the ground closer, then loping along behind him when the man from the Eagle Clan had satisfied himself they were still on the trail.

It was one such time, when the tracker was kneeling beside several tracks, that Eric noticed a worried look on the other man's face.

"What is wrong?" Eric questioned sharply.

"A small band of warriors found the trail left by the girls. See!" Jumping Hare directed Eric's attention to several tracks that seemed fresher than the others. "They are Wolf Clan."

"How can you tell?"

Jumping Hare pointed to several round indentations, deeper than the rest of the print. "The women of the Wolf Clan sew colored beads around the heels of the warrior's moccasins. They leave a print like that."

Eric hated to ask, but knew he must have an answer to the question that plagued him. "Are the Wolf Clan friends of the Eagle Clan?"

Instead of answering the question, Jumping Hare asked one of his own. "Is the hawk friend to the rabbit?"

Raw with tension, his nerves stretched almost to the point of breaking, Eric loped along beside Jumping Hare as they followed the tracks of the warriors of the Wolf Clan and the two girls. Eric refused to allow himself to dwell on what was happening to Shala. Whatever it was, he would deal with it whenever he found her. If he found her alive . . .

Twenty-two

Shala led the way back down the trail, her eyes darting here and there, searching frantically for some way out of the trap they were in. When she first saw the split in the face of the cliff, she was unaware of its possibilities. It was only a narrow gap partially hidden by a scraggly juniper that grew in a place where there was not enough soil to sustain any other plant.

Pushing aside the lower branches of the juniper, Shala peered into the knee-high crevice. The gray light extended several feet, then darkened considerably, preventing her from seeing the end of the passage.

Could they hide from their enemies inside? Was it wide enough to allow them to enter? It seemed a dubious haven at best, but it was the only chance they had.

With fast beating heart, Shala shoved her head and shoulders inside, measuring the width of the passage with her eyes. Although they were both slender, neither Nama's shoulders nor her own would fit through. But if they turned sideways it just might work.

She strained her eyes, trying again to determine the length of the passage, but the shadowy darkness prevented her from doing so.

Never mind, she consoled herself. The split went deep enough to hide them from the eyes of their enemies, and a few feet within, it became a little higher and wider.

"Snala." Nama pulled at her shoulder. "What have you found? Is it a way out?"

Shala pulled back from the hole and looked up at her friend. "Perhaps," she replied. "There is no way of knowing how far the split goes. It is too dark in there to see."

"We are going inside?" Nama's voice quivered slightly. "Will the man who follows us be so easily fooled? Will he not search for us until he finds the gap in the rocks? You found it quite easily, Shala. Could he not do so as well?"

"If he looks," Shala replied. "So we must take care that he does not search for us. We must make it appear we have fallen over the edge of the cliff."

"How can we do that?" Nama asked quickly. "You have a plan?"

"Yes," Shala assured the other girl. "We will go back up the path until we reach the widest place—you know, just before the pathway narrows so sharply. We will stomp heavily as we go. That way our footprints will be plain for him to see." Her voice became tinged with scorn. "Even a fool such as Hooked Nose would be unable to miss the sign we will leave on the ground."

"Do not underestimate that man, Shala." She looked pointedly at Shala's bruises. "He is cruel, but hardly a fool."

"He is a fool!" Shala spat out. "We walked out of the enemy camp as easily as a duck glides through water. Only a fool would allow us to do so."

"Then there were as many fools in that camp as there are fingers on my hand," Nama said with a wide grin. "For none of the Wolf band woke when we left."

"They are all fools," Shala said grimly. "All of them."

"All of the Wolf Clan?" Nama raised an inquiring eyebrow. "How can you condemn a whole clan without prior knowledge of them?"

"Not the whole clan. Just the men. All men." Her words sounded bitter, as were her thoughts, for they had returned to her reason for being here in the first place.

Eric.

He was the reason she had left the mesa.

It was because of her golden-haired Viking that she was in this mess. Him and his strange, savage customs.

Shala felt a quick movement in her belly as though her anger had unsettled the babe nestled there. She forced herself to forget Eric, to concentrate instead on covering their trail.

Nama followed her instructions exactly and the girls returned to the end of the trail, where several large rocks that had fallen from the top of the mountain were balanced precariously. Shala pointed to a particularly large rock and said, "Help me move that one, Nama. If we get behind it and push hard, it should roll over the edge of the cliff. Make sure you step on the rocks though." She pointed the way. "Hooked Nose must believe the rockslide was an accident."

Taking care where they stepped, the two girls pushed and shoved, straining their muscles and backs, trying to budge the large rock that seemed immovable. Beads of sweat popped out on Shala's forehead, caused by the effort she expended, but the rock remained immobile, seeming to be frozen to the spot.

"It is no use," Nama finally said. "We cannot move it."

"Yes, we can!" Shala snapped, then was instantly sorry. "We can do it," she said in a kinder tone of voice. "We must do it, Nama. Our lives depend upon it." She bunched her muscles again, putting everything she had into the effort. "Shove!" she grunted.

Did the rock shift ever so slightly, Shala wondered. "Again," she grunted, straining against the massive boulder. The rock gave slightly, then seemed to shiver. Then it rolled, stopping after a quarter turn. "It moved!" she cried, elation surging forth. "Do it again!" Gritting her teeth and setting her jaw, she pushed with all her might. The rock turned again, then rolled another quarter, stopped and quivered, then rolled again gathering momentum as it went, carrying along smaller rocks and debris that lay in its path.

"We did it!" Nama cried, throwing her arms around her friend and jumping excitedly from one foot to another. "Do you see it, Shala? We did it! We actually did it!"

With their arms around each other, they watched the boulder go over the edge, breaking off a good part of the ledge as it went.

Crash!

The sound of the boulder reaching the canyon floor echoed through the mountains. Realizing the man following them might very well have heard it, they knew there was little time to spare. They began the second part of their plan, stepping backward in their own footprints until they finally reached the juniper that covered the split in the cliff. After checking for any telltale sign and deciding there was nothing to give them away, Shala urged Nama into the crack, then followed her, pulling several fallen branches behind her and wedging them into the entrance, hoping there would be nothing left to give away their presence to the man who followed them.

As the dead branches covered the entrance, the interior became darker, the shadows thicker around them.

Realizing they must get as far away from the entrance as possible lest the very breath that left their bodies give away their presence, Shala urged her friend farther down the passage.

"How far must we go?" Nama asked.

"As far as we can," Shala replied.

Their feet crunched over a heavy carpet of leaves, and Shala knew they must hurry, must put as much distance between them and the exit and their pursuer as possible.

Suddenly Nama seemed to lose her balance momentarily and flung out both hands to steady herself against the rock walls.

"Is that the end of the passage?" Shala whispered, casting a quick look behind her toward the entrance.

"No," the other girl replied. "It seems to go on, but it makes a bend here."

"Go on!" Shala said urgently. "Maybe there is another way out."

"I cannot," Nama replied. "The rocks are too slippery ahead. There must be water seeping in from somewhere."

Shala strained her eyes to see in the shadowy darkness. Was there a trace of light coming from ahead of them? If so there must be another exit ahead. Hope beat strong in her breast as she gripped Nama's arm.

The passage had widened at this point until there was room enough for Shala to pass. "Press as close as you can against the rock wall," she whispered. "Let me in front so I can lead the way."

It was a tight squeeze, hard to make with both of them on their haunches, but the feat was finally accomplished. Although Shala found the rock slippery, there were places where she could gain a firm foothold. She edged around the bend and her eyes widened slightly, traveling around the enclosure. It was a large space, about the width of two men placed side by side. And it was high, so high that ten men might stand atop each other and still not reach the crack at the top that allowed sunlight to filter through. It was a good hiding place she had found. It would shelter them until the man who pursued them had made his departure.

"Come on," Shala urged. "This is a good place to rest. We will be safe here."

Nama followed her into the chamber and the two girls dropped to the ground. Shala's fingers loosened around her spear, and she laid it beside her and let her head slump against the rock wall. "We will be safe here," she said again, trying to convince herself she was right.

Her heart slowed its heavy pounding as she began to relax slightly, and she became aware of another noise . . . a dull roaring that was somewhere not too distant. She knew instantly what she was hearing.

The waterfall.

She felt grateful for the sound, knew it should cover any noise they might inadvertently make. But it had its downside too. It would also cover the approach of their enemy if he found their hiding place. If they could not hear him, they would not know when he came or when he departed.

That worried her more than she cared to admit. They had been through so much already; yet there would surely be more perils unless they found a safe haven, a place that was hidden well enough so that no others would ever find them.

Was there such a place? she wondered uneasily. There had to be, otherwise everything she had been through, the pain of leaving those she loved—the Viking . . . her mother—would all have been for nothing.

A deep sense of loneliness washed over her as she thought of Eric. She would never see him again, never feel his warm embrace. Her eyes welled with tears, but she blinked them away furiously, remembering the child nestled within her belly. It was foolish to cry over what must be! she chided herself. But even though her mind approved of her actions, her heart sang a different song.

Eric! Oh, Eric, my love! Life will be endless without you by my side!

Cold rage washed over Bull Elk when he reached the broken ledge and realized what had happened. His quarry had been within reach. They could have gone no farther. Now, because of a freak accident, because they had been careless, they had escaped by falling into a chasm.

He peered over the edge, saw the boulder that had obviously broken apart on the bottom of the chasm so far below him. Although he could see no sign of the two girls, he knew they must be there, probably crushed beneath the rocks. There was certainly no way they could have survived such a fall.

Raising his head, he bellowed out his rage, curling his fingers tight as eagle talons gripping the rock of a precarious roost.

The sound struck the mountain across from him and reverberated, echoing over and over again until he had completely spent his fury and nothing remained except his overwhelming disappointment at the loss of the girls from the Eagle Clan.

Bull Elk turned to go, then stopped abruptly, his gaze fixed on the place where the boulder had originally rested. Something about it bothered him. How had it come to fall from that position? What had caused it to move?

He bent over the ground and studied it closer. The sign was there, plain enough for a child to read. Perhaps that was what bothered him. Almost as though it had been deliberately made to set him off the trail.

But that was inconceivable. His quarry were only women. Young girls who had barely reached womanhood. They would have no knowledge of signs . . . of hiding trails to fool their enemies.

Would they?

Bending over the rocky ground, he studied the tracks at length, but try as he would, he could make nothing else out of them. The two girls had traveled this far and were attempting to go around the curve when they dislodged a boulder.

See, an inner voice chided. *Look where it lay. See how their attempts to pass the rock disturbed it and sent it rolling toward the edge!*

Yes. He did see. Still, something disturbed him.

He worried over the tracks as he turned to go

back down the mountain. It was near dark. Father Sun was in a hurry now, anxious to seek his rest, and Bull Elk knew he should do the same. But perhaps he would not go far, he decided. Perhaps he would camp at the bottom of the trail. If the sign had been deliberately put there for him to read—if the two girls were actually knowledgeable about such things—then they would still be trapped, because they could not go farther on the ledge. Their only recourse would be to descend the mountain again.

Yes, he thought with great satisfaction. If they were still alive, he would soon have them in hand. Then they would learn the price of crossing him.

Twenty-three

Shala scrambled through the split in the rock, feeling a sense of urgency brought on by fear. She was conscious of her thudding heart, knew that something terrible followed close behind her but was unable to see whatever it was, could not even determine whether it was man or beast.

Eric, *she screamed, but curiously, no sound left her throat.* Help me, Eric! *Again, there was no sound save the heavy beating of her heart. What had happened to her voice? Why could she not call out for help? Even now the dark presence loomed closer. She knew it, could feel it . . . only a few feet distant.*

She must find Eric! Only he could save her!

Suddenly, in the blink of an eye, the scene changed. Shala was no longer in the crevice, instead, she was running through a dark forest, running with stumbling feet over moss that gave beneath her bare feet, running toward a sunshiny glade where no evil would dare to follow.

Her heart filled with gladness. She would be safe there. But even as she reassured herself, she became aware of the coalescing darkness behind her again. It had found her, a pulsating, mass of evil that sought to keep her from sunshine.

Her heart pumped madly as fingers of darkness began to surround her, clutching at her clothing, ripping at her flesh. She would not make it.

Eric! She struggled again to vocalize the name, but as before, there was only silence. That terrible, tormenting silence, broken only by the heavy pounding of her own heart. She struggled to gain release from the coalescing evil, felt her clothing tear as she ripped free. Just a few more feet and she would reach the safety of the golden, sunshiny glade that beckoned, the glade that promised safety.

She dashed toward it, her legs moving with the swiftness of a land turtle. Why could she not gain any speed? her mind screamed. Although her movements seemed to be in slow motion, her breathing was spasmodic, coming in short, gasping bursts.

Nearly there! she silently cried. Almost there! The darkness was breathing down her neck again. She had to run faster, must do it, must do it, must do it!

Then suddenly, Shala was there, bursting through the shadows into the golden glade. . . . And there was Eric, standing near the edge of a pool of water that was fed by an enchanted waterfall.

As though he had been expecting her, he beckoned with his hand, smiling an invitation.

Incredible joy washed over Shala, and she unfastened her hide dress and allowed it to fall carelessly at her feet. Eric was here, his gaze caressing the intimate curves of her breasts before moving lower to dwell on the shapely curves of her hips. Shala's heart thudded with pleasure . . . and something else, something barely remembered.

When she recognized the feeling as dread, she wondered at it. Why should she feel so when Eric was nearby, waiting with outstretched hand for her to join him in that peaceful pool with water cascading so gently–

No! Her mind recoiled in horror. The water was not peaceful! It roared, tumbled and roiled. It was turbulent and stormy and dark, and Eric must get out at once before it swallowed him.

Eric? Can you not see the evil around you? Oh, Great Spirit! She had forgotten the evil! Lost in Eric's eyes, she had forgotten that it followed so close behind her! Now it was too late to escape. . . . Too late . . .

Shala woke abruptly from the nightmare, almost overcome with fear. It washed over her in torrents. It made the fine hairs on the back of her neck stand up. Where was she? What had awakened her so abruptly?

Feeling completely disoriented, her pulse throbbing and her heart pounding, she pushed herself to her elbows and tried to penetrate the blackness surrounding her, but that was impossible because the darkness was absolute.

The heavy drumming in her ears continued. Was her heart still pounding so heavily? It sounded like a dull roar instead of a heartbeat.

Becoming aware of hard edges beneath her buttocks, she ran a hand over the floor. Rocks. Instead of her sleeping mat, she lay on a bed of rocks. Why was she–?

Suddenly, memory slammed into her brain and

she knew exactly where she was, but that knowledge did nothing to lessen her fear.

How long had she slept? she wondered. And had their plan worked? Had they succeeded in fooling the man who pursued them? Would it be safe to leave the small cave now?

Suddenly, Shala felt an awful emptiness inside and knew it for what it was. Hunger. "Be patient, little one," she muttered, rubbing a light hand across her belly. "You must wait awhile for your meal."

Shala's gaze probed the area again. Was the darkness a shade lighter, perhaps not quite so thick, directly above her? Yes, she was almost certain of it. There was a soft gray light filtering through from somewhere above.

It must be early morn, and if that were true, it was past time they went on their way.

Crawling over to the other girl, Shala called her name. "Nama," she whispered. "Wake up. We must go now."

Nama remained still, unmoving.

Shala reached out, intending to wake the other girl, but stopped suddenly, wondering again what had awakened her so abruptly. Had there been some kind of noise? Her heart gave a sudden jerk. Had their pursuer found their hiding place? Was he, even now, working his way down the crevice toward them?

She strained her eyes, trying to penetrate the shadowy darkness, but again, to no avail.

Perhaps she should not wake Nama just yet. The girl might cry out in fear, and if the man who followed them was still around, any sound might give away their position.

No. Leave Nama sleeping while you look for danger, an inner voice warned.

Shala listened to the voice of caution and slowly retraced her steps along the crack until she had almost reached the end of the tunnel. And there, only a few feet inside the entrance, she paused to listen for any sound that would give away the presence of her enemy. But it was useless, she now realized. The roar of the waterfall that she had mistaken for her fearful heartbeat covered any other sound.

Cautiously, Shala poked her head outside and peered down the trail leading off the mountain. Her heart skipped a beat. Nothing. She looked the other way. Still nothing. Slowly, a grin spread across her face.

They had escaped him!

Elated, her gaze slid along the path directly in front of her, and she was on the point of exiting the crevice when she saw moccasin-clad feet standing near the edge of the canyon.

Oh, Great Creator! It was him! Hooked Nose! It had to be him!

She covered her mouth to stifle the gasp that would have given away her presence and jerked her head back into the crevice and waited there, her heart pounding with fear.

What could she do now? They were trapped!

Hiding her face in her hands, fearing that at any moment she would do something—make some sound—that would alert Hooked Nose to her presence, Shala slowly, cautiously, worked her way back to the small chamber where she had left Nama.

What could they do now? she wondered. With Hooked Nose waiting outside the crevice, there was no escape.

Eric, she silently cried. *Help me, Eric! My spirit guide has deserted me and I am alone!*

Eric! Help me, Eric!

With the words still echoing in his mind, Eric fought his way from the cobwebs of sleep. It had been a sleep of complete exhaustion that had befuddled his brain and had him seeking the girl who had cried out to him even while he realized that she was not with him. He knew he was not really hearing her. Not with his ears. No! It was his heart that continually listened, his mind that told him of her danger, and he was certain in every fiber of his being, everything combined that made up the whole man—his vital organs, his bones, his flesh and his blood—that he would shrivel up and die if he lost her.

Feeling it urgent that he continue on, he leapt to his feet and nudged Jumping Hare. "Get up!" he growled. "It is past time we left!"

Jumping Hare's eyes snapped open as swiftly as Eric's own had. He stared up at Eric for a moment, and something flickered in his dark eyes—something very much like animosity. Then, as quickly as it had come, it was gone. Heaving a deep sigh, Jumping Hare pushed himself upright, then dropped to his haunches with a groan, rubbing his right ankle with both palms.

Eric frowned down at him. "What is wrong?" He realized the situation even as he asked the question. The tracker had stepped into a gopher hole yesterday and had finished the day out with a decided limp although he had uttered no word of complaint.

The Viking stooped over the other man and examined the injured ankle. It was swollen to twice its normal size. "You cannot walk on this," he said. "You will have to stay behind." Although he spoke calmly, Eric was worried about leaving Jumping Hare. Not because he thought harm would befall him—the man, although thin and wiry, had proven he could take care of himself—but because Eric's tracking skills were not equal to those of the man from the Eagle Clan. Still, he had no choice. He must go on without Jumping Hare, because Shala needed him now. Right at this very moment. Eric knew he was not imagining things. She was in danger, and she had cried out to him for help.

Eric looked toward the northern horizon, then back to the other man. "You understand that I have no choice. I must go on, Jumping Hare. Shala is out there somewhere . . . facing something terrible."

"Go," Jumping Hare muttered, settling down again. "Do not trouble yourself about me, Eric. Our water guts are both almost full. Mine will last until I am able to travel, and there is enough dried meat to keep me from starving." When Eric still hesitated, Jumping Hare picked up a thin stick and made several marks upon the ground with it. "Look here, Eric," he said, pointing to several wavy lines. "You will save time if you ignore the tracks and head straight for this place. See the pass?" He pointed to the place. "You must go through there. Beyond that place is the village of the Wolf Clan."

"How far is it?"

"At least three days' travel. Two days beyond the big river."

"I dare not leave her alone with them for that long," Eric growled. "There is no telling what might happen. She might not reach the village alive."

"Then follow the trail," Jumping Hare said. "Be assured that I will take the same path you have trod whenever I am able to travel."

Eric nodded abruptly, gave the tracker's shoulder a gentle squeeze and set off at a loping run, his mind having already dismissed the man he left behind and zoomed forward to the girl who continually cried out to him, begging him for help.

He must find her before it was too late.

With the interior of the cave so dark, it was pure luck that allowed Shala to see the crack in the farthest wall. Her heartbeat picked up speed. She crossed the cavern and bent closer, running her palms over the roughness of the stones, slipping her hand inside the crevice and measuring its width.

Too narrow. There was no way they could get through.

Despairing, she slumped down against the rocky floor, her hand still against the wall. That was the only reason she found the opening. It was small, rounded, perhaps the size of Shala's waist. But it was large enough to squeeze through!

Calm down, she told herself. *A hole cannot help you unless it leads out of this place.*

She stuck her head inside and swept her hand through the darkness before her, feeling the rock walls on both sides. Granted, the hole was small, but it seemed to be deep and there was enough room to pass through it.

Should she check it out before waking Nama and getting her hopes up? She thought not. She dare not leave Nama alone, unaware of the man lingering outside the entrance to the passage.

Behind her, Nama stirred. Realizing the need for quiet, Shala reached out, grasped the other girl's arm and squeezed it lightly. "Shhhh," Shala whispered. "Be calm, Nama."

Nama's reaction was instant. She jerked upright, uttering a gasp of fear. "Shala!" Her voice quivered. "Where are you?"

"Be calm," Shala urged again. "I am here. But we must go now. And we must be quiet lest other ears hear us." She decided not to tell Nama about the man waiting just outside the entrance to the passage. Not yet. Time enough to do that later, but she must make certain Nama knew the wisdom of keeping quiet.

Nama gave a delicate shudder. "Do you think anyone is still about?"

"We dare not take the chance," Shala replied. "That is why we are not going back yet. First we will try another way."

"Another way?"

"Yes. The passage does not end here as we thought. It continues on. I am hoping it goes all the way through the mountains."

"Is that possible?" Nama asked, her voice suddenly quivering with excitement. "Oh, Shala. I hope you are right. I have tried so hard to be brave, but at heart I am such a coward, and the very thought of going back, of being taken captive again by those animals that call themselves men . . . well, the mere thought of such a possibility makes me sick with fear. If this is another way out. . . . Maybe it leads to the top of the mountain. It could, you know, because the floor of the crevice slants upward. What do you think we will find up there? It will surely be safe, because the ledge is too narrow to be traveled by anyone and the cliffs are too steep to climb."

Her voice became wistful. "Do you think the mountain top is like our own mesa? Will there be plants and roots for us to eat, and game to hunt?" She became silently thoughtful for a moment, then continued. "You will have to do the hunting for now, Shala, and I will dig up the roots. But that situation will not last long. You must teach me to hunt as soon as possible."

"I am glad you wish to learn," Shala replied, hoping Nama would be able to keep her enthusiasm instead of regressing to the black mood of yesterday. So much hung on this passage. If it did prove to be a way out, then perhaps the Wise One above was guiding their steps after all. Who knew what He had in store for them?

"Watch yourself now," Shala told the other girl. "And follow close behind me." Without waiting for Nama to speak, she entered the narrow passage, feeling her way carefully along the walls, hoping the dull roar of the waterfall would keep their pursuer from hearing the sound they made as they traveled.

The tunnel was long, seeming to be endless, and it curved to the left, then to the right, then curved back again, always with a slight upward twist. Could Nama be right? Would the passage take them to the top of the mountain?

"How much farther is it?" Nama asked from behind her. "Can you see the end of the passage?"

"No."

"Why is it so dark now?"

"The split in the ceiling that allowed light to filter through is no longer there," Shala explained.

"If the bottom suddenly dropped away beneath us, we would be unaware of it until it was too late to save ourselves."

"Do not think about it," Shala said. "And be quiet. You should save your breath!"

Nama fell silent and only a little time had passed before Shala regretted having shushed the other girl. The sound of her voice had helped cover the dull roaring of the distant waterfall, and her constant questions that required answers had left little time to think.

Nama, unused to such strenuous exercise, finally asked Shala to stop so they could rest.

Although Shala felt the need to hurry, she also knew they must not be exhausted when—or if—they found an exit from the tunnel. There was no way of knowing what waited for them outside.

"We will stop," she said. "But only for a few moments." Uttering a weary sigh, she slumped down on the rocky floor of the passage.

They sat in silence until they regained their breath; then Nama suddenly spoke. "Are you sorry you left with me?" she asked. "Do you wish you had stayed with Eric?"

Did she? Yes. The Wise One above knew how badly Shala wanted to be with Eric again, knew how much she wanted to feel his body pressed against hers, his arms holding her tightly against him. At this moment her reasons for leaving seemed senseless. Why had she not spoken her thoughts aloud to Eric? Why had she not told him of her fears? She might have been wrong about him. Must have been, for surely he would want their babe. A man such as he, who had shown such tenderness to her, such consideration, would not deliberately harm their child.

No! She had been wrong to leave!

"I love him," she whispered. "And I think we may have been wrong to have come away. I should have gone to Eric and spoken with him about the babe, about your problem. He would have reassured me and would have found a way to help you."

"I have never loved a man," Nama said, uttering a wistful sigh. "During last planting, when Walks Fast expressed an interest in me, I tried hard to love him. But nothing happened."

"What did you expect to happen?"

"How could I know what to expect when I know nothing of the feelings between a woman and her man. Nothing except what I have heard by listening to the other maidens who tell about their own feelings."

"What do they say?" Shala asked curiously, for she had always been too busy with her own concerns to hang around with the maidens and listen to them giggle about the men they knew.

"They speak of many things, Shala. They speak of the strength contained in the male body, of a warrior's prowess with a weapon, and they speak of a man's skill at hunting, and talk about the magnitude of male parts."

"Magnitude?" Shala laughed.

"I wondered about that," Nama admitted. "I have seen none of great magnitude. The men do well to hide the things behind their loincloths, because, to my eyes, they resemble worms . . . shriveled and tiny and wrinkled." She shrugged her shoulders. "But then, perhaps all of them are not alike. No!" she said, fear edging into her voice. "I had forgotten for a moment about the man from the Wolf Clan." Her voice became almost tearful. "How could I have forgotten such a thing, Shala. It was horrible! And that thing! It was so ugly, and I know it would have—"

"Stop it!" Shala commanded. "It serves no purpose to remember!"

"No," Nama agreed. "It serves no purpose, except to make me more cautious. We must not fall into their hands again."

"We will not." Shala uttered the words, hoping they were true. "Forget them, Nama. Tell me more about what you have heard from the other maidens."

"They speak of their admiration," Nama muttered, her voice still tense with fear, but as she continued to speak, it began to lose the taut, worried sound. "They seem to think their men are without fault, Shala. That is the reason I knew I did not love Walks Fast. He has a bad body smell. Have you not noticed?"

"Yes. But a good smell means little. He is a good hunter, is he not? You should think less about his smell and more of his hunting skills."

"That is easy for you to say. You would not be obliged to take him to your sleeping mat."

"There are other available men, Nama. Walks Fast need not be your choice. What about Nampeyo? What do you think of him?"

"We are friends," Nama replied. "There has never been anything else between us. It has always been so."

"I know. But I thought perhaps. . . . Well, never mind. There will come a day when you will know love. But it cannot be forced. It is something that happens when you least expect it."

Nama was silent.

Shala wondered what the girl was thinking about, and although she knew it was too dark to see her, she turned her eyes in Nama's direction. As she did so, something flickered on the edge of her vision and her eyes swung back, staring, trying to penetrate the darkness, trying to bring the tiny speck of light closer.

Light? Was it an illusion? No, she decided. It was really there. Light. A narrow point of light so small that she had almost missed it.

"Nama!" she exclaimed. "Look there! Light! We are nearly out! See it? See the light? There! Ahead of us . . . in the distance."

"A light? Are you sure? Where? I cannot see it!"

Shala knew it was too dark to point the way, so she fumbled through the darkness until she found Nama and turned her head until she faced the light. "It is small," she said, still hardly able to believe her eyes. "But it is there. We have found the other way out! We are nearly there!"

Oh let it be true, she whispered silently. *Let it be the way out of this place!*

She hurried forward, unmindful of the noise she made now, almost certain they were far enough away from their pursuer to have completely eluded him. As they drew nearer the light, the dull roaring became louder, more intense.

Were they beyond the waterfall? They must certainly be!

Thank you, Great Creator, she silently exulted. *Thank you for guiding my footsteps. Thank you for showing me the way out!*

Suddenly, the way narrowed sharply, the ceiling lowered. But Shala remained untroubled. After all, had they not seen the exit? She knew it was there. Knew as well that it was big enough to allow them to leave the crevice. She stooped lower, lower still.

"What has happened?" Nama asked dropping to her knees behind her friend.

"The roof is lower ahead, but we can get out by crawling."

"I will squirm along on my belly like a snake if it becomes necessary," Nama said, her voice high and excited.

It seemed it was necessary. The ceiling lowered drastically until it was no higher than Shala's knees. She dropped to her belly, squirming over the rough rocks until she reached the exit.

"We are there," she said triumphantly. "We are there, Nama! We have reached the exit." Laying aside the spear she had been pulling along beside her, Shala crawled out of the hole, stood up and blinked, trying to adjust her eyes to the harsh sunlight.

Her smile faded away like wisps of smoke blown in the wind when she looked around her. As she had suspected, the roaring came from the waterfall. But they were not ahead of it. They were behind it.

Her heart began to thump with dread. They were not on the mountain's top. Instead, they had exited at a very familiar place. It was here they had pushed the boulder from the path, sending it into the canyon below. Here, beneath her feet, the ledge narrowed so dramatically that it could not be traversed. All of the twists and curves had confused her, and they were now only a short distance from where she had last seen Hooked Nose.

"Is it the mountain top?" Nama's voice was jerky as she climbed from the hole. "You left your spear behind, Shala. You are growing careless. We will need your weapon to hunt game." Her voice was muffled slightly, as though she had stuck her head into the hole again.

You are growing careless! Nama's words echoed in her mind. *Careless, careless, careless.*

They were very true. Shala had been careless when she had left her weapon in the passage. And it was a mistake they would both regret. She knew that, even before the hairs on the nape of her neck stood up. Knew it before she heard the noise that spun her around—

—to face her enemy.

The man who stood behind her, blocking her path.

Hooked Nose!

Twenty-four

"So . . . you thought to escape me!"

The words brought Nama's head around, and she stared at the man who had uttered them. *Hooked Nose! Oh, Great Creator! We are found!*

Nama's heart skipped a beat, then began a rapid tattoo beneath her breastbone, thundering loudly in her ears, threatening to burst from her chest. The man stood on the narrow path, just beyond where Shala stood, her body rigid, her face expressionless as she faced the warrior who would surely use them unmercifully, then cast their lifeless bodies aside with no more regret than he would feel at throwing the ashes from his firepit after they had served their purpose.

Why did Shala continue to stand so rigid? Why did she not scream, or try to escape? As though Nama's thoughts had penetrated her frozen state, Shala cast a quick look at Nama, then allowed her eyes to drift to the crevice they had just left before they returned to the man she referred to as Hooked Nose.

Suddenly, Shala sighed heavily, and her expression became one of defeat. "I should have known we could not escape you," she said in a dejected voice. "We have only wasted our energy by trying to do so." Her tone became mournful, pitiful sounding. "We have been without food for a long time now. We are very near to starving. Have you brought anything to eat with you? Could we have some of it?"

Nama was surprised to hear the whine in Shala's voice. How could the girl, who had been so brave during the time she was an outcast, resort to such a cowardly demeanor because of mere hunger?

Remembering Shala's enigmatic look toward the passage, Nama glanced that way. Her searching gaze found the spear left inside, and she realized then what the other girl was about. She was only playing for time, trying to keep the man unaware of her friend's actions.

Surely she did not expect Nama, who had always been a cowering, quivering mass of cowardice, to save them? Nama had been unable to dredge up enough courage to save herself, so how could Shala expect anything from her now?

Still, if she did not act, the result would be terrible.

He pays no attention to you, a silent voice said. *You could leave the way you came while he is occupied with Shala. You might be able to fool him, might be able to reach the other side of the mountain, might get away before he could stop you.*

Even as the thought occurred, Nama dismissed

it as unworthy of her. Shala was her friend. How could she even consider leaving her behind?

Remembering the way the warrior's manhood looked as it tried to penetrate Shala who lay helpless on the ground, Nama knew even death would be preferable to such a fate.

From somewhere deep within, she summoned up enough courage to reach for the spear. Her fingers wrapped around the smooth wooden shaft, and with one sinuous movement, she drew back her arm and hurled the weapon, sending it speeding toward the warrior from the Wolf Clan.

But she was unskilled with the weapon, and the spear whooshed past Hooked Nose's left shoulder and fell to the ground, landing with a clatter against the rocks.

Shala dashed forward, evading the warrior's clutching hands long enough to snatch up the spear, but before she could launch it, he was upon her, wrapping both hands around her spear hand and squeezing, until with a cry of pain she dropped the weapon.

Immediately, Nama launched herself at him, lashing out with both fists, using every ounce of strength she possessed, attempting to throw him off balance, to push him over the cliff.

But her efforts were puny in the face of his strength. He remained fixed on the path, the fingers of one hand locked tightly around Shala's wrist while, with the other hand, he knocked Nama carelessly aside, sending her sprawling on the ground, hard enough to knock the breath from her body.

"You will suffer for having made me wait for this," the warrior growled, pushing Shala to the ground and throwing himself atop her.

Was he going to attack her right there on the ledge?

Rage flowed through her. The warrior was so intent on getting revenge on Shala, that he treated Nama as of no more consequence than a fly he would swat with one finger.

Well, Nama would show him that she was not a fly but a buzzing, angry wasp who could leave a mark if ignored too long.

Scrambling to her feet, she snatched up a fist-sized rock and struck out. If the blow had landed the enemy would have been rendered unconscious, but he saw it coming and jerked aside at the last moment, taking the brunt of the blow on his shoulder.

With a howl of pain, he lashed out with his feet, catching Nama a hard blow against one knee. Her leg buckled beneath her, and she flailed out with both arms, trying to keep her balance.

He kicked again, knocking her sideways, closer to the rim of the gorge. "Shala!" she cried in terror.

Shala's voice rang out, filled with panic as she realized the extent of her friend's danger. "Leave her alone!" she screamed at the warrior, crawling toward him.

But Nama knew it was too late to stop him. Knew it when he picked her up as though she weighed no more than a feather and tossed her over the edge.

A sense of fatality came over Nama as she plummeted down, down, down into the canyon, to what was most certainly her death. She should have known it would end this way. Even so, as she fell, her last thought was for Shala, who would be left to face the brunt of Hooked Nose's anger. At least Nama's own death would be quick.

Not so her friend's. Hooked Nose would see that Shala suffered greatly before she died.

"Nama!" Shala screamed, the word bursting from her lungs. It struck the mountain across from them and sent an echo back again. *Nama, Nama, Nama!*

Horror filled Shala as she realized her friend was gone. Had been flung to certain death by the man who stood staring over the edge of the cliff with a satisfied smile on his face.

Rage flowed through her. He must not be allowed to gloat over the killing of Nama. Her eyes fell on the spear that had fallen a short distance away. If she could just reach it while he was still—

She crawled toward it, felt loose rubble beneath her knees just before she heard the sound of its clatter.

He was alerted.

He turned to her, saw at once her intention and lunged forward, wrapping his fingers through her hair, yanking her painfully toward him.

She turned on him like a she-cat, fighting with every ounce of strength she possessed, using fists, feet and teeth. Adrenaline surged through her, giving her the strength of a madwoman. But he was too strong; she was fighting a losing battle.

If only she had a weapon of some kind . . .

No sooner had the thought come to mind than her skittering gaze touched on the man's weapons, placed a few feet distant down the path.

Why had she not seen them before? Why had she not even wondered where they were?

And yet, what good were they to her? She could never reach them in time.

His knees were pinning her down now, his hands sliding her skirt up her hips. His lips, drawn back into a snarl, were only a few inches above her own. Her gaze slid lower, for she was unwilling to see his eyes when he entered that most secret part of her.

If only she had died first! Before he soiled her with his touch.

His throat worked as harsh gasps left it, forced out by the efforts he was making to keep her subdued for she still fought hard.

His breath!

Her eyes narrowed on his throat.

Without allowing herself time to consider the action, she lifted her head slightly, opened her mouth and clamped her teeth over his jugular vein.

With a howl of pain, he gripped her hair, yanking it hard as he tried to pry her loose from his neck. To no avail. Shala's rage made her strong, and she twisted her head as though she were a maddened beast intent on ripping through flesh and bone to the soft tissue beneath.

A hard blow to the side of her head set her ears to ringing, and spots now floated in front of her eyes.

Wrapping her arms around his neck, she brought him closer, dug her teeth deeper, tasting the coppery flow of blood in her mouth.

Howling with rage and pain he pummeled her with his fist, pulling at her, trying to rip her loose, but when he finally succeeded, she came away with a mouth full of flesh and blood.

He stared at her as though he could not believe what he was seeing. A hand went to the gaping hole in his neck that was pumping blood so fast, lingered there for only a moment, then came away, drenched. He looked at the bright red liquid on it, then lifted agonized eyes to the woman who faced him, still breathing heavily from her exertions.

His mouth worked as though he wanted to speak, but no word was uttered. The light in his eyes began to dim, and he slumped against the ground, his eyes wide and staring.

Shala waited for a long moment, trying to gather courage to face another attack, knowing she had used up all her strength in the last one.

When the assault did not come, she looked closer at him, saw him staring up at the sky, his blood pouring into the ground around him. It was only then she realized what she had done.

She had killed him, but too late for Nama, who had given her life to save her friend.

Silently, Shala mourned. Nama had called herself a coward, but it had not been so. Because of her, Shala still lived.

Oh, Eric, she silently cried. *Now I am truly alone. Have you already gone back to your homeland?*

She wanted him, needed him badly. She had been foolish to leave without a word of explanation. If only she had told him of her fears.

But it was not too late. She could return to the cliff dwellings. To her home, to her people—and Eric.

She turned to go back down the trail, to retrace the path that she and her friend had so recently traveled. It was then she discovered that she was no longer alone.

The tall, red-haired warrior—Red Fox—stood blocking her path.

Consciousness slowly returned to Shala. Groaning, she opened her eyes and stared up at the Blessed Star People who glittered brightly against Sky Man's black velvet cloak. They wavered fuzzily and she squinted, attempting to bring them into focus.

Why did her head pound with such vigor? she wondered. And why did her body seem to be a mass of bruises?

She tried to straighten her arms and legs . . . and discovered she could not. Strips of rawhide bound her wrists and ankles, making movement next to impossible.

Terror streaked through her as memory returned, striking her with the force of a hard blow. She had been captured by hunters from the north, and Nama was dead.

Grief and despair tore at her. She felt weighted down by a terrible guilt. It was all her fault! All her fault. She should have been more careful, more observant, before stepping out of the passage. If she had, then perhaps Nama would still be alive.

Eric! she silently cried, squeezing her eyes shut tight to hold back the tears that threatened to fall. *What have I done, Eric? What have I done?*

Her heart thudded rapidly beneath her rib cage, fluttering like a butterfly caught in a spider web, throbbing so loudly in her ears that it covered all other sound.

Thrum! Thrum, thrum, thrum. Thrum! Thrum, thrum, thrum. The sound had a curious rhythm to it. Was it really her heart she was hearing?

She thought not, suspected the sound was made by drums.

Where had her captors brought her? She remembered nothing after seeing Red Fox, knew her senses must have left her.

She turned her head slightly, saw nothing but hide dwellings of a conical shape. Turning her head again, she saw more of the dwellings, too many to count. The sight struck terror into her heart, cutting into that vital organ just as surely as an obsidian blade with a keen edge. Apparently her captors had finished the journey home while she was unconscious.

But where were the people who occupied the

village? No sooner had the thought occurred than an old woman left the nearest dwelling, noticed Shala was awake and, with a shrill cry, snatched up a stick and rushed toward her.

As though they had only been waiting for the woman's call, people poured from the hide dwellings, like water flowing through a broken dam. They rushed toward Shala, reaching out to her. Harsh hands clutched at her, nails scratching her legs, ripping her clothing as she strained at her bonds, trying to twist away from their cruel touches.

But it was an impossible task. The leather thongs tied around her ankles and wrists were too tight. She was unable to escape the hands that beat at her, unable to escape the drums that thundered in time with their fists.

My baby! she silently shrieked as she was struck, prodded and pinched. *Leave me alone! My baby will be killed!* Her pulse raced with fear, her heart thundering in her breast in time to the pulsating drumbeats, and she strained against the bonds that fastened her wrists to the wooden stakes, even though she knew her efforts were useless.

Eric! she cried inwardly. *They are killing our baby! Help me!*

A hard blow struck the side of her head, sending her senses reeling. She felt the encroaching darkness and knew it was too late. Her time had come. She closed her eyes to embrace death.

Red Fox sat in the circle amidst the elders of the council, wondering if he could convince them to spare the girl's life, wondering as well why it meant so much for him to do so.

Apparently others wondered as well.

"Why do you speak for the girl, Red Fox?" asked Chief Tall Tree.

"Because there is no other to do so," Red Fox replied.

"Of course there is no other. She tore out Bull Elk's throat like a she-wolf. Bull Elk's family want revenge for his death, and they are entitled to it."

"Can she be blamed for killing him? He would have taken her life had he been able," Red Fox pointed out.

"How can you know that? His intention may have been to catch her, to bring her back!"

"Why then did he leave the camp like a thief in the night? Why did he not wake the rest of us?" Without waiting for a reply, he went on. "There can only be one reason. He did not want us to know he was gone until it was too late to stop him. He wanted to use the two women for his own purpose."

"Why should he not use them?" inquired Howling Wolf, a cousin of the deceased. "Why else were they captured, if not for that purpose?" He pinned Red Fox with a hard gaze. "Running Wolf has told us that you stopped Bull Elk from taking the girl before."

"Of course. It is our custom to bring all captives here and let the council decide their fate." Red Fox infused the right amount of sarcasm into his voice when he added, "As you would surely know had you been born into the Wolf Clan."

His intention was to remind everyone who sat on the council that Bull Elk and his relatives had only been with the clan for a year and, therefore, were not truly clan.

Obviously aware of Red Fox's intent and fearing that his wishes would be ignored, Howling Wolf raised his voice and pointed an accusing finger at the red-haired warrior. "Bull Elk was a powerful warrior, and his skill as hunter brought much food into this camp. We were eagerly accepted by the Wolf Clan when we came here. And we *are* Wolf Clan now. When the woman killed Bull Elk, she killed a Wolf Clan warrior. The punishment for that is death." His eyes blazed with hatred as he glared at Red Fox. "Bull Elk's death must be revenged."

"Killing her will not bring him back," Red Fox said harshly. "At this very moment your relatives are exacting revenge for what she has done." He knew it for a fact, could hear the savage yells coming from outside and knew as well that he could be speaking for nothing. The woman might already be dead.

"That is so," Chief Tall Tree said thoughtfully. "They are meting out punishment when the council has not yet decided her fate." He looked across at Red Fox. "Go remove the woman to a safe place and keep her there until her fate has been decided."

Without seeming to hurry, Red Fox rose to his feet and left the council chamber. Outside, his steps quickened. He feared it was already too late for the girl, but if it was not, he would take her to his own dwelling and assign a guard that he could trust.

If she was still alive . . .

When he saw the crowd surrounding the girl, his harsh voice rang out, startling them, causing the ones who had been beating her to cease their cruel torment.

She lay upon the ground, motionless, her body bruised and broken. Had her spirit already taken leave of this world? he wondered. Was it journeying now to the land of the Great Beyond?

Perhaps he had arrived too late to save her . . .

Twenty-five

A cold breeze skimmed through the pine trees that grew along the edge of the river, tousling Eric's hair and blowing an errant curl across his cheek. From his vantage point—a rocky outcrop on the side of a tall mountain—he could see across a wide river to the distant shore where the hazy green of vegetation carpeted a valley nestling between two mountains.

Was Jumping Hare right? Eric wondered. Could that be where the Wolf Clan had taken Shala and her friend?

A movement at his elbow told Eric that Jumping Hare had joined him on his high rocky perch. The tracker had caught up to him this morning, seeming to appear out of nowhere when the Viking had completely lost the trail.

Without Jumping Hare to guide him, Eric would never have found the faint trace of footprints the Wolf Clan had left behind. Not across such rocky ground. The Viking knew he was lucky the other man's ankle had healed so quickly, lucky as well that Jumping Hare had honored his promise to follow as soon as he was capable of doing so, instead of returning to the cliff city.

Turning to face the tracker, Eric noticed the other man's gaze was fastened on the far distant mountains, somewhere near the snowline where the green growth ended so abruptly.

What was he staring at so intently? The snow that still lingered? Or the dark clouds that were building there.

"The cloud spirits are displeased," Jumping Hare said brusquely, his gaze meeting the Viking's for one short moment, before returning to study the fast-moving clouds. "See how they gather over the mountains, Eric. See how they seethe with violence. Their anger is fed by those who disobey the laws set down by First Man. Those very same laws were given to First Man by the Creator, and they were meant to be obeyed. The cloud spirits speak together of man's disobedience, of his complete disregard for those laws. Soon they will release their fury upon the earth. Then all living creatures will be forced to seek shelter from their wrath."

Eric studied the clouds, seeing them through the tracker's eyes. Yes. They did seem to be seething with violence. A humorless smile crept across his lips. The *skraelings* beliefs were not really so different from those held by the Vikings before Christianity had come to them, and the clouds did take on peculiar shapes. Spirits? Perhaps. But Eric did not see the same spirits as the tracker. Instead, he saw the ancient gods of Norway. He saw Odin and Thor, the spirit warriors and the Valkyries. But, unlike Jumping Hare, Eric knew this was only fanciful thinking.

The *skraelings* were still living in the dark ages, as the Vikings would have been had they not realized the weakness of the heathen religion when it came into contact with Christianity. Of course, there were those, like Eric, who chose one of the deities for his special friend and protector, with whom he entered into a kind of partnership, and although it was to God Eric prayed, it was to Odin he told his innermost thoughts.

Was it the same with the Eagle Clan? Eric wondered. He knew they believed in one supreme being they referred to as the Creator. But they also believed spirits existed in each and every living thing—the wind, the trees, the grass and even the earth upon which they trod.

And how could Eric dispute those beliefs? Had not the white wolf—Shala's spirit guide—come to guard her when help was needed? Eric still found that fact a source of amazement, something he could not easily explain to his satisfaction.

His gaze probed the valley nestled between the two mountains. Was the wolf with Shala now? Now when she undoubtedly needed him so badly?

If the wolf was not with her, would the supreme being that she believed in become personally involved in her situation?

"Anyone who trespasses on that mountain will face great danger," Jumping Hare said gruffly, jerking Eric back to the present. "The warriors who bear the sign of the Wolf Clan are fierce, strong in numbers, and they jealously guard everything—and everyone—they consider their own."

"A little danger adds spice to life," Eric said with a quick grin. "My blade and bow are eager for battle." His grin slowly faded as he considered the other man. "You have done well, my friend, by bringing me this far, but it is not necessary for you to continue on with me."

"You would have me turn back now?" Jumping Hare questioned. "Just when my curiosity has been aroused?"

"Your curiosity?"

"Yes. It has always been my desire to journey to the other side of that river."

"You have never been there? How do you know, then, where the village of the Wolf Clan lies?"

"I have ears, my friend." A grin pulled the tracker's lips wide. "And they know when to listen. There are many traders who come to our city bringing goods we could not otherwise obtain . . . and they bring stories as well, tales about other people and other lands. It was from one such trader that I learned where to find the village of the Wolf Clan."

"Lucky for me you have such good ears and the ability to keep them open," Eric commented.

The two had become fast friends during the two weeks they had been searching for the two women from the Eagle Clan. Even so, Eric would have placed no blame on Jumping Hare had the tracker decided to return to his home, because, although Jumping Hare was not married, he had left an extensive family behind. Sometimes, when the two men's bodies succumbed to weariness and they were forced to stop and rest, if the tracker felt inclined to conversation, he would speak of this family . . . of his mother and sisters and his young nieces and nephews, all depending upon him for their livelihood.

Eric studied the tracker's wiry frame, wondering what his family would do if Jumping Hare did not return to them.

Suddenly, Eric's brows pulled into a worried frown. He had not looked closely at the tracker for some time, but now that he did, he realized Jumping Hare looked almost gaunt.

Was he sickening for something? Or was it only the long journey that was taking its toll on the other man?

Granted, the trail had not been easy. Not on either one of them. Both men were bone weary, had often gone hungry for long periods of time. And there might be more of the same ahead of them. There was no way of knowing what they faced, no way of knowing, Eric realized, if the two girls were even alive.

As quick as that thought came, he forced himself to cast it away, fearing that to allow the thought to exist might actually bring about the death of one, or perhaps even both, of them. And, at the moment, hope was all he had left.

He must cling to that with every ounce of strength he possessed; otherwise, he feared for his own sanity.

Shala was alive. He knew it. And he must continue to hold on to that belief.

She was alive and somehow, wherever she was, he would find her.

A buffalo hide dwelling.

A shield with a wolf's head painted upon it.

The aroma of roasted meat.

The round yellow ball of Sister Moon's face peeping through a smoke hole.

Shala drifted in and out of consciousness, and each time that she opened her eyes, she saw the same man hovering over her; a tall, slender man with fiery lights in his dark hair.

Sometimes the man gently worked an ointment into her bruised flesh, and sometimes he applied compresses soaked in cold water to her swollen eyes. One time he even lifted her head and forced her to drink some foul-tasting concoction that she was unable to recognize; yet she knew instinctively that the brew would not cause her harm. Not if it came from this man who exhibited such regard for her welfare and who looked at her with such concern and kindness.

"No!" Eric protested aloud, staring in consternation at the river that was already swollen beyond its banks. The water was muddy, swirling and foaming as it moved swiftly, carrying logs and other debris along on its winding way downriver.

How could they possibly cross it?

"We cannot cross now," Jumping Hare said from beside him, vocalizing the Viking's thoughts. "We must wait until the water runs smooth again."

"It may be too late then," Eric said grimly, pacing back and forth along the riverbank. "Too much time has already passed since they were captured." Too much time. So much that it might already be too late.

"If the Wolf Clan has kept them alive this long they have a purpose in doing so," Jumping Hare remarked.

"A purpose?" Hope flared strong within the Viking. "Do you think that likely?"

"Yes." The tracker's voice was hesitant, as though he wondered how Eric would take his words. "The Wolf Clan need women from other clans to perpetuate their line. Otherwise there is too much inbreeding among the clan. It is a practice that eventually leads to stillborn—or afflicted—babes."

Eric listened in silence to the tracker's words and found a small measure of comfort in the explanation. He had always known that Shala would most likely be raped. But if the Wolf Clan wanted new blood, wanted women to produce healthy sons for them, surely they would not do her great harm. Surely she would survive until he could reach her!

Shala woke gradually, her body chilled. Every muscle in her body ached and the skin on her face felt swollen, stretched taut as a drum. She lifted her eyelids, staring up at the hide covering with eyes that were sore.

Then, rolling over to a sitting position, she pulled her legs up against her breasts and brushed at the grit on her face. Even had she been unable to see, the fur beneath her buttocks would have told her she was no longer in the center of the compound. Instead, she was inside a dwelling with brightly colored pottery and baskets hanging from the lodgepoles, alongside a multitude of shields and masks and hide pouches obviously used for storage purposes.

"How do you feel?" A deep, male voice asked from somewhere nearby.

Slowly, she turned her head toward the man who had spoken. He sat beside the firepit, his legs crossed beneath him. She recognized him immediately. He was Red Fox, the man responsible for her situation. "How would you feel if you were in my place?" she asked bitterly, glaring at him from swollen eyes.

His mouth twisted slightly. Was he amused by her situation? "Not very good, I expect. But you were lucky."

"Lucky? How can you say that?"

"It is true," he insisted. "They could have killed you, or broken your bones, but they did not. Instead, you are only bruised and cut; your flesh is swollen, but skin is resilient. In time the bruises will fade, the cuts will heal. You will recover from the beating."

Uncurling his legs, he crossed to a large clay

jug that had been splashed with vivid yellow and red dye. Hanging above it on the nearest lodge-pole, was a gourd dipper. He lowered the gourd into the jug and then brought it to Shala. "The water is fresh. It will cool your throat."

Although her pride demanded that she refuse the offer, her parched, dry throat would not allow her to do so. She sipped slowly, feeling the cooling liquid slip past the lacerated places in her mouth where she had bitten through the flesh to stop her silent cries of pain from being released. When she had quenched her thirst, she studied the purpling bruises on her bare arms.

"Why did they stop beating me?" she asked.

"It was our leader, Chief Tall Tree's decision."

"Why did he interfere on my behalf?" Her voice was wary; yet deep within her breast, a spark of hope flared to life. "Am I to be spared?"

"Your fate has not yet been decided by the council of elders." Even as he spoke, he looked away from her.

Why did he avoid her gaze? she wondered. Was it because he feared she would read his thoughts there, that she would know her fate was already sealed?

"Perhaps it would have been kinder had your chief allowed them to end my life," she said wearily. "Surely my death has only been delayed for a short time." She waited for him to confirm her suspicions.

"Perhaps not." He seemed unwilling to speak of her future and changed the subject. "Your recovery requires plenty of rest. You should sleep again while you have the chance. Are you cold? There are plenty of furs to keep you warm. Would you like one now?"

His demeanor was kind, contrary to the attitude he had displayed when she was first captured. Why had he changed toward her?

"I am not cold," she replied. "And I do not require sleep. How long have I been here?"

"Only two days," he replied. "Are you hungry? Perhaps you could rest better if you eat something?"

Just the thought of food made her salivate. There was no way she could refuse it. "Yes," she admitted. "My belly has been without food for a very long time."

"Shall I bring it to you?"

"No." She pushed herself to her knees, then tried to stand and found she had little strength to do so. Her legs were sore, obviously badly bruised, and they wobbled like those of a newborn fawn.

Determinedly, she locked her knees in place and straightened her body, then crouched again involuntarily, feeling as though an invisible band had squeezed the left side of her lower belly.

"Are you in pain?"

The spasm subsided and she stumbled forward, crumpling against the pile of furs, leaning back and gulping in deep breaths.

"Are you in pain?" he asked again, dropping to his haunches beside her.

"Are you surprised?" she asked. "How could it be otherwise when your people beat me so badly."

"The people who beat you were Bull Elk's relatives," he explained, dipping a soft cloth into a bowl of water and placing it against her face, wiping away the grime and blood that had dried there. "They cannot be blamed for their feelings."

"Do they know what he did to my friend?" she asked bitterly. "Do they know that he would have killed me, too, had he been able to do so?"

"They know, but it does not matter to them." Something dark flickered in his eyes. "Why should they let it trouble them? You are not of our clan. You mean less than nothing to them. Unlike Bull Elk, who was an excellent hunter. His relatives number more than the fingers of both my hands and most of them depended on him for their very existence. Now that he is gone they are wondering how they will survive the harsh winters."

His hands continued to move, the damp cloth gentle on her bruised flesh. She winced as he touched a particularly sore spot.

"Does that hurt?"

"A little," she muttered, unwilling for him to know how much pain she was feeling. She closed her eyes against him, turning her face away, hating to have him near her, tending her needs, and yet, at the same time, dreading the thought of being left alone with her thoughts. "How long before the council decides my fate?" she asked, voicing the question that was uppermost in her mind, pretending to be unconcerned by his answer.

He hesitated, as though reluctant to reply. At

last he said, "Tonight. When Father Sun seeks his rest the council will meet again. Then your fate will be decided."

Despair washed over Shala, taking away what little hope she had managed to cling to. It was too soon. Too soon. She was not ready to die yet, but that must surely be what fate held in store for her. And it was not fair. Hooked Nose—she could not help thinking of him that way—had deserved to die. But the Wolf Clan would not take that into account. They would see she was punished for his death, and if his relatives had any say in the matter, her death would be a long, painful one.

Cra-a-ack!

The sound was loud above them and the rain that had been threatening throughout the day poured down with the fury of a waterfall.

Crack! Boom! Crack!

Thunder sounded again, reverberating off the mountains, and Wind Woman began to howl with fury, lashing the hide dwellings and making them sway beneath her anger.

Red Fox ignored the storm raging outside, carefully filling a gourd bowl with thin gruel that should slip easily down her sore throat. Shala watched him with hungry eyes, wondering all the while why she bothered filling her belly. If she was going to die anyway . . .

She forced the thought from her mind, reaching eagerly for the bowl of gruel. As their fingers touched, another boom sounded outside, and, startled, she dropped the gruel on a brightly colored rug that covered the dirt floor near the sleeping mat.

"Never mind," Red Fox said, rolling the rug out of the way. "This can be cleaned later." He refilled the bowl and brought it to her again, speaking soothingly of inconsequential things, of the severity of winter, of the beauty of spring, obviously attempting to calm her jangled nerves.

While he talked, Wind Woman continued to lash the teepee, and rain continued to fall in torrents; but with his voice washing over her, Shala felt safe inside the hide dwelling, secure from those who would seek to harm her. Slowly, the tension that had stretched her nerves taut began to lessen. Whether it was the food in her belly or Red Fox's gentle voice that soothed her, Shala had no way of knowing. Nor did she care. She only cared that she was safe and dry within the hide dwelling, for the moment at least. And, she suspected, as long as the elements continued to rage around them, she would probably be left alone by the people of the Wolf Clan.

"You need not fear the storm," Red Fox said, reaching out to clasp her hand in his.

"I have no fear of such things," she said, even as she flinched at the loud booming thunder around them. "It is only Eric's god, Odin, and his men of war riding through the spirit world." She spoke the words so easily, wondering how they came to sound so right to her. Surely she did not believe them. No! She could not! But to speak of Eric's gods made the Viking seem closer to her.

And she needed to feel close to him. Needed it desperately.

Suddenly, a memory surfaced in her mind, a memory of Eric, of the night they spent together in the abandoned city on the mesa. That was a night she would always remember, because it was then he made her his woman.

"Who is Eric?" Red Fox asked, pulling her from her memories. "Is he one of your clansmen?"

"No. Not a clansman." She would not have answered him, but speaking aloud of Eric made him seem less distant. "Eric came to our land a stranger, unfamiliar with our ways. He told me of his home, a land far away, beyond the big salt water." Her lips pulled into a smile that never reached her eyes, and she jerked her hand away from Red Fox's. "Eric is a man to be feared. Big as Brother Black Bear, and be warned, he will come after me. He is my husband. A golden-haired Viking whose anger is great to behold. If any harm comes to me, he will never rest until he has taken revenge on the Wolf Clan."

"There is no such man as that which you have described. If there were, he would not have allowed you to travel," Red Fox growled, his gaze boring into hers as though he would read the truth written on her soul.

"I was running away from him," she admitted.

"Running away? Was he cruel to you, then?" Red Fox asked.

"No," she whispered, her gaze turning inward to the last time Eric had held her in his arms.

"He was always kind to me. It was only my foolishness that caused me to leave him."

Suddenly remembering her reason for leaving, she put her hands over her stomach, wondering if her child had already ceased breathing?

The thought caused a hard stab of pain somewhere in the region of her heart. How could she have so easily forgotten the babe? she wondered. For some reason, she suddenly wanted someone other than herself to know about it. "The babe," she muttered, her eyes meeting those of the man beside her. "I am with child, and I am afraid for the babe."

He frowned down at her. "A child?" He looked at her slightly rounded stomach. "Is that the reason you left your clan? Was your husband not the father?"

"The babe is his, but he is not of the clan."

"What does that matter?"

"His ways are different from ours. In his country a man must accept the babe at birth. Otherwise it is not allowed to survive."

Comprehension dawned in his dark eyes. "And you thought he might not accept the babe?"

"There is always that possibility."

"Do you have a reason for believing such a thing?" he asked kindly.

"He would not accept a child if it was less than perfect."

"Do you know this for certain?"

"My own ears have heard him say so."

"Do you have reason to believe the child will not be perfect?"

"No. But I dared not take the chance."

"Your man's belief is not so strange," he said slowly. "There are others in our land who share his feelings. Think about it for a moment. A child must be strong to survive the harsh weather winter often brings. And there are times when meat is hard to find, when the people endure long periods without food. Those who are not strong enough cannot last through those periods. Death claims the old ones then, those who are the weakest. And death claims the lives of too many of our children. It is hard for those left behind, Shala. And it makes me think that, perhaps, it would be better not to love than to lose that which is most precious to one's heart."

"Every living creature has a right to life," Shala said accusingly. "Only the Creator has a right to take that life away."

"What about the animals we kill?" he chided gently. "The Creator is not responsible for their deaths."

"That is different," she argued. "We do what is necessary for our survival. And we do not take the animal's life without first apologizing to it, and asking for blessing of the meat. The Creator meant for us to use them in that manner."

"Yes," he agreed. "And we do so . . . because it is necessary." He took her hand again, stroking the back with his fingers. "Let us agree to speak no more of this at present. Just think about what I have said."

"You cannot convince me it is right to let a

babe die," she said firmly, allowing her hand to lie beneath his. "Certainly not mine."

"Then let us agree to disagree."

"As you wish."

"I am curious about this man of yours. Tell me more about him."

She glanced at him, recognized his curiosity as more than an idle one and wondered why that should be. "I am not so sure I want to speak with you anymore. After all, you are to blame for my being here."

"Yes. I am to blame. And, I must admit that, when we captured you, I had no thought for your welfare. But I have had second thoughts since then. I realize you could have acted no differently. Captured as you were, violently attacked by one of us, you would naturally protect yourself in any way you could." He held her gaze for a long moment. "I feel the weight of guilt resting heavy upon my shoulders, but there is nothing I can do to help you. Your only hope rests with your man. I think the storm will delay the council's decision for a while, and your man just might have time to save you."

"Then there is no hope." Shala was unaware that, sunk in the depths of despair, she was admitting the telling of a falsehood. "Eric will not come for me."

"He will come," he said, tilting her chin and forcing her to meet his eyes. "Only the river separates him from the village."

Eric was coming for her? Hope surged forth, washing away the despair that had been her constant companion for so long. "How do you know?" she whispered.

"I have always known we were being followed."

"You know it is Eric?"

"No. But if he is all you say, then it is he who follows."

"It is more than likely Nama they are seeking." A sudden thought struck her. "Do others of your clan know they are coming?"

"No. The men who followed our trail numbered only two. Since it is obvious they are greatly outnumbered I decided to hold my own council for a while."

"If they come here you would allow me to leave with them?"

"If that is the only way to save your life," he said gravely. "Yes. I would see you leave."

"My life is important to you?"

He shrugged his shoulders. "Perhaps. I am not sure." His dark eyes glittered, belying his words. "Perhaps I feel guilty that you are in this situation."

"Your people would never allow me to leave."

"No. But if care were taken they might not know until it was too late."

She studied him for a long moment, wondering why he would allow the approach of an enemy. Was he only tormenting her? Perhaps so. Perhaps his words about Eric coming were false. "You could help me now," she said slowly. "You could turn your back and allow me to leave here while the storm is upon us."

"And where would you go?" he asked softly.

"You are in no condition to travel far." He shook his head. "No. We must wait until you are better, more able to face the long journey that awaits you."

Shala knew then that it was all a lie. Red Fox, for some unknown reason, was pretending a sympathy toward her that he was far from feeling.

But, she silently decided, for the moment she would hold her silence, would make the warrior from the Wolf Clan think that she had accepted his words. And when the time was right, she would make her escape from this place. She would return home to the place of her birth, and she would try to forget the Viking that had occupied a place in her heart for such a short time.

Even as Shala's mind denied her love, her heart cried out with the pain of losing him, making her wonder just how long it would take to forget her Viking lover.

Twenty-six

The torrential rain continued to fall. For three days and nights it fell, flooding the village and forcing the Wolf Clan to seek higher ground.

Shala felt no alarm when the village crier—the man who was responsible for passing on important news to members of the clan—stuck his head into Red Fox's dwelling and told him of the move. Instead, she felt a momentary surge of hope. The time might well be approaching when she could make her attempt at escape.

"It would be foolish to try to leave now," Red Fox said the moment the crier disappeared, apparently guessing the path along which her mind had wandered. "The storm is too intense. You would be wandering in circles and would very soon be caught. And in the heat of the moment who could say what would happen?" He squeezed her shoulder gently. "You cannot escape alone. Wait. Your man will come for you."

Again, she remained silent. What good would it do to tell him Eric had long since departed for his homeland? Better to let him think she believed her Viking would come for her. Perhaps then Red Fox would think she had accepted the inevitable, that she would remain passive until Eric made his appearance, and so he would not be expecting it when she made her escape.

Shala, unused to dismantling hide dwellings, looked to Red Fox for direction. The People of the Wolf Clan scurried about the encampment, buffeted by high winds and pounded by rains that came down in sheets as they hurried to move their conical-shaped dwellings. They paid no attention to Shala and Red Fox, who worked side by side to take down his teepee, while all about them the elements raged, thunder and lightning splitting the heavens apart with their fury.

Red Fox took only what was necessary, making a travois out of the teepee poles and the hide covering of the dwelling, then loading it with food, furs and weapons. When he was finished, Red Fox stepped between the two poles and, with Shala's help, moved slowly toward the nearest mountain that had been previously selected for such an emergency as this.

Wind Woman's breath was so strong that Shala had to brace herself before it. Angry gusts ripped at her clothing, flattening it against her body and threatening to tear it apart.

All thought of escaping had flown from Shala's mind. She had no choice except to stay, for Red Fox was right. No one could possibly survive if exposed to such a storm.

An eternity seemed to pass before they reached

the selected site. Then eons crept by while they erected the new lodges. Shala was completely worn out by the time they had finished and quickly sought her rest as soon as she entered the teepee, too tired to move a muscle, too weary of body and mind to even consider what fate held in store. The moment she closed her eyes she was fast asleep.

The storm struck while Eric contemplated the swollen river. Jagged lightning reached for the earth and thunder boomed across the sky. He realized then there was no way they could cross the river at this point in time. They would surely drown if they tried to swim, and the likelihood of a raft, however carefully it was constructed, staying together long enough to reach the other side was too minimal to even consider this option.

It seemed there was really no choice. They would have to wait out the storm, wait until the water level was lower, the river less swollen.

They sought shelter in a small cave located in the side of the mountain. After building a fire from the few sticks of dry wood he was able to find, Eric extended his cold hands toward the flames. "How long do you think the storm will last?" he asked Jumping Hare.

"There is no way of knowing," Jumping Hare replied. "Wind Woman is very angry. She must have time to spend her fury on those around her."

"Why do you refer to the wind as a person?" Eric asked, intent on keeping the conversation going, unwilling to dwell on Shala's plight, for there was little he could do to help her at the moment. "You speak as though the wind were a living being."

"She is," Jumping Hare replied. "Did you not already know that? We are all one with nature, Eric. The earth is our mother and the sun is our father and all the creatures around us—great or small—are related to us in one way or another."

"Shala once told me the same thing, but her words fell on deaf ears."

"Deaf? Or ears that were only closed to the truth?"

"Who can say what is true? The Eagle Clan believe the animals have spirits, that beneath the outer wrapping of flesh all living creatures are the same."

"That is so."

"Even if it is true, how can you possibly include the wind?"

Jumping Hare's lips spread into a wide smile, and his teeth showed white in his deeply tanned skin. "Is not the wind a living thing, Eric?"

"Of course not."

"Listen to her now," Jumping Hare commanded. "Listen to Wind Woman howl her fury and deny that she is alive. Can you not hear her?" He fell silent, waiting for Eric to respond.

Whoooo, whooo, whooo. The wind sent chills down Eric's spine as its sounds rose in volume, seeming uncannily like the wailing of a multitude of spirits.

"Listen to her, Eric! See how she wails! Hear

her rage? It is obvious that she is angry. Someone has caused her great displeasure."

"The wind blows because of the elements around us . . . the clouds in the sky . . . and other things," Eric said, becoming suddenly aware of how little he really knew about such things.

Jumping Hare ignored the Viking's weak explanation, obviously preferring his own. "If Wind Woman could reach into this cave, she would tear at our clothing, would rip it from our bodies and leave us standing naked, completely exposed to her wrath." He held Eric's eyes for a long moment. "But when her fury is spent, when she has vented her anger on those who have displeased her, she will become almost loving. She will apologize to those she has abused by caressing them with her warm, soft touch."

Comprehension dawned on Eric. "Warm, soft, loving," he repeated. "Like a woman. One moment caressingly tender, the next scratching and biting, spitting out her fury. No wonder you refer to the wind as a woman."

"Yes, no wonder," Jumping Hare agreed. "Exactly like a woman. One moment caressing, the next passionate, sometimes full of fury."

Eric leaned back against the cavern walls and contemplated the flames, allowing his thoughts to turn inward. Jumping Hare's words had summoned up memories of Shala.

Shala! The way she looked during their tender moments together.

Shala! The way she laughed.

Shala! With her midnight dark hair tumbling

across bared shoulders, reaching down her coppery skin to caress taut nipples.

Shala! Standing before him with his sword clutched in both hands, her dark eyes blazing with fury.

The memories continued to come, bringing with them a deep abiding loss that pierced him anew. He had failed her somehow. Had failed to recognize her needs. He should have known something was wrong on that last night they were together.

But how could he? his heart argued. That was the night she had loved him so passionately, so thoroughly.

She must have known, even then, that she was leaving you, his mind said.

"Yes," he muttered aloud. "She must have known."

Eric, too occupied with his thoughts of Shala and of how she would react to him when he finally caught up to her, was unaware of the look sent him by the tracker from the Eagle Clan.

Red Fox watched the girl sleeping on his bed of furs. Outside, the storm had abated, having spent its fury. His thoughts were troubled, occupied by worries over Shala's future.

There had been no sign of her man, no sign of anyone coming to her rescue.

Had the two who followed them lost the trail? Or had they somehow perished? It had to be one or the other, because her man would not have abandoned Shala to her fate.

Red Fox uttered a deep sigh. Somehow, he must devise a plan for helping her. He could not allow her to be put to death. And yet, how could he stop it if that was the council's decision?

His eyes traveled over the hair tumbling softly about her face. She was such a delicate creature to be so strong. How could one such as she have killed a man with the strength that Bull Elk possessed?

Surely the council would take that into consideration, would see that one who possessed such bravery would be an asset to any tribe. She could give them many sons to swell their numbers . . . sons that would surely grow into brave young men, fierce fighters that would help the tribe fight off their enemies.

Red Fox felt an urgent need to speak to the council. He had to make them see that the woman should be allowed to live among them. Just the thought of her death was more than he could bear.

No! That must not be. He must do whatever he could to keep her alive, to prevent the torture that Bull Elk's relatives would be sure to demand.

Leaving Shala sleeping, the warrior from the Wolf Clan hurried across the compound, headed for the dwelling that housed Chief Tall Tree.

When the storm was finally over, Eric could wait no longer to cross the river. He began to build a raft to carry him across, dragging logs from a small creek where the storm had partially dislodged a beaver dam.

After the raft was completed to the best of his ability, considering they had only a short length of rope to work with and must, of necessity, use vines to bind the logs together, Eric turned to the other man.

"You need not accompany me," he said grimly. "But I can wait no more. I have this feeling that, if I do not go now, it will be too late."

Jumping Hare's gaze held the Viking's for a long moment. "When such feelings are too strong to be ignored, they must be obeyed. But I cannot turn back now, no matter what lies before us." He wrapped his fingers around a log. "We are wasting time, Eric. Help me push this craft into the water."

Eric needed no further urging. Gathering up his weapons, he secured his sword to the raft by wedging the blade between two logs. Then, looping his crossbow over it, he gripped the raft from the front and put his back into the effort to move it. Behind him, the water flowed swift and deep, dark and dangerous, the river still swollen, water running bank to bank.

Beads of sweat broke out on his upper lip as he continued to strain against the weight of the raft while Jumping Hare stood behind it and pushed.

Moments later it was caught by the dark and furious water, pulled into its current, and even as the men fought to climb on, the river fought just as eagerly to wrench the raft from their grasp.

Eric's knuckles whitened as he fought to retain his grip on the logs while he threw one long, muscular leg across the raft. He clung there for a few moments, breathing heavily; then, his strength somewhat renewed, he pulled himself aboard the makeshift vessel and lay upon it for a long moment, vaguely aware that Jumping Hare had joined him on the flimsy craft.

The raft swirled around and jerked awkwardly, plunging this way and that, veering wildly to the left, rearing up on one end, then plunging downward into a deep trough between waves that seemed insurmountable.

Pushing himself to his haunches, Eric freed the long paddle Jumping Hare had made while the Viking built the raft, and pushed it into the water, attempting to maneuver the raft to the other shore, but his efforts were in vain. The current was too strong, his strength too puny against the raging fury of the river.

He swayed with the heaving raft, trying to maintain his stance, but the craft was too unsteady. They swirled downstream at a furious pace, unable to break free of the swift current. Then, suddenly, Eric yelled a warning when he saw the rock emerging from the angry water. But it was already too late to brace himself.

The raft struck the rock with a mighty impact that sent him sprawling headlong into the foaming water.

He felt the shock of the cold river as his body

hit the surface, then it was closing around him, swallowing him, sucking him under to its icy depths where the light was dim and no air could be found.

The current twisted and turned, pulling at him, rolling his body over and over, drawing him deeper and deeper into its murky depths until his lungs burned for lack of the oxygen they so desperately needed.

He fought desperately to reach the surface, to break free of the clutching, grasping river for just one brief moment, to suck in enough of that life-giving air and ease the terrible burning of his lungs.

A dull roar began in his ears, and he was aware of bright, sparkling flashes behind his eyelids. Was it over then? he wondered.

Had the end finally come?

Some sound woke Shala from her restless sleep. Fearing the worst, she turned her head and searched for the source. Other than herself, the teepee was empty.

Where was Red Fox? she wondered. And, even more important, how long would he be gone?

Flinging back the confining covers, she hurried to the entrance flap and pushed it aside a bare slit, she searched for the man assigned to guard her. He stood only a few feet distant, his back to her, obviously watching something out of the range of Shala's vision.

Carefully, she pulled the hide flap until the gap

was wider, until she could find the focus of the guard's interest. It was then she saw the girl approaching, carrying a laden basket. Her dark hair was tied up with bands of braided deerhide in the manner of the other women of the clan. And even from this distance, Shala realized an enormous amount of work had been expended in making the graceful garment she wore. It was crafted from fine antelope skin; soft, velvety, fringed, and worked and embroidered with porcupine quills. And around her neck, she wore several turquoise bead necklaces.

Unlike the other women Shala saw moving around the compound, the girl seemed to be dressed for some ceremonial occasion.

Suddenly, she paused beside an old man. They spoke together for a moment; then the girl turned her steps toward the dwelling that housed Shala. Had she been seen spying on them? Shala wondered. She was about to resettle the hide flap in place, intent on covering the fact that she had wakened, when something beyond the girl's left shoulder caught her attention. A movement near the edge of a thickly wooded area, near the big blue spruce. Forgetting her danger, she fixed her gaze on the spot. There was something white there, hidden by the lower limbs of the spruce.

Her heartbeats picked up speed. Was it Wolf? Could her spirit guide have come to her rescue? She strained her eyes, trying to bring the object into focus. It was Wolf. No, wait! It was something else, bending over, hiding itself from the people who went about the business of clearing up after the storm.

Eric! It was Eric, her Viking! He had *come for her!*

A sharp voice near to hand broke her concentration, made her aware that she had been discovered spying on the Wolf Clan. She jerked her eyes up and met those of her guard. But it was not he who had spoken. It was the old man.

"Back inside!" he ordered unnecessarily, for she had never left the dwelling. "Stay away from the entrance!" he gave her a hard push that sent her sprawling on the ground. "Why is she not bound?" he asked the guard.

"Red Fox did not think it was necessary," the guard explained.

"Red Fox is a fool!" the ancient one said. "Bind her!"

Apparently this old man was someone of importance, because the guard hurried to do exactly that. Even so, Shala could not be brought down from the emotional heights she had reached when she had realized Eric had come for her. She knew her Viking. If he had come this far to find her, then he would stop at nothing to set her free.

Twenty-seven

After checking to make certain her bindings were secure, the old man left the teepee, the guard following close behind him. They had no sooner left the dwelling than the girl Shala had noticed earlier stepped inside.

"I am Pale Fawn," she said, setting her basket down beside Shala. She took a moment to study the girl who was bound so tightly. "I am a relative of Bull Elk."

Shala felt a cold, icy chill slide down her spine. Had the girl come to exact revenge for the death of her kinsman?

"They say you killed Bull Elk," the other girl went on, her face expressionless and her voice possessing no more feeling than if she had been discussing the weather. "They say you tore the flesh away from his neck until the blood that gave him life ran swiftly from his veins. Is that true?"

Bound the way she was, Shala hated to admit the truth of that. She was unsure of the other girl's reaction and could not protect herself if attacked. But, realizing it would do no good to deny the charges, since everyone in the village was more than likely in possession of the facts surrounding Bull Elk's death, Shala slowly nodded her head, admitting to everything.

A wide grin spread across the other girl's face. "I wish I could have been there," she said, her dark eyes flashing. "For the past three years it has been my wish to see him dead. I would have killed him myself had I the courage to do so."

"Why?" Shala asked. "You said he was your relative."

"That fact is a matter of birth," the girl replied, "not of choice."

"But he is still your relative."

"Yes. And he was my sister's relative too. But that did not stop him from raping her."

"Raping her?" Shala stared at the other girl in horror. "The Wolf Clan allows such horrible things to happen among them? Rape is taboo among the Eagle Clan."

"We did not live with the Wolf Clan when it happened. We lived with the Round Hoof Clan. They do not allow rape either. Bull Elk became an outcast for his misdeeds."

"That was when he came to live with the Wolf Clan?"

"Yes. But they were unaware of his evil nature. Unaware that he had been cast out of his own clan."

"Why did you come with him?"

"I had no choice. Since my mother died when I was born, both my sister and I lived with my uncle—Bull Elk's father. Although my uncle did not approve of his son's actions, he could do nothing about them. He is old and crippled, unable to hunt. When Bull Elk left the Round Hoof Clan, we came with him."

"And your sister came too?"

"My sister could not come. She is dead."

"He killed her?"

"She killed herself."

Shala recoiled in horror. "She could not live with the shame," she whispered.

"No. She could not."

"How could you live with him, knowing all that?"

"It was easy. I stayed to exact revenge. You cheated me of it, but it is just as well. I fear I do not have the courage you possess."

"Would you help me, then?" Shala asked, holding her bound hands out to the other girl.

"I cannot."

"Why? You admit you had no love for Bull Elk, that you wanted to see him suffer. Well, he did. And at my hands. Surely that very fact would make you want to help me. Please, release me. Allow me to go free."

"I cannot," the girl repeated.

Shala could not accept that. Pale Fawn was her only hope. She must be convinced. "Why not? You bear me no ill will for killing him. You said yourself that he deserved it."

"Yes. But the others do not feel the same. They want revenge for his death." The look in her eyes was one of compassion. "I only came to speak to you . . . and to bring you food to eat."

"I have no need for your food," Shala said sharply. "Red Fox has provided that for me."

"He is a good man," Pale Fawn said softly.

"You must help me."

"I can do nothing," Pale Fawn replied. For some reason, she seemed in no hurry to leave; instead, she settled down beside Shala. "Tell me something of yourself," she said. "I have heard stories of the Eagle Clan, told by the traders who come to our village. They say your people build their homes among the rocks."

Although Shala felt uninclined to idle conversation, she found herself telling the other girl—Pale Fawn—about her life, about the people who dwelled among the cliffs and cultivated the ground to grow corn and beans and squash.

She was unaware of the passing of time until the drums began to sound. *Thrum, thrum, thrum. Thrum, thrum, thrum.* She listened to their throbbing beat, a feeling of dread coming over her. What did it mean? she wondered. Why had the drummers been called upon to beat the drums?

She was well aware of Pale Fawn's scrutiny, but gave no sign, preferring to remain silent, although she was unable to continue their conversation, unable to pretend her life was not on the line.

"The council has been called to their chambers," Pale Fawn said gently. "You will soon know what they have decided. If you are put to death, then I will go out into the forest and sing your soul to the spirits."

Shala felt the other girl's palm against her upper arm, a gentle touch; then it was gone as quickly as it came.

She remained still, frozen in place for a long moment, then, sensing an emptiness around her that was new, she turned her head, searching the shadowy interior. The dwelling was empty.

Shala waited with held breath, wondering if Pale Fawn would return, but as the moments slowly passed and she remained absent, Shala realized the girl had gone on her way.

Her heart gave a crazy jolt, then picked up speed. She was alone again, and although her hands were bound, she might be able to release them. Could she escape from this place before anyone knew she was gone?

Hurriedly, she jerked upright, searching around the firepit until she found a stone with a sharp side. Placing her bound hands over it, she began to work the leather thongs back and forth, back and forth, seeking to wear the hide down until it parted.

Thrum, thrum, thrum. Her pounding heart beat in time with the drums as she worked the leather over the stone. She stopped occasionally to test the strips, but the thongs were still strong, they refused to part.

She searched around the firepit for something to cut through them. Nothing. Everything that could have been of use had been removed.

Realizing she could do nothing more, nothing but accept her fate, she dropped down on the pile of furs again. Her foot struck something hard then, something hidden beneath the edge of a brightly colored blanket. Leaning forward, she used her heels to push aside the edge of the covering and exposed a gleaming obsidian blade.

Hope surged through her as, eagerly, she maneuvered until she could wrap her fingers around it. Then, with the blade firmly within her grasp, she sawed away at her bonds until they parted.

She was free!

Dashing across the dwelling, she pushed aside the hide flap and peered out. Her gaze swept the compound, counting the people outside. There were only as many as the fingers on one hand, and they were all occupied with other things, none of them looking her way . . . except one. Pale Fawn. For a moment their eyes locked, then the other girl turned away from Shala, began a conversation with the old man who had ordered Shala bound.

Was she telling him about Shala? Or was Pale Fawn bent on keeping his attention diverted until Shala could escape? Suddenly, a thought struck Shala. Where had the knife come from? It was not one she had seen before, did not look like any of Red Fox's weapons. Could Pale Fawn have brought it with her?

Realizing that was a distinct possibility, Shala's fear of exposure lessened slightly. Pale Fawn must have supplied the knife. And if she had, she would not give her away now. Shala slipped outside, waiting only until the flap fell back into place before she dashed around the dwelling and hid herself from prying eyes.

She stood still for a moment, the thought of discovery keeping her frozen to the spot, afraid to move lest she be seen, and yet, knowing she must before her absence was discovered. But where could she go? Her desperate gaze skittered back and forth, measured the clearing, knowing all the time it was too open while the cover of the forest was too distant. She would surely be seen if she attempted to reach the trees, would surely be caught again.

Oh, Great Creator, she silently prayed. *Help me! I have been abandoned by my spirit guide.*

Even as she uttered the prayer, she saw Wolf. And, standing beside him, near the edge of the forest, was a man whose bronzed skin was only a shade darker than his golden hair. Eric! It was really Eric. Her Viking lover had come for her.

Happiness flowed through her. It was true then. Even though she had doubted Red Fox's words, Eric had come for her! And he had brought Wolf with him.

Confidence surged through her, overwhelming the fear that had been her companion for so long. Eric was here. He would see her safely home. Without another thought, she made a quick dash toward the trees that sheltered her love. As the branches closed in around her, she heard a shout and knew that her enemies had learned of her departure.

"Hurry, Eric!" she shouted, knowing there was no time for a reunion. "There are too many of them to fight. We must flee!"

Taking it for granted that he and Wolf would

follow her, she fled into the dense forest, secure in the knowledge that they could easily elude the warriors of the Wolf Clan.

Chief Tall Tree listened carefully to what Red Fox had to say, then nodded his head in agreement. "Your words make sense," he said slowly. "The woman does show great courage. And since you are willing to make yourself responsible for her, the council may be willing to allow her to live. Still, there is no way to predict which way the council will vote. Bull Elk's relations will not be happy if the woman is spared."

"I know. But they are not the only ones to be considered. They will not go hungry. Our hunters always share their kill with the less fortunate ones. It has always been our way." He knew he need not explain their customs to his chief, but felt he must say the words aloud, must remind Tall Tree of the facts. "The woman will be no problem for us. I have spoken to her at length these past few days. She will harm no other of our tribe."

"You can be sure of that?"

"I will personally see to it."

"Then I will speak on her behalf."

With Tall Tree's words ringing in his ears, Red Fox felt better about Shala's future, but even as he assured the chief of the Wolf Clan that Shala would do no harm, she was condemning herself by her own actions.

* * *

Shala had only gone a short way before she realized she had lost sight of Eric. But he was close by, she reassured herself, most likely only searching out the enemy with some idea in mind of lessening their numbers.

Knowing that he would find her wherever she was, she raced on, intent on putting as much distance between herself and the village as possible.

She leapt over a fallen log, then circled around several high bushes. It was there she found herself confronted with a warrior who seemed to come out of nowhere.

Shala reacted quickly, drawing back the knife she had had sense enough to keep and thrusting the deadly weapon at him. The blade entered his flesh, slashing a long path across his middle. Blood spurted out of the wound, and he looked at her with shocked eyes. His legs wobbled then crumpled beneath him, and his body crashed into a nearby bush, where it broke through the limbs and struck the ground with a heavy thud.

He lay still.

Shala stared at him, and had she been able to see her face, she would have recognized the expression there. It was the same one the warrior wore. Shocked, disbelieving.

She had not felt that way when Bull Elk lay dead at her feet, but this was different. She hated Bull Elk with a passion that covered all else. He had deserved to die. But this man at her feet . . . she had never seen him before.

A shout in the distance reminded her of her peril, and Shala cast one quick desperate look behind her before she turned away and darted through the forest of pine trees, speeding away as fast as her legs could carry her.

She realized how little time she had when only moments later she heard her pursuers crashing through the underbrush, drawing closer all the time.

Where is Eric? her mind screamed.

Where is Wolf?

Had they deserted her, left her to fend for herself?

She heard a howl in the distance and for a moment, her steps faltered. Was it Wolf who called to her? Was it his way of answering her, of assuring her that she was not alone?

Another howl sounded, eerie, searching, and yet she realized the sound came from a great distance. If it was Wolf who called to her, he was too far away to be of any help. And, with no sign of the Viking, she had only herself to rely on again.

Shala raced on, running mindlessly through the forest, unaware that she still clutched the bloody knife in her hand.

Branches reached out, slashing at her, tearing at her clothing, her flesh. She raised her elbows, protecting her face from them, her ears thundering to the throb of her heartbeat.

Escape! her mind screamed. *Run! Get away! Hide!*

Where? Her gaze skittered back and forth, searching for a place of concealment. There were bushes, trees, but there was no safety there. Those who pursued her would soon find her if she tried to hide herself among them.

Her sides ached, her chest felt tight, constricted, her breath came in short, painful gasps, but she dared not stop to rest, could not. She forced herself to go on, mindlessly, half-blinded by the perspiration brought on by exertion.

Suddenly, Shala tripped, flailing out both arms to regain her balance, and lost her grip on the knife. She heard it clatter as it struck something hard. A stone? Dropping to her knees, she swept her hands among the dead leaves covering the forest floor. *Where is it?* her mind screamed, even while she knew she was losing precious time.

Too late! an inner voice chided. *No time to find it!* Her heart thumped in time with the voice inside her head that continued to scream a warning. *Hurry, hurry, hurry!*

Crash! The footsteps stomping through the underbrush reminded her she had run out of time. She could not stay here! There was no place to hide. No place that offered safety of any kind!

Crash! They were even closer now, gaining on her, the pursuers uncaring of the noise they made.

Run! Run! Get away while you can! her mind screamed. *Leave the knife behind!*

In an instant she was up again, dashing away from the threat of being taken captive again. Her dark hair tumbled wildly about her shoulders as she ran, her eyes wide and terrified.

How close were they now? she wondered fearfully. Why had Eric or Wolf not come to her aid?

The answer eluded her as she stumbled on.

***

When Red Fox was told about the escape and the death of one of their people, he knew everything he had accomplished by his meeting with Tall Tree was now undone. Shala's fate had been sealed the very moment her knife had penetrated Black Cloud's flesh.

Her only hope lay in her ability to elude the warriors who pursued her. Perhaps he could aid her in some way if he could reach her before the others did.

Somehow, he knew that she would head for the mountain south of them. The way she had talked about her home, with so much longing in her voice, told him she would seek out the mesa.

But she would not escape. There was no way she, a mere woman, could avoid the trackers of the Wolf Clan. No others had such skill as theirs, a fact that had given him great pride. But not at the moment. At the moment he wished their skill would dissolve like mist before the morning sun. Because that would be the only way the woman from the Eagle Clan could escape them.

It was pure luck that saved Shala. She would not have seen the opening in the rocky cliff had she not stopped to catch her breath. Even then, she nearly missed it, would have if the stitch in her side had not been bad enough to double her over at that particular point.

It was a small opening, barely big enough for

her to squeeze inside. But it was so close to the ground that there was a chance her trackers might not spot the hole. The thought had barely occurred when Shala heard a shout from nearby.

She immediately crawled inside the opening and curled herself into the smallest ball possible.

She had only just accomplished that feat when the trackers broke through the forest and came together in the middle of the clearing. They spoke together for a short time while one of their fellows dropped to his haunches to search the ground. Then, amazing though it was, they hurried on across the clearing and entered the heavily wooded forest again.

Realizing that they would soon learn of their mistake and return to look for her, Shala doubled back on her trail until she found a place where rocks covered the ground. Then, carefully, she retraced her steps, walking backward for a short way, then using a low-hanging branch to cover the fact that she had changed directions at that point.

Although Shala was tired to the point of dropping in her tracks, she forced herself to go on, always traveling now in a southerly direction.

Father Sun blazed a path through the western sky, but she ignored the darkening twilight. She traveled throughout the night, with only the stars above to guide her, stopping occasionally for a short rest before making herself get up again and continue her journey.

The first light before dawn gave her a glimpse of the wide, muddy river. She was near the edge of a hillock, where the pine trees thinned because of a landslide that had occurred sometime in the past.

She stared down at the river that looked like a wide band of silver winding through the mountains as it made its way in a southeasterly direction downstream. Even from this distance the current looked swift, dangerous, but Shala knew she must find a way to cross it, for beyond the river lay safety.

Exhausted though she was, Shala again thought of Eric. Had she only imagined him there . . . near the edge of the forest? No! She could not have done so. He had been there, his golden hair gleaming beneath the sun. Why had he not joined her? What kept him from her so long?

Knowing she had no choice, she went on, slipping and sliding down the hillside, winding her way through thickets of pine, of blue spruce and aspen, and a tangled growth of assorted vines. She could hear the river now, and her heart quickened with anticipation. Somehow she would cross that turbulent stream, would return to the place of her birth. The mesa. Her home.

She would do it. Somehow. Some way.

The big, muddy river ran swift and deep where the current was strong, but enough time had passed since the recent storm that there was now a gentler side to it as well. One such place lay near the northern shore where the constant barrage of water and debris had eroded the riverbank and created a small circular pool that was edged with aspen and spruce and pine.

The forest was silent and still around the pool, and the golden light of morning filtered softly through the pine trees, dappling the makeshift raft that had come to rest there, making lacy patterns across the face of the man who lay so quietly, upon it, unaware of his surroundings. The creatures of the forest were silent, curious about the man who had invaded their territory. A squirrel peeped out from behind a tree. A raven flew closer to the raft, stopping to rest on a limb of the nearest tree, its beady eyes fixed on the object that sparkled so brightly beneath the rays of the sun. The raven had no way of knowing it was a weapon. Broad-edged and sharp, the blade of the sword was still firmly wedged between the two logs.

Shala felt a sense of freedom. The river was within her reach now, near enough that safety would surely be hers.

Crash! Crack!

Shala's head jerked around, her gaze searching the brush for the source of the noise. Eric? Was it Eric finally joining her? She dared not call out, lest it be the enemy who approached.

Crash, crack, crack! There it was again. Too many sounds to be one man. A bear?

But it was not a bear. Instead, her searching gaze focused on a man just then emerging from the dense forest, and Shala knew, with a certainty, that the Wolf Clan had found her again.

Her heart beat with the speed of a rabbit's when the creature was trying to escape from a trap. She spun around, preparing to take flight, but before she could do so, two men stepped abruptly into her path.

Uttering a shrill scream, Shala darted sideways, trying to escape their clutches, but as though anticipating her actions, another man appeared out of nowhere.

Before she could react to the newest threat, arms wrapped around her, jerking her against a hard male body. Overcome with horror, Shala uttered another scream that was quickly stifled by a hand over her mouth. She bit down hard, feeling a small measure of content when she heard a grunt of pain. The hand was quickly removed.

Her captor snarled something at her, grasping her hair and yanking hard enough to bring tears to her eyes. She screamed again, louder this time, even though she knew it was useless to resist. Hysteria drove her as she used her fists, pounding against her captor's shoulders, lashing out with her feet, trying to kick whatever part of him was within reach.

"Hold her!" one of the warriors, a short, heavyset man, snarled. "Do you want her to get away again?"

"She is not so easy to hold!" her captor complained. "If you can do better, then take her!" He pushed her toward the heavyset man, and Shala would have fallen if the warrior had not caught her in time. Then, before she could regain her senses, she was bound hand and foot and tossed beneath the nearest tree. While she lay there, breathless, her captor wound a long strip of hide around her wrists, added several knots, then secured it to the tree.

The nearest man laughed when he saw the way she had been tied. "Do you need another strip of leather?" he taunted.

"You would not laugh if she managed to escape," said the man who was busy adding another knot to the leather straps. "How would you explain such an event? A mere girl escaping from four strong warriors of the Wolf Clan?"

His words silenced the other fellow. After checking the leather bindings one last time, the heavy-set warrior finally joined the other men who, it seemed, had every intention of making camp where they stood.

Why? she wondered, as a thousand butterflies tried to beat their way out of her stomach. Why were they in no hurry to return to their village?

The scream, long and piercing, sounded throughout the forest, reaching the riverbank and rousing the man who lay on the raft. He stirred, his golden eyelashes fluttering against his bronzed skin. At first the movement was barely more than a quiver; then, slowly, his lashes lifted, revealing dazed green eyes.

With a heavy frown, he studied the pine trees that rose majestically all around him, partially obscuring the morning sky. His frown deepened. What was he doing here? he wondered. Why was his bed so hard, and why did it sway so gently beneath him?

Even as he puzzled over the matter, a scream sounded, long and shrill, filled with extreme terror, making him feel it had been ripped from a throat that could no longer hold it back.

Realizing he could not ignore that scream, that he must respond to the threat behind it, he pushed himself erect, shaking his head as he did so, trying to clear his mind while he fought the vertigo that threatened to render him unconscious again.

Shala, having convinced herself the warriors intended to sleep, watched in amazement as one of them drew a small circle in the dirt, then stepped back to join the others who stood a goodly distance away.

"Me first," a slender young man said. He tossed a small stone toward the circle. It landed just outside the line.

The other men seemed amused. They laughed and taunted the warrior who had thrown the stone. Another warrior took his turn. It landed just inside the line. He turned to the other men. "Looks like she is mine!" he cried.

"We are not yet finished," said yet another man.

Only then did Shala understand what was happening. They were playing a game, gambling on which of them would be the first to possess her!

She closed her eyes against the sight. She would kill herself if she were able, for she could not stand the thought of any of them touching her in that way. Only Eric had the right to do so.

Eric, she silently cried. *Where are you? Why did you leave me alone?*

When she first heard the noise, it was a mere whisper, a soft sound that could have been nothing more than the sighing of Wind Woman. But there was something different about it, something subtle; something that demanded her attention.

Swiveling her head, she tried to locate the source, and immediately sucked in a sharp breath, her body tense, her eyes disbelieving.

Eric? Although her lips formed the words, her voice made no sound.

He put a finger to his lips, miming a shush. At the same moment, Shala felt a tug on the leather thongs that bound her wrists. Another tug and they parted beneath his blade.

Wanting nothing more than to rush into his arms, but realizing that she dare not do so lest the mere sound of her flesh touching his alert the men whose attention was still focused on their game, Shala contented herself with looking at him, with dwelling once again on his compelling grass green eyes and firm features, on the confident set of his shoulders that told her his strength would be enough to save her.

Suddenly, one of the warriors, apparently considering himself the winner, looked toward her with a grin that quickly faded at the sight of Eric. Before he could react, the Viking lifted his sword and, with an angry roar, hurled himself among them, swinging his mighty blade before him, cutting the warriors down as though they had no more substance than the morning mist. And when he finally stood among their blood-covered remains, he turned his back on them and walked away.

"E-Eric." Shala's voice trembled as she sought reassurance from the man who had wrought such savage destruction, the man whose cold eyes now stared at her . . . through her. "Eric," she said again, wanting the look to leave his face, worrying that it was there for good, a reminder of the easy way in which he had dispatched his enemies.

"Did they hurt you?" he questioned, his voice as grim as his expression.

His words brought her relief. It was only concern for her that hardened his expression, that had made him destroy so many with never a thought for the families that might suffer as a result of his deeds.

"Shala!" His cold eyes bored through her, demanded an answer. "Did they hurt you?"

His obvious concern brought tears to her eyes. "A little," she admitted shakily. "But I will survive their treatment." She could not move, could do nothing except stare at him with misty eyes. "I never believed you would follow me. I had no idea you were anywhere near until Red Fox told me. I . . . I—" She broke off, unable to continue, her heart too full for words.

He came to her then. Crossed the distance that separated them. Extending a finger, he caught a tear that hung on the end of her dark lashes. "You said someone told you I was coming?"

"Yes. It was Red Fox. He said there were two men who followed."

"There were two. Jumping Hare is dead. At least he was thrown from the raft. I never saw him again." His eyes swept her face, touched on her disheveled hair, on the scratches and purpling bruises that marred her skin. "Were you beaten, Shala?" he asked harshly. "Did they treat you badly?"

She sniffed, lowered her lashes and turned her head away, ashamed of her tears. When she spoke, her voice was strained. "What they did to me is of little consequence." She looked up at him again. "I am still alive. But they killed Nama." Her lips trembled, and tears ran swiftly down her cheeks. "They killed her, Eric, and I helped them do it." She slung her arms around his neck and began to weep uncontrollably. "I helped them do it," she babbled over and over again. "I helped them do it."

Although he remained silent, his arms slid around her waist, holding her against him, giving her the comfort that she needed so desperately. "Ssshhhh!" he whispered huskily. "Stop your weeping, Shala. Your tears will not bring back your friend."

No. Tears would not bring Nama back. Nothing would. That knowledge gnawed at Shala's insides, and her sobbing continued as mindlessly, almost helplessly, she clung to her Viking lover.

Red Fox silently watched the reunion from his place of concealment. His feelings were mixed. He had arrived too late to help his clansmen, and now he was in a quandary. It was his duty to revenge the warriors; yet the golden one was powerful, would be almost impossible to defeat. And there was the fact that Red Fox wanted Shala to survive. Whatever happened, he would not see her dead.

He turned away from them, having already made his decision. He would return to the village, would tell them of the golden-haired Viking who had single-handedly defeated four warriors and of his subsequent escape with the woman from the Eagle Clan, and perhaps the council would deem it wiser to allow the matter to rest.

Red Fox looked once again toward the embracing couple, knowing that he would always carry that last glimpse of Shala hidden deep inside his memory. And no matter how long he lived, his heart would never forget the woman from the Eagle Clan.

Twenty-eight

Since the river was still too swift to cross, they went downstream, following ridge trails and creekbeds, keeping the river in sight as much as possible, yet every sense alert to the need to stay hidden from anyone who might seek to pursue them.

Eric set a pace that Shala found hard to maintain. Hard as she tried to keep up, she kept falling behind, but she forced herself to remain silent, unwilling to beg a reprieve from the man who had changed so drastically from the one she had left on the mesa.

What had happened to change him? she wondered. To make his expression so grim, his eyes so cold and hard? It was true he must be constantly alert, could never let down his guard lest they walk into an ambush, and yet, surely that was not the whole of it.

Was he angry with her for leaving him? That must be it, she decided. He was angry because she had run away. Well, never mind. She could explain it all. When there was time, she could tell him of her fears, could make him see why she had felt she must go.

He would listen to her, and he would understand. And her explanation would take away the grim look that seemed almost carved into his face.

Shala had no liking for the man who stood beside her now. He had changed drastically since they had first met. And she realized it was her fault. Because she did not trust enough. She wanted him back—that other man. She could not endure the thought that he might always be this hard man who faced her now, so cold, so ruthless, so unforgiving.

Would he understand when she explained? she wondered, throwing a quick look his way. They were resting at the moment, having climbed a hill that had been in their way. Eric stood near the brow of a canyon while Shala leaned against the trunk of a large pine, trying to ease the pain in her lower back.

"Eric."

He turned to face her, his eyes dark and unfathomable.

"You never said how you came to be with Wolf," Shala said, feeling the need of easy conversation.

"Wolf?" His brows pulled into a frown. "The white wolf you refer to as your spirit guide?"

"Yes."

"I have not been with him. He has not been near me since he left the mesa."

"But you *were* with him!" she exclaimed. "You

came to the village of the Wolf Clan and beckoned me to follow you. Wolf stood beside you."

"You are mistaken, Shala. I never reached that village. I never went beyond that riverbank. I have no idea how much time passed . . . how long I was unconscious, but you woke me when you screamed—when the warriors attacked you."

"That cannot be," she whispered. "I saw you there. And you were with a white wolf. It had to be Wolf beside you."

"Not me," he said shortly. "If anyone was there, it was someone else." He reached out a hand and pulled her to her feet, frowning as she gave a short cry of pain.

"What is wrong? Are you in pain?"

"No." She was unwilling to admit to the pain in her belly, hoping it would go away if she ignored it. "I am fine."

Without another word, they resumed their journey south.

They traveled until nightfall, then stopped in a thicket of pines that would offer some concealment. Eric allowed her only a few hours of sleep before he woke her and said they must go on. They continued that way for several days, journeying throughout the day with little rest, then stopping at dark for a few hours' sleep.

It was several days later when, one morning, after checking their backtrail, the Viking told Shala he was certain they were no longer being followed.

"Apparently the people of the Wolf Clan have decided not to pursue us farther."

"That is a great relief," she said. "Maybe there will be no need to travel so fast now." She was mentally and physically exhausted. There had been times when she could not have gone on if Eric had not been there to offer his strength to her.

Now that she was no longer worried about the Wolf Clan, Shala began to wonder about their destination. Were they returning to the mesa? Or was it his intention to return to the longboat?

That night, while they enjoyed a meal of roasted rabbit, she put the question to him.

"We must return to the mesa," he told her. "At least long enough to inform Jumping Hare's relatives of his death."

"He may have survived, Eric," she pointed out. "You never saw his body."

"No. But I am sure he perished. There is no way he could have survived that river."

"You had become friends," she said softly. "Like Nama and myself. It is sad to lose a friend."

"Yes," he agreed, contemplating the chunk of meat he was holding. "It is sad to lose a friend. But there are other things that are equally sad when lost."

Suddenly, he flung aside the meat and reached out, curving his hand around her neck. His mood was such, his expression so dark, that she feared he meant her harm. But instead of tightening his fingers around her throat, he gave her a shove that sent her sprawling across the bed of pine needles she had previously prepared.

"No, Eric!" she said quickly, fearing his mood would cause a roughness that would hurt the babe nestled within her belly.

"Yes," he breathed harshly against her neck. "Yes, yes, yes."

That night he taught her a way of loving that she had never before even dreamed of. It began with a kiss, placed behind her left ear. She felt the wet moistness of his tongue touch her flesh and shivered, uttering a short gasp as goose pimples broke out on her skin. "That tickles," she said, her fear melting away as though it had never been. She flashed him a sultry look from beneath dark lashes.

"Tickles?" he queried, repeating the action, but more decisively this time. Instead of a quick touch of the tongue, he deliberately made a wet circle behind her ear.

"Aaaahh!" She shivered, the word escaping out of her mouth.

Although his touch was teasing, she felt fire coursing through her veins like a raging river.

She made a quick, involuntary appraisal of his features. He had lost that harsh, unforgiving look. "Do it again," she whispered hoarsely. "It felt nice."

"Nice?"

His mouth dipped down, his tongue streaking her neck, dipping into the deep slash of her neckline, encountering the valley between her breasts.

Her breath quickened, and her body felt as if it were ice and flame. Her heart picked up speed.

Noticing her reaction, he pulled at her garments, intent on getting them and his own out of the way. A few moments later he was beside her again, his lips and mouth creating havoc within her as he kissed her taut nipples, arousing a melting sweetness within.

Then his mouth was on her belly, his tongue dipping into the cleft there, and she gasped with shock, quivering with an explosion of fiery sensations. Waves of ecstasy throbbed through her. She desperately needed more of him, must have him inside her, must feel herself filled with his need.

Her impatience grew to explosive proportions, and she pulled at his arms, trying to drag him upward, but he resisted, his mouth moving lower, his teeth nipping at her soft flesh.

"Eric," she moaned, thrashing beneath his roving tongue. "Do not make me wait, Eric. I cannot stand it. Take me now."

He laughed low in his throat and went even lower, his tongue sliding into her most secret parts. Love flowed in her like warm honey, and she cried out for release, felt a wet hot spurt gushing forth.

Passion pounded the blood through her heart, through her chest, her head, leaving her almost mindless when he pulled back, mounted her, and pushed into her with his throbbing rod. It was accomplished with ease since she was so wet from his ministrations.

Her exhaustion was as though it had never been. She bumped and twisted, urging him onward with greater speed, wanting more and more of him within her.

When she came, it was a blinding explosion, as though the heavens had opened suddenly and released its fury upon them. And yet there was no fear in the explosions. Nothing but ecstasy, pure and simple. At that very moment he exploded within her and sent his seed flying through her body. Shala felt that had she not already been with child she would surely have conceived several at that moment.

When it was over they lay together, completely satiated, too exhausted to do more than hold each other with contentment.

Shala knew as long as she lived she would never forget that moment. It was one to lock away in her memory and bring out when she was old and gray . . . too precious to share with others.

Sighing with pleasure, she snuggled close in his arms and closed her eyes and fell into a deep, dreamless sleep.

Eric woke in the half-light before dawn, feeling there was something wrong, some danger that threatened nearby. He eased his way out of Shala's arms, thinking to allow her to sleep a little longer.

With his sword in hand, he paced the perimeter of the camp, searching for some sign of what threatened them. He had almost convinced himself he was imagining things when he heard the rustle of dry leaves. Someone was moving nearby.

His eyes pinpointed the position—a plumbush that was greening out enough to offer concealment.

With his blade poised for battle, he called out in the Anasazi language. "Reveal yourself to me."

A male voice rang out in the same language. "Hold on! I mean you no harm! It is only chance that brings me here." A tall, slender man dressed in an elkhide shirt and trousers stepped out of the brush with his arms spread wide. He was weaponless, carrying nothing but a crooked walking stick. "Put down your weapon," he added. "I am no enemy."

"Then why were you hiding in the bushes?"

"A man would be foolish to approach a camp without first knowing who is in it."

"And do you know now?"

"No." The stranger's gaze was keen, and although it touched on Eric's weapon again, he seemed unafraid. "But it is obvious that although you speak the language of the People you are not one of us." His eyes swept over Eric's golden locks before returning to meet his gaze. "Who are you? And how do you come to know our tongue?"

"I could ask the same of you," Eric said. "You are the intruder here."

"Well said," the stranger replied, ignoring Eric and striding away from him.

Eric frowned at the man. "Stay!" he commanded. "I have not finished with you."

"I am not leaving," the man said, kneeling beside the firepit and raking through the coals with a stick. "Good. There are still some coals here." He reached for the wood laid nearby and put several sticks on the coals, leaning over them to blow hard.

"What are you about?" Eric growled, starting toward the intruder.

"Eric!" Shala called quickly.

Thinking perhaps the man's actions had been a way of diverting his attention while another man attacked Shala, Eric spun quickly, bringing his weapon up before him.

But there was no one with Shala. She stood alone, clutching her garment in front of her naked body. It was only then that Eric realized he wore not a stitch of clothing.

But his nakedness did not bother him half as much as the man who was still occupied with blowing at their fire.

"He is a trader," Shala whispered, her voice barely carrying across the space between them. "Leave him alone. He must not be harmed."

"Why?" His gaze went from her to the man she called a trader.

"Because." For a moment she looked confused. "Traders can go wherever they please, Eric. It is the way of our People."

"You know him?" he asked.

"No. Not him. But he is a trader," she said with certainty. "His staff is that of a trader."

"Trader or not, he has yet to prove himself a friend."

"Come, dress yourself," she commanded. "We must feed our guest."

Eric frowned at her, watching as she turned her back and struggled to don her clothing while keeping as much of her body hidden as was possible. Although he still was unsure about the man who had entered their camp, he knew he would feel more at ease were he not quite so naked.

Which presented a dilemma. He had to put the sword down before he could dress himself. And he was not so sure he could trust the man who was still busy building up their fire.

Seeming to realize Eric's predicament, even with his back turned, the stranger suddenly said, "Give the weapon to Shala if you distrust me. If she is half the warrior I am told, then you can surely trust her to keep me at bay until you have dressed yourself." He looked around with a wide smile. "Unless you feel better without your clothing. I do not mind your state of undress."

Uttering a choked expletive, Eric threw his sword down within easy reach and quickly donned his trousers. He did feel better able to face the man when dressed.

"Now, by Thor, you will tell me what you are doing here and how you come to know Shala when she claims not to know you."

"I am Black Crow. And, as Shala has guessed, I am a trader," the other man said. "I hear many stories in my travels. Like many others, I have heard of Shala, the woman who rejected her clan shaman and was cast out to live apart." He looked at Shala with admiring eyes. "It is said that you survived very well on your own. You are much admired by others."

Eric relaxed slightly. "Since you know so much, why do you not know who I am?"

The trader grinned. "I am not a spirit or the divine being. I can only know what others have learned before me. It seems this time I am to be the first with the knowledge. If you decide to tell me," he added.

When Eric remained silent, Shala hurried to explain who Eric was. When she had finished with her explanations, the trader said, "I know of the longboat. But I do not know where it came from."

"You have seen it?" Eric was interested now. "Do you know of my crew? How do my men fare?"

"I know nothing of your crew. Only that there are others like yourself there. Some with the same color of hair and others that have hair the color of flames."

"Where did you hear about them?"

"From other traders," Black Crow explained. "Two have spoken of your boat. One of them actually traded with the people who live near the great muddy water. The other trader heard the news from one of our own."

Even though the trader could tell him nothing more, it was obvious to Eric that his men were still there and still surviving if that much was known. He was so pleased that he actually smiled. "We will be going there soon," he said. "My men are waiting for me to return so we can go home."

"Why are you so far from your boat?"

"I wanted to explore the land," Eric said. He thought it better not to mention that he had hoped to take slaves and treasures back to his homeland.

They talked while Shala prepared a meal from the trader's supplies. After they finished eating, Black Crow brought out a small white bag. He opened it and pulled out several blue stones. "Perhaps we might make a trade," he said, holding his hand out to Eric. "The People of this land hold these stones of great value. Perhaps your people would value them as well."

Eric sucked in a sharp breath. "I have seen these stones," he said. "Do you know where they come from?"

Black Crow shrugged his shoulders. "From many places. The stones are sacred to the People of this land and cannot easily be found."

"What will you take for those?" Eric asked.

Instead of answering the question, Black Crow asked one of his own. "What do you have to offer?"

And so the haggling began.

Twenty-nine

In the early light of dawn, the trader gathered his belongings together and made ready to leave.

"Where are you going from here?" Eric asked. His animosity had been completely forgotten. Instead, he was pleased with their meeting, for, although he had had little of value to trade except his sword, he held a pouch containing several small turquoise stones in his hand.

Black Crow was equally pleased with himself. He had obtained an engraved bronzed buckle in the exchange. "I have a desire to visit the Wolf Clan," the trader answered. "But have no worry that I will give away your location. Traders never mix in the conflicts of others. If we did we could not travel so freely across this land without fear of attack from those who might seek revenge." Leaning over, he picked up his staff and, after wishing them good luck on their journey, went on his way.

Shala watched him go with mixed feelings. Eric had been so withdrawn of late, distant and definitely not inclined to idle conversation, quite unlike the genial trader whose cordial nature and quick smile served to lift her spirits, making her forget the ordeal that she had so recently come through.

The air around them was hot and heavy as they continued to follow the river downstream, traveling along the narrow bank for miles until that way finally became completely impassable, blocked by a densely wooded mountain that rose high into the air.

"The river cuts through the two mountains at the gorge," Eric said, pointing to limestone bluffs ahead of them. "We must go over the mountain and hope there will be a place to cross over beyond it."

They went up a steep ridge and into a deep forest, then across a high meadow. All the while, Shala searched in vain for one small glimpse of the river.

Father Sun was high overhead when they came around the brow of the mountain and saw a glimpse of silver far below them. The river. It muttered and rushed below, foaming with whitecaps, turbulent, angry looking.

After a short rest, they continued on again, changing direction every now and then to seek the edge of the cliff, reassuring themselves the river was still there, although it remained several hundred feet below them.

It was late in the evening when they descended into a long ravine and came out from between two hills to find themselves at the river's edge, bluffs and mountains towering on both sides. Here, the river flowed deep and fast from between limestone cliffs. Still swollen, turbulent, and yet, the rocks forced the water to narrow drastically at this point.

"We will cross here," Eric said, studying the gorge with his searching gaze.

"We cannot swim across," she said.

"No," he said slowly. "We will have to build a raft."

Was he remembering Jumping Hare and the way he had perished? "We have no rope with which to bind the logs together," she protested.

"We will use vines." His searching gaze found three logs piled nearby, held there between several large rocks. He pulled them out and tested them for strength. One broke in half, the other two held firm.

"Bring me some of those grapevines," he said, nodding toward a tree around which they were entwined.

She hurried toward it and pulled as many vines free as she could, selecting the smallest ones possible, knowing they would be easier to work with.

They spent the rest of the day gathering together logs for the vessel and lashing them together with the strong vines. By the time they had finished, the sun was a red ball hanging over the western horizon.

"Do you plan on crossing the river tonight?" Shala asked, eying the turbulent water with dismay.

"Yes. We can rest easier over there, knowing the river is between us and the Wolf Clan."

"The trader can be trusted," she said. "He will not mention seeing us."

"Perhaps not intentionally," he agreed. "But he might say something to give away our position, and we would not know until the enemy attacks." Gripping the raft with both hands, he strained to pull it toward the water. "Help me, Shala. The mud keeps the logs from sliding smoothly."

Together, they pushed the crude raft into the shallows until it would float. "Get on!" Eric ordered.

"What about you?" Shala asked, climbing aboard and slipping her fingers around one of the logs.

"I will soon join you." He pushed the makeshift raft farther into the water where it bobbed gently for a moment, then swirled around as it was caught by the current.

"Get on!" she shouted, fearing she would be sent downstream without him.

Eric braced his arms against the raft and gave a mighty heave that brought him halfway out of the water. His biceps strained with effort as he hung onto the raft while at the same time pulling his body over the edge. "Whoomph!" The air was forced out of his throat as he landed belly down across the logs that were lashed together. He had no time to gather his wits before the raft crashed against the rocky cliff and shuddered beneath the impact.

The crash loosened Shala's grip and sent her

sliding toward the edge of the craft. Fear sliced through her, but she was unable to utter a sound. All her efforts were focused toward securing another hold on the raft. Her fingers found an opening between the logs and darted through, hooked around the heavy wood.

Her peril had gone unnoticed by Eric, who had grabbed up the stout pole brought along to keep them off the rocky sides of the gorge. It had taken all his strength to keep the raft away from the rocks that would soon have torn their vessel apart.

The ride through the gorge was a wild one. Whitecapped waters splashed over them, rolling the raft, spinning it around and continually forcing it toward the rocky cliffs that seemed to wait ominously, like a living thing intent on destroying them, for that moment in time when Eric could no longer keep them away from the sharp rocks. But that time did not come. Each time they neared the jutting rocks, Eric managed somehow to push them away with the pole, sending them back into the current again. This in turn sent them sailing downstream with amazing speed, spinning them around like a whirligig until Shala was so dizzy that she had of necessity to close her eyes.

The journey seemed endless, and her knuckles whitened with the effort she exerted to keep herself on the raft.

When the spinning finally stopped, Shala was unaware of it because her head was still whirling.

"Get off!" Eric commanded gruffly.

"Off?" She opened her eyes and stared at him. "In the water?"

"It is safe," he said, sliding over the edge to show her. "The raft is caught on something, but I think we only have a moment before the current catches it again." Even as he spoke, the raft turned halfway around.

"Get off!" he shouted urgently.

Becoming aware of the danger she faced by remaining on the flimsy craft, Shala rolled toward the edge. But she was not as lucky as Eric had been. Her feet did not find firm ground, and she was swept away.

"Shala!"

She heard him call her name as water closed over her head, flooding her nose; then her mouth opened in a silent scream. The cold liquid was flooding her lungs as she fought to reach the surface, flailing out with both arms even while she knew it was too late. The pull of the current was too strong . . . too strong . . . too strong.

An eternity seemed to pass before Eric was able to reach Shala. Wrapping his arms around her waist, he kicked against the river bottom and surged upward until his head broke surface. Turning Shala on her back, he put one hand beneath her chin, holding her head out of the water as he swam toward the bank, fighting desperately to escape the current that fought equally hard to capture them in its watery embrace.

His heart thudded heavily with exertion when

his feet finally scraped against the gravel shoal that had temporarily captured the raft. Sweeping Shala into his arms, he carried her out of the water and laid her on the ground beneath the shade of a willow tree.

"Shala!" His voice was hoarse, raspy, as he tried to wake her. When she lay unmoving, he slapped her face gently. She drew in a sharp breath of air, then coughed repeatedly as water flooded from her mouth.

Her eyelids lifted, and she stared up at him. "Eric?" she whispered.

Incredible joy swept through him as he realized she was all right. How close he had come to losing her! The very thought sent chills through his body. She was too precious to lose, too important to his future. His awareness of how nearly he had lost her colored his voice when he spoke again. "Have you no sense, woman? You very nearly drowned."

Immediately, she retaliated, pushing herself upright and glaring at him. "You told me to get off!"

Although he knew she was right, he took exception to her tone. "Any fool would have made certain it was safe before turning loose of the raft."

"I am not a fool." She turned away from him. "And I object to being called one." Her voice became distant, cold. "The mesa should be no more than two days from here. You need not accompany me there."

"What does that mean?"

"You can go back to your boat. I can find my own way home."

His grass green eyes became cold as ice. "You go nowhere alone, Shala. When I reach my longboat it will be with you beside me."

"No! I will not go!"

"Not go?" His voice held the surprise he felt at her words. "Of course you will go."

"No. I do not wish to leave my people. I told you that, but you chose not to concern yourself with my feelings."

"So you left." The voice was flat, unemotional. "Without a word of explanation, you left me, sneaking away like a thief in the night, uncaring whether or not I worried about you."

"Did you worry?"

"Of course." His look was hard. "You belong to me, Shala. We belong together."

You belong to me. Somehow the words sounded wrong. Was that the way he thought of her, then? As a possession? The possibility caused her great concern. She had always considered possessions to be inanimate objects. They certainly had no say in their own behalf. She found the question arising again that had plagued her so much in the past. Exactly how was she to be treated in his world? Would she have no rights? No say in her own future?

"I belong to no man," she said harshly, lifting her chin and straightening her back. "I am Shala . . . a woman of the Eagle Clan who has earned the right to control my own life."

"And I am Eric, the Viking warrior, who has

just saved that life," Eric said, his voice equally harsh. "Does that not give me some rights?"

Realizing he was right, remembering as well that he had saved her not only once but three times, Shala conceded his point. "Yes. It does." There was resignation in her voice, and was there something else as well? Perhaps an acceptance? He certainly hoped so.

When Shala realized Eric had every right to control her destiny, since without his aid there would be no future for her, she uttered a long sigh. She felt the tenseness drain away from her, to be replaced by acceptance and something else that she could not yet define.

"There is something else we must talk about," Eric said slowly. "We have put it off long enough. We must speak about your time of captivity."

"No. I want only to forget it ever happened," she said, barely controlling a shudder.

"It must be spoken of," he said firmly. "Otherwise, it will fester and grow. It must be brought out into the open. There should be no secrets between us, Shala. Not now. Not ever!"

"It will not fester and grow within me," she denied.

"It will be spoken of!" he commanded. "You cannot lightly dismiss that time." His expression hardened. "Tell me now, and leave nothing out. When it is spoken of we will put it aside. But I need to know what happened to you there."

There was something in his voice that should

have warned her. "They found us while we were sleeping," she whispered.

"How many?"

"All the fingers of one hand and one on the other."

"Six." His voice was grimmer now. "And did all of them attack you?"

She was puzzled, knew her face reflected her bewilderment. "All of them? Yes. They were all there."

"Did they all attack you at once, or did they come one at a time?" His voice was strained.

"They were all there. All together."

"So you were raped by all of them." The words sounded as though they had been squeezed through a tight throat. "How many times?"

"Raped? I was not raped." She threw the words at him like stones. "I was possessed by none of them."

Something dark flickered in his eyes. "That is hard to believe."

She glared at him with burning, reproachful eyes. "It is true. Their leader, Red Fox, stopped them. He was a kind man and tried to help me. If not for him, I would have been tortured to death. It was his intervention that kept me alive for so long."

"I suppose he was repaid for his kindness." His curt voice lashed out at her.

"Repaid? I carried nothing with me that would have repaid him for my life. I had nothing except the clothes on my body."

His expression darkened. "Where were you kept?"

"In his dwelling."

He looked away from her. "You stayed there until you escaped?"

"Yes."

He turned away from her. "I have learned enough. We will speak no more of it."

Shala had no quarrel with that, had never wanted to speak about her ordeal in the first place. But there was something that must be told, she decided. Something that should have been told long before now.

"Eric," she said, her voice barely above a whisper. "There is something that you must know. A babe grows within my body."

His movements stilled, and long moments passed before he turned to her. When he did, his face was gray. But it was his eyes that caught her attention. They lashed her with barely contained fury. "Are you sure?"

She flinched away from his anger. "Yes," she muttered, nodding her dark head.

"Who is the child's father?" His expression was grim.

A horrified gasp was torn from her throat. "You are!" she cried.

"Me?" There was no change in his expression. "How can you be so sure, Shala?"

"Because no other has had me," she cried, glaring furiously at him. "I told you that." She leapt to her feet, her hands instinctively going over her stomach to protect the life sheltered there.

He reached out a hand, but she stepped back, avoiding his touch.

"The babe does not belong to another man," she insisted. "It is yours . . . and mine." Her mouth twisted bitterly. "I told you no other had me. But it is apparent now that you did not believe me."

She turned away from him, staring at the far distant mountains. "I will go no farther with you. I shall return to my people and you can return alone to your world."

He clutched her shoulder and turned her around. "You shall not leave me again, Shala!" His voice was dark with emotion. "Never again! Put that thought out of your mind—right now!"

She tried to shrug his hand away, but he tightened his grip and pulled her back against him. "If you say the child is mine, then I must accept that."

She heard him say the words, but she did not believe them.

He held her in his arms for a long moment, his chin resting on top of her head, then, almost reluctantly, he released her. "It is late, Shala. Past time that we slept."

Shala had been unaware of the purpling twilight until he spoke, unaware that night was upon them. She ached with weariness, tired in both mind and body. She needed time to rest, time to think, to consider the future that lay ahead. No matter that she owed Eric her life. There was another life to be considered as well. The life of her unborn child.

Seeming aware of her exhausted state, Eric left

her alone while he pulled enough of the long grass growing nearby to protect them from the damp earth.

Shala lay awake long into the night, and although he remained still beside her, she knew he was awake, too. Finally, his voice broke the stillness.

"Go to sleep, Shala. You have nothing to fear from me." He gave a heavy sigh. "I could not harm the babe. No matter who has fathered the child, it is your flesh and blood." He drew her close against him and kissed the tip of her nose, then her lips, gently, then more firmly. But Shala could not respond to him, dared not, lest she be swayed by his loving.

Finding her unresponsive, Eric sighed heavily and turned his back to her.

She lay there beside him, her body crying out its need while her mind told her she had been right in refusing him. She had wanted the loving, too, needed it as much as he did, but she would not allow it to happen, had come to a decision even before he spoke. She would have to leave him, as she had done once before. She realized she could not trust his words. He had been raised in a different world, one where a child was left in the elements to die if it was born less than perfect. How could a man who condoned such practices be trusted to keep a child he imagined was born from another man's seed?

No. She could not trust him. Dared not! And that left her with no choice.

She must leave him again, must hide herself away where he could never find her.

Thirty

It was never Shala's intention to fall asleep, but the day had taken its toll and had brought her to the point of exhaustion. When she had closed her eyes Shala had only meant to rest them for a moment, but when she opened them again, it was the half-light before dawn.

The cobwebs of sleep scattered like fall leaves blown by a strong wind as her eyes flew to the man beside her. His heavy breathing told her he was not yet awake.

Carefully, feeling an urgent need to hurry, Shala left the bed of grass and scooped up the knife he had left beside his sword. After another quick glance at the sleeping man, she crept away on silent feet.

Father Sun was peeking over the slope of the mountain east of her when she heard something that brought her to a standstill.

"Sha-a-a-la!"

Even though Shala was several miles away on the slope of the northern mountain, the canyons around her echoed out the name.

"Sha-a-a-la!" The voice came again, startling a family of quail so that they erupted from a nearby bush and flew away, their wings flapping furiously to escape from the sound.

Shala heard the fury in the voice and imagined she heard something else as well. Was there pain there, too? Just the thought that there might be sent moisture welling into her eyes. The tears brimmed over and slid down her face. Her heart was a heavy ball of pain in her chest, and she fought the urge to scurry down the mountain as fast as she could, to hurry back to her love on winged feet, knowing all the while that she dare not do so. Not with the life of their child at stake.

She faced forward again, realizing that she must go on, could not allow Eric to stop her from leaving.

As time passed, the path she followed became more difficult. But still she continued on, knowing she must. She stopped frequently to rest, finding the climb sapping her strength.

One such time when she had stopped to rest, she turned to look behind her, and her heart gave a jerk of fear when she realized the dot on the valley below was Eric. If he continued to travel at that speed, he would surely catch her before midday.

"Oh, Creator," she muttered, "help me. He will kill the child."

Her breath rasped harshly as she resumed her climb, hurrying as fast as she could. But it was not fast enough. Eric continued to gain steadily on her.

Panic filled her world as she forced her weary legs to carry her over uneven ground. She must go on, must reach the mesa, must reach the cliff dwellings. Only there could she find safety for herself and the child.

Even as she climbed, dread settled over her. There was no safety from one such as the Viking. Nowhere. Eric would never stop until he found her, and he would deal harshly with the both of them. Herself and her unborn babe.

She could hear his footsteps now, thundering loudly in her ears. Or was that her heart?

A swift look back told her he was getting closer, ever closer. And there was something different about—Oh, Creator! He had left his sword behind in order to gain speed. She knew then how badly he wanted her. She tried to hurry faster, but her legs ached, her chest was tight, her throat constricted. She could not go faster. He was nearly upon her. His hands reached out, grasping, tangling in her clothing.

"No, Eric!" she screamed, forcing the words through her tortured throat.

His hands circled her, tightened; he lifted her off the ground, raised her high into the air.

Was he going to crush her against the ground?

"No!" she cried again. "Do not hurt me!"

Slowly, his expression changed, becoming one of bewilderment. He lowered her slowly, pulling her against his chest and holding her tightly there for a long, heart-stopping moment. Then he cupped her chin and tilted her head upward, forcing her eyes to meet his. "Hurt you? Why do you think I would hurt you?"

"You . . . you were chasing me."

"How else could I stop you?" he asked harshly. "Why did you leave me?"

"I was afraid."

"Afraid of me?"

"Yes."

"Why?"

"You were so angry. And the babe . . ." Her voice trailed off into nothingness.

"You feared I would harm the babe?" He held her closer and smoothed her hair. "How could you think that of me, Shala? I could never harm your child. I told you so."

"You will never accept it."

"It is yours." He hesitated, then added softly, "And mine."

"You believe me now?"

"You would not lie to me."

"Oh, Eric." She looked up at him with longing. "I love you so much. But I am so afraid. Even now. Suppose you feel differently when the child is born. I would be gone from my home, unprotected by my own people. I cannot take such a chance. Not with the life of my child."

His expression became dark and brooding. "You have no need to be protected by others, Shala."

She shrank away from him, and immediately his expression changed. "Be calm," he said, smoothing back her tangled hair. "You have nothing to fear from me. Neither has the babe. But we will never be parted. If you are so afraid to leave with me, then we will not go."

Her eyes widened. "You mean that, Eric? You would stay here with me? Live with me among the cliffs?"

"If you so desire. I want you happy, Shala. Surely you know that." His gaze turned inward. "My family will think me dead and will mourn my passing, but their grief would not be as great as mine, should I lose you." His arms tightened around her. "I cannot bear the thought of losing you again, Shala. Life would not be worth living without you."

"You love me?"

"Of course I love you. Have I not told you so?"

"No."

His expression became tender. "Would it have made a difference, Shala?"

"Yes."

"Then I am telling you now, love. And I will tell anyone who cares to listen. Everyone will know that I love Shala, woman of the Eagle Clan." Although he smiled at her, she sensed there was still a deep sadness within him.

"You will miss your family," she whispered.

"Yes. I will miss them. But not nearly as much as I would miss you . . . and the child." She saw acceptance in his eyes and knew suddenly that everything would be all right. Whatever happened in the future, Eric would not harm the babe, and in time, he would surely come to love it as she already did.

When that day came, perhaps they could build

a longboat that would be capable of carrying them across the big salt water to where his people lived. It was a good thought. One that she would have to consider carefully.

But there was plenty of time to do that.

Right now, she had an urgent need to wrap herself around this Viking of hers. She lifted her face and read that same desire in his eyes, knew that he felt the same way she did and exulted in that knowledge.

When she raised her face for his kiss, his lips were already lowering to cover hers. Their lips clinging together, they sank down onto the ground and were soon lost in the ecstasy they could only find in each other's arms.

Epilogue

The wind blew softly against his cheek as Eric paced back and forth before the small cave in the cliff. How long had it been now? he wondered. How long had Shala been laboring to have the babe that refused to make its way into the world. Too long, he knew. That was the reason, despite her objection, he had gone for Gryla, Keeper of Memories. Shala could not birth the child alone. He knew that she needed help, and as soon as Shala's mother examined her daughter, she confirmed his suspicions. The babe was turned wrong.

Had Gryla come in time to help her? Eric wondered. What would he do if Shala did not survive the ordeal of birth? He refused to even consider such an event.

He resumed his pacing.

A shrill cry jerked his head around, and he stared at the entrance, frozen in place. Had that been Shala? If so, it was the first cry she had uttered since going into labor.

The cry came again, louder this time, and he realized it was not Shala. It was a babe.

Ripping aside the hide flap that had barred his entrance, he hurried inside, afraid of what he would see.

Relief swept over him as he saw her, smiling at him over the head of the babe she held in her arms.

"Give him to me," he said, kneeling beside her. "Let me hold the babe."

Uncertainty flickered in her eyes, but only for a moment. "You would not harm the babe?" she whispered. "Would you, Eric? It is a healthy child, Eric. Look. See the fingers and toes. They are all there."

"Yes. I see. Give the boy to me."

"The child is a female," Gryla spoke up, staring at him with dark eyes. "Do you object to that?"

"I object to nothing about this babe," he said, trying to reassure both women. "Give her to me, Shala."

"Her hair is dark," Shala said, her voice wobbling slightly. "Now there is no proof that she is yours. Only my word that no other could have sired her."

His heart felt heavy. Not because of himself, but because of Shala. Although he had tried his best to reassure her of his love, she was still uncertain enough of him to need proof about the child. He had hoped, for her sake, that the babe would have blond hair.

"You will accept her?" Shala asked.

"Have I not already said so?" he asked calmly.

"Do you not know me well enough yet, wife, to know that I could never harm a child, whoever it belonged to."

Whoever it belonged to. The words hung there between them, and he wished them unsaid. "I did not mean to imply—" he began, but quickly broke off as the babe opened her eyes and stared up at him with eyes the color of new spring grass.

A grin slowly spread across his face. "Look, Shala," he said, holding the babe closer to her. "Behold. My daughter smiles at me."

Joy spread across Shala's face. The uncertainty was gone. There could no longer be any doubt in her Viking's mind that the babe was his. Now Shala could sleep, knowing that all would be well for the three of them. For herself, for Eric and for their child.